Walking
DISASTER

ALSO BY JAMIE McGUIRE

Beautiful Disaster

Walking DISASTER

JAMIE McGUIRE

SIMON & SCHUSTER

London · New York · Sydney · Toronto · New Delhi

First published in Great Britain in 2013 by Simon & Schuster UK Ltd

3 5 7 9 10 8 6 4 2

Simon & Schuster UK Ltd
1st Floor
222 Gray's Inn Road
London
WC1X 8HB

www.simonandschuster.co.uk

Simon & Schuster Australia, Sydney
Simon & Schuster India, New Delhi

A CIP catalogue copy for this book is available
from the British Library.

ISBN: 978-1-4711-3084-7
eBook ISBN: 978-1-47111-515-8

Printed and bound by CPI Group (UK) Ltd, Croydon, CR0 4YY

To Jeff,

my very own

BEAUTIFUL *disaster*

Walking DISASTER

PROLOGUE

EVEN WITH THE SWEAT ON HER FOREHEAD AND THE skip in her breath, she didn't look sick. Her skin didn't have the peachy glow I was used to, and her eyes weren't as bright, but she was still beautiful. The most beautiful woman I would ever see.

Her hand flopped off the bed, and her finger twitched. My eyes trailed from her brittle, yellowing nails, up her thin arm, to her bony shoulder, finally settling on her eyes. She was looking down at me, her lids two slits, just enough to let me know she knew I was there. That's what I loved about her. When she looked at me, she really saw me. She didn't look past me to the other dozens of things she needed to do with her day, or tune out my stupid stories. She listened, and it made her really happy. Everyone else seemed to nod without listening, but not her. Never her.

"Travis," she said, her voice raspy. She cleared her throat, and the corners of her mouth turned up. "Come here, baby. It's okay. C'mere."

Dad put a few fingers on the base of my neck and pushed me forward while listening to the nurse. Dad called her Becky. She came to the house for the first time a few days ago. Her words were soft, and her eyes were kinda nice, but I didn't like Becky. I couldn't explain it, but her being there was scary. I knew she might have been there to help, but it wasn't a good thing, even though Dad was okay with her.

Dad's nudge shoved me forward several steps, close enough to where Mommy could touch me. She stretched her long, elegant fingers, and brushed my arm. "It's okay, Travis," she whispered. "Mommy wants to tell you something."

I stuck my finger in my mouth, and pushed it around on my gums, fidgeting. Nodding made her small smile bigger, so I made sure to make big movements with my head as I stepped toward her face.

She used what was left of her strength to scoot closer to me, and then she took a breath. "What I'm going to ask you will be very hard, son. I know you can do it, because you're a big boy now."

I nodded again, mirroring her smile, even if I didn't mean it. Smiling when she looked so tired and uncomfortable didn't feel right, but being brave made her happy. So I was brave.

"Travis, I need you to listen to what I'm going to say, and even more important, I need you to remember. This will be very hard. I've been trying to remember things from when I was three, and I . . ." She trailed off, the pain too big for a bit.

"Pain getting unmanageable, Diane?" Becky said, pushing a needle into Mom's IV.

After a few moments, Mommy relaxed. She took another breath, and tried again.

"Can you do that for Mommy? Can you remember what I'm about to say?" I nodded again, and she raised a hand to my cheek. Her skin wasn't very warm, and she could only keep her hand in place for a few seconds before it got shaky and fell to the bed. "First, it's okay to be sad. It's okay to feel things. Remember that. Second, be a kid for as long as you can. Play games, Travis. Be silly"—her eyes glossed over—"and you and your brothers take care of each other, and your father. Even when you grow up and move away, it's important to come home. Okay?"

My head bobbed up and down, desperate to please her.

"One of these days you're going to fall in love, son. Don't settle for just anyone. Choose the girl that doesn't come easy, the one you have to fight for, and then never stop fighting. Never"—she took a deep breath—"stop fighting for what you want. And never"—her eyebrows pulled in—"forget that Mommy loves you. Even if you can't see me." A tear fell down her cheek. "I will always, *always* love you."

She took a choppy breath, and then coughed.

"Okay," Becky said, sticking a funny-looking thing in her ears. She held the other end to Mommy's chest. "Time to rest."

"No time," Mommy whispered.

Becky looked at my dad. "We're getting close, Mr. Maddox. You should probably bring the rest of the boys in to say goodbye."

Dad's lips made a hard line, and he shook his head. "I'm not ready," he choked out.

"You'll never be ready to lose your wife, Jim. But you don't want to let her go without the boys saying their goodbyes."

Dad thought for a minute, wiped his nose with his sleeve, and then nodded. He stomped out of the room, like he was mad.

I watched Mommy, watched her try to breathe, and watched Becky checking the numbers on the box beside her. I touched Mommy's wrist. Becky's eyes seemed to know something I didn't, and that made my stomach feel sick.

"You know, Travis," Becky said, leaning down so she could look me in the eyes, "the medicine I'm giving your mommy will make her sleep, but even though she's sleeping, she can still hear you. You can still tell Mommy that you love her and that you'll miss her, and she'll hear everything you say."

I looked at Mommy but quickly shook my head. "I don't want to miss her."

Becky put her soft, warm hand on my shoulder, just like Mommy used to when I was upset. "Your mom wants to be here with you. She wants that very much. But Jesus wants her with him right now."

I frowned. "I need her more than Jesus does."

Becky smiled, and then kissed the top of my hair.

Dad knocked on the door, and then it opened. My brothers crowded around him in the hallway, and Becky led me by the hand to join them.

Trenton's eyes didn't leave Mommy's bed, and Taylor and Tyler looked everywhere *but* the bed. It made me feel better somehow that they all looked as scared as I felt.

Thomas stood next to me, a little bit in front, like the time he protected me when we were playing in the front yard, and the neighbor boys tried to pick a fight with Tyler. "She doesn't look good," Thomas said.

Dad cleared his throat. "Mom's been real sick for a long time, boys, and it's time for her . . . it's time she . . ." He trailed off.

Becky offered a small, sympathetic smile. "Your mom hasn't been eating or drinking. Her body is letting go. This is going to be very hard, but it's a good time to tell your mom that you love her, and you're going to miss her, and that it's okay for her to go. She needs to know that it's okay."

My brothers nodded their heads in unison. All of them but me. It wasn't okay. I didn't want her to leave. I didn't care if Jesus wanted her or not. She was my mommy. He could take an old mommy. One that didn't have little boys to take care of. I tried to remember everything she told me. I tried to glue it to the inside of my head: Play. Visit Dad. Fight for what I love. That last thing bothered me. I loved Mommy, but I didn't know how to fight for her.

Becky leaned into my dad's ear. He shook his head, and then nodded to my brothers. "Okay, boys. Let's go say goodbye, and then you need to get your brothers in bed, Thomas. They don't need to be here for the rest."

"Yes, sir," Thomas said. I knew he was faking a brave face. His eyes were as sad as mine.

Thomas talked to her for a while, and then Taylor and Tyler whispered things in each of her ears. Trenton cried and hugged her for a long time. Everyone told her it was okay for her to leave us. Everyone but me. Mommy didn't say anything back this time.

Thomas pulled on my hand, leading me out of her bedroom. I walked backward until we were in the hall. I tried to pretend she was just going to sleep, but my head went fuzzy. Thomas picked me up and carried me up the stairs. His feet climbed faster when Dad's wails carried through the walls.

"What did she say to you?" Thomas asked, turning on the tub faucet.

I didn't answer. I heard him ask, and I remembered like she told me to, but my tears wouldn't work, and my mouth didn't either.

Thomas pulled my dirt-soiled shirt over my head, and my shorts and Thomas the Train Underoos down to the floor.

"Time to get in the tub, bubby." He lifted me off the floor and sat me in the warm water, soaking the rag, and squeezing it over my head. I didn't blink. I didn't even try to get the water off of my face, even though I hated it.

"Yesterday, Mom told me to take care of you and the twins, and to take care of Dad." Thomas folded his hands on the rim of the tub and rested his chin on them, looking at me. "So that's what I'm gonna do, Trav, okay? I'm going to take care of you. So don't you worry. We're going to miss Mom together, but don't be scared. I'm going to make sure everything's okay. I promise."

I wanted to nod, or hug him, but nothing worked. Even though I should have been fighting for her, I was upstairs, in a tub full of water, still as a statue. I had already let her down. I promised her in the very back of my head that I would do all the things she had told me as soon as my body worked again. When the sad went away, I would always play, and I would always fight. Hard.

CHAPTER ONE

Pigeon

Fucking vultures. They could wait you out for hours. Days. Nights, too. Staring right through you, picking which parts of you they will pull away first, which pieces will be the sweetest, the most tender, or just which part will be most convenient.

What they don't know, what they've never anticipated, is that the prey is faking. It's the vultures that are easy. Just when they think all they have to do is be patient, to sit back and wait for you to expire, that's when you hit them. That's when you bring in the secret weapon: an utter lack of respect for the status quo; a refusal to give in to the order of things.

That's when you shock them with how much you just don't give a fuck.

An opponent in the Circle, some random douche bag trying to expose your weakness with insults, a woman trying to tie you down; gets them every time.

I'd been very careful from a very young age to live my life this way. These bleeding heart assholes that went around giving their soul to every gold-digging banshee that smiled at them had it all wrong. But somehow I was the one swimming upstream. I was the man out. Their way was the hard way if you ask me. Leaving emotion at the door, and replacing it with numbness, or anger—which was much easier to control—was easy. Letting yourself feel made you vulnerable. As many times as I tried to explain this error to my brothers, my cousins, or my friends, I was met with skepticism. As many times as I had seen them crying or losing sleep over some dumb bitch in a pair of fuck-me heels that never gave a shit about them anyway, I couldn't understand it. The women that were worth that kind of heartbreak wouldn't let you fall for them so easy. They wouldn't bend over your couch, or allow you to charm them into their bedroom on the first night—or even the tenth.

My theories were ignored because that wasn't the way of things. Attraction, sex, infatuation, love, and then heartbreak. That was the logical order. And, it was always the order.

But not for me. No. Fucking. Way.

I decided a long time ago I would feed on the vultures until a dove came along. A pigeon. The kind of soul that didn't impede on anyone; just walked around worrying about its own business, trying to get through life without pulling everyone else down with its own needs and selfish habits. Brave. A communicator. Intelligent. Beautiful. Soft-spoken. A creature that mates for life. Unattainable until she has a reason to trust you.

As I stood at my open apartment door, flicking the last bit of ashes off my cigarette, the girl in the bloody, pink cardigan from the Circle flashed in my memory. Without thinking, I'd called her Pigeon. At the time it was just a stupid nickname to make her even more uncomfortable than she already was. Her crimson-spattered face, her eyes wide, outwardly she seemed innocent, but I could tell it was just the clothes. I pushed her memory away as I stared blankly into the living room.

Megan lay on my couch lazily, watching TV. She looked bored, and I wondered why she was still in my apartment. She usually got her crap and left right after I bagged her.

The door complained when I pushed it a little wider. I cleared my throat and picked up my backpack by the straps. "Megan. I'm out."

She sat up and stretched, and then gripped the chain of her excessively large purse. I couldn't imagine she had enough belongings to fill it. Megan slung the silver links over her shoulder, and then slipped on her wedge heels, sauntering out the door.

"Text me if you're bored," she said without glancing in my direction. She slipped on her oversize sunglasses, and then descended the stairs, completely unaffected by my dismissal. Her indifference was exactly why Megan was one of my few frequent flyers. She didn't cry about commitment, or throw a tantrum. She took our arrangement for what it was, and then went about her day.

My Harley glistened in the morning autumn sun. I waited for Megan to pull away from the parking lot of my apartment, and then jogged down the stairs, zipping up my jacket. Dr. Rueser's humanities class was in half an hour, but he didn't care if I was late. If it didn't piss him off, I didn't really see a point in killing myself to get there.

"Wait up!" a voice called from behind me.

Shepley stood at the front door of our apartment, shirtless and balancing on one foot while trying to pull a sock onto the other. "I meant to ask you last night. What did you say to

Marek? You leaned into his ear and said something. He looked like he swallowed his tongue."

"I thanked him for taking off out of town a few weekends before, because his mother was a wildcat."

Shepley stared at me, dubious. "Dude. You didn't."

"No. I heard from Cami that he got a Minor In Possession in Jones County."

He shook his head, and then nodded toward the couch. "Did you let Megan spend the night this time?"

"No, Shep. You know better than that."

"She just came over to get some morning nookie before class, huh? That's an interesting way to claim you for the day."

"You think that's it?"

"Anyone else gets her sloppy seconds." Shepley shrugged. "It's Megan. Who knows. Listen, I've gotta take America back to campus. Want a ride?"

"I'll meet you later," I said, slipping on my Oakleys. "I can take Mare if you want."

Shepley's face contorted. "Uh . . . no."

Amused at his reaction, I saddled up on the Harley and ripped the engine. Even though I had the bad habit of seducing his girlfriend's friends, there was one line I wouldn't cross. America was his, and once he showed interest in a girl, she was off my radar, never to be considered again. He knew that. He just liked to give me shit.

I met Adam behind Sig Tau. He ran the Circle. After the initial payout the first night, I'd let him pick up the tote returns the following day, and then give him a cut for his trouble. He kept the cover; I kept the winnings. Our relationship was strictly business, and we both preferred to keep it simple. As long as he kept paying me, I stayed out of his face, and as long as he didn't want to get his ass kicked, he stayed out of mine.

I made my way across campus to the cafeteria. Just before I reached the double metal doors, Lexi and Ashley stepped in front of me.

"Hey, Trav," Lexi said, standing with perfect posture. Perfectly tanned, silicone-endowed breasts peeked from her pink T-shirt. Those irresistible, bouncing mounds were what begged me to bag her in the first place, but once was enough. Her voice reminded me of the sound made by air being slowly let out of a balloon, and Nathan Squalor bagged her the night after I did.

"Hey, Lex."

I pinched the cherry off my cigarette and threw it into the bin before walking quickly past her through the doors. Not that I was eager to tackle the buffet of limp vegetables, dry meat, and overripe fruits. Jesus. Her voice made dogs howl, and children perk up to see what cartoon character had come to life.

Regardless of my dismissal, both girls followed.

"Shep." I nodded. He was sitting with America, laughing with the people around him. The pigeon from the fight sat across from him, poking at her food with a plastic fork. My voice seemed to pique her curiosity. I could feel her big eyes follow me to the end of the table where I tossed my tray.

I heard Lexi giggle, forcing me to restrain the irritation boiling inside me. When I sat, she used my knee for a chair.

Some of the guys from the football team sitting at our table watched in awe, as if being followed by two inarticulate tarts was an unattainable aspiration for them.

Lexi slid her hand under the table and then pressed her fingers into my thigh as she made her way up the inseam of my jeans. I spread my legs a little wider, waiting for her to reach her mark.

Just before I felt her hands on me, America's loud murmurs traveled down the table.

"I think I just threw up a little bit in my mouth."

Lexi turned, her entire body rigid. "I heard that, skank."

A dinner roll flew past Lexi's face and bounced off the floor. Shepley and I traded glances, and then I let my knee give way.

Lexi's ass bounced off the cafeteria tile. I admit, it turned me on a little hearing the sound of her skin slap against the ceramic.

She didn't complain much before walking away. Shepley seemed to appreciate my gesture, and that was good enough for me. My toleration for girls like Lexi only lasted so long. I had one rule: respect. For me, my family, and for my friends. Hell, even some of my enemies deserved respect. I didn't see a reason to associate longer than necessary with people who didn't understand that life lesson. It might sound hypocritical to the women that have passed through my apartment door, but if they carried themselves with respect, I would have given it to them.

I winked at America, who seemed satisfied, nodded to Shepley, and then took another bite of whatever was on my plate.

"Nice job last night, Mad Dog," Chris Jenks said, flicking a crouton across the table.

"Shut up, dumb ass," Brazil said in his typical low voice. "Adam will never let you back in if he hears you're talking."

"Oh. Yeah," he said, shrugging.

I took my tray to the trash, and then returned to my seat with a frown. "And don't call me that."

"What? Mad Dog?"

"Yeah."

"Why not? I thought that was your Circle name. Kind of like your stripper name."

My eyes targeted Jenks. "Why don't you shut up and give that hole in your face a chance to heal."

I'd never liked that little worm.

"Sure thing, Travis. All you had to do was say so." He chuckled nervously before gathering his trash and heading out.

Before long, most of the lunchroom was empty. I glanced down to see Shepley and America still hanging around, talking with her friend. She had long, wavy hair, and her skin was still bronzed from summer break. She didn't have the biggest tits I'd ever seen, but her eyes . . . they were a weird gray color. Familiar somehow.

There was no way I'd met her before, but something about her face reminded me of something I couldn't put my finger on.

I stood up and walked toward her. She had the hair of a porn star, and the face of an angel. Her eyes were almond shaped and uniquely beautiful. That was when I saw it: behind the beauty and fake innocence was something else, something cold and calculating. Even when she smiled, I could see sin so deeply ingrained in her that no cardigan could hide it. Those eyes floated above her tiny nose, and smooth features. To anyone else, she was pure and naive, but this girl was hiding something. I knew only because the same sin had dwelled in me my entire life. The difference was she held it deep within her, and I let mine out of its cage on a regular basis.

I watched Shepley until he felt me staring at him. When he looked my way, I nodded in the pigeon's direction.

Who's that? I mouthed.

Shepley only responded with a confused frown.

Her, I silently mouthed again.

Shepley's mouth turned up into the annoying asshole grin he always made when he was about to do something to piss me off.

"What?" Shepley asked, a lot louder than necessary.

I could tell the girl knew we were talking about her, because she kept her head down, pretending not to hear.

After spending sixty seconds in Abby Abernathy's presence, I discerned two things: she didn't talk much, and when she did she was kind of a bitch. But I don't know . . . I kind of dug that about her. She put on a front to keep assholes like me away, but that made me even more determined.

She rolled her eyes at me for the third or fourth time. I was annoying her and found it pretty amusing. Girls didn't usually treat me with unadulterated loathing, even when I was showing them the door.

When even my best smiles didn't work, I turned it up a notch.

"Do you have a twitch?"

"A what?" she asked.

"A twitch. Your eyes keep wiggling around." If she could have murdered me with her glare, I would have bled out on the floor. I couldn't help but laugh. She was a smart-ass and rude as hell. I liked her more every second.

I leaned closer to her face. "Those are some amazing eyes, though. What color is that, anyway? Gray?"

She immediately ducked her head, letting her hair cover her face. Score. I made her uncomfortable, and that meant I was getting somewhere.

America immediately jumped in, warning me away. I couldn't blame her. She'd seen the endless line of girls come in and out of the apartment. I didn't want to piss America off, but she didn't look angry. More like amused.

"You're not her type," America said.

My mouth fell open, playing into her game. "I'm everyone's type!"

The pigeon peeked over at me and grinned. A warm feeling—probably just the insane urge to throw this girl on my couch—came over me. She was different, and it was refreshing.

"Ah! A smile," I said. Simply calling it a smile, like it wasn't the most beautiful thing I'd ever seen, seemed wrong, but I wasn't about to fuck up my game when I was just getting ahead. "I'm not a rotten bastard after all. It was nice to meet you, Pidge."

I stood, walked around the table, and leaned into America's ear. "Help me out here, would ya? I'll behave, I swear."

A French fry came hurdling toward my face.

"Get your lips outta my girl's ear, Trav!" Shepley said.

I backed away, holding my hands up to highlight the most innocent expression on my face that I could manage. "Networking! I'm networking!" I walked backward a few steps to the door, noticing a small group of girls. I opened the door, and they swarmed through like a herd of water buffalo before I could let myself out.

It had been a long time since I'd had a challenge. The weird thing was, I wasn't out to fuck her. It bothered me that she might think I was a piece of shit, but it bothered me more that I cared. Either way, for the first time in a long time, someone was unpredictable. Pigeon was the total opposite of the girls I'd met here, and I had to know why.

CHANEY'S CLASS WAS FULL. I TOOK THE STEPS TO MY seat two at a time, and then waded through the bare legs crowding my desk.

I nodded. "Ladies."

They hummed and sighed in harmony.

Vultures. Half of them I'd bagged my freshman year, the other half had been on my couch well before fall break. Except the girl on the end. Sophia flashed a crooked smile. It looked like her face had caught fire and someone had tried to put it out with a fork. She had been with a few of my frat brothers. Knowing their track records and her lack of concern for safety, it was best to consider her an unnecessary risk, even if I was habitually careful.

She leaned forward on her elbows to make better eye contact. I felt the urge to shudder with disgust, but I resisted. *No. Not even close to being worth it.*

The brunette in front of me turned around and batted her lashes. "Hey, Travis. I hear there's a date party coming up at Sig Tau."

"No," I said without pause.

Her bottom lip formed a pout. "But . . . when you told me about it, I thought you might want to go."

I laughed once. "I was bitching about it. Not the same."

The blonde next to me leaned forward. "Everyone knows Travis Maddox doesn't go to date parties. You're barking up the wrong tree, Chrissy."

"Oh yeah? Well, no one asked you," Chrissy said with a frown.

As the women argued back and forth, I noticed Abby rush in. She practically threw herself into a front-row desk just before the bell rang.

Before I took a second to ask myself why, I grabbed my paper and popped my pen in my mouth, and then jogged down the steps, sliding into the desk next to her.

The look on Abby's face surpassed amusing, and for a reason I couldn't explain, it caused adrenaline to rush through my body—the kind that I used to experience before a fight.

"Good. You can take notes for me."

She was utterly disgusted, and that only pleased me more. Most girls bored me outta my gourd, but this girl was intriguing. Entertaining, even. I didn't faze her, at least not in a positive way. My very presence seemed to make her want to puke, and I found that strangely endearing.

The urge came over me to find out if it was really hate she felt for me, or if she was just a hard-ass. I leaned in close. "I'm sorry . . . did I offend you in some way?"

Her eyes softened before she shook her head. She didn't hate me. She just *wanted* to hate me. I was way ahead of her. If she wanted to play, I could play.

"Then what is your problem?"

She seemed embarrassed to say what came next. "I'm not sleeping with you. You should give up, now."

Oh yeah. This was going to be fun. "I haven't asked you to sleep with me . . . have I?" I let my eyes drift to the ceiling, as if I had to think about it. "Why don't you come over with America tonight?"

Abby's lip turned up, as if she'd smelled something rotten.

"I won't even flirt with you, I swear."

"I'll think about it."

I tried not to smile too much and give myself away. She wasn't going to roll over like the vultures above. I glanced behind me, and they were all glaring at the back of Abby's head. They knew it as well as I did. Abby was different, and I was going to have to work for this one. For once.

Three doodles of potential tattoos, and two dozen 3-D boxes later, class dismissed. I slid through the halls before anyone could stop me. I made good time, but Abby had somehow ended up outside, a good twenty yards ahead of me.

I'll be damned. She was trying to avoid me. I quickened my pace until I was next to her. "Have you thought about it?"

"Travis!" A girl said, playing with her hair. Abby kept going, leaving me stuck listening to this girl's irritating babble.

"Sorry, uh . . ."

"Heather."

"Sorry, Heather . . . I'm . . . I've gotta go."

She wrapped her arms around me. I patted her backside, shrugged out of her grasp, and kept walking, wondering who she was.

Before I could figure out who Heather was, Abby's long, tan legs came into view. I popped a Marlboro into my mouth and jogged to her side. "Where was I? Oh yeah . . . you were thinking."

"What are you talking about?"

"Have you thought about coming over?"

"If I say yes, will you quit following me?"

I pretended to mull it over, and then nodded. "Yes."

"Then I'll come over."

Bullshit. She wasn't that easy. "When?"

"Tonight. I'll come over tonight."

I stopped midstep. She was up to something. I hadn't anticipated her going on the offensive. "Sweet," I said, playing off my surprise. "See you then, Pidge."

She walked away without looking back, not the least bit affected by the conversation. She disappeared behind other students making their own way to class.

Shepley's white ball cap came into view. He was in no hurry to get to our computer class. My eyebrows pressed together. I hated that class. Who doesn't know how to work a fucking computer anymore?

I joined Shepley and America as they merged into the flow of students on the main walkway. She giggled and watched him yap at me with stars in her eyes. America was no vulture. She was hot, yeah, but she could have a conversation without saying *like* after every word, and she was pretty funny at times. What I liked most about her is she wouldn't come to the apartment for several weeks after their first date, and even after they watched a movie all snuggled up at the apartment, she went back to her dorm room.

I had a feeling the probationary period before Shepley could bag her was about to end, though.

"Hey, Mare," I said, nodding.

"How's it going, Trav?" she asked. She acknowledged me with a friendly smile, but then her eyes were right back on Shepley.

He was one of the lucky ones. Girls like that didn't come along very often.

"This is me," America said, gesturing to her dorm around the corner. She wrapped her arms around Shepley's neck and kissed him. He gripped her shirt on each side and pulled her close before letting her go.

America waved one last time at both of us, and then joined her friend Finch at the front entrance.

"You're falling for her, aren't you?" I asked, punching Shepley in the arm.

He shoved me. "None of your business, dick."

"Does she have a sister?"

"She's an only child. Leave her friends alone, too, Trav. I mean it."

Shepley's last words were unnecessary. His eyes were a billboard for his emotions and thoughts most of the time, and he was clearly serious—maybe even a little desperate. He wasn't just falling for her. He was in love.

"You mean Abby."

He frowned. "I mean any of her friends. Even Finch. Just stay away."

"Cousin!" I said, hooking my elbow around his neck. "Are you in love? You're making me all misty-eyed!"

"Shut up," Shepley grumbled. "Just promise me you'll stay away from her friends."

I grinned. "I promise nothing."

CHAPTER TWO

Backfire

"What are you doing?" Shepley asked. He stood in the middle of the room, a pair of sneakers in one hand, a dirty pair of underwear in the other.

"Uh, cleaning?" I asked, shoving shot glasses into the dishwasher.

"I see that. But . . . why?"

I smiled, my back turned to Shepley. He was going to kick my ass. "I'm expecting company."

"So?"

"The pigeon."

"Huh?"

"Abby, Shep. I invited Abby."

"Dude, no. No! Don't fuck this up for me, man. Please don't."

I turned, crossing my arms across my chest. "I tried, Shep. I did. But, I don't know." I shrugged. "There's something about her. I couldn't help myself."

Shepley's jaw worked under his skin, and then he stomped into his room, slamming the door behind him.

I finished loading the dishwasher, and then circled the couch to make sure I hadn't missed any visible empty condom wrappers. That was never fun to explain.

The fact that I had bagged a good portion of beautiful coeds at this school was no secret, but I didn't see a reason to remind them when they came to my apartment. It was all about presentation.

Pigeon, though. It would take far more than false advertising to bag her on my couch. At this point, the strategy was to take her one step at a time. If I focused on the end result, the process could easily be fucked up. She noticed things. She was farther from naive than I was; light-years away. This operation was nothing less than precarious.

I was in my bedroom sorting dirty laundry when I heard the front door open. Shepley usually listened for America's car to pull in so he could greet her at the door.

Pussy.

Murmuring, and then the closing of Shepley's door was my signal. I walked into the front room, and there she sat: glasses, her hair all piled on top of her head, and what might have been pajamas. I wouldn't have been surprised if they'd been molding in the bottom of her laundry hamper.

It was so hard not to bust into laughter. Never once had a female come to my apartment dressed like that. My front door had seen jean skirts, dresses, even a see-through tube dress over a string bikini. A handful of times, spackled-on makeup and glitter lotion. Never pajamas.

Her appearance immediately explained why she'd so easily agreed to come over. She was going to try to nauseate me into leaving her alone. If she didn't look absolutely sexy like that, it might have worked, but her skin was impeccable, and the lack of makeup and the frames of her glasses just made her eye color stand out even more.

"It's about time you showed up," I said, falling onto the couch.

At first she seemed proud of her idea, but as we talked and I remained impervious, it was clear that she knew her plan had failed. The less she smiled, the more I had to stop myself from grinning from ear to ear. She was so much fun. I just couldn't get over it.

Shepley and America joined us ten minutes later. Abby was flustered, and I was damn near light-headed. Our conversation had gone from her doubting that I could write a simple paper to her questioning my penchant for fighting. I kind of liked talking to her about normal stuff. It was preferable to the awkward task of asking her to leave once I bagged her. She didn't understand me, and I kind of wanted her to, even though I seemed to piss her off.

"What are you, the Karate Kid? Where did you learn to fight?"

Shepley and America seemed to be embarrassed for Abby. I don't know why; I sure as hell didn't mind. Just because I didn't talk about my childhood much didn't mean I was ashamed.

"I had a dad with a drinking problem and a bad temper, and four older brothers that carried the asshole gene."

"Oh," she said simply. Her cheeks turned red, and at that moment, I felt a twinge in my chest. I wasn't sure what it was, but it bugged me. "Don't be embarrassed, Pidge. Dad quit drinking. The brothers grew up."

"I'm not embarrassed." Her body language didn't match her words. I struggled to think of something to change the subject, and then her sexy, frumpy look came to mind. Her embarrassment was immediately replaced by irritation, something I was far more comfortable with.

America suggested watching TV. The last thing I wanted to do was to be in a room with Abby but unable to talk to her. I stood. "You hungry, Pidge?"

"I already ate."

America's eyebrows pulled in. "No, you haven't. Oh . . . er . . . that's right. I forgot. You grabbed a . . . pizza? Before we left."

Abby was embarrassed again, but her anger quickly covered it. Learning her emotional pattern didn't take long.

I opened the door, trying to keep my voice casual. I'd never been so eager to get a girl alone—especially to *not* have sex with her. "C'mon. You've gotta be hungry."

Her shoulders relaxed a bit. "Where are you going?"

"Wherever you want. We can hit a pizza place." I inwardly cringed. That might have been too eager.

She looked down at her sweatpants. "I'm not really dressed."

She had no idea how beautiful she was. That made her even more appealing. "You look fine. Let's go, I'm starvin'."

Once she was on the back of my Harley, I could finally think straight again. My thoughts were usually more relaxed on my bike. Abby's legs had my hips in a vise grip, but that was oddly relaxing, too. Almost a relief.

This weird sensation I felt around her was disorienting. I didn't like it, but then again it reminded me that she was around, so it was as comforting as it was unsettling. I decided to get my shit together. Abby might be a pigeon, but she was just a fucking girl. No need to get my boxers in a bunch.

Besides, there was something under the good girl facade. She hated me on sight because she'd been burned by someone like me before. No way was she a slut, though. Not even a reformed slut. I could spot them a mile away. My game face slowly melted away. I'd finally found a girl that was interesting enough to get to know, and a version of me had already hurt her.

Even though we'd just met, the thought of some jackhole hurting Pidge infuriated me. Abby associating me with someone that would hurt her was even worse. I gunned the throttle as I pulled into the Pizza Shack. That ride wasn't long enough to sort out the clusterfuck in my head.

I wasn't even thinking about my speed, so when Abby jumped off my bike and started yelling, I couldn't help but laugh.

"I went the speed limit."

"Yeah, if we were on the autobahn!" She ripped the wild bun down from the crown of her head, and then brushed her long hair with her fingers.

I couldn't stop staring while she rewrapped it and tied it back again. I imagined that this was what she looked like in the morning, and then had to think about the first ten minutes of *Saving Private Ryan* to keep my dick from getting hard. Blood. Screaming. Visible intestines. Grenades. Gunfire. More blood.

I held the door open. "I wouldn't let anything happen to you, Pigeon."

She angrily stomped past me and into the restaurant, ignoring my gesture. It was a damn shame; she was the first girl that I had ever wanted to open the door for. I'd been looking forward to that moment, and she didn't even notice.

After following her inside, I headed for the corner booth I usually commandeered. The soccer team was seated at several tables pushed together in the middle of the room. They were already howling that I had walked in with a date, and I gritted my teeth. I didn't want Abby to hear.

For the first time ever, I found myself embarrassed about my behavior. But it didn't last long. Seeing Abby sit across the table, cranky and annoyed, cheered me right up.

I ordered two beers. The look of disgust on Abby's face caught me off guard. The waitress was blatantly flirting with me, and Abby was unhappy. Apparently I could piss her off without even trying.

"Come here often?" she snapped, glancing at the waitress.

Hell, yeah. She was jealous. Wait. Maybe the way I was treated by women was a turnoff. That wouldn't surprise me, either. This chick made my head spin.

I leaned on the table with my elbows, refusing to let her see she was getting to me. "So what's your story, Pidge? Are you a man-hater in general, or do you just hate me?"

"I think it's just you."

I had to laugh. "I can't figure you out. You're the first girl that's ever been disgusted with me *before* sex. You don't get all flustered when you talk to me, and you don't try to get my attention."

"It's not a ploy. I just don't like you."

Ouch. "You wouldn't be here if you didn't like me."

My persistence paid off. Her scowl smoothed, and the skin around her eyes relaxed.

"I didn't say you're a bad person. I just don't like being a foregone conclusion for the sole reason of having a vagina."

Whatever it was that had come over me, I couldn't contain it. I choked back my laughter to no avail, and then burst out laughing. She didn't think I was a dick after all; she just didn't like my approach. Easily fixed. A wave of relief washed over me, and I laughed harder than I'd laughed in years. Maybe ever.

"Oh my *God*! You're killing me! That's it. We have to be friends. I won't take no for an answer."

"I don't mind being friends, but that doesn't mean you have to try to get in my panties every five seconds."

"You're not sleeping with me. I get it."

That was it. She smiled, and in that moment, a whole new world of possibilities opened up. My brain flashed like channels through Pigeon porn, and then the whole system crashed, and an infomercial about nobility and not wanting to screw up this weird friendship we'd just begun appeared in its place.

I smiled back. "You have my word. I won't even think about your panties . . . unless you want me to."

She rested her small elbows on the table and leaned onto them. Of course my eyes went right to her tits, and the way they now pressed against the edge of the table.

"And that won't happen, so we can be friends."

Challenge accepted.

"So what's *your* story?" Abby asked. "Have you always been *Travis 'Mad Dog' Maddox*, or is that just since you came here?" She used two fingers on each hand as quotation marks when she said that god-awful fucking nickname.

I cringed. "No. Adam started that after my first fight." I hated that name, but it stuck. Everyone else seemed to like it, so Adam kept using it.

After an awkward silence, Abby finally spoke. "That's it? You're not going to tell me anything about yourself?"

She didn't seem to mind the nickname, or else she just accepted the backstory. I never knew when she was going to get offended and freak out, or when she would be rational and stay cool. Holy hell, I couldn't get enough of it.

"What do you wanna know?"

Abby shrugged. "The normal stuff. Where you're from, what you want to be when you grow up . . . things like that."

I was having to work at keeping the tension out of my shoulders. Talking about myself—especially my past—was out of my comfort zone. I gave some vague answers and left it at that, but then I heard one of the soccer players make a crack. It wouldn't have bothered me nearly as much if I wasn't dreading the moment Abby realized what they were laughing about. Okay, that was a lie. That would have pissed me off whether she was there or not.

She kept wanting to know about my family and my major, and I was trying not to jump out of my seat and take them all out in a one-man stampede. As my anger came to a boil, focusing on our conversation became more difficult.

"What are they laughing about?" she finally asked, gesturing to the rowdy table.

I shook my head.

"Tell me," she insisted.

My lips pressed together into a thin line. If she walked out, I'd probably never get another chance, and those cheese dicks would have something more to laugh about.

She watched me expectantly.

Fuck it. "They're laughing about me having to take you to dinner, first. It's not usually . . . my thing."

"First?"

When the meaning sunk in, her face froze. She was mortified to be there with me.

I winced, waiting for her to storm out.

Her shoulders fell. "I was afraid they were laughing about

you being seen with me dressed like this, and they think I'm going to sleep with you," she grumbled.

Wait. What? "Why wouldn't I be seen with you?"

Abby's cheeks flushed pink, and she looked down to the table. "What were we talking about?"

I sighed. She was worried about me. She thought they were laughing about the way she looked. The Pigeon wasn't a hard-ass, after all. I decided to ask another question before she could reconsider.

"You. What's your major?"

"Oh, er, general ed, for now. I'm still undecided, but I'm leaning toward accounting."

"You're not a local, though. You must be a transplant."

"Wichita. Same as America."

"How did you end up here from Kansas?"

"We just had to get away."

"From what?"

"My parents."

She was running. I had a feeling the cardigan and pearls she wore the night we met were a front. But, to hide what? She got irritated pretty quick with the personal questions, but before I could change the subject, Kyle from the soccer team shot off his mouth.

I nodded. "So, why here?"

Abby snapped something back. I missed whatever it was. The chuckles and asshole comments from the soccer team drowned out her words.

"Dude, you're supposed to get a doggie bag, not bag the doggie."

I couldn't hold back anymore. They weren't just being disrespectful to me, they were disrespecting Abby. I stood up and took a few steps, and they started to shove each other out the door, tripping and stumbling over a dozen pairs of feet.

Abby's eyes penetrated the back of my head, bringing me back to my senses, and I planted myself back in the booth. She raised an eyebrow, and immediately my frustration and anger melted away.

"You were going to say why you chose this school," I said. Pretending that little sideshow didn't happen was probably the best way to continue.

"It's hard to explain," she said, shrugging. "I guess it just felt right."

If there was a phrase to explain the way I felt at that moment, that was it. I didn't know what the hell I was doing or why, but something about sitting across from her in that booth brought me a weird sense of calm. Even in the middle of a rage.

I smiled and opened my menu. "I know what you mean."

CHAPTER THREE

White Knight

SHEPLEY STOOD AT THE DOOR LIKE A LOVESICK IDIOT, waving to America as she pulled out of the parking lot. He shut the door, and then collapsed in the recliner with the most ridiculous smile on his face.

"You're dumb," I said.

"Me? You should have seen you. Abby couldn't get out of here quick enough."

I frowned. Abby didn't seem in a hurry to me, but now that Shepley had said something, I remembered that she *was* pretty quiet when we got back. "You think so?"

Shepley laughed, stretching back in the chair and pulling the footrest up. "She hates you. Give it up."

"She doesn't hate me. I nailed that date—dinner."

Shepley's eyebrows shot up. "Date? Trav. What are you doing? Because if this is just a game to you and you fuck this up for me, I'm going to kill you in your sleep."

I fell against the couch and grabbed the remote. "I don't know what I'm doing, but I'm not doing that."

Shepley looked confused. I wouldn't let him see that I was just as baffled as he was.

"I wasn't kidding," he said, keeping his eyes on the TV screen. "I'll smother you."

"I heard you," I snapped. The whole feeling-out-of-my-element thing was pissing me off, and then I had Pepé Le Pew over there threatening my death. Shepley with a crush was annoying. Shepley in love was almost intolerable.

"Remember Anya?"

"It's not like that," Shepley said, exasperated. "It's different with Mare. She's the one."

"You know that after a couple of months?" I asked, dubious.

"I knew it when I saw her."

I shook my head. I hated it when he was like this. Unicorns and butterflies flying out of his ass and hearts floating in the air. He always ended up getting his heart broken, and then I had to make sure he didn't drink himself to death for six months solid. America seemed to like it, though.

Whatever. No woman could make me blubber and get slobbering drunk over losing her. If they didn't stick around, they weren't worth it anyway.

Shepley stood and stretched, and then ambled toward his room.

"You're full of shit, Shep."

"How would you know?" he asked.

He was right. I'd never been in love, but I couldn't imagine it changing me that much.

I decided to turn in, too. I stripped down and lay back on the mattress in a huff. The second my head hit the pillow, I thought of Abby. Our conversation replayed verbatim in my mind. A few times she had showed a glint of interest. She didn't totally hate me, and that helped me relax. I wasn't exactly apologetic about my reputation, but she didn't expect me to pretend. Women didn't make me nervous. Abby made me feel distracted and focused at the same time. Agitated and relaxed. Pissed off and damn near giddy. I'd never felt so at odds with myself. Something about that feeling made me want to be around her more.

After two hours of staring at the ceiling, wondering if I would see her the next day, I decided to get up and find the bottle of Jack Daniel's in the kitchen.

The shot glasses were clean in the dishwasher, so I pulled out one and filled it to the brim. After hammering it back, I poured another. I tossed it back, set the glass in the sink, and turned around. Shepley stood in his doorway with a smirk on his face.

"And so it begins."

"The day you appeared on our family tree, I wanted to cut it down."

Shepley laughed once and shut his door.

I trudged to my bedroom, pissed that I couldn't argue.

MORNING CLASSES TOOK FOREVER, AND I WAS A LITTLE disgusted with myself that I had all but run to the cafeteria. I didn't even know if Abby would be there.

But, she was.

Brazil was sitting directly across from her, chatting it up with Shepley. A smirk touched my face, and then I sighed, both relieved and resigned to the fact that I was lame.

The lunch lady filled my tray with god-knows-what, and then I walked over to the table, standing directly across from Abby.

"You're sittin' in my chair, Brazil."

"Oh, is she one of your girls, Trav?"

Abby shook her head. "Absolutely not."

I waited, and then Brazil complied, taking his tray to an empty seat at the end of the long table.

"What's up, Pidge?" I asked, waiting for her to spit venom in my direction. To my extreme surprise, she showed no signs of anger.

"What is that?" She stared at my tray.

I looked down at the steaming concoction. She was making random conversation. Yet another good sign. "The cafeteria ladies scare me. I'm not about to critique their cooking skills."

Abby watched me poke around with my fork for something edible, and then seemed distracted by the murmurings of those around us. Granted, it was new for my fellow students to see me make a fuss over sitting across from someone. I still wasn't sure why I did.

"*Ugh* . . . that bio test is after lunch." America groaned.

"Did you study?" Abby asked.

America's nose wrinkled. "God, no. I spent the night reassuring my boyfriend that you weren't going to sleep with Travis."

Shepley immediately became sullen at the mention of the previous night's conversation.

The football players seated at the end of our table quieted down to hear our conversation, and Abby sunk down into her seat, shooting a glare at America.

She was embarrassed. For whatever reason, she was mortified by any attention whatsoever.

America ignored Abby and nudged Shepley with her shoulder, but Shepley's frown didn't fade.

"Jesus, Shep. You've got it that bad, huh?" I threw a packet of ketchup at him, trying to lighten the mood. The surrounding students turned their attention to Shepley and America then, hoping for something to talk about.

Shepley didn't answer, but Abby's gray eyes peeked up at me over a small smile. I was on a roll today. She couldn't hate me if she tried. I don't know why I was so worried. It wasn't like I wanted to date her or anything. She just seemed like the perfect platonic experiment. She was basically a good girl—albeit slightly angry—and didn't need me fucking up her five-year plan. If she had one.

America rubbed Shepley's back. "He's going to be okay. It's just going to take him a while to believe Abby is resistant to your charms."

"I haven't *tried* to charm her," I said. I was just getting ahead, and America was sinking my battleship. "She's my friend."

Abby looked to Shepley. "I told you. You have nothing to worry about."

Shepley met Abby's eyes, and then his expression smoothed. Crisis averted. Abby saved the day.

I waited for a minute, trying to think of something to say. I wanted to ask Abby to come over later, but it would be lame after America's comment. A brilliant idea popped into my head, and I didn't hesitate. "Did *you* study?"

Abby frowned. "No amount of studying is going to help me with biology. It's just not something I can wrap my head around."

I stood, nodding toward the door. "C'mon."

"What?"

"Let's go get your notes. I'm going to help you study."

"Travis . . ."

"Get your ass up, Pidge. You're gonna ace that test."

The next three seconds might have been the longest of my life. Abby finally stood. She passed America and tugged on her hair. "See you in class, Mare."

She smiled. "I'll save you a seat. I'll need all the help I can get."

I held the door open for her as we left the cafeteria, but she didn't seem to notice. Again, I was only horrifically disappointed.

Shoving my hands in my pockets, I kept pace with her during the short walk to Morgan Hall, and then I watched as she fidgeted with her door key.

Abby finally pushed the door open, and then tossed her biology book onto the bed. She sat down and crossed her legs, and I fell onto the mattress, noting how stiff and uncomfortable it was. No wonder all the girls at this school were cranky. They couldn't possibly get a good night's rest on these damn mattresses. Jesus.

Abby turned to the correct page of her textbook, and I went to work. We went over the key points of the chapter. It was kind of cool how she watched me while I talked. Almost like she was both hanging on to every word, and amazed that I knew how to read. A few times I could tell by her expression that she didn't understand, so I'd go back over it, and then her eyes would brighten. I started working hard for the lights-on look on her face after that.

Before I knew it, it was time for her to go to class. I sighed, and then smacked her playfully on the head with her study guide.

"You got this. You know this study guide backward and forward."

"Well . . . we'll see."

"I'm going to walk you to class. I'll quiz you on the way." I waited for a polite rejection, but she offered a small smile and nodded.

We walked into the hall, and she sighed. "You're not going to be mad if I flunk this test, are you?"

She was worried if I was going to be mad at her? I wasn't sure what I should think about that, but it felt pretty fucking awesome.

"You're not going to flunk, Pidge. We need to start earlier for the next one, though," I said, walking along with her to the science building. I asked her question after question. She answered most right away, some she hesitated about, but she got them all correct.

We reached the door of her classroom, and I could see the appreciation on her face. She was too proud to admit it, though.

"Kick ass," I said, not really knowing what else to say.

Parker Hayes passed by and nodded. "Hey, Trav."

I hated that douche. "Parker," I said, nodding back.

Parker was one of those guys that liked to follow me around and use his White Knight status to get laid. He liked to refer to me as a womanizer, but the truth was, Parker just played a more sophisticated game. He wasn't honest about his conquests. He pretended to care and then let them down easy.

One night our freshman year, I took Janet Littleton home from the Red Door to my apartment. Parker was trying to get lucky with her friend. We went our separate ways from the club, and after I bagged her and didn't pretend to want a relationship afterward, she called her friend all pissed off to come get her. The friend was still with Parker, so he ended up taking Janet home.

After that, Parker had a new story to tell his conquests. Whatever girl I bagged, he usually swept up my sloppy seconds by recounting the time he saved Janet.

I tolerated him, but only just barely.

Parker's eyes targeted Pigeon and immediately lit up. "Hey, Abby."

I didn't understand why Parker was so insistent on seeing if he could land the same girls I did, but he'd had class with her for several weeks and was just now showing interest. Knowing it was because he saw her talking to me nearly sent me into a fury.

"Hi," Abby said, taken off guard. She clearly didn't know why he was suddenly talking to her. It was written all over her face. "Who's that?" she asked me.

I shrugged casually, but I wanted to tear across the room and beat his preppy ass. "Parker Hayes," I said. His name left a bad taste in my mouth. "He's one of my Sig Tau brothers." That left a bad taste, too. I had brothers, both frat and blood. Parker felt like neither. More like an archenemy that you kept close enough to keep an eye on.

"*You're* in a *frat*?" she asked, her little nose wrinkling up.

"Sigma Tau, same as Shep. I thought you knew."

"Well . . . you don't seem the . . . fraternity type," she said, eyeing the tattoos on my forearms.

The fact that Abby's eyes were back on me immediately put me in a better mood. "My dad is an alumnus, and my brothers are all Sig Tau. It's a family thing."

"And they expected you to pledge?" she asked, skeptical.

"Not really. They're just good guys," I said, flicking her papers. I handed them to her. "Better get to class."

She flashed that flawless smile. "Thanks for helping me." She nudged me with her elbow, and I couldn't help but smile back.

She walked into the classroom and sat next to America. Parker was staring at her, watching the girls talking. I fantasized about picking up a desk and hurling it at his head as I walked down the hall. With no more classes for the day, there was no reason for me to stick around. A long ride on the Harley would help keep the thought of Parker sleazing his way into Abby's good graces from driving me crazy, so I made sure to take the long way home to give me more time to think. A few couch-worthy coeds crossed my path, but Abby's face kept popping into my mind—so many times that I began to annoy myself.

I had notoriously been a piece of shit to every girl with whom I'd had a private conversation over the age of sixteen—since I was fifteen. Our story might have been typical: Bad boy falls for good girl, but Abby was no princess. She was hiding something. Maybe that was our connection: whatever it was that she had left behind.

I pulled into the apartment parking lot and climbed off the bike. So much for thinking better on the Harley. Everything I'd just unraveled in my head made no fucking sense. I was just trying to justify my weird obsession with her.

Suddenly in a very bad mood, I slammed the door behind me and sat on the couch, and became even more pissed off when I couldn't find the remote right away.

Black plastic landed beside me as Shepley passed to sit in the recliner. I picked up the remote and pointed it at the TV, turning it on.

"Why do you take the remote to your bedroom? You just have to bring it back in here," I snapped.

"I don't know, man, it's just habit. What's your problem?"

"I don't know," I grumbled, flipping on the TV. I pressed the mute button. "Abby Abernathy."

Shepley's eyebrow pushed up. "What about her?"

"She gets under my skin. I think I just need to bag her and get it over with."

Shepley eyed me for a while, unsure. "It's not that I don't appreciate you not fucking up my life with your newfound restraint, but you've never needed my permission before . . . unless . . . don't tell me you finally give a shit about someone."

"Don't be a dick."

Shepley couldn't contain his grin. "You care about her. I guess it just took a girl refusing to sleeping with you for more than a twenty-four-hour period."

"Laura made me wait a week."

"Abby won't give you the time of day, though?"

"She just wants to be friends. I guess I'm lucky she doesn't treat me like a leper."

After an awkward silence, Shepley nodded. "You're scared."

"Of what?" I asked with a dubious smirk.

"Rejection. *Mad Dog* is one of us after all."

My eye twitched. "You know I fucking hate that, Shep."

Shepley smiled. "I know. Almost as much as you hate the way you feel right now."

"You're not making me feel any better."

"So you like her and you're scared. Now what?"

"Nothing. It just sucks that I finally found the girl worth having and she's too good for me."

Shepley tried to stifle a laugh. It was irritating that he was so amused about my predicament. He straightened his smile and then said, "Why don't you let her make that decision for herself?"

"Because I care about her just enough to want to make it for her."

Shepley stretched and then stood, his bare feet dragging across the carpet. "You want a beer?"

"Yeah. Let's drink to friendship."

"So you're going to keep hanging out with her? Why? That sounds like torture to me."

I thought about it for a minute. It did sound like torture, but not as bad as just watching her from afar. "I don't want her to end up with me . . . or any other dick."

"You mean or anyone else. Dude, that's nuts."

"Get my fuckin' beer and shut up."

Shepley shrugged. Unlike Chris Jenks, Shepley knew when to shut up.

CHAPTER FOUR

Distracted

THE DECISION WAS CRAZY, BUT FREEING. THE NEXT DAY I walked into the cafeteria, and without a second thought, sat in the empty seat across from Abby. Being around her was natural and easy, and other than having to put up with the prodding eyes of the general student population, and even some professors, she seemed to like having me around.

"We studying today or what?"

"We are," she said, unfazed.

The only negative about hanging out with her as friends was the more time I spent with her, the more I liked her. It was harder to forget the color and shape of her eyes, and the way her lotion smelled on her skin. I also noticed more about her, like how long her legs were, and the colors she wore most often. I even got a pretty good handle on which week I shouldn't give her any extra shit, which fortunately for Shepley, was the same week not to fuck with America. That way, we had three weeks to not be on guard instead of two, and we could give each other fair warning.

Even at her worst, Abby wasn't fussy like most girls. The only thing that seemed to affect her was the occasional questions about our relationship, but as long as I took care of it, she got over it pretty fast.

As more time passed, people speculated less. We ate lunch together on most days, and on the nights when we studied, I'd take her out to dinner. Shepley and America invited us to a movie once. It was never awkward, never a question of whether we were more than friends. I wasn't sure how I felt about that, especially since my decision not to pursue her in that way didn't stop me from fantasizing about making her moan on my couch—until one night I was watching her and America poke and tickle each other at the apartment and I imagined Abby in my bed.

She needed to get outta my head.

The only cure was to stop thinking about her long enough to land my next conquest.

A few days later, a familiar face caught my eye. I'd seen her before with Janet Littleton. Lucy was fairly hot, never missed a chance to show off her cleavage, and very vocal about hating my guts. Fortunately it took me thirty minutes and a tentative invite to the Red to get her home. I'd barely shut the front door before she was removing my clothes. So much for the deep well of hatred she had harbored toward me since last year. She left with a smile on her face and disappointment in her eyes.

I still had Abby on my mind.

Not even postorgasm fatigue was going to cure it, and I felt something new: guilt.

The next day, I rushed to history class and slid into the desk next to Abby. She already had out her laptop and book, barely acknowledging my presence when I sat down.

The classroom was darker than usual; the clouds outside robbed the room of the natural light that usually poured in through the windows. I nudged her elbow, but she wasn't as receptive as usual, so I snatched her pencil out of her hand and began doodling in the margins. Tattoos, mostly, but I scrawled her name in cool letters. She peeked over at me with an appreciative smile.

I leaned over and whispered in her ear. "You wanna grab lunch off campus today?"

I can't, she mouthed.

I scribbled in her book.

Y?

Because I have to make use of my meal plan.

Bullshit.

Seriously.

I wanted to argue but was running out of room on the page. *Fine. Another mystery meal. Can't wait.*

She giggled, and I enjoyed that on-top-of-the-world feeling I experienced whenever I made her smile. A few more doodles and a legit drawing of a dragon later, Chaney dismissed class.

I tossed Abby's pencil in her backpack as she packed away the rest of her things, and then we walked to the cafeteria.

We didn't get as many stares as we had in the past. The student populace had grown accustomed to seeing us together on a regular basis. When we went through the line, we made small talk about the new history paper Chaney had assigned. Abby ran her meal card and then made her way to the table. I immediately noticed one thing missing from her tray: the can of OJ she picked up every day.

I scanned the line of husky, no-nonsense servers who stood behind the buffet. Once the stern-looking woman behind the register came into view, I knew I'd found my target.

"Hey, Miss . . . uh . . . Miss . . ."

The cafeteria lady sized me up once before deciding I was going to cause her trouble, as most women did right before I made their thighs tingle.

"Armstrong," she said in a gruff voice.

I tried to subdue my disgust as the thought of her thighs appeared in the dark corners of my mind.

I flashed my most charming smile. "That's lovely. I was wondering, because you seem like the boss here . . . No OJ today?"

"There's some in the back. I've been too busy to bring any more to the front."

I nodded. "You're always running your ass off. They should give you a raise. No one else works as hard as you do. We all notice."

She lifted her chin, minimizing the folds on her neck. "Thank you. It's about time someone did. Did you need orange juice?"

"Just a can . . . if you don't mind, of course."

She winked. "Not at all. I'll be right back."

I brought the can to the table and sat it on Abby's tray.

"You didn't have to do that. I was going to grab one." She peeled off her jacket and laid it across her lap, exposing her shoulders. They were still tan from the summer, and a little shiny, begging me to touch them.

A dozen dirty things flashed in my mind.

"Well, now you don't have to," I said. I offered one of my best smiles, but this time it was genuine. It was another one of those Happy Abby moments I sort of wished for these days.

Brazil snorted. "Did she turn you into a cabana boy, Travis? What's next, fanning her with a palm tree leaf, wearing a Speedo?"

I craned my neck down the table to see Brazil with a smart-ass grin. He didn't mean anything by it, but he ruined my moment, and it pissed me off. I probably did look a little bit like a pussy, bringing her a drink.

Abby leaned forward. "You couldn't *fill* a Speedo, Brazil. Shut the hell up."

"Easy, Abby! I was kidding!" Brazil said, holding up his hands.

"Just . . . don't talk about him like that," she said, frowning.

I stared for a moment, watching her anger subside a tiny bit as she turned her attention to me. That was definitely a first. "Now I've seen it all. I was just defended by a girl." I offered her a small smile and then stood, glaring at Brazil one last time before leaving to dump my tray. I wasn't that hungry, anyway.

The heavy metal doors easily gave way when I shoved through them. I pulled my cigarettes from my pocket and lit one up, trying to forget what had just happened.

I'd just made an ass of myself over a girl, and it was particularly satisfying to my frat brothers because I had been the one giving them a hard time for two years for even mentioning they might want to do more than just bag a girl. It was my turn now, and I couldn't do a damn thing about it—because I couldn't. Even worse? I didn't want to.

When the other smokers around me laughed, I did the same, even though I had no clue what they were talking about. Inside I was pissed off and humiliated, or pissed off that I was humiliated. Whichever. The girls pawed at me and took turns trying to make conversation. I nodded and smiled to be nice, but I really just wanted to get out of there and punch something. A public tantrum would show weakness, and I wasn't havin' that shit.

Abby passed, and I cut off one of the girls in midsentence to catch up with her. "Wait up, Pidge. I'll walk you."

"You don't have to walk me to every class, Travis. I know how to get there on my own."

I admit it: That stung a little. She didn't even look at me when she said it, completely dismissive.

Just then a girl with a short skirt and mile-high legs passed by. Her shiny dark hair swayed against her back as she walked. That's when it hit me: I had to give up. Bagging a random hot chick was what I did best, and Abby wanted nothing more than to be friends with me. I planned to do the right thing and keep things platonic, but if I didn't do something drastic, that plan would get lost in the mess of conflicting thoughts and emotions swirling inside of me.

It was time to finally draw a line. I didn't deserve Abby, anyway. What was the point?

I threw my cigarette to the ground. "I'll catch up with you later, Pidge."

I put on my game face, but it wouldn't take much. She had crossed my path on purpose, hoping her short skirt and hooker heels would get my attention. I got ahead of her and turned around, shoving my hands in my pockets.

"You in a hurry?"

She smiled. I already had her. "I'm going to class."

"Oh yeah? What class?"

She stopped, one side of her mouth pulling to the side. "Travis Maddox, right?"

"Right. My reputation precedes me?"

"It does."

"Guilty."

She shook her head. "I have to get to class."

I sighed, feigning disappointment. "That's a shame. I was just going to ask you for some help."

"With what?" Her tone was dubious, but she was still smiling. I could have just asked her to follow me home for a quick fuck and she probably would have gone for it, but a certain amount of charm went a long way for later.

"Getting to my apartment. I have a terrible sense of direction."

"Is that so?" she asked, nodding, frowning, and then smiling. She was trying hard not to be flattered.

Her top two buttons were loose, leaving the bottom curve of her breasts and a few inches of her bra visible. I felt that familiar swelling in my jeans, and I switched my weight to the other foot.

"Terrible." I smiled, watching her gaze drift to the dimple in my cheek. I don't know why, but the dimple always seemed to seal the deal.

She shrugged, trying to remain cool. "Lead the way. If I see you veering off course, I'll honk."

"I'm this way," I said, nodding in the direction of the parking lot.

She had her tongue down my throat before we got all the way up the apartment stairs and was pulling off my jacket before I could single out the right key. We were clumsy, but it was fun. I had plenty of practice opening the lock on the apartment door with my lips on someone else's. She shoved me into the living room the second the bolt unlatched, and I grabbed her hips and pushed her against the door to close it. She wrapped her legs around my waist, and I lifted her up, pressing my pelvis against hers.

She kissed me like she'd been starving and she knew there was food in my mouth. I don't know, I kinda dug it. She bit my bottom lip, and I took a step back, losing my footing and crashing into the end table beside the recliner. Various items knocked to the floor.

"Oops," she said, giggling.

I smiled and watched as she walked over to the couch and leaned forward over the back so her ass cheeks became visible along with the slightest trace of a thin strip of white lace.

I unbuckled my belt and took a step. She was going to make this easy. She arched her neck and whipped her long dark hair against her back. She was hot as hell, I'd give her that. My zipper could barely contain what was underneath.

She turned to look at me and I leaned over, planting my lips on hers.

"Maybe I should tell you my name?" she breathed.

"Why?" I panted. "I kinda like this."

She smiled, hooked her thumbs onto each side of her panties and then pulled them down until they fell down to her ankles. Her eyes connected with mine, refreshingly wicked.

Abby's disapproving eyes flashed in my mind.

"What are you waiting for?" she asked, excited and impatient.

"Absolutely nothing," I said, shaking my head. I tried to concentrate on her bare backside against my thighs. Having to concentrate to stay hard was definitely something new and different, and it was all Abby's fault.

She turned around and yanked my shirt over my head, and then finished unzipping my jeans. Damn. I was either working at a turtle's pace, or this woman was the female version of me. I kicked off my boots and then stepped out of the denim, kicking it all to the side.

One of her legs pulled up, and her knee hooked around my hip. "I've wanted this for a long time," she whispered against my ear. "Since I saw you at freshman orientation last year."

I ran my hand up her thigh, trying to think if I'd talked to her before. By the time my fingers reached the end of the line, they were drenched. She wasn't kidding. A year's worth of mental foreplay made my job a lot easier.

She moaned the second my fingertips touched her tender skin. She was so wet my fingers didn't get much traction, and my balls were starting to hurt. I had only bagged two women in as many weeks. This chick, and Janet's friend Lucy. Oh wait. Megan made three. The morning after I met Abby. Abby. Guilt swept over me, and it had a rather negative effect on my hard on.

"Don't move," I said, running in only boxers to my bedroom. I fished out a square package from my nightstand, and then jogged back to where the brunette stunner was standing, exactly the way I'd left her. She snatched the package out of my hand, and then got on her knees. After some creativity and rather surprising tricks with her tongue, I had the green light to put her on the couch.

So I did. Facedown with a reach around, and she loved every minute of it.

CHAPTER FIVE

Roommates

THE SEXAHOLIC WAS IN THE BATHROOM, GETTING dressed and primping. She didn't say much after we finished, and I was thinking I was going to have to get her number and put her on the very short list of girls—like Megan—that didn't require a relationship to have sex, and were also worth a repeat.

Shepley's phone chirped. It was a kiss noise, so it must have been America. She changed her text tone on his phone, and Shepley was more than happy to comply. They were good together, but they also made me wanna puke.

I was sitting on the couch clicking through channels, waiting for the girl to come out so I could send her home, when I noticed that Shepley was buzzing around the apartment.

My eyebrows pushed together. "What are you doing?"

"You might want to pick up your shit. Mare's coming over with Abby."

That got my attention. "Abby?"

"Yeah. The boiler went out again at Morgan."

"So?"

"So they're going to be staying here for a few days."

I sat up. "They? As in Abby's going to stay here? In our apartment?"

"Yes, buttmunch. Get your mind out of Jenna Jameson's ass and listen to what I'm saying. They will be here in ten minutes. With luggage."

"No fuckin' way."

Shepley stopped in his tracks and looked at me from under his brow. "Get your ass up and help me, and take your trash out," he said, pointing to the bathroom.

"Oh, fuck," I said, hopping to my feet.

Shepley nodded his head, his eyes wide. "Yeah."

It finally hit. If it pissed America off that I had a straggler still here when she arrived with Abby, it would put Shepley in a bad spot. If Abby didn't want to stay here because of it, it would become his problem—and mine.

My eyes focused on the bathroom door. The faucet had been running since she'd gone in there. I didn't know if she was taking a shit or a shower. No way was I going to get her out of the apartment before the girls came. It would look worse if I was caught trying to sweep her out, so I decided to change the sheets on my bed and pick up a little bit, instead.

"Where is Abby going to sleep?" I asked, looking at the couch. I wasn't going to let her sprawl out on fourteen months of body fluids.

"I don't know. The recliner?"

"She's not sleeping on the fucking recliner, assclown." I scratched my head. "I guess she'll sleep in my bed."

Shepley howled, his laughter spanning at least two blocks. He bent over and grabbed his knees, his face turning red.

"What?"

He stood up and pointed, shaking his finger and his head at me. He was too amused to talk, so he just walked away, trying to continue cleaning while his body shuddered.

Eleven minutes later, Shepley was jogging across the front room to the door. He made his way down the stairs, and then nothing. The faucet in the bathroom finally shut off, and it became very quiet.

After a few minutes more, I heard the door bang open, and Shepley complaining between grunts.

"Christ, baby! Your suitcase is twenty pounds more than Abby's!"

I walked into the hall, seeing my latest conquest emerge from the bathroom. She froze in the hallway, took one look at Abby and America, and then finished buttoning her blouse. She definitely wasn't freshening up in there. She still had makeup smeared all over her face.

For a minute, I was completely distracted from the awkwardness by the letters *W, T,* and *F.* I guess she wasn't as uncomplicated as previously thought, making America and Abby's unannounced visit even more welcome. Even if I was still in my boxers.

"Hi," she said to the girls. She looked down at their luggage, her surprise turning to total confusion.

America glared at Shepley.

He held up his hands. "She's with Travis!"

That was my cue. I turned the corner and yawned, patting my guest's ass. "My company's here. You'd better go."

She seemed to relax a bit and smiled. She wrapped her arms around me, and then kissed my neck. Her lips felt soft and warm not an hour ago. In front of Abby, they were like two sticky buns lined with barbed wire.

"I'll leave my number on the counter."

"Eh . . . don't worry about it," I said, purposefully nonchalant.

"What?" she asked, leaning back. The rejection in her eyes shone bright, searching mine for something other than what I truly meant. Glad this was coming out now. I might have called her again and made things very messy. Mistaking her for a possible frequent flyer was a bit startling. I was usually a better judge than that.

"*Every* time!" America said. She looked at the woman. "*How* are you surprised by this? He's Travis Fucking Maddox! He is *famous* for this very thing, and *every* time they're surprised!" she said, turning to Shepley. He put his arm around her, gesturing for her to calm down.

The woman's eyes narrowed, on fire with anger and embarrassment, and then she stormed out, grabbing her purse on the way.

The door slammed, and Shepley's shoulders tensed. Those moments bothered him. I, on the other hand, had a shrew to tame, so I strolled into the kitchen and opened the fridge as if nothing had happened. The hell in her eyes foretold a wrath like I had never experienced (not because I hadn't come across a woman who wanted to hand my ass to me on a silver platter, but because I'd never cared to stick around to hear it).

America shook her head and walked down the hall. Shepley followed her, angling his body to compensate for the weight of her suitcase as he trailed behind her.

Just when I thought Abby would strike, she collapsed into the recliner. *Huh. Well . . . she's pissed. Might as well get it over with.*

I crossed my arms, keeping a minimum safe distance from her by staying in the kitchen. "What's wrong, Pidge? Hard day?"

"No, I'm thoroughly disgusted."

It was a start.

"With me?" I asked with a smile.

"Yes, *you*. How can you just use someone like that and treat them that way?"

And so it began. "How did I treat her? She offered her number, I declined."

Her mouth fell open. I tried not to laugh. I don't know why it amused me so much to see her flustered and appalled at my behavior, but it did. "You'll have sex with her, but you won't take her number?"

"Why would I want her number if I'm not going to call her?"

"Why would you sleep with her if you're not going to call her?"

"I don't promise anyone anything, Pidge. She didn't stipulate a relationship before she spread-eagled on my couch."

She stared at the couch with revulsion. "She's someone's daughter, Travis. What if, down the line, someone treats *your* daughter like that?"

The thought had crossed my mind, and I was prepared. "My daughter better not drop her panties for some jackass she just met, let's put it that way."

That was the truth. Did women deserve to be treated like sluts? No. Did sluts deserve to be treated like sluts? Yes. I was a slut. The first time I bagged Megan and she left without so much as a cuddle, I didn't cry about it and eat a gallon of ice cream. I didn't complain to my frat brothers that I put out on the first date and Megan treated me according to the way I behaved. It is what it is, no sense in pretending to protect your dignity if you set out to destroy it. Girls are notorious for judging each other, anyway, only taking a break long enough to judge a guy for doing it. I'd hear them label a classmate a whore before the thought ever crossed my mind. However, if I took that whore home, bagged her, and released her strings-free, I was suddenly the bad guy. Nonsense.

Abby crossed her arms, noticeably unable to argue, and that made her even angrier. "So, besides admitting that you're a jackass, you're saying that because she slept with you, she deserved to be tossed out like a stray cat?"

"I'm saying that I was honest with her. She's an adult, it was consensual . . . she was a little too eager about it, if you want to know the truth. You act like I committed a crime."

"She didn't seem as clear about your intentions, Travis."

"Women usually justify their actions with whatever they make up in their heads. She didn't tell me up front that she expected a relationship any more than I told her I expected sex with no strings. How is it any different?"

"You're a pig."

I shrugged. "I've been called worse." Regardless of my indifference, to hear her say that felt about as good as her shoving a two-by-four under my thumb nail. Even if it was true.

She stared at the couch, and then recoiled. "I guess I'm sleeping on the recliner."

"Why?"

"I'm not sleeping on that thing! God knows what I'd be lying in!"

I lifted her duffel bag off the floor. "You're not sleeping on the couch or the recliner. You're sleeping in my bed."

"Which is more unsanitary than the couch, I'm sure."

"There's never been anyone in my bed but me."

She rolled her eyes. "Give me a break!"

"I'm absolutely serious. I bag 'em on the couch. I don't let them in my room."

"Then why am *I* allowed in your bed?"

I wanted to tell her. Jesus, did I ever want to mouth the words, but I could barely admit it to myself, much less her. Deep down I knew I was a piece of shit, and she deserved better. Part of me wanted to carry her to the bedroom and *show* her why she was different, but that was also the one thing that stopped me. She was my opposite: innocent on the surface, and damaged deep within. There was something about her I needed in my life, and even though I wasn't sure what it was, I couldn't give into my bad habits and fuck it up. She was the forgiving type, I could see, but she had lines drawn that I knew better than to cross.

A better option popped into my head, and I smirked. "Are you planning on having sex with me tonight?"

"No!"

"That's why. Now get your cranky ass up, take your hot shower, and then we can study some bio."

Abby's eyes stared me down, but she complied. She nearly shoved her shoulder into me as she passed, and then slammed the bathroom door. The pipes under the apartment immediately whined in response to her turning on the water.

She packed light: only the essentials. I found some shorts and a T-shirt and a pair of white cotton panties with purple stripes. I held them up in front of me, and then dug a little further. They were all cotton. She really didn't plan to get naked with me, or even to tease. A little disappointing, but at the same time it made me like her even more. I wondered if she had any thongs at all.

Was she a virgin?

I laughed. A virgin in college was unheard of these days.

A tube of toothpaste and her toothbrush, and a small tub of some sort of face cream was packed, too, so I took them with me down the hall, grabbing a clean towel from the hall linen closet on the way.

I knocked once, but she didn't answer, so I just walked in. She was behind the curtain, anyway, and she didn't have anything I hadn't seen before.

"Mare?"

"No, it's me," I said, setting her stuff on the counter beside the sink.

"What are you doing in here? Get out!" she squealed.

I laughed once. What a baby. "You forgot a towel, and I brought your clothes, and your toothbrush, and some weird face cream I found in your bag."

"You went through my stuff?" Her voice went up an octave.

The sudden laughter caught in my throat and I choked it back. I brought in Prudezilla's things to be a nice guy, and she was freaking out. Not like I was going to find anything interesting in her bag, anyway. She was about as naughty as a Sunday school teacher.

I squeezed some of her toothpaste onto my toothbrush and turned on the faucet.

Abby was strangely quiet until her forehead and eyes popped out from behind the curtain. I tried to ignore her, feeling her eyes burning a hole in the back of my head.

Her irritation was a mystery. To me, the whole scenario was oddly relaxing. That thought caused me to pause; domesticity was not something I thought I'd enjoy.

"Get out, Travis," she growled.

"I can't go to bed without brushing my teeth."

"If you come within two feet of this curtain, I will poke out your eyes while you sleep."

"I won't peek, Pidge." Actually, the thought of her leaning over me, even with a knife in her hand, was kind of hot. More the leaning over part than the knife.

I finished brushing my teeth and then made my way to the bedroom, smiling the whole way. Within minutes the pipes silenced, but it took forever for her to come out.

Impatient, I poked my head through the bathroom door. "C'mon, Pidge! I'm gettin' old, here!" Her appearance surprised me. I'd seen her without makeup on before, but her skin was pink and shiny, and her long, wet hair was slicked back away from her face. I couldn't help but stare.

Abby reared back her arm and chucked her comb at me. I ducked, and then shut the door, chuckling all the way down the hall.

I could hear her small feet padding down the hall to my room, and my heart began to pound in my chest.

"Night, Abby," America called from Shepley's room.

"Night, Mare."

I had to laugh. Nightmare was right. Shepley's girlfriend had introduced me to my very own form of crack. I couldn't get enough, and I didn't want to quit. Even though I couldn't call it anything but an addiction, I didn't dare sample even a crumb. I only kept her close, feeling better just knowing she was around. There was no hope for me.

Two small knocks brought me back to reality.

"Come in, Pidge. You don't have to knock."

Abby slipped in, her hair dark and damp, in a gray T-shirt

and plaid boxer shorts. Wide eyes wandered about the room as she decided different things about me based on the bareness of my walls. It was the first time a woman had been in there. That moment wasn't something I had thought about, but Abby changing the way the room felt was not something I expected.

Before, it was just where I slept. A place where I'd never spent much time at all. Abby's presence made the white, clutter-less walls obvious, to the point where I felt a lesser version of embarrassment. Abby being in my room made it feel like home, and the emptiness no longer seemed right.

"Nice pj's," I said finally, sitting on the bed. "Well, come on. I'm not going to bite you."

Her chin lowered and she raised her brows. "I'm not afraid of you." Her biology book landed beside me with a *thud*, and then she stopped. "Do you have a pen?"

I nodded to the night table. "Top drawer." The second I said the words, my blood turned cold. She was going to find my stash. I readied myself for the impending death match that would quickly follow.

She put one knee on the bed and reached over, pulling open the drawer and fishing around until her hand lurched back. In the next second, she grabbed the pen and then slammed the drawer shut.

"What?" I asked, pretending to scan over the words in the biology book.

"Did you rob the health clinic?"

How does a pigeon know where to get condoms? "No. Why?"

Her face twisted. "Your lifetime supply of condoms."

Here it comes. "Better safe than sorry, right?" She couldn't possibly argue with that.

Instead of the yelling and name calling I expected, she rolled her eyes. I turned the pages of the biology book, trying not to look too relieved.

"Okay, we can start here. Jesus . . . photosynthesis? Didn't you learn this in high school?"

"Kind of," she said, defensively. "It's Biology 101, Trav. I didn't pick the curriculum."

"And you're in calculus? How can you be so advanced in math and behind in science?"

"I'm not behind. The first half is always review."

I raised an eyebrow. "Not really."

She listened while I went over the basics of photosynthesis, and then the anatomy of plant cells. It didn't matter how long I talked, or what I said, she hung on to every word. It was easy to pretend that she was interested in me and not a passing grade.

"Lipids. Not lipides. Tell me what they are again."

She pulled off her glasses. "I'm beat. I can't memorize one more macromolecule."

Fuckin' A. Bedtime. "All right."

Abby suddenly looked nervous, which was curiously soothing to me.

I left her alone with her nerves to take a shower. Knowing she had just been standing naked in the same spot made for some arousing thoughts, so for the five minutes before I got out, the water had to be ice cold. It was uncomfortable, but at least it got rid of my hard-on.

When I returned to the bedroom, Abby was lying on her side, eyes closed, and stiff as a board. I dropped my towel, changed into my boxers, and then crawled into bed, flipping off the light. Abby didn't move, but she wasn't asleep.

Every muscle in her body was tense, but they tightened even more just before she turned to face me.

"You're sleeping in here, too?"

"Well, yeah. This is my bed."

"I know, but I . . ." she trailed off, weighing her options.

"Don't you trust me by now? I'll be on my best behavior, I swear." I held up my index, middle, and pinky finger, affectionately known by my frat brothers as the "shocker." She didn't get it.

As much as being good would suck, I wasn't going to run her off the first night by doing something stupid.

Abby was a delicate balance of tough and tender. Pushing her too far seemed to garner the same reaction as a cornered animal. It was fun to walk the tightrope she required, in a terrifying, driving-at-a-thousand-miles-per-hour, backward-on-a-motorcycle kind of way.

She turned away from me, karate chopping the blanket around every curve of her body. Another smile crept across my face, and I leaned into her ear.

"Good night, Pigeon."

CHAPTER SIX

Shots

THE SUN HAD JUST BEGUN TO CAST SHADOWS ON THE walls of my bedroom when I opened my eyes. Abby's hair was tangled and messy, and covering my face. I took a deep breath through my nose.

Dude. What are you doing . . . besides being creepy? I thought. I turned onto my back, but before I could stop myself, took in another breath. She still smelled like shampoo and lotion.

A few seconds later, the alarm bleated, and Abby began to rouse. Her hand ran across my chest, and then lurched back.

"Travis?" she said, groggily. "Your alarm." She waited for a minute, and then sighed, reaching across me, straining until she finally reached the clock, and then pounded against the plastic until the noise stopped.

She fell against her pillow and puffed. A chuckle escaped my lips, and she gasped.

"You were awake?"

"I promised I'd behave. I didn't say anything about letting you lay on me."

"I didn't lay on you. I couldn't reach the clock. That has to be the most annoying alarm I've ever heard. It sounds like a dying animal."

"You want breakfast?" I tucked my hands behind my head.

"I'm not hungry."

She seemed pissed about something, but I ignored it. She probably just wasn't a morning person. Although with that logic, she wasn't really an afternoon or night person, either. Come to think of it, she was kind of a cranky bitch . . . and I *liked* it.

"Well, I am. Why don't you ride with me down the street to the café?"

"I don't think I can handle your lack of driving skills this early in the morning." She wiggled her bony little feet into her slippers, and then shuffled to the door.

"Where are you going?"

She was instantly annoyed. "To get dressed and go to class. Do you need an itinerary while I'm here?"

She wanted to play hardball? Okay. I'd play. I walked over to her and cupped her shoulders in my hands. Damn, her skin felt good against mine. "Are you always so temperamental, or will that taper off once you believe I'm not just creating some elaborate scheme to get in your pants?"

"I'm *not* temperamental."

I leaned in, whispering in her ear. "I don't want to sleep with you, Pidge. I like you too much."

Her body grew tense, and then I left without another word. Jumping up and down to celebrate the thrill of victory would have been a bit obvious, so I restrained myself until I was sufficiently hidden behind the door, and then made a few celebratory air punches. Keeping her on her toes was never easy, but when it worked, I felt like I was one step closer to . . .

To what? I wasn't exactly sure. It just felt right.

It had been a while since I'd done any grocery shopping, so breakfast wasn't quite gourmet, but it was good enough. I scrambled eggs in a bowl, throwing in a concoction of onion, green and red pepper, and then poured it into a skillet.

Abby walked in and sat on a stool.

"You sure you don't want some?"

"I'm sure. Thanks, though."

She had just rolled out of bed and was still gorgeous. It was ridiculous. I was sure that couldn't be typical, but I wouldn't know, either. The only girls I'd seen in the morning were Shepley's, and I didn't look at any of them close enough to have an opinion.

Shepley grabbed some plates and held them in front of me. I scooped up eggs in the spatula and flopped them onto each plate. Abby watched with mild interest.

America puffed as Shepley sat the plate in front of her. "Don't look at me like that, Shep. I'm sorry, I just don't want to go."

Shepley had been moping for days about America's rejection of his invitation to the date party. I didn't blame her. Date parties were torture. The fact that she didn't want to go was kinda impressive. Most girls fell all over themselves to be invited to those things.

"Baby," Shepley whined, "the House has a date party twice a year. It's a month away. You'll have plenty of time to find a dress and do all that girl stuff."

America wasn't going for it. I tuned them out until I realized America had agreed to go only if Abby would. If Abby went, that meant she'd go with a date. America looked to me, and I raised an eyebrow.

Shepley didn't hesitate. "Trav doesn't go to the date parties. It's something you take your girlfriend to . . . and Travis doesn't . . . you know."

America shrugged. "We could set her up with someone."

I started to speak up, but Abby clearly wasn't happy. "I can hear you, you know," she grumbled.

America pouted. That was the face Shepley couldn't deny.

"Please, Abby? We'll find you a nice guy who's funny and witty, and you know I'll make sure he's hot. I promise you'll have a good time! And who knows? Maybe you'll hit it off."

I frowned. America would find her a guy? For the date party. One of my frat brothers. Oh, fuck, no. The thought of her hitting it off with *anyone* made the hairs on the back of my neck stand on end.

The pan made a clanging noise when I threw it into the sink. "I didn't say I wouldn't take her."

Abby rolled her eyes. "Don't do me any favors, Travis."

I took a step. "That's not what I meant, Pidge. Date parties are for the guys with girlfriends, and it's common knowledge that I don't do the girlfriend thing. But I won't have to worry about you expecting an engagement ring afterward."

America pouted again. "Pretty please, Abby?"

Abby looked like she was in pain. "Don't look at me like that! Travis doesn't want to go. I don't want to go . . . we won't be much fun."

The more I thought about it, the more I warmed to the idea. I crossed my arms and leaned back against the sink. "I didn't say I didn't want to go. I think it'd be fun if the four of us went."

Abby recoiled when all eyes turned to her. "Why don't we hang out here?"

I was okay with that.

America's shoulders slumped, and Shepley leaned forward.

"Because I have to go, Abby," Shepley said. "I'm a freshman. I have to make sure everything's running smoothly, everyone has a beer in their hand, things like that."

Abby was mortified. She clearly didn't want to go, but what scared me was that she couldn't say no to America, and Shepley was willing to say anything for his girlfriend to go. If Abby didn't go with me, she could end up spending the evening—or night—with one of my frat brothers. They weren't bad guys, but listening to the stories they've told, and imagining them talking about Abby was something I couldn't stand.

I walked across the tile and wrapped my arms around Abby's shoulders. "C'mon Pidge. Will you go with me?"

Abby looked to America, then to Shepley. It was only a few seconds until she looked into my eyes, but it felt like a goddamn eternity.

When her eyes finally met mine, her walls came crashing down.

"Yes." She sighed. The enthusiasm in her voice was nonexistent, but it didn't matter. She was going with me, and that knowledge allowed me to breathe again.

America screamed like girls do, clapped her hands, and then grabbed Abby to hug her.

Shepley offered an appreciative smile to me, and then to Pigeon. "Thanks, Abby," he said, placing his hand on her back.

I'd never seen someone less happy to go on a date with me, but then again, it wasn't me she was unhappy about.

The girls finished getting ready and left early for their eight o'clock class. Shepley stuck around to do the dishes, happy that he'd finally gotten his way.

"Dude, thank you. I didn't think America would go."

"What the fuck, Chuck? You guys are trying to set Pidge up with someone?"

"No. I mean, America might have. I don't know. What does it matter?"

"It matters."

"It does?"

"Just don't . . . don't do that, okay? I don't wanna see her making out in a dark corner with Parker Hayes."

Shepley nodded, scrubbing the egg from the skillet. "Or anyone else."

"So?"

"How long do you think that's going to fly?"

I frowned. "I don't know. As long as it can. Just don't step on my toes."

"Travis, do you want her or not? Doing what you can to keep her from dating someone else when you're not even with her is kind of an asshole thing to do."

"We're just friends."

Shepley shot a dubious smirk in my direction. "Friends talk about a weekend fuck. Somehow, I don't see that happening for you two."

"No, but that doesn't mean we can't be friends."

Shepley's eyebrows shot up in disbelief. "It kinda does, bro."

He wasn't wrong. I just didn't want to admit it. "There's just . . ." I paused, glancing to see Shepley's expression. Of all people, he would judge me the least, but it felt weak to admit what I'd been thinking about, and how often thoughts of Abby had crossed my mind. Shepley would understand, but it didn't make me feel any better about saying it out loud. "There's something about her I need. That's all. Is it weird that I think she's cool as hell and I don't want to share?"

"You can't share her if she's not yours."

"What do I know about dating, Shep? You. You and your twisted, obsessive, needy relationships. If she meets someone else and starts dating them, I'll lose her."

"So date her."

I shook my head. "Not ready yet."

"Why's that? Scared?" Shepley asked, throwing the dish towel in my face. It fell to the floor, and I bent down to pick it up. The fabric twisted and pulled tight in my hands as I wrung it back and forth.

"She's different, Shepley. She's good."

"What are you waiting for?"

I shrugged. "Just one more reason, I guess."

Shepley grimaced with disapproval, and then bent down to start the dishwasher. A mixture of mechanical and fluid sounds filled the room, and Shepley made his way to his room. "Her birthday's coming up, you know. Mare wants to put something together."

"Abby's birthday?"

"Yeah. In a little over a week."

"Well, we gotta do something. Do you know what she likes? Does America have something in mind? I guess I better buy her something. What the fuck do I get her?"

Shepley smiled as he closed his bedroom door. "You'll figure it out. Class starts in five. You riding in the Charger?"

"Nah. I'm going to see if I can get Abby on the back of my bike again. It's the closest I can get to the inside of her thighs."

Shepley laughed, and then shut the door behind him.

I headed to my bedroom, and slipped on a pair of jeans and a T-shirt. Wallet, phone, keys. I couldn't imagine being a girl. The bullshit routine they had to go through just to get out the door consumed half of their lives.

Class took for fucking ever, and then I rushed across campus to Morgan Hall. Abby was standing at the front entrance with some guy, and my blood instantly boiled. A few seconds later, I recognized Finch and sighed with relief. She was waiting for him to finish his cigarette, and laughing at whatever he was saying. Finch was waving his arms around, obviously in the middle of a grand story, the only pauses he took were to take drags of his cigarette.

When I approached, Finch winked at Abby. I took that as a good sign. "Hey, Travis," he sang.

"Finch." I nodded, quickly turning my attention to Abby. "I'm headed home, Pidge. You need a ride?"

"I was just going in," she said, grinning up at me.

My stomach sank, and I spoke before thinking. "You're not staying with me tonight?"

"No, I am. I just had to grab a few things that I forgot."

"Like what?"

"Well, my razor for one. What do you care?"

Damn, I liked her. "It's about time you shaved your legs. They've been tearing the hell outta mine."

Finch's eyes nearly popped out of their sockets.

Abby frowned. "That's how rumors get started!" She looked to Finch. "I'm sleeping in his bed . . . *just* sleeping."

"Right," Finch said with a smug smile.

Before I knew what happened, she was inside, tromping up the stairs to her room. I took two steps at a time to catch up with her.

"Oh, don't be mad. I was just kidding."

"Everyone already assumes we're having sex. You're making it worse."

Apparently her having sex with me was a bad thing. If I had questions of whether she was into me like that at all, she'd just given the answer: not just no, but hell no. "Who cares what they think?"

"I do, Travis! I do!" She pushed open the door to her dorm room, and then zoomed from one side of the room to the other, opening and shutting drawers, and shoving things into a bag. I was suddenly drowning in an intense feeling of loss, the kind where you either have to laugh or cry. A chuckle escaped from my throat.

Abby's gray eyes darkened and targeted me. "It's not funny. Do you want the whole school to think I'm one of your sluts?"

My sluts? They weren't mine. Hence them being sluts.

I took the bag from her hands. This wasn't going well. To her, being associated with me, not to mention being in a relationship with me, meant sinking her reputation. Why did she still want to be my friend if that was how she felt?

"No one thinks that. And if they do, they better hope I don't hear about it."

I held open the door, and she stomped through. Just as I let go and began to follow her, she stopped, forcing me to balance on the tips of my toes to keep from running into her. The door closed behind me, shoving me forward. "Whoa!" I said, bumping into her.

She turned. "Oh my God!" At first I thought our collision had hurt her. The shocked look on her face had me worried for a second, but then she continued, "People probably think we're together and you're shamelessly continuing your . . . *lifestyle*. I must look pathetic!" She paused, lost in the horror of her realization, and then shook her head. "I don't think I should stay with you anymore. We should just stay away from each other in general for a while."

She took her bag from my hands, and I grabbed it back. "No one thinks we're together, Pidge. You don't have to quit talking to me to prove a point." I felt a little desperate, which was nothing less than unsettling.

She pulled on her bag. Determined, I yanked it back. After a few tugs, she growled in frustration.

"Have you ever had a girl—that's a friend—stay with you? Have you ever given girls rides to and from school? Have you eaten lunch with them every day? No one knows what to think about us, even when we tell them!"

I walked to the parking lot with her bag, my mind racing. "I'll fix this, okay? I don't want anyone thinking less of you because of me."

Abby was always a mystery, but the grieved look in her eyes took me by surprise. It was disturbing to the point where I wanted to make anything that didn't make her smile go away. She was fidgeting, and clearly upset. I hated it so much that it made me regret every questionable thing I'd ever done because it was just one more thing that got in the way.

That's when the realization hit: as a couple, we weren't going to work. No matter what I did, or how I finagled my way into her good graces, I would never be good enough for her. I didn't want her to end up with someone like me. I would just have to settle for whatever scraps of time I could get with her.

Admitting that to myself was a jagged pill to swallow, but at the same time, a familiar voice whispered from the dark corners of my mind that I needed to fight for what I wanted. Fighting seemed much easier than the alternative.

"Let me make it up to you," I said. "Why don't we go to the Dutch tonight?" The Dutch was a hole-in-the-wall, but a lot less crowded than the Red. Not as many vultures hanging around.

"That's a biker bar." She frowned.

"Okay, then let's go to the club. I'll take you to dinner and then we can go to the Red Door. My treat."

"How will going out to dinner and then to a club fix the problem? When people see us out together, it will make it worse."

I finished tying her bag to the back of my bike and then straddled the seat. She didn't argue about the bag this time. That was always promising.

"Think about it. Me, drunk, in a room full of scantily clad women? It won't take long for people to figure out we're not a couple."

"So what am I supposed to do? Take a guy home from the bar to drive the point home?"

I frowned. The thought of her leaving with a guy made my jaw tense, as if I'd poured lemon juice in my mouth. "I didn't say that. No need to get carried away."

She rolled her eyes, and then climbed onto the seat, wrapping her arms around my middle. "Some random girl is going to follow us home from the bar? *That's* how you're going to make it up to me?"

"You're not jealous, are you, Pigeon?"

"Jealous of *what?* The STD-infested imbecile you're going to piss off in the morning?"

I chuckled, and then started the engine. If she only knew how impossible that was. When she was around, everyone else seemed to disappear. It took all of my focus and concentration to stay a step ahead of her.

We informed Shepley and America of our plans, and then the girls began their routine. I hopped in the shower first, realizing too late that I should have been last, because the girls took a lot longer than me and Shepley to get ready.

Me, Shepley, and America waited for an eternity for Abby to come out of the bathroom, but when she finally emerged, I nearly lost my balance. Her legs looked like they went on forever in her short, black dress. Her tits were playing peek-a-boo, just barely making their presence known when she turned a certain way, and her long curls hung off to the side instead of over her chest.

I didn't remember her being that tan, but her skin had a healthy glow against the dark fabric of her dress.

"Nice legs," I said.

She smiled. "Did I mention the razor is magic?"

Magic my ass. She was fucking gorgeous. "I don't think it's the razor."

I pulled her out the door by her hand, leading her to Shepley's Charger. She didn't pull it away, and I held it in mine until we got to the car. It felt wrong to let go. When we got to the sushi restaurant, I interlaced my fingers between hers as we walked in.

I ordered one round of sake, and then another. The waitress didn't card us until I ordered beer. I knew America had a fake ID, and I was impressed when Abby whipped hers out like a champ.

Once the waitress looked it over and walked away, I grabbed it. Her picture was in the corner, and everything looked legit as far as I knew. I'd never seen a Kansas ID before, but this one was flawless. The name read Jessica James, and for some reason, that turned me on. Hard.

Abby flicked the ID, and it popped out of my grasp, but she caught it midflight to the floor, and within seconds it was hidden away inside her wallet.

She smiled, and I smiled back, leaning on my elbows. "Jessica James?"

She mirrored my position, leaning on her elbows and matching my stare. She was so confident. It was incredibly sexy.

"Yeah. So?"

"Interesting choice."

"So is the California Roll. Pansy."

Shepley burst into laughter, but stopped abruptly when America chugged her beer. "Slow down, baby. The sake hits late."

America wiped her mouth and grinned. "I've had sake, Shep. Stop worrying."

The more we drank, the louder we became. The waitstaff didn't seem to mind, but that was probably because it was late and there were only a few others on the far side of the restaurant, and they were almost as drunk as we were. Except Shepley. He was too protective of his car to drink too much while driving, and he loved America more than his car. When she came along, he not only watched his intake, but he also followed every traffic law and used his blinkers.

Whipped.

The waitress brought the check, and I tossed some cash on the table, nudging Abby until she scooted out of the booth. She elbowed me back playfully, and I nonchalantly threw my arm around her while we walked across the parking lot.

America slid into the front seat next to her boyfriend, and began licking his ear. Abby looked at me and rolled her eyes, but regardless of being a captive audience to the peep show, she was having a good time.

After Shepley pulled into the Red, he drove through the rows of cars two or three times.

"Sometime tonight, Shep," America muttered.

"Hey. I have to find a wide space. I don't want some drunken idiot dinging the paint."

Maybe. Or he was just prolonging the tongue bath his inner ear was getting from America. Sick.

Shepley parked on the edge of the lot, and I helped Abby out. She pulled and tugged at her dress, and then shook her hips a little bit before taking my hand.

"I meant to ask you about your IDs," I said. "They're flawless. You didn't get them around here." I would know. I'd purchased many.

"Yeah, we've had them for a while. It was necessary . . ."

Why in the hell would it be necessary for her to have a fake ID?

". . . in Wichita."

The gravel crunched under our feet as we walked, and Abby's hand squeezed mine as she navigated the rocks under her heels.

America tripped. I let go of Abby's hand in reaction, but Shepley caught his girlfriend before she hit the ground.

"It's a good thing you have connections," America said, giggling.

"Dear God, woman," Shepley said, holding her arm before she fell over. "I think you're already done for the night."

I frowned, wondering what the hell it all meant. "What are you talking about, Mare? What connections?"

"Abby has some old friends that—"

"They're fake IDs, Trav," Abby said, interrupting before America could finish. "You have to know the right people if you want them done right, right?"

I looked to America, knowing something wasn't right, but she looked everywhere but at me. Pushing the issue didn't seem smart, especially since Abby had just called me Trav. I could get used to that, coming from her.

I held out my hand. "Right."

She took it, smiling with the expression of a hustler. She thought she'd just pulled one over on me. I'd definitely have to revisit that later.

"I need another drink!" she said, pulling me toward the big red door of the club.

"Shots!" America yelled.

Shepley sighed. "Oh, yeah. That's what you need. Another shot."

Every head in the room turned when Abby walked in, even a few guys with their girlfriends were shamelessly breaking their necks or leaning back in their chairs to get a longer look.

Oh, fuck. This is going to be a bad night, I thought, tightening my hand around Abby's.

We walked to the bar closest to the dance floor. Megan stood in the smoky shadows by the pool tables. Her usual hunting ground. Her big, blue eyes locked on me before I even recognized it was her standing there. She didn't watch me long. Abby's hand was still in mine, and Megan's expression changed the moment she saw. I nodded at her, and she smirked.

My usual seat at the bar was open, but it was the only one open along the bar. Cami saw me coming with Abby trailing behind, so she laughed once, and then brought my arrival to the attention of the people sitting on the surrounding stools, warning them of their impending eviction. They left without complaint.

Say what you want. Being a psychotic asshole had its perks.

CHAPTER SEVEN

Seeing Red

BEFORE WE REACHED THE BAR, AMERICA PULLED HER best friend to the dance floor. Abby's hot pink stilettos glowed in the black light, and I smiled when she laughed at America's wild dance moves. My eyes traveled down her black dress, stopping on her hips. She had moves, I'd give her that. A sexual thought popped into my mind, and I had to look away.

The Red Door was fairly crowded. Some new faces, but mostly regulars. Anyone new walking in was like fresh meat to those of us who didn't have the imagination for anything but showing up at the bar every weekend. Especially girls that looked like Abby and America.

I ordered a beer, chugged half of it, and then turned my attention back to the dance floor. Staring wasn't voluntary, especially knowing I probably had the same expression on my face as every schmuck watching them.

The song ended, and Abby pulled America back to the bar. They were panting, smiling, and just sweaty enough to be sexy.

"It's going to be like this all night, Mare. Just ignore them," Shepley said.

America's face was screwed in disgust, staring behind me. I could only imagine who was back there. Couldn't have been Megan. She wasn't one to wait in the wings.

"It looks like Vegas threw up on a flock of vultures," America sneered.

I glanced over my shoulder, and three of Lexi's sorority sisters were standing shoulder to shoulder. Another of them stood next to me with a bright smile. They all grinned when I made eye contact, but I quickly turned around, chugging the last half of my beer. For whatever reason, girls that acted that way around me made America pretty cranky. I couldn't disagree with her vulture reference, though.

I lit a cigarette, and then ordered two more beers. The blonde next to me, Brooke, smiled and bit her lip. I paused, unsure if she was going to cry or hug me. It wasn't until Cami popped the tops and slid the bottles over that I knew why Brooke had that ridiculous look on her face. She picked up the beer and started to take a sip, but I grabbed it from her before she could, and handed it to Abby.

"Uh . . . not yours."

Brooke stomped off to join her friends. Abby, however, seemed perfectly content, taking man-size gulps.

"Like I would buy a beer for some chick at a bar," I said. I thought it would add to Abby's amusement, but instead she held up her beer with a sour look on her face.

"You're different," I said with a half smile.

She clinked her bottle against mine, clearly irritated. "To being the only girl a guy with no standards doesn't want to sleep with." She took a swig, but I pulled the bottle from her mouth.

"Are you serious?" When she didn't respond, I leaned in closer for full effect. "First of all . . . I have standards. I've never been with an ugly woman. Ever. Second of all, I wanted to sleep with you. I thought about throwing you over my couch fifty different ways, but I haven't because I don't see you that way anymore. It's not that I'm not attracted to you, I just think you're better than that."

A smug smile crept across her face. "You think I'm too good for you."

Unbelievable. She really didn't get it. "I can't think of a single guy I know that's good enough for you."

The smugness melted away, replaced with a touched, appreciative smile. "Thanks, Trav," she said, setting her empty bottle on the bar. She could really put them back when she wanted to. Normally I would call that sloppy, but she carried herself with such confidence . . . I don't know . . . anything she did was hot.

I stood and grabbed her hand. "C'mon." I pulled her to the dance floor, and she followed behind me.

"I've had a lot to drink! I'm going to fall!"

Now on the dance floor, I grabbed her hips and pulled her body tight against mine, leaving no room between us. "Shut up and dance."

All the giggles and smiles left her face, and her body began to move against mine to the music. I couldn't keep my hands off of her. The closer we were, the closer I needed her to be. Her hair was in my face, and even though I'd drunk enough to call it a night, all of my senses were alert. The way her ass felt against me, the different directions and motions her hips made to the music, the way she leaned back against my chest and rested the back of her head on my shoulder. I wanted to pull her to some dark corner and taste the inside of her mouth.

Abby turned to face me with a mischievous smile. Her hands began at my shoulders, and then she let her fingers run down my chest and stomach. I nearly went insane, wanting her right then and there. She turned her back to me, and my heart beat even faster against my rib cage. She was closer that way. I gripped her hips and pulled her tighter into me.

I wrapped my arms around her waist and buried my face in her hair. It was saturated with sweat, and combined with her perfume. Any rational thought disappeared. The song was ending, but she showed no signs of stopping.

Abby leaned back, her head against my shoulder. Some of her hair fell away, exposing the glistening skin of her neck. All willpower vanished. I touched my lips to the delicate spot just behind her ear. I couldn't stop there, opening my mouth to let my tongue lick the salty moisture from her skin.

Abby's body tensed, and she pulled away.

"What, Pidge?" I asked. I had to chuckle. She looked like she wanted to hit me. I thought we were having a good time, and she was angrier than I'd ever seen her.

Instead of letting her temper fly, she pushed through the crowd, retreating to the bar. I followed, knowing I would find out soon enough what exactly I had done wrong.

Taking the empty stool beside her, I watched as Abby signaled to Cami that she wanted another beer. I ordered one for myself, and then watched her chug half of hers. The bottle clanged against the counter when she slammed it down.

"You think *that* is going to change anyone's mind about us?"

I laughed once. After all that bumping and grinding against my dick, she was suddenly worried about appearances? "I don't give a damn what they think about us."

She shot me a dirty look, and then turned to face forward.

"Pigeon," I said, touching her arm.

She jerked away. "Don't. I could *never* get drunk enough to let you get me on that couch."

Instant rage consumed me. I had never treated her like that. Never. She led me on, and then I gave her one or two little kisses on the neck, and she freaks out?

I started to speak, but Megan appeared next to me.

"Well. If it isn't Travis Maddox."

"Hey, Megan."

Abby eyed Megan, clearly taken off guard. Megan was an old pro at tipping the scales in her favor.

"Introduce me to your girlfriend," Megan said, smiling.

She knew damn good and well Abby wasn't my girlfriend. Ho 101: If the man in your sights is on a date or with a female friend, force him to admit to lack of commitment. Creates insecurity and instability.

I knew where this was going. Hell, if Abby really thought I was a criminal-grade douche bag, I might as well act like one. I slid my beer down the bar, and it fell off the edge, clinking into the full trash can at the end. "She's not my girlfriend."

Purposefully ignoring Abby's reaction, I grabbed Megan's hand and led her to the dance floor. She complied, happily swinging our arms until our feet hit the wood. Megan was always entertaining to dance with. She had no shame and let me do anything to her that I wanted, on and off the dance floor. As usual, most of the other dancers stopped to watch.

We usually made a spectacle, but I was feeling exceptionally lewd. Megan's dark hair slapped me in the face more than once, but I was numb. I picked her up and she wrapped her legs around my waist, and then bent back, stretching her arms over her head. She smiled as I pumped her in front of the entire bar, and when I set her on her feet, she turned and bent over, grabbing her ankles.

Sweat poured down my face. Megan's skin was so wet, my hands slipped away every time I tried to touch her. Her shirt was soaked, and so was mine. She leaned in for a kiss, her mouth slightly open, but I leaned back, looking toward the bar.

That was when I saw him. Ethan Coats. Abby was leaned in toward him, smiling with that drunken, flirty, take-me-home smile I could spot in a crowd of a thousand women.

Leaving Megan on the dance floor, I pushed through the mass that had gathered around us. Just before I reached Abby, Ethan reached over to touch her knee. Remembering what he'd gotten away with the year before, I balled my hand into a fist, standing between them, with my back to Ethan.

"You ready, Pidge?"

Abby put her hand on my stomach and pushed me to the side, smiling the instant Ethan came back into view. "I'm talking, Travis." She held her hand out, feeling how wet it was, and then wiped it on her skirt in dramatic fashion.

"Do you even know this guy?"

She smiled even wider. "This is Ethan."

Ethan extended his hand. "Nice to meet you."

I couldn't take my eyes off of Abby while she stared at that sick and twisted fuck across from her. I left Ethan's hand hanging, waiting for Abby to remember I was standing there.

Dismissive, she waved her hand in my direction. "Ethan, this is Travis." Her voice was decidedly less enthusiastic about my introduction, which just pissed me off more.

I glared down at Ethan, and then at his hand. "Travis Maddox." My voice was as low and menacing as I could manage.

Ethan's eyes grew wide, and he awkwardly pulled back his hand. "Travis *Maddox*?"

I stretched my arm behind Abby to grip the bar. "Yeah, what of it?"

"I saw you fight Shawn Smith last year, man. I thought I was about to witness someone's death!"

My eyes narrowed, and my teeth clenched. "You wanna see it again?"

Ethan laughed once, his eyes darting back and forth between us. When he realized I wasn't kidding, he smiled awkwardly at Abby, and then walked away.

"Are you ready, now?" I snapped.

"You are a complete asshole, you know that?"

"I've been called worse." I held out my hand and she took it, letting me help her from the stool. She couldn't have been that pissed.

With a loud whistle, I signaled Shepley, who saw my expression and immediately knew that it was time to leave. I used my shoulder to cut through the crowd, shamelessly knocking over a few innocent bystanders to let off steam until Shepley headed us off and took over for me.

Once outside, I took Abby's hand, but she jerked it away.

I wheeled around and yelled in her face. "I should just kiss you and get it over with! You're being ridiculous! I kissed your neck, so what?"

Abby leaned back, and when that didn't create enough space, she pushed me away. No matter how pissed I was, she knew no fear. It was kinda hot.

"I'm not your fuck buddy, Travis."

I shook my head, stunned. If there was anything else I could do to keep her from thinking that, I didn't know what it was. She was special to me from the second I laid eyes on her, and I tried to let her know it every chance I got. How else could I get that across to her? How much different from everyone else could I treat her? "I never said you were! You're around me 24-7, you sleep in my bed, but half the time you act like you don't wanna be seen with me!"

"I *came* here with you!"

"I have never treated you with anything but respect, Pidge."

"No, you just treat me like your property. You had no right to run Ethan off like that!"

"Do you know who Ethan is?" When she shook her head, I leaned in. "I *do*. He was arrested last year for sexual battery, but the charges were dropped."

She crossed her arms. "Oh, so you have something in common?"

A red veil covered my eyes, and for less than a second, the rage inside me boiled over. I took a deep breath, willing it away. "Are you calling me a *rapist*?"

Abby paused in thought, and her hesitation made the anger melt away. She was the only one that had that effect on me. Every other time I'd been that angry, I had punched something or someone. I had never hit a woman, but I would have definitely taken a swing at the truck parked next to us.

"No, I'm just pissed at you!" she said, pressing her lips together.

"I've been drinking, all right? Your skin was three inches from my face, and you're beautiful, and you smell fucking awesome when you sweat. I kissed you! I'm sorry! Get over yourself!"

My answer made her pause, and the corners of her mouth turned up. "You think I'm beautiful?"

I frowned. What a stupid question. "You're gorgeous and you know it. What are you smiling about?"

The harder she tried not to smile, the more she did. "Nothing. Let's go."

I laughed once, and then shook my head. "Wha . . . ? You . . . ? You're a pain in my *ass*!"

She was grinning from ear to ear from my compliment, and the fact that I had gone from psycho to ridiculous in less than five minutes. She tried to stop smiling, and, in turn, that made me smile.

I hooked my arm around her neck, wishing to God I *had* just kissed her. "You're making me crazy. You know that, right?"

The ride home was quiet, and when we finally arrived at the apartment, Abby went straight to the bathroom, turning on the shower. My mind was too fuzzy to rifle through her shit, so I grabbed a pair of my boxers and a T-shirt. I knocked on the door, but she didn't answer, so I went ahead and walked in, laid it on the sink, and then left. I wasn't sure what to say to her anyway.

She walked in, swallowed by my clothes, and fell into bed, a residual smile still on her face.

I watched her for a moment, and she stared back, clearly wondering what I was thinking. The trouble was, even *I* didn't know. Her eyes slowly traveled down my face to my lips, and then I knew.

"Night, Pidge," I whispered, turning over, cussing at myself like never before. She was incredibly drunk, though, and I wasn't going to take advantage. Especially not after she'd forgiven me for the spectacle I'd made with Megan.

Abby fidgeted for several minutes before finally taking a breath. "Trav?" She leaned up on her elbow.

"Yeah?" I said, not moving. I was afraid if I looked into her eyes, all rational thought would go out the window.

"I know I'm drunk, and we just got into a ginormous fight over this, but . . ."

"I'm not having sex with you, so quit asking."

"What? No!"

I laughed and turned, looking at her sweet, horrified expression. "What, Pigeon?"

"This," she said, laying her head on my chest and stretching her arm across my stomach, hugging me close.

Not what I was expecting. At all. I held up my hand and froze in place, unsure what the hell to do. "You *are* drunk."

"I know," she said, shameless.

No matter how pissed she would be in the morning, I couldn't say no. I relaxed one hand against her back, and the other on her wet hair, and then kissed her forehead. "You are the most confusing woman I've ever met."

"It's the least you can do after scaring off the only guy that approached me tonight."

"You mean Ethan the rapist? Yeah, *I* owe *you* for that one."

"Never mind," she said, beginning to pull away.

My reaction was instantaneous. I held her arm against my stomach. "No, I'm serious. You need to be more careful. If I wasn't there . . . I don't even want to think about it. And now you expect me to apologize for running him off?"

"I don't want you to apologize. It's not even about that."

"Then what's it about?" I asked. I'd never begged for anything in my life, but I was silently begging for her to tell me she wanted me. That she cared about me. Something. We were so close. It would just take another inch or so for our lips to touch, and it was a mental feat not to give in to that inch.

She frowned. "I'm drunk, Travis. It's the only excuse I have."

"You just want me to hold you until you fall asleep?"

She didn't answer.

I turned, looking straight into her eyes. "I should say no to prove a point," I said, my eyebrows pulling together. "But I would hate myself later if I said no and you never asked me again."

She happily nestled her cheek against my chest. With my arms wrapped around her tight, it was hard to keep it together. "You don't need an excuse, Pigeon. All you have to do is ask."

CHAPTER EIGHT

Oz

ABBY PASSED OUT BEFORE I DID. HER BREATHING evened out, and her body relaxed against mine. She was warm, and her nose made the slightest, sweetest buzzing noise when she inhaled. Her body in my arms felt way too good. It was something I could get used to far too easily. As scared as that made me, I couldn't move.

Knowing Abby, she would wake up and remember she was a hard-ass, and yell at me for letting it happen or, worse, resolve to never let it happen again.

I wasn't stupid enough to hope, or strong enough to stop myself from feeling the way I did. Total eye-opener. Not so tough, after all. Not when it came to Abby.

My breathing slowed, and my body sank into the mattress, but I fought the fatigue that steadily overtook me. I didn't want to close my eyes and miss even a second of what it felt like to have Abby so close.

She stirred, and I froze. Her fingers pressed into my skin, and then she hugged herself up against me once before relaxing again. I kissed her hair, and leaned my cheek against her forehead.

Closing my eyes for just a moment, I took a breath.

I opened my eyes again, and it was morning. Fuck. I knew I shouldn't have.

Abby was wiggling around, trying to unwedge herself out from under me. My legs were on top of hers, and my arm still held her.

"Stop it, Pidge. I'm sleepin'," I said, pulling her closer.

She pulled her limbs out from under me, one at a time, and then sat on the bed and sighed.

I slid my hand across the bed, reaching the tips of her small, delicate fingers. Her back was to me, and she didn't turn around.

"What's wrong, Pigeon?"

"I'm going to get a glass of water. You want anything?"

I shook my head, and closed my eyes. Either she was going to pretend it didn't happen, or she was pissed. Neither option a good one.

Abby walked out, and I lay there a while, trying to find the motivation to move. Hangovers sucked, and my head was pounding. I could hear Shepley's muffled, deep voice, so I decided to drag my ass out of bed.

My bare feet slapped against the wood floor as I trudged into the kitchen. Abby stood in my T-shirt and boxers, pouring chocolate syrup into a steaming bowl of oatmeal.

"That's sick, Pidge," I grumbled, trying to blink the blur from my eyes.

"Good morning to you, too."

"I hear your birthday is coming up. Last stand of your teenage years."

She made a face, caught off guard. "Yeah . . . I'm not a big birthday person. I think Mare is going to take me to dinner or something." She smiled. "You can come if you want."

I shrugged, trying to pretend her smile hadn't gotten to me. She wanted me there. "All right. It's a week from Sunday?"

"Yes. When's your birthday?"

"Not 'til April. April first," I said, pouring milk on top of my cereal.

"Shut up."

I took a bite, amused at her surprise. "No, I'm serious."

"Your birthday is on *April Fools'*?"

I laughed. The look on her face was priceless. "Yes! You're gonna be late. I better get dressed."

"I'm riding with Mare."

That small rejection was a lot harder to hear than it should have been. She had been riding to campus with me, and suddenly she was riding with America? It made me wonder if it was because of what had happened the night before. She was probably trying to distance herself from me again, and that was nothing less than disappointing. "Whatever," I said, turning my back to her before she could see the disappointment in my eyes.

The girls grabbed their backpacks in a hurry. America tore out of the parking lot like they had just robbed a bank.

Shepley walked out of his bedroom, pulling a T-shirt over his head. His eyebrows pushed together. "Did they just leave?"

"Yeah," I said absently, rinsing my cereal bowl and dumping Abby's leftover oatmeal in the sink. She'd barely touched it.

"Well, what the hell? Mare didn't even say goodbye."

"You knew she was going to class. Quit being a crybaby."

Shepley pointed to his chest. "I'm the crybaby? Do you remember last night?"

"Shut up."

"That's what I thought." He sat on the couch and slipped on his sneakers. "Did you ask Abby about her birthday?"

"She didn't say much, except that she's not into birthdays."

"So what are we doing?"

"Throwing her a party." Shepley nodded, waiting for me to explain. "I thought we'd surprise her. Invite some of our friends over and have America take her out for a while."

Shepley put on his white ball cap, pulling it down so low over his brows I couldn't see his eyes. "She can manage that. Anything else?"

"How do you feel about a puppy?"

Shepley laughed once. "It's not my birthday, bro."

I walked around the breakfast bar and leaned my hip against the stool. "I know, but she lives in the dorms. She can't have a puppy."

"Keep it here? Seriously? What are we going to do with a dog?"

"I found a cairn terrier online. It's perfect."

"A what?"

"Pidge is from Kansas. It's the same kind of dog Dorothy had in *The Wizard of Oz*."

Shepley's face was blank. "*The Wizard of Oz*."

"What? I liked the scarecrow when I was a little kid, shut the fuck up."

"It's going to crap everywhere, Travis. It'll bark and whine and . . . I don't know."

"So does America . . . minus the crapping."

Shepley wasn't amused.

"I'll take it out and clean up after it. I'll keep it in my room. You won't even know it's here."

"You can't keep it from barking."

"Think about it. You gotta admit it'll win her over."

Shepley smiled. "Is that what this is all about? You're trying to win over Abby?"

My brows pulled together. "Quit it."

His smile widened. "You can get the damn dog . . ."

I grinned. *Yes! Victory!*

". . . if you admit you have feelings for Abby."

I frowned. *Fuck! Defeat!* "C'mon, man!"

"Admit it," Shepley said, crossing his arms. What a tool. He was actually going to make me say it.

I looked to the floor and everywhere else except Shepley's smug ass smile. I fought it for a while, but the puppy was fucking brilliant. Abby would flip out (in a good way for once), and I could keep it at the apartment. She'd want to be there every day.

"I like her," I said through my teeth.

Shepley held his hand to his ear. "What? I couldn't quite hear you."

"You're an asshole! Did you hear that?"

Shepley crossed his arms. "Say it."

"I like her, okay?"

"Not good enough."

"I have feelings for her. I care about her. A lot. I can't stand it when she's not around. Happy?"

"For now," he said, grabbing his backpack off the floor. He slung one strap over his shoulder, and then picked up his cell phone and keys. "See you at lunch, pussy."

"Eat shit," I grumbled.

Shepley was always the idiot in love acting like a fool. He was never going to let me live this down.

It only took a couple of minutes to get dressed, but all that talking had me running late. I slipped on my leather jacket and put my ball cap on backward. My only class that day was Chem II, so bringing my bag wasn't necessary. Someone in class would let me borrow a pencil if we had a quiz.

Sunglasses. Keys. Phone. Wallet. I slipped on my boots and slammed the door behind me, trotting down the stairs. Riding the Harley wasn't nearly as appealing without Abby on the back. Dammit, she was ruining everything.

On campus, I walked a little faster than usual to make it to class on time. With just a second to spare, I slipped into the desk. Dr. Webber rolled her eyes, unimpressed with my timing, and probably a little irritated with my lack of materials. I winked, and the slightest smile touched her lips. She shook her head, and then returned her attention to the papers on her desk.

A pencil wasn't necessary, and once we were dismissed, I took off toward the cafeteria.

Shepley was waiting for the girls in the middle of the greens. I grabbed his ball cap, and before he could take it back, I tossed it like a Frisbee across the lawn.

"Nice, dick," he said, walking the few feet to pick it up.

"Mad Dog," someone called behind me. I knew from the scruffy, deep voice who it was.

Adam approached Shepley and me, his expression all business. "I'm trying to set up a fight. Be ready for a phone call."

"We always are," Shepley said. He was sort of my business

manager. He took care of getting the word out, and he made sure I was in the right place at the right time.

Adam nodded once, and then left for his next destination, whatever that was. I had never been in a class with the guy. I wasn't even sure if he really went to school here. As long as he paid me, I guess I didn't really care.

Shepley watched Adam walk away, and then cleared his throat. "So did you hear?"

"What?"

"They fixed the boilers at Morgan."

"So?"

"America and Abby will probably pack up tonight. We're going to be busy helping them move all their shit back to the dorms."

My face fell. The thought of packing Abby up and taking her back to Morgan felt like a punch in the face. Especially after the night before, she'd probably be happy to leave. She might not even speak to me again. My mind flashed through a million scenarios, but I couldn't think of anything to get her to stay.

"You okay, man?" Shepley asked.

The girls appeared, giggly and smiling. I tried a smile, but Abby was too busy being embarrassed by whatever America was laughing about.

"Hey, baby," America said, kissing Shepley on the mouth.

"What's so funny?" Shepley asked.

"Oh, a guy in class was staring at Abby all hour. It was adorable."

"As long as he was staring at Abby." Shepley winked.

"Who was it?" I asked before thinking.

Abby shifted her weight, readjusting her backpack. It was

overflowing with books, the zipper barely containing the contents. It must have been heavy. I slipped it off her shoulder.

"Mare's imagining things," she said, rolling her eyes.

"Abby! You big fat liar! It was Parker Hayes, and he was being *so* obvious. The guy was practically drooling."

My face twisted. "Parker *Hayes?*"

Shepley pulled on America's hand. "We're headed to lunch. Will you be enjoying the fine cafeteria cuisine this afternoon?"

America kissed him again in answer, and Abby followed behind, prompting me to do the same. We walked together in silence. She was going to find out about the boilers, they would move back to Morgan, and Parker would ask her out.

Parker Hayes was a cream puff, but I could see Abby being interested in him. His parents were stupid rich, he was going to med school, and on the surface he was a nice guy. She was going to end up with him. The rest of her life with him played out in my head, and it was all I could do to calm down. The mental image of tackling my temper and shoving it into a box helped.

Abby placed her tray between America and Finch. An empty chair a few seats down was a better choice for me than attempting to carry on a conversation like I hadn't just lost her. This was going to suck, and I didn't know what to do. So much time had been wasted playing games. Abby didn't have a chance to even get to know me. Hell, even if she had, she was probably better off with someone like Parker.

"Are you okay, Trav?" Abby asked.

"Me? Fine, why?" I asked, trying to get rid of the heavy feeling that settled in every muscle of my face.

"You've just been quiet."

Several members of the football team approached the table and sat down, laughing loudly. Just the sounds of their voices made me want to punch a wall.

Chris Jenks tossed a French fry onto my plate. "What's up, Trav? I heard you bagged Tina Martin. She's been raking your name through the mud today."

"Shut up, Jenks," I said, keeping my eyes on my food. If I looked up at his ridiculous fucking face, I might have knocked him out of his chair.

Abby leaned forward. "Knock it off, Chris."

I looked up at Abby, and for a reason I couldn't explain, became instantly angry. What the fuck was she defending me for? The second she found out about Morgan, she was going to leave me. She'd never talk to me again. Even though it was crazy, I felt betrayed. "I can take care of myself, Abby."

"I'm sorry, I . . ."

"I don't want you to be sorry. I don't want you to be anything," I snapped. Her expression was the final straw. Of course she didn't want to be around me. I was an infantile asshole that had the emotional control of a three-year-old. I shoved away from the table and pushed through the door, not stopping until I was sitting on my bike.

The rubber grips on the handlebars whined under my palms as I twisted my hands back and forth. The engine snarled, and I kicked back the kickstand before taking off like a bat out of hell into the street.

I rode around for an hour, feeling no better than before. The streets were leading to one place, though, and even though it took me that long to give in and just go, I finally pulled into my father's driveway.

Dad walked out of the front door and stood on the porch, giving a short wave.

I took both of the porch stairs at once and stopped just short of where he stood. He didn't hesitate to pull me against his soft, rounded side, before escorting me inside.

"I was just thinking it was about time for a visit," he said with a tired smile. His eyelids hung over his lashes a bit, and the skin beneath his eyes was puffy, matching the rest of his round face.

Dad checked out for a few years after Mom died. Thomas took on a lot more responsibilities than a kid his age should have, but we made do, and finally Dad snapped out of it. He never talked about it, but he never missed a chance to make it up to us.

Even though he was sad and angry for most of my formative years, I wouldn't consider him a bad father, he was just lost without his wife. I knew how he felt, now. I felt maybe a fraction for Pidge what Dad felt for Mom, and the thought of being without her made me feel sick.

He sat on the couch and gestured to the worn-out recliner. "Well? Have a seat, would ya?"

I sat, fidgeting while trying to figure out what I would say.

He watched me for a while before taking a breath. "Something wrong, son?"

"There's a girl, Dad."

He smiled a bit. "A girl."

"She kinda hates me, and I kinda . . ."

"Love her?"

"I don't know. I don't think so. I mean . . . how do you know?"

His smile grew wider. "When you're talking about her with your old dad because you don't know what else to do."

I sighed. "I just met her. Well, a month ago. I don't think it's love."

"Okay."

"Okay?"

"I'll take your word for it," he said without judgment.

"I just . . . I don't think I'm good for her."

Dad leaned forward, then touched a couple of fingers to his lips.

I continued. "I think she's been burned by someone before. By someone like me."

"Like you."

"Yeah." I nodded and sighed. The last thing I wanted was to admit to Dad what I'd been up to.

The front door slammed against the wall. "Look who decided to come home," Trenton said with a wide grin. He hugged two brown paper sacks to his chest.

"Hey, Trent," I said, standing. I followed him into the kitchen and helped him put Dad's groceries away.

We took turns elbowing and shoving each other. Trenton had always been the hardest on me as far as kicking my ass when we disagreed, but I was also closer to him than I was to my other brothers.

"Missed you at the Red the other night. Cami says hi."

"I was busy."

"With that girl Cami saw you with the other night?"

"Yeah," I said. I pulled out an empty ketchup bottle and some molding fruit from the fridge and tossed them in the garbage before we returned to the front room.

Trenton bounced a few times when he fell into the couch, slapping his knees. "What've you been up to, loser?"

"Nothin'," I said, glancing at Dad.

Trenton looked to our father, and then back at me. "Did I interrupt?"

"No," I said, shaking my head.

Dad waved him away. "No, son. How was work?"

"It sucked. I left the rent check on your dresser this morning. Did you see it?"

Dad nodded with a small smile.

Trenton nodded once. "You stayin' for dinner, Trav?"

"Nah," I said, standing. "I think I'm just going to head home."

"I wish you'd stay, son."

My mouth pulled to the side. "I can't. But, thanks, Dad. I appreciate it."

"You appreciate what?" Trenton asked. His head pivoted from side to side like he was watching a tennis match. "What'd I miss?"

I looked at my father. "She's a pigeon. Definitely a pigeon."

"Oh?" Dad said, his eyes brightening a bit.

"The same girl?"

"Yeah, but I was kind of a dick to her earlier. She kind of makes me feel crazy-er."

Trenton's smile started small, and then slowly stretched the entire width of his face. "Little brother!"

"Quit." I frowned.

Dad smacked Trent on the back of the head.

"What?" Trenton cried. "What'd I say?"

Dad followed me out the front door and patted me on the shoulder. "You'll figure it out. I have no doubt. She must be something, though. I don't think I've seen you like this."

"Thanks, Dad." I leaned in, wrapping my arms around his large frame as best I could, and then headed for the Harley.

The ride back to the apartment felt like it took forever. Just a hint of warm summer air remained, uncharacteristic for the time of year, but welcome. The night sky draped darkness all around me, making the dread even worse. I saw America's car parked in her usual spot and was immediately nervous. Each step felt like a foot closer to death row.

Before reaching the door, it flew open, and America stood with a blank look on her face.

"Is she here?"

America nodded. "She's asleep in your room," she said softly.

I slipped past her and sat on the couch. Shepley was on the love seat, and America plopped down beside me.

"She's okay," America said. Her voice was sweet and reassuring.

"I shouldn't have talked to her like that," I said. "One minute I'm pushing her as far as I can to piss her off, and the next I'm terrified she'll wise up and cut me out of her life."

"Give her some credit. She knows exactly what you're doing. You're not her first rodeo."

"Exactly. She deserves better. I know that, and at the same time I can't walk away. I don't know why," I said with a sigh, rubbing my temples. "It doesn't make sense. Nothing about this makes sense."

"Abby gets it, Trav. Don't beat yourself up," Shepley said.

America nudged my arm with her elbow. "You're already going to the date party. What's the harm in asking her out?"

"I don't want to *date* her; I just want to be around her. She's . . . different." It was a lie. America knew it, and I knew it. The truth was, if I really cared about her, I'd leave her the hell alone.

"Different *how?*" America asked, sounding irritated.

"She doesn't put up with my bullshit, it's refreshing. You said it yourself, Mare. I'm not her type. It's just not . . . like that with us." Even if it *was*, it shouldn't be.

"You're closer to her type than you know," America said.

I looked into America's eyes. She was completely serious. America was like a sister to Abby, and protective like a mother bear. They would never encourage anything for each other that could be hurtful. For the first time, I felt a glimmer of hope.

The wooden boards creaked in the hall, and we all froze. My bedroom door shut, and then Abby's footsteps sounded in the hall.

"Hey, Abby," America said with a grin. "How was your nap?"

"I was out for five hours. That's closer to a coma than a nap."

Her mascara was smeared under her eyes, and her hair was matted against her head. She was stunning. She smiled at me, and I stood, took her hand, and led her straight to the bedroom. Abby looked confused and apprehensive, making me even more desperate to make amends.

"I'm so sorry, Pidge. I was an asshole to you earlier."

Her shoulders fell. "I didn't know you were mad at me."

"I wasn't mad at you. I just have a bad habit of lashing out at those I care about. It's a piss-poor excuse, I know, but I *am* sorry," I said, enveloping her in my arms.

"What were you mad about?" she asked, nestling her cheek into my chest. Damn, that felt so good. If I wasn't a dick, I would have explained to her that I knew the boilers had been fixed, and the thought of her leaving here and spending more time with Parker scared the shit out of me, but I couldn't do it. I didn't want to ruin the moment.

"It's not important. The only thing I'm worried about is you."

She looked up at me and smiled. "I can handle your temper tantrums."

I scanned her face for several moments before a small smile spread across my lips. "I don't know why you put up with me, and I don't know what I'd do if you didn't."

Her eyes slowly fell from my eyes to my lips, and her breath caught. Every hair on my skin stood on end, and I wasn't sure if I was breathing or not. I leaned in less than a centimeter, waiting to see if she would protest, but then my fucking phone rang. We both jumped.

"Yeah," I said impatiently.

"Mad Dog. Brady will be at Jefferson in ninety."

"*Hoffman*? Jesus . . . all right. That'll be an easy grand. Jefferson?"

"Jefferson," Adam said. "You in?"

I looked at Abby and winked. "We'll be there." I hung up, stuck my phone in my pocket, and grabbed Abby's hand. "Come with me."

I led her to the living room. "That was Adam," I said to Shepley. "Brady Hoffman will be at Jefferson in ninety minutes."

CHAPTER NINE

Crushed

Shepley's expression changed. He was all business when Adam called with a fight time. His fingers tapped against his phone, clicking away, texting to the people on his list. When Shepley disappeared behind his door, America's eyes widened over her smile.

"Here we go! We'd better freshen up!"

Before I could say anything, America pulled Abby down the hall. The fuss was unnecessary. I'd kick the guy's ass, make the next few months' worth of rent and bills, and life would return to normal. Well, sort of normal. Abby would move back to Morgan Hall, and I would imprison myself to keep from killing Parker.

America was barking at Abby to change, and Shepley was now off the phone, Charger keys in hand. He bent backward to peek down the hall, and then rolled his eyes.

"Let's go!" he yelled.

America ran down the hall, but instead of joining us, she ducked into Shepley's room. He rolled his eyes again but was also smiling.

A few moments later, America burst out of Shepley's room in a short, green dress, and Abby rounded the hall corner in tight jeans and a yellow top, her tits bouncing every time she moved.

"Oh, hell, no. Are you trying to get me killed? You've gotta change, Pidge."

"What?" She looked down at her jeans. The jeans weren't the problem.

"She looks cute, Trav, leave her alone!" America snapped.

I led Abby down the hall. "Get a T-shirt on, and some sneakers. Something comfortable."

"What?" she asked, confusion distorting her face. "Why?"

I stopped at my door. "Because I'll be more worried about who's looking at your tits in that shirt instead of Hoffman," I said. Call it sexist, but it was true. I wouldn't be able to concentrate, and I wasn't going to lose a fight over Abby's rack.

"I thought you said you didn't give a damn about what anyone else thought?" she said, steaming.

She really didn't get it. "That's a different scenario, Pigeon." I looked down at her breasts, proudly pushed up in a white, lacy bra. Canceling the fight suddenly became a tempting idea, if only to spend the rest of the night trying to find a way to get them naked and against my chest.

I snapped out of it, making eye contact again. "You can't wear this to the fight, so please . . . just . . . please just change," I said, shoving her into the room and shutting myself out before I said fuck it and kissed her.

"Travis!" she yelled from the other side of the door. Sounds of scurrying could be heard on the other side of the door, and then what was probably shoes flying across the room. Finally, the door opened. She was in a T-shirt and a pair of Converse. Still hot, but at least I wouldn't be too worried about who was hitting on her to win my damn fight.

"Better?" she puffed.

"Yes! Let's go!"

Shepley and America were already in the Charger, ripping out of the parking lot. I slipped on my shades and waited until Abby was secure before taking off on the Harley into the dark street.

Once we reached campus, I drove down the sidewalk with my lights off, pulling up slowly behind Jefferson.

As I led Abby to the back entrance, her eyes widened, and she laughed once.

"You're joking."

"This is the VIP entrance. You should see how everyone else gets in." I hopped down through the open window into the basement, and then waited in the dark.

"Travis!" she half yelled, half whispered.

"Down here, Pidge. Just come in feetfirst, I'll catch you."

"You're out of your damn mind if you think I'm jumping into the dark!"

"I'll catch you! I promise! Now get your ass in here!"

"This is insane!" she hissed.

In the dim light, I saw her legs wiggle through the small rectangular opening. Even after all her careful maneuvering, she managed to fall instead of jump. A tiny squeal echoed down the concrete walls, and then she landed in my arms. Easiest catch ever.

"You fall like a girl," I said, setting her on her feet.

We walked through the dark maze of the basement until we arrived in the room adjacent to the main room where the fight would be held. Adam was yelling over the noise with his bullhorn, and arms were sticking straight up from the sea of heads, waving cash in the air.

"What are we doing?" she asked, her small hands wrapped tight around my bicep.

"Waiting. Adam has to run through his spiel before I go in."

"Should I wait here, or should I go in? Where do I go when the fight starts? Where's Shep and Mare?"

She looked extremely unsettled. I felt a little bad for leaving her here alone. "They went in the other way. Just follow me out, I'm not sending you into that shark pit without me. Stay by Adam; he'll keep you from getting crushed. I can't look out for you and throw punches at the same time."

"Crushed?"

"There's going to be more people here tonight. Brady Hoffman is from State. They have their own Circle there. It will be our crowd and their crowd, so the room's gonna get crazy."

"Are you nervous?"

I smiled at her. She was particularly beautiful when she was worried about me. "No. You look a little nervous, though."

"Maybe," she said.

I wanted to lean down and kiss her. Something to ease that frightened-lamb expression on her face. I wondered if she worried about me the first night we met, or if it was just because she knew me now—because she cared about me.

"If it'll make you feel better, I won't let him touch me. I won't even let him get one in for his fans."

"How are you going to manage *that?*"

I shrugged. "I usually let them get one in—to make it look fair."

"You . . . ? You *let* people *hit* you?"

"How much fun would it be if I just massacred someone and they never got a punch in? It's not good for business, no one would bet against me."

"What a load of crap," she said, crossing my arms.

I raised an eyebrow. "You think I'm yankin' your chain?"

"I find it hard to believe that you only get hit when you *let* them hit you."

"Would you like to make a wager on that, Abby Abernathy?" I smiled. When I first said the words, it wasn't my intention to use them to my advantage, but when she flashed back an equally wicked smile, the most brilliant fucking idea I'd ever had slipped into my mind.

She smiled. "I'll take that bet. I think he'll get one in on you."

"And if he doesn't? What do I win?" I asked. She shrugged just as the roar of the crowd surrounded us. Adam went over the rules in his usual asshole way.

I stopped a ridiculous grin erupting across my face. "If you win, I'll go without sex for a month." She raised an eyebrow. "But if I win, you have to stay with me for a month."

"*What*? I'm staying with you, anyway! What kind of bet is that?" she shrieked over the noise. She didn't know. No one had told her.

"They fixed the boilers at Morgan today," I said with a smile and a wink.

One side of her mouth turned up. It didn't faze her. "Anything is worth watching you try abstinence for a change."

Her reply sent a rush of adrenaline through my veins that I'd only ever felt during a fight. I kissed her cheek, letting my lips linger against her skin for just a moment longer before walking out into the room. I felt like a king. No way was this fucker going to touch me.

Just as I had anticipated, there was standing room only, and the shoving and shouting amplified once we entered the room. I nodded to Adam in Abby's direction, to signal for him to watch out for her. He immediately understood. Adam was a greedy bastard, but he was once the undefeated monster in the Circle. I had nothing to worry about as long as he watched over her. He would do it so I wouldn't be distracted. Adam would do anything as long as it meant making a shit ton of money.

A path cleared as I walked to the Circle, and then the human gate closed behind me. Brady stood toe to toe with me, breathing hard and shaking like he'd just shot up with Red Bull and Mountain Dew.

Usually I didn't take this shit seriously and made a game of psyching my opponents out, but tonight's fight was important, so I put on my game face.

Adam sounded the horn. I balanced my core, took a few steps back, and waited for Brady to make his first mistake. I dodged his first swing, and then another. Adam popped something off from the back. He was unhappy, but I had anticipated that. Adam liked for fights to entertain. It was the best way to get more heads in the basements. More people meant more money.

I bent my elbow and sent my fist flying into Brady's nose, hard and fast. On a normal fight night, I would hold back, but I wanted to get this over with and spend the rest of the night celebrating with Abby.

I hit Hoffman over and over, and then dodged a few more from him, careful not to get so excited that I would let him hit me and fuck everything up. Brady got a second wind, and came back at me again, but it didn't take long for him to wear himself out throwing punches he couldn't land. I'd dodged punches from Trenton way faster than this bitch could throw.

My patience had run out, and I lured Hoffman to the cement pillar in the center of the room. I stood in front of it, hesitating just long enough for my opponent to think he had a window to nail my face with a devastating blow. I sidestepped as he put everything into his last throw, and slammed his fist straight into the pillar. Surprise registered in Hoffman's eyes just before he doubled over.

That was my cue. I immediately attacked. A loud thud signaled that Hoffman had finally hit the ground, and after a short silence, the room erupted. Adam threw a red flag on Hoffman's face, and then I was surrounded by people.

Most of the time I enjoyed the attention and hell yeahs of those that bet on me, but this time they were just in the way. I tried looking over the sea of people to find Abby, but when I finally got a glimpse of where she was supposed to be, my stomach sank. She was gone.

Smiles turned to shock when I shoved people out of my way. "Get! The fuck! Back!" I yelled, pushing harder as panic came over me.

I finally reached the lantern room, desperately searching for Abby in the darkness. "Pigeon!"

"I'm here!" Her body crashed into mine, and I flung my arms around her. One second I was relieved, the next I was irritated.

"You scared the shit out of me! I almost had to start another fight just to get to you! I finally get here and you're gone!"

"I'm glad you're back. I wasn't looking forward to trying to find my way in the dark."

Her sweet smile made me forget everything else, and I remembered that she was mine. At least for another month. "I believe you lost the bet."

Adam stomped in, looked at Abby, and then glowered at me. "We need to talk."

I winked at Abby. "Stay put. I'll be right back." I followed Adam into the next room. "I know what you're gonna say . . ."

"No you don't," Adam growled. "I don't know what you're doin' with her, but *don't* fuck with my money."

I laughed once. "You made bank tonight. I'll make it up to you."

"You're goddamn straight you will! Don't let it happen again!" Adam slammed cash into my hand, and then shouldered past me.

I shoved the wad of cash into my pocket, and smiled at Abby. "You're going to need more clothes."

"You're really going to make me stay with you for a month?"

"Would you have made me go without sex for a month?"

She laughed. "We better stop at Morgan."

Any attempt at covering my extreme satisfaction was an epic fail. "This should be interesting."

As Adam passed he handed Abby some cash before disappearing into the waning crowd.

"You put in?" I asked, surprised.

"I thought I should get the full experience," she said with a shrug.

I took her by the hand and led her to the window, and then jumped once, pulling myself up. I crawled on the grass, and then turned around, leaning down to pull up Abby.

The walk to Morgan seemed perfect. It was unseasonably warm, and the air had the same electric feel as a summer night.

I was trying not to smile the entire time like an idiot, but it was hard not to.

"Why on earth would you want me to stay with you, anyway?" she asked.

I shrugged. "I don't know. Everything's better when you're around."

Shepley and America waited in the Charger for us to show up with Abby's extra things. Once they took off, we walked to the parking lot and straddled the bike. She wrapped her arms around my chest, and I rested my hand on hers.

I took a breath. "I'm glad you were there tonight, Pidge. I've never had so much fun at a fight in my life." The time it took her to respond felt like an eternity.

She perched her chin on my shoulder. "That was because you were trying to win our bet."

I turned to face her, looking straight in her eyes. "Damn right I was."

Her eyebrows shot up. "Is that why you were in such a bad mood today? Because you knew they'd fixed the boilers, and I would be leaving tonight?"

I got lost in her eyes for moment, and then decided that it was a good time to shut up. I ripped the engine and drove home, slower than I had driven . . . ever. When a stoplight caught us, I found a strange amount of joy in putting my hands on hers, or resting my hand on her knee. She didn't seem to mind, and admittedly, I was pretty fucking close to heaven.

We pulled up to the apartment, and Abby dismounted the bike like an old pro, and then walked to the steps.

"I always hate it when they've been home for a while. I feel like we're going to interrupt them."

"Get used to it. This is your place for the next four weeks," I said, turning around. "Get on."

"What?"

"C'mon, I'll carry you up."

She giggled and hopped onto my back. I gripped her thighs as I ran up the stairs. America opened the door before we made it to the top and smiled.

"Look at you two. If I didn't know better . . ."

"Knock it off, Mare," Shepley said from the couch.

Great. Shepley was in one of his moods.

America smiled as if she'd said too much, and then opened the door wide so we could both fit through. I kept hold of Pidge, and then fell against the recliner. She squealed when I leaned back, playfully pushing my weight against her.

"You're awfully cheerful this evening, Trav. What gives?" America prompted.

"I just won a shitload of money, Mare. Twice as much as I thought I would. What's not to be happy about?"

America grinned. "No, it's something else," she said, watching my hand as I patted Abby's thigh.

"Mare," Shepley warned.

"Fine. I'll talk about something else. Didn't Parker invite you to the Sig Tau party this weekend, Abby?"

The lightness I was feeling immediately went away, and I turned to Abby.

"Er . . . yeah? Aren't we all going?"

"I'll be there," Shepley said, distracted by the television.

"And that means I'm going," America said, looking expectantly at me. She was baiting me, hoping I would volunteer to come along, but I was more concerned with Parker asking Abby out on a fucking date.

"Is he picking you up or something?" I asked.

"No, he just told me about the party."

America's mouth spread into a mischievous grin, almost bobbing in anticipation. "He said he'd see you there, though. He's really cute."

I shot America an irritated glance, and then looked to Abby. "Are you going?"

"I told him I would." She shrugged. "Are you going?"

"Yeah," I said without hesitation. It wasn't a date party, after all, just a weekend kegger. Those I didn't mind. And no fucking way was I going to let Parker have an entire night with her. She'd come back . . . ugh, I didn't even wanna think about it. He'd flash his Abercrombie smile, or take her to his parents' restaurant to parade his money, or find some other way to sleaze into her pants.

Shepley looked at me. "You said last week you weren't."

"I changed my mind, Shep. What's the problem?"

"Nothing," he grumbled, retreating to his bedroom.

America frowned. "You know what the problem is," she said. "Why don't you quit driving him crazy and just get it over with." She joined Shepley in his room, and their voices were reduced to murmuring behind the closed door.

"Well, I'm glad everyone else knows," Abby said.

Abby wasn't the only one confused by Shepley's behavior. Earlier he was teasing me about her, and now he was being a little bitch. What could have happened between then and now that had him freaked out? Maybe he would feel better once he figured out that I'd finally decided I was done with the other girls and just wanted Abby. Maybe the fact that I had actually admitted to caring about her made Shepley worry even more. I wasn't exactly boyfriend material. Yep. That made more sense.

I stood. "I'm going to take a quick shower."

"Is there something going on with them?" Abby asked.

"No, he's just paranoid."

"It's because of us," she guessed.

A weird floating feeling came over me. She said *us.*

"What?" she asked, eyeing me suspiciously.

"You're right. It's because of us. Don't fall asleep, okay? I wanna talk to you about something."

It took less than five minutes for me to wash up, but I stood under the stream of water for at least five more, planning what to say to Abby. Wasting more time wasn't an option. She was here for the next month, and that was the perfect time to prove to her that I wasn't who she thought I was. For her, at least, I was different, and we could spend the next four weeks dispelling any suspicions she might have.

I stepped out of the shower and dried off, excited and nervous as hell about what possibilities could spawn from the conversation we were about to have. Just before opening the door, I could hear a scuffle in the hall.

America said something, her voice desperate. I cracked open the door and listened.

"You promised, Abby. When I told you to spare judgment, I didn't mean for you two to get involved! I thought you were just friends!"

"We are," Abby said.

"No, you're not!" Shepley fumed.

America spoke, "Baby, I told you it will be fine."

"Why are you pushing this, Mare? I told you what's going to happen!"

"And I told you it won't! Don't you trust me?"

Shepley stomped into his room.

After a few seconds of silence, America spoke again. "I just can't get it into his head that whether you and Travis work out or not, it won't affect us. But he's been burned too many times. He doesn't believe me."

Dammit, Shepley. Not the ideal segue. I opened the door a bit more, just enough to see Abby's face.

"What are you talking about, Mare? Travis and I aren't together. We *are* just friends. You heard him earlier . . . he's not interested in me that way."

Fuck. This was getting worse by the minute.

"You heard that?" America asked, surprise evident in her voice.

"Well, yeah."

"And you believe it?"

Abby shrugged. "It doesn't matter. It'll never happen. He told me he doesn't see me like that, anyway. Besides, he's a total commitment-phobe, I'd be hard-pressed to find a girlfriend outside of you that he hasn't slept with, and I can't keep up with his mood swings. I can't believe Shep thinks otherwise."

Every bit of hope I'd had slipped away with her words. The disappointment was crushing. For a few seconds, the pain was unmanageable, until I let the anger take over. Anger was always easier to control.

"Because not only does he know Travis . . . he's talked to Travis, Abby."

"What do you mean?"

"Mare?" Shepley called from the bedroom.

America sighed. "You're my best friend. I think I know you better than you know yourself sometimes. I see you two together, and the only difference between me and Shep and you and Travis is that we're having sex. Other than that? No difference."

"There is a huge, *huge* difference. Is Shep bringing home different girls every night? Are you going to the party tomorrow to hang out with a guy with definite dating potential? You know I can't get involved with Travis, Mare. I don't even know why we're discussing it."

"I'm not seeing things, Abby. You have spent almost every moment with him for the last month. Admit it, you have feelings for him."

I couldn't listen to another word. "Let it go, Mare," I said.

Both girls jumped at the sound of my voice. Abby's eyes met mine. She didn't seem embarrassed or sorry at all, which only pissed me off more. I'd stuck my neck out, and she slit my throat.

Before I said something shitty, I retreated to my room. Sitting didn't help. Neither did standing, pacing, or push-ups. The walls closed in on me more every second. Rage boiled inside of me like an unstable chemical, ready to blow.

Getting out of the apartment was my only option, to clear my head, and try to relax with a few shots. The Red. I could go to the Red. Cami was working the bar. She could tell me what to do. She always knew how to talk me down. Trenton liked her for the same reason. She was the oldest sister of three boys, and didn't flinch when it came to our anger issues.

I slipped on a T-shirt and jeans, and then grabbed sunglasses, my bike keys, and riding jacket, and then shoved my feet inside my boots before heading back down the hall.

Abby's eyes widened when she saw me round the corner. Thank God I had on my shades. I didn't want her to see the hurt in my eyes.

"You're leaving?" she asked, sitting up. "Where are you going?"

I refused to acknowledge the pleading in her voice. "Out."

CHAPTER TEN

Broken

IT DIDN'T TAKE CAMI LONG TO FIGURE OUT I WASN'T good company. She kept the beers coming as I sat in my usual stool at the bar of The Red. Colors from the lights above chased one another around the room, and the music was almost loud enough to drown out my thoughts.

My pack of Marlboro Reds was nearly gone, but that wasn't the reason for the heavy feeling in my chest. A few girls had come and gone, trying to strike up conversation, but I couldn't lift my line of sight from the half-burnt cigarette nestled between two of my fingers. The ash was so long it was just a matter of time until it fell away, so I just watched the remaining embers flicker against the paper, trying to keep my mind off of what sinking feelings the music couldn't muffle.

When the crowd at the bar thinned, and Cami wasn't moving a thousand miles per hour, she sat an empty shot glass in front of me, and then filled it to the brim with Jim Beam. I grabbed for it, but she covered my black leather wristband with her tattooed fingers that spelled BABY DOLL when she held her fists together.

"Okay, Trav. Let's hear it."

"Hear what?" I asked, making a feeble attempt to pull away.

She shook her head. "The girl?"

The glass touched my lips, and I tilted my head back, letting the liquid burn down my throat. "What girl?"

Cami rolled her eyes. "What girl. Seriously? Who do you think you're talking to?"

"All right, all right. It's Pigeon."

"*Pigeon*? You're joking."

I laughed once. "Abby. She's a pigeon. A demonic pigeon that fucks with my head so bad I can't think straight. Nothing makes sense anymore, Cam. Every rule I've ever made's getting broken one by one. I'm a pussy. No . . . worse. I'm Shep."

Cami laughed. "Be nice."

"You're right. Shepley's a good guy."

"Be nice to yourself, too," she said, throwing a rag on the counter and pushing it around in circles. "Falling for someone isn't a sin, Trav, Jesus."

I looked around. "I'm confused. You talking to me or Jesus?"

"I'm serious. So you have feelings for her. So what?"

"She hates me."

"Nah."

"No, I heard her tonight. By accident. She thinks I'm a scumbag."

"She said that?"

"Pretty much."

"Well, you kinda are."

I frowned. "Thanks a lot."

She held out her hands, her elbows on the bar. "Based on your past behavior, do you disagree? My point is . . . maybe for her, you wouldn't be. Maybe for her, you could be a better man." She poured another shot, and I didn't give her the chance to stop me before throwing it back.

"You're right. I've been a scumbag. Could I change? I don't fucking know. Probably not enough to deserve her."

Cami shrugged, holstering the bottle back in its spot. "I think you should let her be the judge of that."

I lit a cigarette, taking a deep breath, and adding my lungfuls of smoke to the already murky room. "Toss me another beer."

"Trav, I think you've had enough already."

"Cami, just fucking do it."

I WOKE UP WITH THE EARLY AFTERNOON SUN SHINING through the blinds, but it might as well have been noon in the middle of a white sand desert. My lids instantly closed, rejecting the light.

A combination of morning breath, chemicals, and cat piss stuck to the inside of my dry mouth. I hated the inevitable cotton mouth that came after a hard night of drinking.

My mind instantly searched for memories from the night before but came up with nothing. Some type of partying was a given, but where or with who was a complete mystery.

I looked to my left, seeing the covers pulled back. Abby was already up. My bare feet felt weird against the floor as I trudged down the hall and found Abby asleep in the recliner. Confusion made me pause, and then panic settled in. My brain sloshed through the alcohol still weighing down my thoughts. Why didn't she sleep in the bed? What had I done to make her sleep in the chair? My heart began beating fast, and then I saw them: two empty condom wrappers.

Fuck. Fuck! The night before came crashing back to me in waves: drinking more, those girls not going away when I told them to, and finally my offer to show them both a good time—at the same time—and their enthusiastic endorsement of the idea.

My hands flew up to my face. I'd brought them here. Bagged them here. Abby had probably heard everything. Oh, God. I couldn't have fucked up any worse. This was beyond bad. As soon as she woke, she would pack her shit and leave.

I sat on the couch, my hands still cupped over my mouth and nose, and watched her sleep. I had to fix this. What could I do to fix this?

One stupid idea after another flipped through my mind. Time was running out. As quietly as I could, I rushed to the bedroom and changed clothes, and then snuck into Shepley's room.

America stirred, and Shepley's head popped up. "What are you doing, Trav?" he whispered.

"I gotta borrow your car. Just for a sec. I have to go pick up a few things."

"Okay . . . ," he said, confused.

His keys jingled when I took them from his dresser, and then I paused. "Do me a favor. If she wakes up before I get back, stall, okay?"

Shepley took a deep breath. "I'll try, Travis, but man . . . last night was . . ."

"It was bad, wasn't it?"

Shepley's mouth pulled to the side. "I don't think she'll stay, cousin, I'm sorry."

I nodded. "Just try."

One last glance at Abby's sleeping face before I left the apartment spurred me to move faster. The Charger could barely keep up with the speed I wanted to go. A red light caught me just before I reached the market and I screamed, hitting the steering wheel.

"God dammit! Turn!"

A few seconds later, the light blinked from red to green, and the tires spun a few times before gaining traction.

I ran into the store from the parking lot, fully aware that I looked like a crazy person as I yanked a grocery cart from the rest. One aisle after another, I grabbed at things that I thought she'd like, or remembered her eating or even talking about. A pink spongy thing hung in a line off of one of the shelves, and that ended up in my basket, too.

An apology wasn't going to make her stay, but maybe a gesture would. Maybe she would see how sorry I was. I stopped a few feet away from the register, feeling hopeless. Nothing was going to work.

"Sir? Are you ready?"

I shook my head, despondent. "I don't . . . I don't know."

The woman watched me for a moment, shoving her hands in the pockets of her white-and-mustard-yellow-striped apron. "Can I help you find something?"

I pushed the cart to her register without responding, watching her scan all of Abby's favorite foods. This was the stupidest idea in the history of ideas, and the only woman alive that I gave a shit about was going to laugh at me while she packed.

"That'll be eighty-four dollars and seventy-seven cents."

A short swipe of my debit card, and the sacks were in my

hands. I bolted into the parking lot, and within seconds the Charger was getting the cobwebs blown out of her pipes all the way back to the apartment.

I took two steps at a time and blew through the door. America's and Shepley's heads were visible over the top of the couch. The television was on, but muted. Thank God. She was still asleep. The sacks crashed against the countertop when I sat them down, and I tried not to let the cabinets crash around too much as I put things away.

"When Pidge wakes up, let me know, okay?" I asked softly. "I got spaghetti, and pancakes, and strawberries, and that oatmeal shit with the chocolate packets, and she likes Fruity Pebbles cereal, right, Mare?" I asked, turning.

Abby was awake, staring at me from the chair. Her mascara was smeared under her eyes. She looked as bad as I felt. "Hey, Pigeon."

She watched me for a few seconds with a blank stare. I took a few steps into the living room, more nervous than I was the night of my first fight.

"You hungry, Pidge? I'll make you some pancakes. Or there's uh . . . there's some oatmeal. And I got you some of that pink foamy shit that girls shave with, and a hairdryer, and a . . . a . . . just a sec, it's in here." I grabbed one of the bags and took it into the bedroom, dumping it out onto the bed.

As I looked for that pink loofah thing I thought she'd like, Abby's luggage, full, zipped, and waiting by the door, caught my eye. My stomach lurched, and the cotton mouth returned. I walked down the hall, trying to keep myself together.

"Your stuff's packed."

"I know," she said.

Physical pain burned through my chest. "You're leaving."

Abby looked to America, who stared at me like she wanted me dead. "You actually expected her to stay?"

"Baby," Shepley whispered.

"Don't fucking start with me, Shep. Don't you dare defend him to me," America seethed.

I swallowed hard. "I am so sorry, Pidge. I don't even know what to say."

"Come on, Abby," America said. She stood and pulled on her arm, but Abby stayed seated.

I took a step, but America pointed her finger. "So help me God, Travis! If you try to stop her, I will douse you with gasoline and light you on fire while you sleep!"

"America," Shepley begged. This was going to get bad from all sides real quick.

"I'm *fine*," Abby said, overwhelmed.

"What do you mean, you're *fine*?" Shepley asked.

Abby rolled her eyes and gestured to me. "Travis brought women home from the bar last night, so what?"

My eyes closed, trying to deflect the pain. As much as I didn't want her to leave, it had never occurred to me that she wouldn't give a fuck.

America frowned. "Huh-uh, Abby. Are you saying you're *okay* with what happened?"

Abby glanced around the room. "Travis can bring home whoever he wants. It's *his* apartment."

I swallowed back the lump that was swelling in my throat. "You didn't pack your things?"

She shook her head and looked at the clock. "No, and now

I'm going to have to unpack it all. I still have to eat, and shower, and get dressed," she said, walking into the bathroom.

America shot a death glare in my direction, but I ignored her and walked over to the bathroom door, tapping lightly. "Pidge?"

"Yeah?" she said, her voice weak.

"You're staying?" I closed my eyes, waiting for punishment.

"I can go if you want me to, but a bet's a bet."

My head fell against the door. "I don't want you to leave, but I wouldn't blame you if you did."

"Are you saying I'm released from the bet?"

The answer was easy, but I didn't want to make her stay if she didn't want to. At the same time, I was terrified to let her go. "If I say yes, will you leave?"

"Well, yeah. I don't live here, silly," she said. A small laugh floated through the wood of the door.

I couldn't tell if she was upset or just tired from spending the night in the recliner, but if it was the former, there was no way I could let her walk away. I'd never see her again.

"Then no, the bet's still in effect."

"Can I take a shower, now?" she asked, her voice small.

"Yeah . . ."

America stomped into the hall and stopped just short of my face. "You're a selfish bastard," she growled, slamming Shepley's door behind her.

I went into the bedroom, grabbed her robe and a pair of slippers, and then returned to the bathroom door. She was apparently staying, but kissing ass was never a bad idea.

"Pigeon? I brought some of your stuff."

"Just set it on the sink. I'll get it."

I opened the door and set her things on the corner of the sink, looking to the floor. "I was mad. I heard you spitting out everything that's wrong with me to America and it pissed me off. I just meant to go out and have a few drinks and try to figure some things out, but before I knew it, I was piss drunk and those girls . . ." I paused, trying to keep my voice from breaking. "I woke up this morning and you weren't in bed, and when I found you on the recliner and saw the wrappers on the floor, I felt sick."

"You could have just asked me instead of spending all that money at the grocery store just to bribe me to stay."

"I don't care about the money, Pidge. I was afraid you'd leave and never speak to me again."

"I didn't mean to hurt your feelings," she said, sincere.

"I know you didn't. And I know it doesn't matter what I say now, because I fucked things up . . . just like I always do."

"Trav?"

"Yeah?"

"Don't drive drunk on your bike anymore, okay?"

I wanted to say more, to apologize again, and to tell her that I was crazy about her—and it was literally driving me insane because I didn't know how to handle what I felt—but the words wouldn't come. My thoughts could only focus on the fact that after everything that had happened, and everything I just said, the only thing she had to say was to scold me about driving home drunk.

"Yeah, okay," I said, shutting the door.

I pretended to stare at the television for hours while Abby primped in the bathroom and bedroom for the frat party, and then decided to get dressed before she needed the bedroom.

A fairly wrinkle-free white shirt was hanging in the closet, so I grabbed it and a pair of jeans. I felt silly, standing in front of the mirror, struggling with the button at the wrist of the shirt. I finally gave up and rolled each sleeve to my elbow. That was more like me, anyway.

I walked down the hall and crashed into the couch again, hearing the bathroom door shut and Abby's bare feet slapping against the floor.

My watch barely moved, and of course nothing was on TV except daring weather rescues and an infomercial about the Slap Chop. I was nervous and bored. Not a good combination for me.

When my patience ran out, I knocked on the bedroom door.

"Come in," Abby called from the other side of the door.

She stood in the middle of the room, a pair of heels sitting side by side on the floor in front of her. Abby was always beautiful, but tonight not a single hair was out of place; she looked like she should be on the cover of one of those fashion magazines you see in the checkout line of the grocery store. Every part of her was lotioned, smooth, polished perfection. Just the sight of her nearly knocked me on my ass. All I could do was stand there, dumbfounded, until I finally managed to form a single word.

"Wow."

She smiled, and looked down at her dress.

Her sweet grin snapped me back to reality. "You look amazing," I said, unable to take my eyes off her.

She bent over to help one foot into her shoe, and then the other. The skintight, black fabric moved slightly upward, exposing just half an inch more of her thighs.

Abby stood and gave me a quick once-over. "You look nice, too."

I shoved my hands in my pocket, refusing to say, *I might be falling for you at this very moment,* or any of the other stupid things that were bombarding my mind.

I stuck out my elbow, and Abby took it, letting me escort her down the hall to the living room.

"Parker is going to piss himself when he sees you," America said. Overall America was a good girl, but I was finding out how nasty she could be if you were on her bad side. I tried not to trip her as we walked to Shepley's Charger, and I kept my mouth shut the entire trip to the Sig Tau house.

The moment Shepley opened the car door, we could hear the loud and obnoxious music from the house. Couples were kissing and mingling; freshmen pledges were running around, trying to keep the damage to the yard at a minimum, and sorority girls carefully walked by hand in hand, in tiny hops, trying to walk across the soft grass without sinking their stilettos.

Shepley and I led the way, with America and Abby just behind us. I kicked a red plastic cup out of the way, and then held the door open. Once again, Abby was totally oblivious to my gesture.

A stack of red cups sat on the kitchen counter beside the keg. I filled two and brought one to Abby. I leaned into her ear. "Don't take these from anyone but me or Shep. I don't want anyone slipping something in your drink."

She rolled her eyes. "No one is going to put anything in my drink, Travis."

She clearly wasn't familiar with some of my frat brothers. I'd heard stories about no one in particular. Which was a good thing, because if I'd ever caught anyone pulling that shit, I would beat the shit out of them without hesitation.

"Just don't drink anything that doesn't come from me, okay? You're not in Kansas anymore, Pigeon."

"I haven't heard that one before," she snapped, throwing back half the cup of beer before she pulled the plastic away from her face. She could drink, I'd give her that.

We stood in the hallway by the stairs, trying to pretend everything was fine. A few of my frat brothers stopped by to chat as they came down the stairs, and so did a few sorority sisters, but I quickly dismissed them, hoping Abby would notice. She didn't.

"Wanna dance?" I asked, tugging on her hand.

"No thanks," she said.

I couldn't blame her, after the night before. I was lucky she was speaking to me at all.

Her thin, elegant fingers touched my shoulder. "I'm just tired, Trav."

I put my hand on hers, ready to apologize again, to tell her that I hated myself for what I'd done, but her eyes drifted away from mine to someone behind me.

"Hey, Abby! You made it!"

The hairs on the back of my neck stood on end. Parker Hayes.

Abby's eyes lit up, and she pulled her hand out from under mine in one quick movement. "Yeah, we've been here for an hour or so."

"You look incredible!" he yelled.

I made a face at him, but he was so preoccupied with Abby, he didn't notice.

"Thanks!" She smiled.

It occurred to me that I wasn't the only one that could make her smile that way, and suddenly I was working to keep my temper in check.

Parker nodded toward the living room and smiled. "You wanna dance?"

"Nah, I'm kinda tired."

A tiny bit of relief dulled my anger a bit. It wasn't me; she really was just too tired to dance, but the anger didn't take long to return. She was tired because she was kept up half the night by the sounds of whoever I'd brought home, and the other half of the night she'd slept in the recliner. Now Parker was here, sweeping in as the knight in shining armor like he always did. Rat bastard.

Parker looked at me, unfazed by my expression. "I thought you weren't coming."

"I changed my mind," I said, trying very hard not to punch him and obliterate four years of orthodontic work.

"I see that," Parker said, looking to Abby. "You wanna get some air?"

She nodded, and I felt like someone had knocked the air out of me. She followed Parker up the stairs. I watched as he paused, reaching to take her hand as they climbed to the second floor. When they reached the top, Parker opened the doors to the balcony.

Abby disappeared, and I squeezed my eyes shut, trying to block out the screaming in my head. Everything in me said to go up there and take her back. I gripped the banister, holding myself back.

"You look pissed," America said, touching her red cup to mine.

My eyes popped open. "No. Why?"

She made a face. "Don't lie to me. Where's Abby?"

"Upstairs. With Parker."

"Oh."

"What is that supposed to mean?"

She shrugged. She'd only been there a little over an hour, and already had that familiar glaze in her eyes. "You're jealous."

I shifted my weight, uncomfortable with someone else besides Shepley being so direct with me. "Where's Shep?"

America rolled her eyes. "Doing his freshman duties."

"At least he doesn't have to stay after and clean up."

She lifted the cup to her mouth and took a sip. I wasn't sure how she could already have a nice buzz drinking like that.

"So are you?"

"Am I what?"

"Jealous?"

I frowned. America wasn't usually so obnoxious. "No."

"Number two."

"Huh?"

"That's lie number two."

I looked around. Shepley would surely rescue me soon.

"You really fucked up last night," she said, her eyes suddenly clear.

"I know."

She squinted, glaring at me so intensely that I wanted to shrink back. America Mason was a tiny blond thing, but she was intimidating as fuck when she wanted to be. "You should walk away, Trav." She looked up, to the top of the stairs. "He's what she thinks she wants."

My teeth clenched together. I already knew that, but it was worse hearing it from America. Before that, I thought maybe she'd be okay with me and Abby, and that somehow meant I wasn't a complete dick for pursuing her. "I know."

She raised an eyebrow. "I don't think you do."

I didn't reply, trying not to make eye contact with her. She grabbed my chin with her hand, squashing my cheeks against my teeth.

"Do you?"

I tried to speak, but her fingers were now squishing my lips together. I jerked back, and then batted her hand away. "Probably not. I'm not exactly notorious for doing the right thing."

America watched me for a few seconds, and then smiled. "Okay, then."

"Huh?"

She slapped my cheek, and then pointed at me. "You, Mad Dog, are exactly what I came here to protect her from. But you know what? We're all broken some way or another. Even with your epic fuckup, you just might be exactly what she needs. You get one more chance," she said, holding up her index finger an inch from my nose. "Just one. Don't mess it up . . . you know . . . more than usual."

America sauntered away, and then disappeared down the hall.

She was so weird.

The party played out as they usually do: drama, a fight or two, girls getting in a tiff, a couple or two getting in an argument resulting in the female leaving in tears, and then the stragglers either passing out or vomiting in an undesignated area.

My eyes drifted to the top of the stairs more times than they should have. Even though the girls were practically begging me to take them home, I kept watch, trying not to imagine Abby and Parker making out, or even worse, him making her laugh.

"Hey, Travis," a high-pitched, singsong voice called from behind me. I didn't turn around, but it didn't take long for the girl to weave herself into my line of sight. She leaned against the wooden posts of the banister. "You looked bored. I think I should keep you company."

"Not bored. You can go," I said, checking the top of the stairs again. Abby stood on the landing, her back to the stairs.

She giggled. "You're so funny."

Abby breezed past me, down the hall to where America stood. I followed, leaving the drunk girl to talk to herself.

"You guys go ahead," Abby said with subdued excitement. "Parker offered me a ride home."

"What?" America said, her tired eyes lit like double bonfires.

"What?" I said, unable to contain my irritation.

America turned. "Is there a problem?"

I glared at her. She knew exactly what my problem was. I took Abby by the elbow and pulled her around the corner.

"You don't even know the guy."

Abby pulled her arm away. "This is none of your business, Travis."

"The hell if it's not. I'm not letting you ride home with a complete stranger. What if he tries something on you?"

"*Good!* He's cute!"

I couldn't believe it. She was really falling for his game. "*Parker Hayes,* Pidge? Really? *Parker Hayes*. What kind of name is that, anyway?"

She crossed her arms and lifted her chin. "Stop it, Trav. You're being a jerk."

I leaned in, livid. "I'll kill him if he touches you."

"I *like* him."

It was one thing to assume she was fooled, it was another to hear her admit it. She was too good for me—damn sure too good for Parker Hayes. Why was she getting all giddy over that idiot? My face tensed in reaction to the rage flowing through my veins. "Fine. If he ends up holding you down in the backseat of his car, don't come crying to me."

Her mouth popped open, she was offended and furious. "Don't worry, I *won't*," she said, shouldering past me.

I realized what I'd said, and then grabbed her arm and sighed, not quite turning around. "I didn't mean it, Pidge. If he hurts you—if he even makes you feel uncomfortable—you let me know."

Her shoulders fell. "I know you didn't. But you have *got* to curb this overprotective big-brother thing you've got going on."

I laughed once. She really didn't get it. "I'm not playing the big brother, Pigeon. Not even close."

Parker rounded the corner and pushed his hands inside his pockets. "All set?"

"Yeah, let's go," Abby said, taking Parker's arm.

I fantasized about running up behind him and shoving my elbow in the back of his head, but then Abby turned and saw me staring him down.

Stop it, she mouthed. She walked with Parker, and he held the door open for her. A wide smile spread across her face in appreciation.

Of course. When he did it, she noticed.

CHAPTER ELEVEN

Cold Bitch

RIDING HOME ALONE IN THE BACKSEAT OF SHEPLEY'S Charger was less than thrilling. America kicked off her heels and giggled as she poked Shepley's cheek with her big toe. He must have been crazy in love with her, because he just smiled, amused by her infectious laughter.

My phone rang. It was Adam. "I got a rookie lined up in an hour. Bottom of Hellerton."

"Yeah, uh . . . I can't."

"What?"

"You heard me. I said I can't."

"Are you sick?" Adam asked, the anger rising in his voice.

"No. I gotta make sure Pidge gets home okay."

"I went to a lot of trouble to set this up, Maddox."

"I know. I'm sorry. Gotta go."

When Shepley pulled into his parking spot in front of the apartment and Parker's Porsche was nowhere to be found, I sighed.

"You coming, cuz?" Shepley asked, turning around in his seat.

"Yeah," I said, looking down at my hands. "Yeah, I guess."

Shepley pulled his seat forward to let me out, and I stopped just short of America's tiny frame.

"You have nothing to worry about, Trav. Trust me."

I nodded once, and then followed them up the stairs. They went straight into Shepley's bedroom and shut the door. I fell into the recliner, listening to America's incessant giggling, and trying not to imagine Parker putting his hand on Abby's knee—or thigh.

Less than ten minutes later, a car engine purred outside, and I made my way to the door, holding the knob. I could hear two pairs of feet walking up the stairs. One set was heels. A wave of relief washed over me. Abby was home.

Only their murmuring filtered through the door. When it got quiet and the knob turned, I twisted it the rest of the way and opened it quickly.

Abby fell through the threshold, and I grabbed her arm. "Easy there, Grace."

She immediately turned to see the expression on Parker's face. It was strained, like he didn't know what to think, but he recovered quickly, pretending to look past me into the apartment.

"Any humiliated, stranded girls in there I need to give a ride?"

I glared at him. He had some damn nerve. "Don't start with me."

Parker smiled and winked at Abby. "I'm always giving him a hard time. I don't get to quite as often since he's realized it's easier if he can get them to drive their own cars."

"I guess that does simplify things," Abby said, turning to me with an amused smile.

"Not funny, Pidge."

"*Pidge?*" Parker asked.

Abby shifted nervously. "It's uh . . . short for Pigeon. It's just a nickname, I don't even know where he came up with it."

"You're going to have to fill me in when you find out. Sounds like a good story." Parker smiled. "Night, Abby."

"Don't you mean good morning?" she asked.

"That, too," he called back with a smile that made me want to puke.

Abby was busy swooning, so to snap her back to reality, I slammed the door without warning. She jerked back.

"*What?*" she snapped.

I stomped down the hall to the bedroom, with Abby on my tail. She stopped just inside the door, hopping on one foot, trying to take off her heel. "He's nice, Trav."

I watched her struggle to balance on one leg, and then finally decided to help before she fell over. "You're gonna hurt yourself," I said, hooking my arm around her waist with one hand, and pulling off her heels with the other. I pulled off my shirt and threw it into the corner.

To my surprise, Abby reached behind her back to unzip her dress, slipped it down, and then yanked a T-shirt over her head. She did some sort of magic bra trick to get it off and out of her shirt. All women seemed to know the same maneuver.

"I'm sure there's nothing I have that you haven't seen before," she said, rolling her eyes. She sat on the mattress, and then pushed her legs between the cover and the sheets. I watched her snuggle into her pillow, and then took off my jeans, kicking them to the corner, too.

She was curled in a ball, waiting for me to come to bed. It irritated me that she'd just rode home with Parker and then undressed in front of me like it was nothing, but at the same time, that was just the kind of fucked-up platonic situation we were in, and it was all my doing.

So many things were building up inside of me. I didn't know what to do with them all. When we'd made the bet, it didn't occur to me that she would be dating Parker. Throwing a tantrum would just drive her straight into his arms. Deep down, I knew I'd do anything to keep her around. If keeping a lid on my jealousy meant more time with Abby, that's what I would have to do.

I crawled into the bed beside her and lifted my hand, resting it on her hip.

"I missed a fight tonight. Adam called. I didn't go."

"*Why?*" she asked, turning over.

"I wanted to make sure you got home."

She wrinkled her nose. "You didn't have to babysit me."

I traced the length of her arm with my finger. She was so warm. "I know. I guess I still feel bad about the other night."

"I told you I didn't care."

"Is that why you slept on the recliner? Because you didn't care?"

"I couldn't fall asleep after your . . . *friends* left."

"You slept just fine in the recliner. Why couldn't you sleep with me?"

"You mean next to a guy who still smelled like the pair of barflies he had just sent home? I don't know! How selfish of me!"

I recoiled, trying to keep the visual out of my head. "I said I was sorry."

"And I said I didn't care. Good night," she said, turning over.

I reached across the pillow to put my hand on hers, caressing the insides of her fingers. I leaned over and kissed her hair. "As worried as I was that you'd never speak to me again . . . I think it's worse that you're indifferent."

"What do you want from me, Travis? You don't want me to be upset about what you did, but you want me to care. You tell America that you don't want to date me, but you get so pissed off when I say the same thing that you storm out and get ridiculously drunk. You don't make any sense."

Her words surprised me. "Is that why you said those things to America? Because I said I wouldn't date you?"

Her expression was a combination of shock and anger. "No, I meant what I said. I just didn't mean it as an insult."

"I just said that because I don't want to ruin anything. I wouldn't even know how to go about being who you deserve. I was just trying to get it worked out in my head."

Saying the words made me feel sick, but they had to be said.

"Whatever that means. I have to get some sleep. I have a date tonight."

"With Parker?"

"Yes. Can I please go to sleep?"

"Sure," I said, shoving myself off the bed. Abby didn't say a word as I left her behind. I sat in the recliner, switching on the television. So much for keeping my temper in check, but damn that woman got under my skin. Talking to her was like having a conversation with a black hole. It didn't matter what I said, even the few times that I was clear about my feelings. Her selective hearing was infuriating. I couldn't get through to her, and being direct just seemed to make her angry.

The sun came up half an hour later. Despite my residual anger, I was able to drift off.

A few moments later, my phone rang. I scrambled to find it, still half asleep, and then held it to my ear. "Yeah?"

"Asshat!" Trenton said, loud in my ear.

"What time is it?" I asked, looking at the TV. Saturday morning cartoons were on.

"Ten something. I need your help with Dad's truck. I think it's the ignition module. It's not even turning over."

"Trent," I said through a yawn. "I don't fucking know about cars. That's why I have a bike."

"Then ask Shepley. I have to go to work in an hour, and I don't want to leave Dad stranded."

I yawned again. "Fuck, Trent, I pulled an all-nighter. What's Tyler doing?"

"Get your ass over here!" he yelled before hanging up.

I tossed my cell to the couch and then stood, looking at the clock on the television. Trent wasn't far off when he guessed the time. It was 10:20.

Shepley's door was closed, so I listened for a minute before I knocked twice and popped my head in. "Hey. Shep. Shepley!"

"What?" Shepley said. His voice sounded like he'd swallowed gravel and chased it with acid.

"I need your help."

America whimpered but didn't stir.

"With what?" Shepley asked. He sat up, grabbing a T-shirt off the floor and slipping it over his head.

"Dad's truck didn't start. Trent thinks it's the ignition."

Shepley finished getting dressed and then leaned over America. "Going to Jim's for a few hours, baby."

"Hmmm?"

Shepley kissed her forehead. "I'm going to help Travis with Jim's truck. I'll be back."

"Okay," America said, falling back asleep before Shepley left the room. He slipped on the pair of sneakers that were in the living room and grabbed his keys.

"You coming or what?" he asked.

I trudged down the hall and into my bedroom, dragging ass like any man that had only four hours of sleep—and not great sleep at that. I slipped on a tank top, and then a hoodie sweatshirt, and some jeans. Trying my best to walk softly, I gently turned the knob of my bedroom door, but paused before leaving. Abby's back was to me, her breathing even, and her bare legs sprawled in opposite directions. I had an almost uncontrollable urge to crawl in bed with her.

"Let's go!" Shepley called.

I shut the door and followed him out to the Charger. We took turns yawning all the way to Dad's, too tired for conversation.

The gravel driveway crunched under the tires of the Charger, and I waved at Trenton and Dad before stepping out into the yard.

Dad's truck was parked in front of the house. I shoved my hands in the front pockets of my hoodie, feeling the chill in the air. Fallen leaves crunched under my boots as I walked across the lawn.

"Well, hello there, Shepley," Dad said with a smile.

"Hey, Uncle Jim. I hear you have an ignition problem."

Dad rested a hand on his round middle. "We think so . . . we think so." He nodded, staring at the engine.

"What makes you think that?" Shepley asked, rolling up his sleeves.

Trenton pointed to the firewall. "Uh . . . it's melted. That was my first clue."

"Good catch," Shepley said. "Me and Trav will run up to the parts store and pick up a new one. I'll put it in and you'll be good to go."

"In theory," I said, handing Shepley a screwdriver.

He unscrewed the bolts of the ignition module and then pulled it off. We all stared at the melted casing.

Shepley pointed to the bare spot where the ignition module was. "We're going to have to replace those wires. See the burn marks?" he asked, touching the metal. "The wire insulation is melted, too."

"Thanks, Shep. I'm gonna go shower. I've gotta get ready for work," Trenton said.

Shepley used the screwdriver to assist in a sloppy salute to Trenton, and then he threw it into the toolbox.

"You boys look like you had a long night," Dad said.

Half of my mouth pulled up. "We did."

"How's your young lady? America?"

Shepley nodded, a wide grin creeping across his face. "She's good, Jim. She's still asleep."

Dad laughed once and nodded. "And your young lady?"

I shrugged. "She's got a date with Parker Hayes tonight. She's not exactly mine, Dad."

Dad winked. "Yet."

Shepley's expression fell. He was fighting a frown.

"What's this, Shep? You don't approve of Travis's pigeon?"

Dad's flippant use of Abby's nickname caught Shepley off guard, and his mouth twitched, threatening a smile. "No, I like Abby just fine. She's just the closest thing America has to a sister. Makes me nervous."

Dad nodded emphatically. "Understandable. I think this one's different, though, don't you?"

Shepley shrugged. "That's kind of the point. Don't really want Trav's first broken heart to be America's best friend. No offense, Travis."

I frowned. "You don't trust me at all, do you?"

"It's not that. Well, it's kind of that."

Dad touched Shepley's shoulder. "You're afraid, since this is Travis's first attempt at a relationship, he's going to screw it up, and that screws things up for you."

Shepley grabbed a dirty rag and wiped his hands. "I feel bad for admitting it, but yeah. Even though I'm rooting for you, bro, I really am."

Trenton let the screen door slam when he jogged out of the house. He punched me in the arm before I even saw him raise a fist.

"Later, losers!" Trenton stopped, and turned on his heels. "I didn't mean you, Dad."

Dad offered a half smile and shook his head. "Didn't think you did, son."

Trent smiled, and then hopped into his car—a dark red, dilapidated Dodge Intrepid. That car wasn't even cool when we were in high school, but he loved it. Mostly because it was paid off.

A small black puppy barked, turning my attention to the house.

Dad smiled, patting his thigh. "Well, c'mon, scaredy-cat."

The puppy took a couple of steps forward, and then backed into the house, barking.

"How's he doing?" I asked.

"He's pissed in the bathroom twice."

I made a face. "Sorry."

Shepley laughed. "At least he's got the right idea."

Dad nodded and waved with concession.

"Just until tomorrow," I said.

"It's fine, son. He's been entertaining us. Trent enjoys him."

"Good." I smiled.

"Where were we?" Dad asked.

I rubbed my arm where it throbbed from Trent's fist. "Shepley was just reminding me of what a failure he thinks I am when it comes to girls."

Shepley laughed once. "You're a lot of things, Trav. A failure is not one of them. I just think you have a long way to go, and between your and Abby's tempers, the odds are against you."

My body tensed, and I stood straight. "Abby doesn't have a bad temper."

Dad waved me away. "Calm down, squirt. He's not badmouthing Abby."

"She doesn't."

"Okay," Dad said with a small smile. He always knew how to handle us boys when things got tense, and he usually tried to mollify us before we were too far gone.

Shepley threw the dirty rag on top of the toolbox. "Let's go get that part."

"Let me know how much I owe you."

I shook my head. "I got it, Dad. We're even for the dog."

Dad smiled and started to pick up the mess Trenton left of the toolbox. "Okay, then. I'll see you in a bit."

Shepley and I left in the Charger, heading to the parts store. A cold front had come through. I clenched the ends of my sleeves in my fists to help keep my hands warm.

"It's a cold bitch today," Shepley said.

"Getting there."

"I think she's going to like the puppy."

"Hope so."

After a few more blocks of silence, Shepley nodded his head. "I didn't mean to insult Abby. You know that, right?"

"I know."

"I know how you feel about her, and I really do hope it works out. I'm just nervous."

"Yep."

Shepley pulled into the parking lot of O'Reilly's and parked, but he didn't turn off the ignition. "She's going on a date with Parker Hayes tonight, Travis. How do you think it's going to go when he picks her up? Have you thought about it?"

"I'm trying not to."

"Well, maybe you should. If you really want this to work, you need to stop reacting the way you want, and react the way that will work for you."

"Like how?"

"Do you think it's going to win you any points if you're pouting while she's getting ready, and then act like a dick to Parker? Or do you think she'll appreciate it if you tell her how amazing she looks and tell her goodbye, like a friend would?"

"I don't want to be just her friend."

"I know that, and you know that, and Abby probably knows it, too . . . and you can be damn sure Parker knows it."

"Do you have to keep saying that fuck stick's name?"

Shepley turned off the ignition. "C'mon, Trav. You and I both know as long as you keep showing Parker he's doing something to drive you nuts, he's going to keep playing the game. Don't give him the satisfaction, and play the game better than he does. He'll show his ass, and Abby will get rid of him on her own."

I thought about what he was saying, and then glanced over at him. "You . . . really think so?"

"Yes, now let's get that part to Jim and get home before America wakes up and blows up my phone because she doesn't remember what I told her when I left."

I laughed and followed Shepley into the store. "He is a fuck stick, though."

It didn't take Shepley long to find the part he was looking for, and not much longer for him to replace it. In just over an hour, Shepley had installed the ignition module, started the truck, and had a sufficiently long visit with Dad. By the time we were waving goodbye as the Charger backed out of the driveway, it was just a few minutes after noon.

As Shepley predicted, America was already awake by the time we made it back to the apartment. She tried to act irritated before Shepley explained our absence, but it was obvious she was just glad to have him home.

"I've been so bored. Abby is still asleep."

"Still?" I asked, kicking off my boots.

America nodded and made a face. "The girl likes her sleep. Unless she gets insanely drunk the night before, she sleeps forever. I've stopped trying to turn her into a morning person."

The door creaked as I slowly pushed it open. Abby was on her stomach, in almost the same position she was in when I left, just on the other side of the bed. Part of her hair was matted against her face, the other in soft, caramel waves across my pillow.

Abby's T-shirt was bunched around her waist, exposing her light blue panties. They were just cotton, not particularly sexy, and she looked comatose, but even so, seeing her crashed haphazardly on my white sheets with the afternoon sun pouring in through the windows, her beauty was indescribable.

"Pidge? You gonna get up today?"

She mumbled and then turned her head. I took a few more steps, deeper into the room.

"Pigeon."

"Hep . . . merf . . . furfon . . . shaw."

America was right. She wasn't waking up anytime soon. I closed the door softly behind me, and then joined Shepley and America in the living room. They were picking at a plate of nachos America had made, watching something girly on TV.

"She up?" America asked.

I shook my head, sitting in the recliner. "Nope. She was talking about something, though."

America smiled, her lips sealed to keep food from falling out. "She does that," she said, her mouth full. "I heard you leave your bedroom last night. What was that about?"

"I was being an ass."

America's brows shot up. "How so?"

"I was frustrated. I pretty much told her how I felt and it was like it went in one ear and out the other."

"How *do* you feel?" she asked.

"Tired at the moment."

A chip flew at my face but fell short, landing on my shirt. I picked it up and popped it in my mouth, crunching the beans, cheese, and sour cream. It wasn't half bad.

"I'm serious. What did you say?"

I shrugged. "I don't remember. Something about being who she deserved."

"Aw," America said, sighing. She leaned away from me, in Shepley's direction, with a wry smile. "That was pretty good. Even you have to admit."

Shepley's mouth pulled to one side; that was the only reaction she would get from him for that comment.

"You are such a grouch," America said with a frown.

Shepley stood. "No, baby. I'm just not feeling all that great." He grabbed a copy of *Car and Driver* from the end table, and headed for the toilet.

With a sympathetic expression America watched Shepley leave, and then turned to me, her face metamorphosing into disgust. "Guess I'll be using your bathroom for the next few hours."

"Unless you want to lose your sense of smell for the rest of your life."

"I might want to after that," she said, shivering.

America took her movie off pause, and we watched the rest of it. I didn't really know what was going on. A woman was talking something about old cows and how her roommate was a man-whore. By the end of the movie, Shepley had rejoined us, and the main character had figured out she had feelings for her roommate, she wasn't an old cow after all, and the man-whore, now reformed, was angry about some stupid misunderstanding. She just had to chase him down the street, kiss him, and it was all good. Not the worst movie I'd ever seen, but it was still a chick flick . . . and still lame.

In the middle of the day, the apartment was well lit, and the TV was on, albeit on mute. Everything seemed normal, but also empty. The stolen signs were still on the walls, hung next to our favorite beer posters with half-naked hot chicks sprawled in various positions. America had cleaned up the apartment, and Shepley was lying on the couch, flipping through channels. It was a normal Saturday. But something was off. Something was missing.

Abby.

Even with her in the next room, passed out, the apartment felt different without her voice, her playful jabs, or even the sound of her picking at her nails. I'd grown accustomed to it all in our short time together.

Just as the credits of the second movie began to roll, I heard the bedroom door open, and Abby's feet dragging along the floor. The bathroom door opened and closed. She was going to start getting ready for her date with Parker.

Instantly, my temper began to boil.

"Trav," Shepley warned.

Shepley's words from earlier in the day replayed in my head. Parker was playing the game, and I had to play it better. My adrenaline died down, and I relaxed against the couch cushion. It was time to put my game face on.

The whining sound of the bathroom pipes signaled Abby's intent to take a shower. America stood, and then nearly danced into my bathroom. I could hear their voices banter back and forth but couldn't quite make out what they were saying.

I walked softly into the hall, and held my ear close to the door.

"I'm not thrilled about you listening to my girl urinate," Shepley said in a loud whisper.

I held my middle finger up to my lips, and then turned my attention back to their voices.

"I explained it to him," Abby said.

The toilet flushed, and the faucet turned on, and then suddenly Abby cried out. Without thinking, I grabbed the doorknob and shoved it open.

"Pidge?"

America laughed. "I just flushed the toilet, Trav, calm down."

"Oh. You all right, Pigeon?"

"I'm great. Get out." I shut the door again and sighed. That was stupid. After a few tense seconds, I realized neither of the girls knew I was just on the other side of the door, so I touched my ear to the wood again.

"Is it too much to ask for locks on the doors?" Abby asked. "Mare?"

"It's really too bad you two couldn't get on the same page. You're the only girl that could have . . ." She sighed. "Never mind. It doesn't matter, now."

The water turned off. "You're as bad as he is," Abby said, her voice thick with frustration. "It's a sickness . . . no one here makes sense. You're pissed at him, remember?"

"I know," America replied.

That was my cue to get back to the living room, but my heart was beating a million miles an hour. For whatever reason, if America thought it was okay, I felt like I had the green light, that I wasn't a total dick for trying to be in Abby's life.

As soon as I sat on the couch, America came out of the bathroom.

"What?" she asked, sensing something was amiss.

"Nothing, baby. Come sit," Shepley said, patting the empty space next to him.

America happily complied, sprawling out next to him, her torso leaning against his chest.

The hairdryer turned on in the bathroom, and I looked at the clock. The only thing worse than having to be okay with Abby leaving on a date with Parker, was Parker having to wait on Abby in my apartment. Keeping my cool for a few minutes while she got her purse and left was one thing. Looking at his ugly mug while he sat on my couch, knowing he was planning how to get into her pants at the end of the night, was another.

A small bit of my anxiety was relieved when Abby walked out of the bathroom. She wore a red dress, and her lips matched perfectly. Her hair in curls, she reminded me of one of those 1950s pinup girls. But, better. Way . . . *way* better.

I smiled, and it wasn't even forced. "You . . . are beautiful."

"Thank you," she said, clearly taken off guard.

The doorbell rang, and instantly adrenaline surged through my veins. I took a deep breath, determined to keep my cool.

Abby opened the door, and it took Parker several seconds to speak.

"You are the most beautiful creature I've ever seen," he cooed.

Yep, I was definitely going to vomit before I ended up throwing a punch. What a loser.

America's grin spread from one ear to the other. Shepley seemed really happy, too. Refusing to turn around, I kept my eyes on the TV. If I saw the smug look on Parker's face, I would climb over the couch and knock him to the first floor without him hitting a step.

The door closed, and I came forward, my elbows on my knees, my head in my hands.

"You did good, Trav," Shepley said.

"I need a drink."

CHAPTER TWELVE

Virgin

LESS THAN A WEEK LATER, I HAD EMPTIED MY SECOND bottle of whiskey. Between trying to cope with Abby spending more and more time with Parker, and her asking me to release her from the bet so she could leave, my lips were touching the mouth of the bottle more than they were my cigarettes.

Parker had ruined the surprise of Abby's surprise birthday party Thursday at lunch, so I had to scramble to move it to Friday night instead of Sunday. I was thankful for the distraction, but it wasn't enough.

Thursday night, Abby and America were chattering in the bathroom. Abby's demeanor toward America was a stark contrast to the way she regarded me: she'd barely spoken to me that evening since I refused to let her out of the bet earlier that day.

Hoping to smooth things over, I popped into the bathroom. "Wanna grab dinner?"

"Shep wants to check out that new Mexican place downtown if you guys wanna go," America said, absently combing through her hair.

"I thought me and Pidge could go alone tonight."

Abby perfected her lipstick. "I'm going out with Parker."

"Again?" I said, feeling my face compress into a frown.

"Again," she lilted.

The doorbell rang, and Abby burst out of the bathroom and rushed across the living room floor to open the front door.

I followed and stood behind her, making a point to give Parker my best death glare.

"Do you ever look less than gorgeous?" Parker asked.

"Based on the first time she came over here, I'm going to say yes," I deadpanned.

Abby held up a finger to Parker, and turned around. I expected her to snap back something shitty, but she was smiling. She threw her arms around my neck and squeezed.

At first I braced myself, thinking she was trying to hit me, but once I recognized she was hugging me, I relaxed, and then pulled her into me.

She pulled away and smiled. "Thanks for organizing my birthday party," she said, genuine appreciation in her voice. "Can I take a rain check on dinner?"

She had the warmth in her eyes I'd missed, but mostly I was surprised that after not speaking to me all afternoon and evening, she was in my arms.

"Tomorrow?"

She hugged me again. "Absolutely." She waved to me as she took Parker's hand and closed the door behind her.

I turned around and rubbed the back of my neck. "I . . . I need a . . ."

"A drink?" Shepley asked, an edge of worry in his voice. He looked to the kitchen. "We're out of everything but beer."

"Then I guess I'm making a trip to the liquor store."

"I'll go with you," America said, jumping up to grab her coat.

"Why don't you drive him in the Charger?" Shepley said, tossing her the keys.

America looked down at the collection of metal in her hand. "You sure?"

Shepley sighed. "I don't think Travis should drive. Anywhere . . . if you get my meaning."

America nodded enthusiastically. "Gotcha." She grabbed my hand. "C'mon, Trav. Let's get you liquored up." I began to follow her out the door, but she stopped abruptly, turning on her heels. "But! You have to promise me something. No fighting tonight. Drowning your sorrows, yes," she said, grabbing my chin and forcing me to nod my head. "Mean drunk, no." She pushed my chin back and forth.

I pulled back, waving her hand away.

"Promise?" She raised one eyebrow.

"Yes."

She smiled. "Then off we go."

My fingers against my lips, my elbow leaning against the door, I watched the world pass my window. The cold front brought with it wild wind, whipping through the trees and bushes, and causing the hanging streetlights to swing back and forth. The skirt of Abby's dress was pretty short. Parker's eyes had better stay in his head if it happened to fly up. The way Abby's bare knees look when she sat next to me in the backseat of the Charger came to mind, and I imagined Parker noticing her soft, shiny skin as I had, but with less appreciation and more salaciousness.

Just as the anger welled up within me, America pulled on the emergency brake. "We're here."

The soft glow of Ugly Fixer Liquor's sign lit the entrance.

America was my shadow down aisle three. It only took me a moment to find what I was looking for. The only bottle that would do for a night like tonight: Jim Beam.

"You sure you wanna go there?" America asked, her voice tinged with warning. "You do have a surprise birthday party to set up tomorrow."

"I'm sure," I said, taking the bottle to the counter.

The second my ass hit the passenger seat of the Charger, I twisted the cap and took a swig, leaning my head back against the headrest.

America watched me for a moment, and then shoved the gear into reverse. "This is going to be fun, I can tell."

By the time we reached the apartment, I'd drunk the whiskey in the neck of the bottle, and made headway at the top.

"You didn't," Shepley said, spotting the bottle.

"I did," I said, taking another swig. "You want some?" I asked, pointing the glass mouth in his direction.

Shepley made a face. "God no. I need to stay sober so I can react fast enough when you go all Travis-on-Jim-Beam on Parker later."

"No, he won't," America said. "He promised."

"I did," I said with a smile, already feeling better. "I promised."

The next hour Shepley and America did their best to keep my mind off things. Mr. Beam did his best to keep me numb. Halfway into hour two, Shepley's words seemed slower. America giggled at the stupid grin on my face.

"See? He's a happy drunk."

I blew air through my lips, and they made a puff sound. "I'm not drunk. Not yet."

Shepley pointed to the diminishing amber liquid. "If you drink the rest of that, you will be."

I held up the bottle, and then looked at the clock. "Three hours. Must be a good date." I lifted the bottle to Shepley, and then touched it to my lips, tilting it all the way back. The rest of the contents passed my numb lips and teeth, and burned all the way to my stomach.

"Jesus, Travis," Shepley said with a frown. "You should go pass out. You don't want to be up when she gets home."

The sound of an engine grew louder as it approached the apartment and then idled outside. I knew the sound well—it was Parker's Porsche.

A sloppy smile spread across my lips. "What for? This is where the magic happens."

America watched me warily. "Trav . . . you promised."

I nodded. "I did. I promised. I'm just going to help her out of the car." My legs were under me, but I couldn't feel them. The back of the couch proved to be a great stabilizer for my drunken attempt at walking.

My hand encompassed the knob, but America gently covered it with her hand. "I'm going to go with you. To make sure you don't break your promise."

"Good idea," I said. I opened the door, and instantly adrenaline burned through the last half of the whiskey. The Porsche rocked once, and the windows were fogged.

Unsure of how my legs moved so fast in my condition, I was suddenly at the bottom of the stairs. America took a fistful of my shirt. As small as she was, she was surprisingly sturdy.

"Travis," she said in a loud whisper. "Abby's not going to let it go too far. Try to calm down, first."

"I'm just going to check that she's okay," I said, taking the few steps to Parker's car. The side of my hand hit the passenger-side window so hard, I was surprised it didn't break. When they didn't open the door, I opened it for them.

Abby was fidgeting with her dress. Her hair a mess and gloss-less lips, a telltale sign of what they'd been doing.

Parker's face tensed. "What the hell, Travis?"

My hands balled into fists, but I could feel America's hand on my shoulder.

"C'mon, Abby. I need to talk to you," America said.

Abby blinked a few times. "About what?"

"Just come on!" America snapped.

Abby looked to Parker. "I'm sorry, I have to go."

Parker shook his head, angry. "No, it's fine. Go ahead."

I took Abby's hand as she stepped from the Porsche, and then kicked the door shut. Abby flipped around and stood between me and the car, shoving my shoulder. "What is *wrong* with you? Knock it off!"

The Porsche squealed out of the parking lot. I pulled my cigs out of my shirt pocket and lit one up. "You can go in, now, Mare."

"C'mon, Abby."

"Why don't you stay, *Abs,*" I said. The word felt ridiculous to say. How Parker could utter it with a straight face was a feat in itself.

Abby nodded for America to go ahead, and she reluctantly complied.

I watched her for a moment, taking a drag or two from my cigarette.

Abby crossed her arms. "Why did you do that?"

"*Why?* Because he was mauling you in front of my apartment!"

"I may be staying with you, but what I do, and who I do it with, is *my* business."

I flicked my cigarette to the ground. "You're so much better than that, Pidge. Don't let him fuck you in a car like a cheap prom date."

"I wasn't going to have sex with him!"

I waved my hand toward the empty space where Parker's car sat. "What were you doing, then?"

"Haven't you ever made out with someone, Travis? Haven't you just messed around without letting it get that far?"

That was stupidest thing I'd ever heard. "What's the point in that?" Blue balls and disappointment. Sounded like a ball.

"The concept exists for a lot of people. Especially those that *date*."

"The windows were all fogged up, the car was bouncing . . . how was I supposed to know?"

"Maybe you shouldn't spy on me!"

Spy on her? She knows we can hear every car that pulls up to the apartment, and she decided that right outside my door was a good place to suck face with a guy I can't stand? I rubbed my face in frustration, trying to keep my cool. "I can't stand this, Pigeon. I feel like I'm going crazy."

"You can't stand *what*?"

"If you sleep with him, I don't wanna know about it. I'll go to prison for a long time if I find out he . . . just don't tell me."

"Travis." She seethed. "I can't *believe* you just said that! That's a big step for me!"

"That's what all girls say!"

"I don't mean the sluts you deal with! I mean *me*!" She held her hand to her chest. "I haven't . . . *ugh*! Never mind." She took a few steps, but I grabbed her arm, turning her to face me.

"You haven't what?" Even in my current state, the answer came to me. "You're a *virgin?*"

"So what?" she said, blushing.

"That's why America was so sure it wouldn't get too far."

"I had the same boyfriend all four years of high school. He was an aspiring Baptist youth minister! It never came up!"

"A youth minister? What happened after all that hard-earned abstinence?"

"He wanted to get married and stay in . . . Kansas. I didn't."

I couldn't believe what Abby was saying. She was almost nineteen, and still a virgin? That was almost unheard of these days. I couldn't remember meeting one since the beginning of high school.

I held each side of her face. "A virgin. I would have never guessed, with the way you danced at the Red."

"Very funny," she said, stomping up the stairs.

I went after her but busted my ass on one of the steps. My elbow cracked against the corner of the concrete stair, but the pain never came. I rolled onto my back, laughing hysterically.

"What are you doing? Get up!" Abby said as she tugged on me until I was upright.

My eyes turned fuzzy, and then we were in Chaney's class. Abby was sitting on his desk wearing something that looked like a prom dress, and I was in my boxer shorts. The room was empty, and it was either dusk or dawn.

"Going somewhere?" I asked, not particularly concerned that I wasn't dressed.

Abby smiled, reaching out to touch my face. "Nope. Not going anywhere. I'm here to stay."

"You promise?" I asked, touching her knees. I spread her legs just enough to fit snugly between her thighs.

"At the end of it all, I'm yours."

I wasn't exactly sure what she meant, but Abby was all over me. Her lips traveled down my neck, and I closed my eyes, in a complete and total state of euphoria. Everything I had worked for was happening. Her fingers traveled down my torso, and I sucked in a bit just as she slipped them between my boxers and settled on my junk.

Whatever awesomeness I'd felt before, it had just been surpassed. I twisted my fingers in her hair, and pressed my lips against hers, wasting no time to caress the inside of her mouth with my tongue.

One of her heels fell to the floor, and I looked down.

"I have to go," Abby said, sad.

"What? I thought you said you weren't going anywhere."

Abby smiled. "Try harder."

"What?"

"Try harder," she echoed, touching my face.

"Wait," I said, not wanting it to end. "I love you, Pigeon."

My eyes blinked slowly. When my eyes focused, I recognized my ceiling fan. My body hurt everywhere, and my head was thumping with every beat of my heart.

From somewhere down the hall, America's excited, shrill voice filled my ears. In contrast, Shepley's low voice was then peppered between America's and Abby's voices.

I closed my eyes, falling into a deep depression. It was just a dream. None of that happiness was real. I rubbed my face, trying to produce enough motivation to drag my ass outta bed.

Whatever party I'd crashed the night before, I hoped it was worth feeling like pulverized meat in the bottom of a trash can.

My feet felt heavy as I dragged them across the floor to pick up a pair of jeans crumpled in the corner. I pulled them on, and then stumbled into the kitchen, recoiling at the sound of their voices.

"You guys are loud as fuck," I said, buttoning my jeans.

"Sorry," Abby said, barely looking at me. No doubt I'd probably done something stupid to embarrass her the night before.

"Who in the hell let me drink that much last night?"

America's face screwed into disgust. "You did. You went and bought a fifth after Abby left with Parker, and killed the whole thing by the time she got back."

Bits of memories came back to me in scrambled pieces. Abby left with Parker. I was depressed. Liquor store stop with America.

"Damn," I said, shaking my head. "Did you have fun?" I asked Abby.

Her cheeks flushed red.

Oh, shit. It must have been worse than I thought.

"Are you serious?" she asked.

"What?" I asked, but the second the word came out, I'd regretted it.

America giggled, clearly amazed at my memory loss. "You pulled her out of Parker's car, seeing red when you caught them making out like high schoolers. They fogged up the windows and everything!"

I pushed my memory as far as it would go into the evening. The making out didn't ring a bell, but the jealousy did.

Abby looked like she was about to blow her top, and I recoiled from her glare.

"How pissed are you?" I asked, waiting for a high-pitched explosion to infiltrate my already throbbing head.

Abby stomped to the bedroom, and I followed her, closing the door softly behind us.

Abby turned. Her expression was different from what I'd seen before. I wasn't sure how to read it. "Do you remember anything you said to me last night?" she asked.

"No. Why? Was I mean to you?"

"No you weren't mean to me! You . . . we . . ." She covered her eyes with her hands.

When her hand went up, a new, shimmering piece of jewelry fell from her wrist to her forearm, catching my eye. "Where'd this come from?" I asked, wrapping my fingers around her wrist.

"It's mine," she said, pulling away.

"I've never seen it before. It looks new."

"It is."

"Where'd you get it?"

"Parker gave it to me about fifteen minutes ago," she said.

Rage welled up within me. The I-need-to-punch-something-before-I'll-feel-better kind. "What the fuck was that douche bag doing *here*? Did he stay the night?"

She crossed her arms, unfazed. "He went shopping for my birthday present this morning and brought it by."

"It's not your birthday, yet." My anger was boiling over, but the fact that she wasn't at all intimidated helped me to keep it in check.

"He couldn't wait," she said, lifting her chin.

"No wonder I had to drag your ass out of his car, sounds like you were . . ." I trailed off, pressing my lips together to keep the rest from coming out. Not a good time to vomit words out of my mouth I couldn't take back.

"What? Sounds like I was *what?*"

I grit my teeth. "Nothing. I'm just pissed off, and I was going to say something shitty that I didn't mean."

"It's never stopped you before."

"I know. I'm working on it," I said, walking to the door. "I'll let you get dressed."

When I reached for the knob, a pain shot from my elbow up my arm. I touched it, and it was tender. Lifting it revealed what I'd suspected: a fresh bruise. My mind raced to figure out what could have caused it, and I recalled Abby telling me she was a virgin, me falling, and laughing, and then Abby helping me to get undressed . . . and then I . . . Oh, God.

"I fell on the stairs last night. And you helped me to bed . . . We," I said, taking a step toward her. The memory of me crashing against her while she stood in front of the closet half naked rushed into my mind.

I had almost fucked her, taken her virginity when I was drunk. The thought of what might have happened made me feel ashamed for the first time since . . . ever.

"No we didn't. Nothing happened," she said, emphatically shaking her head.

I cringed. "You fog up Parker's windows, I pull you out of the car, and then I try to . . ." I tried to shake the memory out of my head. It was sickening. Thankfully, even in my drunken stupor, I'd stopped, but what if I hadn't? Abby didn't deserve for her first time to be like that with anyone, least of all me. Wow. For a while there, I'd really thought I had changed. It only took a bottle of whiskey and the mention of the word *virgin* for me to return to my dick ways.

I turned for the door and grabbed the knob. "You're turning me into a fucking psycho, Pigeon," I growled over my shoulder. "I don't think straight when I'm around you."

"So it's *my* fault?"

I turned. My eyes fell from her face to her robe, to her legs, and then her feet, returning to her eyes. "I don't know. My memory is a little hazy . . . but I don't recall you saying no."

She took a step forward. At first she looked ready to pounce, but her face softened, and her shoulders fell. "What do you want me to say, Travis?"

I glanced at the bracelet, and then back at her. "You were hoping I wouldn't remember?"

"No! I was pissed that you forgot!"

She made No. Fucking. Sense. "*Why?*"

"Because if I would have . . . if we would have . . . and you didn't . . . I don't know why! I just was!"

She was about to admit it. She had to. Abby was pissed at me because she was going to give me her virginity, and I didn't remember what had happened. This was it. This was my moment. We were finally going to get our shit straight, but time was slipping away. Shepley was going to come tell Abby any minute to go run errands with America per our plans for the party.

I rushed toward her, stopping inches away. My hands touched each side of her face. "What are we doin', Pidge?"

Her eyes began at my belt, and then traveled slowly up to my eyes. "You tell me."

Her face went blank, as if admitting deep feelings for me would make her whole system shut down.

A knock on the door triggered my anger, but I stayed focused.

"Abby?" Shepley said. "Mare was going to run some errands; she wanted me to let you know in case you needed to go."

"Pidge?" I said, staring into her eyes.

"Yeah," she called to Shepley. "I have some stuff I need to take care of."

"All right, she's ready to go when you are," Shepley said, his footsteps disappearing down the hall.

"Pidge?" I said, desperate to stay on track.

She took a few steps backward, pulled a few things from the closet, and then slid past me. "Can we talk about this later? I have a lot to do today."

"Sure," I said, deflated.

CHAPTER THIRTEEN

Porcelain

ABBY DIDN'T STAY IN THE BATHROOM LONG. AS A MATter of fact, she couldn't leave the apartment fast enough. I tried not to let it throw me. Abby usually spazzed out whenever something serious came up.

The front door shut, and America's car pulled out of the parking lot. Once again, the apartment seemed stuffy and too empty at the same time. I hated being there without her and wondered what I had done before we met.

I walked over to a small plastic bag from the pharmacy that I'd picked up a few days before. I'd uploaded some pics of me and Abby from my phone, and ordered some prints.

The white walls finally had some color. Just as the last picture was tacked in place, Shepley knocked on the door.

"Hey, man."

"Yeah?"

"We've got shit to do."

"I know."

We drove to Brazil's apartment, mostly in silence. When we arrived, Brazil opened the door, holding at least two dozen balloons. The long silver strings blew into his face, and he waved them away, spitting some away from his lips.

"I was wondering if you guys had canceled. Gruver is bringing the cake and liquor."

We walked past him into the front room. Their walls didn't look much different from mine, but their apartment had either come "fully furnished" or they got their couch from the Salvation Army.

Brazil continued, "I had some redshirts grab some food and Mikey's kick-ass speakers. One of the Sigma Cappa girls has some lights we can borrow—don't worry, I didn't invite them. I said it was for a party next weekend. We should be set."

"Good," Shepley said. "America would shit a wildcat if she showed up and we were here with a bunch of sorority girls."

Brazil smiled. "The only girls here will be a few of Abby's classmates and girlfriends of the team. I think Abby's going to love it."

I smiled, watching Brazil spread the balloons across the ceiling, letting the strings hang down. "I think so, too. Shep?"

"Yeah?"

"Don't call Parker until the last minute. That way, we invited him, but if he makes it at all, at least he won't be here the whole time."

"Got it."

Brazil took a breath. "Wanna help me move furniture, Trav?"

"Sure," I said, following him into the next room. The dining room and kitchen were one room, and the walls were already lined with chairs. The counter had a row of clean shot glasses and an unopened bottle of Patrón.

Shepley stopped, staring at the bottle. "This isn't for Abby, is it?"

Brazil smiled, his white teeth standing out against his dark olive skin. "Uh . . . yeah. It's tradition. If the football team is throwing her a party, she's getting the team treatment.

"You can't make her drink that many shots," Shepley said. "Travis. Tell him."

Brazil held up his hand. "I'm not making her do anything. For every shot she drinks, she gets a twenty. It's our present to her." His smile faded when he noticed Shepley's frown.

"Your present is alcohol poisoning?"

I nodded once. "We'll see if she wants to take a birthday shot for twenty bucks, Shep. No harm in that."

We moved the dining table to the side, and then helped the redshirts bring in the food and speakers. One of the guys' girlfriends started spraying air freshener around the apartment.

"Nikki! Knock that shit off!"

She put her hand on her hips. "If you guys didn't smell so bad, I wouldn't have to. Ten sweaty boys in one apartment starts stinking pretty quick! You don't want her walking in here when it smells like a locker room, do you?"

"She's right," I said. "Speaking of that, I need to get back and shower. See you in half an hour."

Shepley wiped his brow and nodded, pulling his cell phone from one jeans pocket, his keys from the other.

He tapped out a quick text to America. Within seconds, his phone beeped. He smiled. "I'll be damned. They're right on schedule."

"That's a good sign."

We rushed back to our apartment. Within fifteen minutes, I was showered, shaved, and dressed. Shepley didn't take much longer, but I kept checking my watch.

"Calm down," Shepley said, buttoning up his green plaid shirt. "They're still shopping."

A loud engine pulled up out front, a car door slammed shut, and then footsteps climbed the iron steps outside our door.

I opened it, and smiled. "Good timing."

Trenton smiled, holding a medium-size box with holes cut into the sides and a lid. "He's been fed, watered, took his daily man crap. He should be good to go for a while."

"You're awesome, Trent. Thanks." I looked past him to see my dad sitting behind the wheel of his pickup. He waved, and I waved back.

Trenton open the lid a bit and grinned. "Be good, little man. I'm sure we'll see each other again."

The puppy's tail banged against the box while I replaced the top, and then took him inside.

"Aw, man. Why my room?" Shepley asked, whining.

"In case Pidge happens to go into mine before I'm ready." I pulled out my cell and dialed Abby's number. The phone buzzed once, and then again.

"Hello?"

"It's dinnertime! Where the hell did you two run off to?"

"We indulged in a little pampering. You and Shep knew how to eat before we came along. I'm sure you can manage."

"Well, no shit. We worry about you, ya know."

"We're fine," she said, a smile in her voice.

America spoke somewhere close to Abby. "Tell him I'll have you back in no time. I have to stop by Brazil's to pick up some notes for Shep, and then we'll be home."

"Did you get that?" Abby asked.

"Yeah. See you then, Pidge."

I hung up and quickly followed Shepley out to the Charger. I wasn't sure why, but I was nervous.

"Did you call the douche bag?"

Shepley nodded, putting his car in gear. "While you were in the shower."

"Is he coming?"

"Later. He wasn't happy that it was late notice, but when I reminded him that it was necessary because of his big fucking mouth, he didn't have much to say after that."

I smiled. Parker had always rubbed me the wrong way. Not inviting him would make Abby unhappy, so I had to go against my better judgment and let Shepley give him a call.

"Don't get drunk and punch him," Shepley said.

"No promises. Park over there, where she won't see," I said, pointing to the side lot.

We jogged around the corner to Brazil's apartment, and I knocked. It was quiet.

"It's us! Open up."

The door opened, and Chris Jenks stood in the doorway with a stupid grin on his face. He weaved back and forth, already drunk. He was the only person I liked less than Parker. No one could prove it, but Jenks was rumored to have slipped something in a girl's drink once at a frat party. Most believed it, since that was the only way he could get laid. No one had come forward to say he had, so I just tried to keep an eye on him.

I shot a glare at Shepley, who raised his hands. He obviously wasn't aware Jenks was going to be there either.

I glanced at my watch, and we waited in the dark with dozens of silver strings in our faces. Everyone was so close together, smashed into the living room waiting for Abby, that just one person's movement made us all list one way or the other.

A few knocks at the door made us all freeze. I was expecting America to walk in, but nothing happened. People were whispering while others were shushing them.

Another knock spurred Brazil into action, and he took several quick steps to the door, swinging it wide open, revealing America and Abby in the doorway.

"HAPPY BIRTHDAY!" we all yelled in unison.

Abby's eyes grew wide, and then she smiled, quickly covering her mouth. America nudged her inside, and everyone gathered around.

As I made my way to Abby, the crowd split. She looked phenomenal, wearing a gray dress and yellow heels. The palms of my hands cupped each side of her smiling face, and I pressed my lips against her forehead.

"Happy birthday, Pigeon."

"It's not 'til tomorrow," she said, smiling at everyone around us.

"Well, since you were tipped off, we had to make some last-minute changes to surprise you. Surprised?"

"Very!"

Finch rushed up to wish her a happy birthday, and America elbowed her side. "Good thing I got you to run errands with me today or you would have shown up looking like ass!"

"You look great," I said, making a show of looking her over. *Great* wasn't the most poetic word I could have used, but I didn't wanna overdo it.

Brazil came over to give Abby a bear hug. "And I hope you know America's Brazil-is-creepy story was just a line to get you in here."

America laughed. "It worked, didn't it?"

Abby shook her head, still grinning and wide-eyed from the shock of it all. She leaned into America's ear and whispered something, and then America whispered back. I was going to have to ask her later what that was about.

Brazil cranked up the volume on the stereo, and everyone screamed. "Come here, Abby!" he said, walking to the kitchen. He picked up the bottle of tequila from the bar, and stood before the shot glasses lined up on the counter. "Happy birthday from the football team, baby girl," he smiled, pouring each shot glass full of Patrón. "This is the way we do birthdays: You turn nineteen, you have nineteen shots. You can drink 'em or give 'em away, but the more you drink, the more of these you get," he said, fanning out a handful of twenties.

"Oh my God!" Abby squealed. Her eyes lit up at the site of so much green.

"Drink 'em up, Pidge!" I said.

Abby looked to Brazil, suspicious. "I get a twenty for every shot I drink?"

"That's right, lightweight. Gauging by the size of you, I'm going to say we'll get away with losing sixty bucks by the end of the night."

"Think again, Brazil," Abby said. She lifted the first shot glass to her mouth and rolled the rim from the side of her bottom lip to the middle of her mouth. Her head tipped back to empty the glass, and then she rolled the rim across the rest of her lip, dropping it into her other hand. It was the sexiest thing I'd ever seen.

"Holy shit!" I said, suddenly turned on.

"This is really a waste, Brazil," Abby said, wiping the corners of her mouth. "You shoot Cuervo, not Patrón."

The smug smile on Brazil's face faded, and he shook his head and shrugged. "Get after it, then. I've got the wallets of twelve football players that say you can't finish ten."

She narrowed her eyes. "Double or nothing says I can drink fifteen."

I couldn't help but smile, and at the same time wondered how in God's name I was going to behave myself if she kept acting like a fucking Vegas hustler. It was hot as hell.

"Whoa!" Shepley cried. "You're not allowed to hospitalize yourself on your birthday, Abby!"

"She can do it," America said, staring at Brazil.

"Forty bucks a shot?" Brazil asked, looking unsure.

"Are you scared?" Abby asked.

"Hell no! I'll give you twenty a shot, and when you make it to fifteen, I'll double your total."

She popped back another shot. "That's how Kansans do birthdays."

The music was loud, and I made sure to dance with Abby to every song she'd agree to. The whole apartment was full of smiling college kids, a beer in one hand, and a shot glass in the other. Abby would veer off occasionally to hammer back another shot, and then return with me to our makeshift dance floor in the living room.

The birthday gods must have been pleased with my efforts, because just when Abby was getting a good buzz, a slow song came on. One of my favorites. I kept my lips close to her ear, singing to her, and leaning back to mouth the important parts I wanted her to understand were from me. She probably didn't catch that part, but that didn't stop me from trying.

I leaned her back, and her arms fell behind her, her fingers nearly touching the floor. She laughed out loud, and then we were upright, swaying back and forth again. She wrapped her arms around my neck and sighed against my skin. She smelled so good, it was ridiculous.

"You can't do that when I start getting into the double-digit shots." She giggled.

"Did I tell you how incredible you look tonight?"

She shook her head and hugged me, laying her head on my shoulder. I squeezed her to me, and buried my face in her neck. When we were like that, quiet, happy, ignoring the fact that we weren't supposed to be anything more than friends, it was the only place I wanted to be.

The door opened, and Abby's arms fell away. "Parker!" she squealed, running over to hug him.

He kissed her lips, and I went from feeling like a king to a man on the edge of murder.

Parker lifted her wrist and smiled, mouthing something to her about that stupid bracelet.

"Hey," America said loudly in my ear. Even though the volume of her voice was louder than normal, no one else could hear.

"Hey," I said back, still staring at Parker and Abby.

"Keep your cool. Shepley said Parker is just stopping by. He has something to do tomorrow morning, so he can't stay long."

"Oh, yeah?"

"Yeah, so keep it together. Take a breath. He'll be gone before you know it."

Abby pulled Parker to the counter, picked up another shot glass, and killed it, slamming it on the counter upside down like the five times before. Brazil handed her another twenty, and she danced into the living room.

Without hesitation, I grabbed her, and we danced with America and Shepley.

Shepley slapped her on the butt. "One!"

America added a second swat, and then the entire party joined in.

At number nineteen, I rubbed my hands together, making her think I was going to bust her a good one. "My turn!"

She rubbed her posterior. "Be easy! My ass hurts!"

Unable to contain my amusement, I reared my hand far above my shoulder. Abby closed her eyes, and after a moment, peeked back. I stopped just short of her ass, and gave her a gentle pat.

"Nineteen!" I yelled.

The guests cheered, and America started a drunken rendition of "Happy Birthday to You." When it got to the part for her name, the entire room sang "Pigeon." It made me kinda proud.

Another slow song came over the stereo, but this time Parker pulled her to the middle of the room for a dance. He looked like a robot with two left feet, stiff and clumsy.

I tried not the watch, but before the song was over, I caught them slip off to the hallway. My eyes met America's. She smiled, winked, and shook her head, silently telling me not to do anything stupid.

She was right. Abby wasn't alone with him for more than five minutes before they were walking to the front door.

The uncomfortable, embarrassed expression on Abby's face told me that Parker had tried to make those few minutes memorable.

He kissed her cheek, and then Abby shut the door behind him.

"Daddy's gone!" I yelled, pulling Abby to the center of the living room. "Time to get the party started!"

The room exploded into cheering.

"Hang on! I'm on a schedule!" Abby said, walking into the kitchen. She took another shot.

Seeing how many she had left, I grabbed one from the end and drank it. Abby took another shot, so I did the same.

"Seven more, Abby," Brazil said, handing her more cash.

The next hour we danced, laughed, and talked about nothing particularly important. Abby's lips were locked in a smile, and I couldn't help but stare at her all night.

One in a while, I thought I'd catch her glance at me, and it made me wonder what would happen when we got back to the apartment.

Abby took her time drinking the next few shots, but by her tenth, she was in bad shape. She danced on the couch with America, bouncing and giggling, but then lost her balance.

I caught her before she fell.

"You've made your point," I said. "You've drunk more than any girl we've ever seen. I'm cutting you off."

"The hell you are," she said, slurring her words. "I have six hundred bucks waiting on me at the bottom of that shot glass, and you of all people aren't going to tell me I can't do something extreme for cash."

"If you're that hard up for money, Pidge . . ."

"I'm not borrowing money from you," she sneered.

"I was gonna suggest pawning that bracelet." I smiled.

She smacked me on the arm just as America started the countdown to midnight. When the hands of the clock superimposed on the twelve, we all celebrated.

I had never wanted to kiss a girl so much in my life.

America and Shepley beat me to it, kissing each of her cheeks. I lifted her off the ground, twirling her around.

"Happy birthday, Pigeon," I said, trying very hard not to press my lips against hers.

Everyone at the party knew what she was up to in the hall with Parker. It would be pretty shitty of me to make her look bad in front of them.

She watched me with her big gray eyes, and I melted inside of them.

"Shots!" she said, stumbling to the kitchen.

Her shout startled me, bringing all the noise and motion around us back into my reality again.

"You look torn up, Abby. I think it's time to call it a night," Brazil said when she arrived at the counter.

"I'm not a quitter," she said. "I wanna see my money."

I joined her as Brazil placed a twenty under the last two glasses. He yelled at his teammates, "She's gonna drink 'em! I need fifteen!"

They all groaned and rolled their eyes, pulling out their wallets to stack a pile of twenties behind the last shot glass.

"I would have never believed that I could lose fifty bucks on a fifteen-shot bet with a girl," Chris complained.

"Believe it, Jenks," she said, picking up a glass in each hand.

She knocked back each of the glasses, one at a time, but then paused.

"Pigeon?" I asked, taking a step in her direction.

She raised a finger, and Brazil smiled. "She's going to lose it," he said.

"No, she won't." America shook her head. "Deep breath, Abby."

She closed her eyes and inhaled, picking up the last shot remaining on the counter.

"Holy God, Abby! You're going to die of alcohol poisoning!" Shepley cried.

"She's got this," America assured him.

She tipped her head back, and let the tequila flow down her throat. The entire party erupted into whistles and yells behind us as Brazil handed her the stack of money.

"Thank you," she said with pride, tucking the money away in her bra.

I'd never seen anything like it in my life. "You are incredibly sexy right now," I said in her ear as we walked to the living room.

She wrapped her arms around me, probably letting the tequila settle.

"You sure you're okay?"

She meant to say "I'm fine," but the words came out garbled.

"You need to make her go throw up, Trav. Get some of that out of her system."

"God, Shep. Leave her alone. She's fine," America said, annoyed.

Shepley's brows pulled in. "I'm just trying to keep something really bad from happening."

"Abby? You okay?" America asked.

Abby managed a smile, looking half asleep.

America looked at Shepley. "Just let it run through her system, she'll sober up. It's not her first rodeo. Calm down."

"Unbelievable," Shepley said. "Travis?"

I touched my cheek to Abby's forehead. "Pidge? You want to play it safe and purge?"

"No," she said. "I wanna dance." She wrapped her arms around me tighter.

I looked at Shepley and shrugged. "As long as she's up and moving . . ."

Unhappy, Shepley barreled through the crowd on the makeshift dance floor until he was out of sight. America clicked her tongue and rolled her eyes, and then followed after him.

Abby pressed her body against mine. Even though the song was fast, we were slow dancing in the middle of the room, surrounded by people bouncing around and waving their arms. Blue, purple, and green lights danced with us, on the floor and along the walls. The blue lights reflected on Abby's face, and I had to really concentrate through the liquor not to kiss her.

When the party began to wind down a few hours later, Abby and I were still on the dance floor. She had sobered up a bit after I fed her some crackers and cheese, and tried to dance with America to some stupid pop song, but other than that, Abby was in my arms, her wrists locked behind my neck.

The bulk of the party had either left or passed out somewhere in the apartment, and Shepley and America's bickering had gradually gotten worse.

"If you're riding with me, I'm leaving," Shepley said, tearing toward the door.

"I'm not ready to leave," Abby mumbled, her eyes half closed.

"I think this night is spent. Let's go home." When I took a step toward the door, Abby didn't move. She was staring at the floor, looking a bit green.

"You're going to throw up, aren't you?"

She looked up at me, her eyes half closed. "It's about that time."

She weaved back and forth a few times before I scooped her up in my arms.

"You, Travis Maddox, are kinda sexy when you're not being a whore," she said, a ridiculous, drunken grin twisting her mouth in different directions.

"Uh . . . thanks," I said, readjusting her so I had a better grip.

Abby touched her palm to my cheek. "You know what, Mr. Maddox?"

"What, baby?"

Her expression turned serious. "In another life, I could love you."

I watched her for a moment, staring into her glassed-over eyes. She was drunk, but just for a moment it didn't seem wrong to pretend that she meant it.

"I might love you in this one."

She tilted her head, and pressed her lips against the corner of my mouth. She'd meant to kiss me, but missed. She pulled back, and then let her head fall against my shoulder.

I looked around, and everyone still conscious was frozen, staring in shock at what they'd just witnessed.

Without a word, I carried her out of the apartment to the Charger, where America stood, her arms crossed.

Shepley gestured to Abby. "Look at her! She's your friend, and you let her do something insanely dangerous! You encouraged it!"

America pointed at herself. "I know her, Shep! I've seen her do way more than that for money!"

I shot her a glance.

"Shots. I've seen her do more shots for money," she qualified. "You know what I mean."

"Listen to yourself!" Shepley yelled. "You followed Abby all the way from Kansas to keep her out of trouble. Look at her! She has a dangerous level of alcohol in her system, and she is unconscious! That isn't behavior you should be okay with!"

America's eyes narrowed. "Oh! Thanks for the public service announcement about what not to do in college, Mr. Eighteen-year-old-frat-boy-with-eleventy-billion-'serious'-girlfriends-under-his-belt!" She used her fingers to mark invisible quotations when she said *serious*.

Shepley's mouth popped open, unamused. "Get in the fucking car. You're a mean drunk."

America laughed. "You haven't seen me mean, mama's boy!"

"I told you we're close!"

"Yeah, so are me and my asshole! Doesn't mean I'm going to call it twice a day!"

"You're a bitch!"

All color left America's face. "Take. Me. Home."

"I'd love to, if you'd *get in the fucking car*!" Shepley screamed the last bit. His face turned red, and veins were popping out on his neck.

America opened the door and climbed into the back, leaving the door open. She helped me slide Abby in beside her, and then I fell into the passenger seat.

The ride home was short and completely silent. When Shepley pulled into his parking spot and threw the shifter in Park, I scrambled out of the car and pulled the seat forward.

Abby's head was on America's shoulder, her hair covering her face. I reached in and pulled Abby out, throwing her over my shoulder. America crawled out quickly after, and she walked straight to her car, pulling her keys from her purse.

"Mare," Shepley said, regret already obvious from the break of his voice.

America sat in the driver's seat, slammed the door in Shepley's face, and then backed away.

Abby was ass up, her arms dangling behind me.

"She's gotta come back for Abby, right?" Shepley asked, his face desperate.

Abby moaned, and then her body lurched. The awful groan/growl that always accompanied vomit preceded a splashing sound. The back of my legs felt wet.

"Tell me she didn't," I said, frozen.

Shepley bent back for a second, and then righted himself. "She did."

I jogged up the stairs two at a time, and rushed Shepley as he tried to find the apartment key. He opened it, and I raced into the bathroom.

Abby leaned over the toilet, emptying the contents of her stomach liters at a time. Her hair was already wet with puke from the incident outside, but I grabbed one of those round, black, stretchy things off the sink and pulled her long hair back into a ponytail. The damp pieces clung together in thick clumps, but I pulled it all back with my hands, anyway, and secured it with the black hair holder thingy. I'd seen enough girls twist it and pull their hair back through in class, it didn't take long for me to figure it out.

Abby's body lurched again. I wet a washrag from the hall closet, and then sat back down beside her, holding it against her forehead. She leaned against the tub and groaned.

I gently wiped her face with the wet rag, and then tried to sit still when she lay her head on my shoulder.

"You gonna make it?" I asked.

She frowned, and then gagged, keeping her lips together just long enough to position her head over the toilet. She heaved again, and more liquid splashed into it.

Abby was so small, and the amount she was expelling didn't seem normal. Worry crept into my mind.

I scrambled from the bathroom and returned with two towels, an extra sheet, three blankets, and four pillows in my arms. Abby moaned over the toilet bowl, her body trembling. I fashioned the linens against the tub in a pallet and waited, knowing we would more than likely end up spending the night in that little corner of the bathroom.

Shepley stood in the doorway. "Should I . . . call someone?"

"Not yet. I'm going to keep an eye on her."

"I'm fine," Abby said. "This is me not getting alcohol poisoning."

Shepley frowned. "No, this is *stupid*. That's what this is."

"Hey, you got the uh . . . her uh . . ."

"Present?" he said with one eyebrow up.

"Yeah."

"I got it," he said, clearly unhappy.

"Thanks, man."

Abby fell back against the tub once more, and I promptly wiped her face. Shepley wet a fresh rag and tossed it to me.

"Thanks."

"Yell if you need me," Shepley said. "I'm going to lie awake in bed, trying to think of a way to get Mare to forgive me."

I relaxed against the tub as best I could, and pulled Abby against me. She sighed, letting her body melt into mine. Even with her covered in vomit, close to her was the only place I wanted to be. Her words at the party replayed in my mind.

In another life, I could love you.

Abby was lying weak and sick in my arms, depending on me to take care of her. In that moment I recognized that my feelings for her were a lot stronger than I thought. Sometime between the moment we met, and holding her on that bathroom floor, I had fallen in love with her.

Abby sighed, and then rested her head in my lap. I made sure she was completely covered with blankets before I let myself nod off.

"Trav?" she whispered.

"Yeah?"

She didn't answer. Her breathing evened out, and her head fell heavily against my legs. The cold porcelain against my back and the unforgiving tile under my ass were brutal, but I didn't dare move. She was comfortable, and she would stay that way. Twenty minutes into watching her breathe, the parts of me that hurt started to numb, and my eyes closed.

CHAPTER FOURTEEN

Oz

ALREADY, THE DAY HADN'T STARTED OFF WELL. ABBY was somewhere with America, trying to talk her out of dumping Shepley, and Shepley was chewing off his fingernails in the living room, waiting for Abby to work a miracle.

I'd taken the puppy out once, paranoid that America would pull up at any moment and ruin the surprise. Even though I'd fed him and given him a towel to snuggle up with, he was whining.

Sympathy wasn't my strong point, but no one could blame him. Sitting in a tiny box wasn't anyone's idea of a good time. Thankfully, seconds before they returned, the little mongrel had quieted down and gone to sleep.

"They're back!" Shepley said, jumping off the couch.

"Okay," I said, quietly shutting Shepley's door behind me. "Play it coo—"

Before my sentence was complete, Shepley had opened the door and run down the stairs. The doorway was a great spot to watch Abby smile at Shepley and America's eager reconciliation. Abby shoved her hands into her back pockets and walked to the apartment.

The fall clouds cast a gray shadow over everything, but Abby's smile was like summertime. With each step she took that brought her closer to where I stood, my heart pounded harder against my chest.

"And they lived happily ever after," I said, closing the door behind her.

We sat together on the couch, and I pulled her legs onto my lap.

"What do you wanna do today, Pidge?"

"Sleep. Or rest . . . or sleep."

"Can I give you your present, first?"

She pushed my shoulder. "Shut up. You got me a present?"

"It's not a diamond bracelet, but I thought you'd like it."

"I'll love it, sight unseen."

I lifted her legs off of my lap and went to retrieve her gift. I tried not to shake the box, hoping the puppy wouldn't wake up and make any noises to tip her off. "Ssshhhh, little man. No crying, okay? Be a good boy."

I sat the box at her feet, crouching behind it. "Hurry, I want you to be surprised."

"*Hurry*?" she asked, lifting the lid. Her mouth fell open. "A *puppy*?" she shrieked, reaching into the box. She lifted the puppy to her face, trying to keep hold of it as it wiggled and stretched its neck, desperate to cover her mouth with kisses.

"You like him?"

"Him? I love him! You got me a puppy!"

"It's a cairn terrier. I had to drive three hours to pick him up Thursday after class."

"So when you said you were going with Shepley to take his car to the shop . . ."

"We went to get your present." I nodded.

"He's wiggly!" She laughed.

"Every girl from Kansas needs a Toto," I said, trying to keep the fur ball from falling off her lap.

"He does look like Toto! That's what I'm going to call him," she said, wrinkling her nose at him.

She was happy, and that made me happy.

"You can keep him here. I'll take care of him for you when you're back at Morgan, and it's my security that you'll visit when your month is up."

"I would have come back anyway, Trav."

"I'd do anything for that smile that's on your face right now."

My words made her pause, but she quickly turned her attention back to the dog. "I think you need a nap, Toto. Yes, you do."

I nodded, pulled her onto my lap, and then lifted her with me as I stood. "Come on, then."

I carried her to the bedroom, pulled back the covers, and then lowered her to the mattress. The action itself would have been a turn-on, but I was too tired. I reached over her to pull the curtains closed, and then fell onto my pillow.

"Thanks for staying with me last night," she said, her voice a bit hoarse and sleepy. "You didn't have to sleep on the bathroom floor."

"Last night was one of the best nights of my life."

She turned to shoot me a dubious look. "Sleeping in between the toilet and the tub on a cold, hard tile floor with a vomiting idiot was one of your best nights? That's sad, Trav."

"No, sitting up with you when you were sick, and you falling asleep in my lap, was one of my best nights. It wasn't comfortable, I didn't sleep worth a shit, but I brought in your nineteenth birthday with you, and you're actually pretty sweet when you're drunk."

"I'm sure between the heaving and purging I was very charming."

I pulled her close, patting Toto, who was snuggled up to her neck. "You're the only woman I know that still looks incredible with your head in the toilet. That's saying something."

"Thanks, Trav. I won't make you babysit me again."

I leaned against my pillow. "Whatever. No one can hold your hair back like I can."

She giggled and closed her eyes. As tired as I was, it was difficult to stop watching her. Her face was makeup free except for the thin skin under her lower lashes that was still a little stained with mascara. She fidgeted a bit before her shoulders relaxed.

I blinked a few times, my eyes getting heavier each time they closed. It seemed I'd just fallen asleep when I heard the doorbell.

Abby didn't even stir.

Two male voices murmured in the living room, one of them Shepley's. America's voice was a high-pitched break between the two, but none of them sounded happy. Whoever it was wasn't just making a social call.

Footsteps sounded in the hall, and then the door blew open. Parker stood in the doorway. He looked at me, and then at Abby, his jaw tense.

I knew what he thought, and it crossed my mind to explain why Abby was in my bed, but I didn't. Instead I reached over and rested my hand on her hip.

"Shut the door when you're finished being in my business," I said, resting my head next to Abby's.

Parker walked away without a word. He didn't slam my door, instead putting his full force behind closing the front door.

Shepley peeked into my room. "Shit, bro. That's not good."

It was done; couldn't change it now. The consequences weren't a concern in the moment, but lying next to Abby, scanning over her perfectly content, beautiful face, the panic slowly crept in. When she found out what I'd done, she would hate me.

THE GIRLS LEFT FOR CLASS THE NEXT MORNING IN A rush. Pidge barely had time to speak to me before she left, so her feelings about the day before were definitely less than clear.

I brushed my teeth and got dressed, and then found Shepley in the kitchen.

He sat on a stool in front of the breakfast bar, slurping milk from his spoon. He wore a hoodie and the pink boxers America had bought him because she thought they were "sexy."

I pulled a glass from the dishwasher and filled it with OJ. "Looks like you two worked it out."

Shepley smiled, looking nearly drunk with contentment. "We did. Have I ever told you what America is like in bed right after we argue?"

I made a face. "No, and please don't."

"Fighting with her like that is scary as hell, but tempting if we make up like that every time." When I didn't answer, Shepley continued. "I'm going to marry that woman."

"Yeah. Well, when you're done being a pansy ass, we need to be on our way."

"Shut your face, Travis. Don't think I'm oblivious to what's going on with you."

I crossed my arms. "And what's going on with me?"

"You're in love with Abby."

"*Pft.* You were obviously making shit up in your head to keep your mind off America."

"You're denying it?" Shepley's eyes didn't flinch, and I tried to look everywhere but into them.

After a full minute, I shifted nervously but remained silent.

"Who's being a pansy ass, now?"

"Fuck you."

"Admit it."

"No."

"No, you're not denying that you're in love with Abby, or no you won't admit it? Because either way, asshole, you're in love with her."

". . . So?"

"I KNEW IT!" Shepley said, kicking the stool back, making it skid to where the wood floor met the rug in the living room.

"I . . . just . . . shut up, Shep," I said. My lips formed a hard line.

Shepley pointed at me while walking to his room. "You just admitted to it. Travis Maddox in love. Now I've heard everything."

"Just put your panties on, and let's go!"

Shepley chuckled to himself in his bedroom, and I stared at the floor. Saying it out loud—to someone else—made it real, and I wasn't sure what to do with it.

Less than five minutes later, I was fiddling with the radio in the Charger while Shepley was pulling out of the parking lot of our apartment complex.

Shepley seemed to be in an exceptionally good mood as we weaved through traffic and slowed down just enough to keep from tossing pedestrians over the hood. He finally found a suitable parking space, and we headed to English Comp II—the one class we shared.

The top row had been me and Shepley's new seating arrangement for several weeks in an attempt to break free of the flock of baggable females that usually crowded my desk.

Dr. Park breezed into the classroom, dumping off a tote bag, a briefcase, and a cup of coffee onto her desk. "Christ! It's cold!" she said, pulling her coat tighter around her tiny frame. "Is everyone here?" Hands shot up, and she nodded, not really paying attention. "Great. Good news. Pop quiz!"

Everyone groaned, and she smiled. "You'll still love me. Paper and pen, people, I don't have all day."

The room filled with the same sound as everyone reached for their supplies. I scribbled my name at the top of my paper and smiled at Shepley's panicked whispers.

"Why? Pop quiz in Comp Two? Fucking ridiculous," he hissed.

The quiz was fairly harmless, and her lecture ended with another paper being due by the end of the week. In the last minutes of class, a guy in the row directly ahead of me craned his neck back. I recognized him from class. His name was Levi, but I only knew that because I'd heard Dr. Park call on him several times. His greasy dark hair was always slicked back, away from his pockmarked face. Levi was never in the cafeteria, or in any fraternity. He wasn't on the football team, either, and never at any parties. Not any that I frequented, anyway.

I looked down at him, and then turned my attention back to Dr. Park, who was sharing a story about the latest visit from her favorite gay friend.

My eyes drifted down again. He was still staring.

"Need something?" I asked.

"I just heard about Brazil's party this weekend. Well played."

"Huh?"

The girl to his right, Elizabeth, turned too, her light brown hair bouncing. Elizabeth was the girlfriend of one of my frat brothers. Her eyes lit up. "Yeah. Sorry I missed that show."

Shepley leaned forward. "What? Me and Mare's fight?"

The guy chuckled. "No. Abby's party."

"The birthday party?" I asked, trying to think of what he could be referring to. Several things had happened that would have the rumor mills churning, but nothing some random guy from oblivion would hear about.

Elizabeth checked to see if Dr. Park was looking in our direction, and then turned back around. "Abby and Parker."

Another girl turned. "Oh, yeah. I heard Parker walked in on you two the next morning. Is it true?"

"You heard where?" I asked, adrenaline screaming through my veins.

Elizabeth shrugged. "Everywhere. People were talking about it in my class this morning."

"Mine, too," Levi said.

The other girl just nodded.

Elizabeth turned around a bit more, leaning in my direction. "Did she really go at it with Parker in Brazil's hallway, and then go home with you?"

Shepley frowned. "She's staying with us."

"No," the girl beside Elizabeth said. "Her and Parker were making out on Brazil's couch, and then she got up, danced with Travis, Parker left all pissed, and she left with Travis . . . and Shepley."

"That's not what I heard," Elizabeth said, visibly trying to contain her enthusiasm. "I heard it was a threesome sort of deal. So . . . which is it, Travis?"

Levi seemed to be enjoying the conversation. "I'd always heard it was the other way around."

"What's that?" I asked, already irritated with his tone.

"Parker getting *your* sloppy seconds."

I narrowed my eyes. Whoever this guy was, he knew way more about me than he should. I leaned down. "That's some more of your fucking business, asshole."

"Okay," Shepley said, putting his hand on my desk.

Levi immediately turned, and Elizabeth's eyebrows shot up before she followed behind him.

"Fucking dirtbag," I grumbled. I looked to Shepley. "Lunch is next. Someone's going to say something to her. They're saying we both bagged her. Fuck. *Fuck*, Shepley what do I do?"

Shepley immediately began shoving his things in his backpack, and I did the same.

"Dismissed," Dr. Park said. "Get the hell out and be productive citizens today."

My backpack thumped against my lower back as I sprinted across campus, making a beeline for the cafeteria. America and Abby came into sight, just a few steps from the entrance.

Shepley grabbed America's arm. "Mare," he puffed.

I grabbed my hips, trying to catch my breath.

"Is there a mob of angry women chasing you?" Abby teased.

I shook my head. My hands were trembling, so I gripped the straps of my backpack. "I was trying to catch you . . . before you . . . went in," I breathed.

"What's going on?" America asked Shepley.

"There's a rumor," Shepley began. "Everyone's saying that Travis took Abby home and . . . the details are different, but it's pretty bad."

"*What?* Are you serious?" Abby cried.

America rolled her eyes. "Who cares, Abby? People have been speculating about you and Trav for weeks. It's not the first time someone has accused you two of sleeping together."

I looked at Shepley, hoping he'd figured a way out of the predicament I'd gotten myself into.

"What?" Abby said. "There's something else, isn't there?"

Shepley winced. "They're saying you slept with Parker at Brazil's, and then you let Travis . . . take you home, if you know what I mean."

Her mouth fell open. "Great! So I'm the school slut now?"

I had done this, and of course it was Abby that was getting the shit end of the stick. "This is my fault. If it was anyone else, they wouldn't be saying that about you." I walked into the cafeteria, my hands in fists at my sides.

Abby sat, and I made sure to sit a few seats across and down from her. Rumors had been spread about me bagging girls before, and sometimes Parker's name was even mentioned, too, but I never cared until now. Abby didn't deserve to be thought of that way just because she was my friend.

"You don't have to sit down there, Trav. Come on, come sit," Abby said, patting the empty table space in front of her.

"I heard you had quite a birthday, Abby," Chris Jenks said, throwing a piece of lettuce onto my plate.

"Don't start with her, Jenks," I warned, glowering.

Chris smiled, pushing up his round, pink cheeks. "I heard Parker is furious. He said he came by your apartment yesterday, and you and Travis were still in bed."

"They were taking a nap, Chris," America sneered.

Abby's eyes darted to me. "Parker came by?"

I shifted uncomfortably in my chair. "I was gonna tell you."

"*When*?" she snapped.

America leaned into her ear, probably explaining what everyone else but Abby knew.

Abby put her elbows on the table, covering her face with her hands. "This just keeps getting better."

"So you guys really didn't do the deed?" Chris asked. "Damn, that sucks. Here I thought Abby was right for you after all, Trav."

"You better stop now, Chris," Shepley warned.

"If you didn't sleep with her, mind if I take a shot?" Chris said, chuckling to his teammates.

Without thinking, I jumped from my seat, and climbed over the table at Chris. His face metamorphosed in slow motion from smiling to wide eyes and an open mouth. I grabbed Chris by the throat with one hand, and a fistful of his T-shirt in the other. My knuckles barely felt the connection with his face. My rage was full blown and I was just short of letting everything fly. Chris covered his face, but I kept whaling on him.

"Travis!" Abby screamed, running around the table.

My fist froze midflight, and then I released Chris's shirt, letting him crumble into a ball on the floor. Abby's expression made me falter; she was afraid of what she'd just seen. She swallowed, and took a step back. Her fear only made me more angry, not at her, but because I was ashamed of myself.

I shouldered past her and shoved through everyone else in my way. Two for two. First, I'd managed to help start a rumor about the girl I was in love with, and then scared her half to death.

The solitude of my bedroom seemed like the only place fit for me. I was too ashamed to even seek the advice of my father. Shepley caught up with me. Without a word, he got into the Charger next to me and started the engine.

We didn't speak as Shepley drove to the apartment. The scene that would inevitably go down when Abby decided to come home was something my mind didn't want to process.

Shepley brought his car to a stop in its usual parking spot, and I got out, walking up the stairs like a zombie. There was no possible good ending. Either Abby was going to leave because she was afraid of what she saw, or even worse—I had to release her from the bet so she could leave, even if she didn't want to.

My heart had been back and forth between leaving Abby alone and deciding it was okay to pursue her more times than a freshly single sorority girl on the second floor of a frat house. Once inside, I threw my backpack against the wall, and made sure to slam the bedroom door behind me. It didn't make me feel better, in fact, stomping around like a toddler reminded me just how much of Abby's time I was wasting by pursuing her—if it could be called that.

The high-pitched hum of America's Honda idled briefly before she cut the engine. Abby would be with her. She would either come in screaming, or the complete opposite. I wasn't sure which would make me feel worse.

"Travis?" Shepley said, opening the door.

I shook my head, and then sat on the edge of the bed. It sank under my weight.

"You don't even know what she's going to say. She could just be checking on you."

"I said no."

Shepley closed the door. The trees outside were brown and beginning to shed what color remained. Soon they would be leafless. By the time the last leaves fell, Abby would be gone. Damn, I felt depressed.

A few minutes later, another knock on the door. "Travis? It's me. Open up."

I sighed. "Walk away, Pidge."

The door creaked when she cracked it open. I didn't turn around. I didn't have to. Toto was behind me, and his small tail was beating my back at the sight of her.

"What is going on with you, Trav?" she asked.

I didn't know how to tell her the truth, and part of me knew she wouldn't hear me, anyway, so I just stared out the window, counting the falling leaves. With each one that detached and floated to the ground, we were one more closer to Abby disappearing from my life. My own natural hourglass.

Abby stood beside me, crossing her arms. I waited for her to yell, or chastise me somehow for the meltdown in the cafeteria.

"You're not going to talk to me about this?"

She began to turn for the door, and I sighed. "You know the other day when Brazil mouthed off to me and you rushed to my defense? Well . . . that's what happened. I just got a little carried away."

"You were angry before Chris said anything," she said, sitting next to me on the bed. Toto immediately crawled into her lap, begging for attention. I knew the feeling. All the antics, my stupid stunts; everything was to somehow get her attention, and she seemed oblivious to it all. Even my crazy behavior.

"I meant what I said before. You need to walk away, Pidge. God knows I can't walk away from you."

She reached for my arm. "You don't want me to leave."

She had no idea how right—and how wrong—she was. My conflicted feelings about her were maddening. I was in love with her; couldn't imagine a life without her in it; but at the same time, I wanted her to have better. With that in mind, the thought of Abby with someone else was unbearable. Neither one of us could win, and yet I couldn't lose her. The constant back and forth made me exhausted.

I pulled Abby against me, and then kissed her forehead. "It doesn't matter how hard I try. You're going to hate me when it's all said and done."

She wrapped her arms around me, linking her fingers around the cusp of my shoulder. "We have to be friends. I won't take no for an answer."

She'd stolen my line from our first date at the Pizza Shack. That seemed like a hundred lifetimes ago. I wasn't sure when things had become so complicated.

"I watch you sleeping a lot," I said, wrapping her in both of my arms. "You always look so peaceful. I don't have that kind of quiet. I have all this anger and rage boiling inside of me—except when I watch you sleep.

"That's what I was doing when Parker walked in. I was awake, and he walked in, and just stood there with this shocked look on his face. I knew what he thought, but I didn't set him straight. I didn't explain because I *wanted* him to think something happened. Now the whole school thinks you were with us both in the same night. I'm sorry."

Abby shrugged. "If he believes the gossip, it's his own fault."

"It's hard to think anything else when he sees us in bed together."

"He knows I'm staying with you. I was fully clothed, for Christ's sake."

I sighed. "He was probably too pissed to notice. I know you like him, Pidge. I should have explained. I owe you that much."

"It doesn't matter."

"You're not mad?" I asked, surprised.

"Is that what you're so upset about? You thought I'd be mad at you when you told me the truth?"

"You should be. If someone single-handedly sunk my reputation, I'd be a little pissed."

"You don't care about reputations. What happened to the Travis that doesn't give a shit what anyone thinks?" she teased, nudging me with her elbow.

"That was before I saw the look on your face when you heard what everyone's saying. I don't want you to get hurt because of me."

"You would never do anything to hurt me."

"I'd rather cut off my arm." I sighed.

I relaxed my cheek against her hair. She always smelled so good, felt so good. Being near her was like a sedative. My entire body relaxed, and I was suddenly so tired, I didn't want to move. We sat together, our arms around each other, her head tucked in against my neck, for the longest time. Nothing beyond that moment was guaranteed, so I stayed there inside of it, with Pigeon.

When the sun began to set, I heard a faint knock at the door.

"Abby?" America's voice sounded small on the other side of the wood.

"Come in, Mare," I said, knowing she was probably worried about why we were so quiet.

America walked in with Shepley, and she smiled at the sight of us tangled in each other's arms. "We were going to grab a bite to eat. You two feel like making a Pei Wei run?"

"*Ugh* . . . Asian *again,* Mare? Really?" I asked.

"Yes, really," she said, seeming a little more relaxed. "You guys coming or not?"

"I'm starving," Abby said.

"Of course you are, you didn't get to eat lunch," I said, frowning. I stood, raising her up with me. "Come on. Let's get you some food."

I wasn't ready to let go of her yet, so I kept my arm around her for the ride to Pei Wei. She didn't seem to mind, and even leaned against me in the car while I conceded to share a number-four meal with her.

As soon as we found a booth, I unloaded my coat beside Abby and went to the bathroom. It was weird how everyone was pretending I hadn't just pummeled someone a few hours ago, like nothing had happened. My hands formed a cup under the water, and I splashed my face, looking into the mirror. The water dripped from my nose and chin. Once again, I was going to have to swallow the dysphoria and go along with everyone else's fake mood. As if we had to keep up pretenses to help Abby move through reality in her little bubble of ignorance where no one felt anything too strongly, and everything was cut-and-dried.

"Damn it! The food's not here yet?" I asked, sliding into the booth next to Abby. Her phone lay on the table, so I picked it up, turned on the camera, made a stupid face, and snapped a picture.

"What the hell are you doing?" Abby said with a giggle.

I searched for my name, and then attached the picture. "So you'll remember how much you adore me when I call."

"Or what a dork you are," America said.

America and Shepley talked most of the time about their classes and the latest gossip, taking care not to mention anyone involved in the scuffle earlier.

Abby watched them talk with her chin rested on her fist, smiling and effortlessly beautiful. Her fingers were tiny, and I caught myself noticing how naked her ring finger looked. She glanced over at me and leaned over to playfully shove me with her shoulder. She then righted herself, continuing to listen to America's chatter.

We laughed and joked until the restaurant closed, and then crowded into the Charger to head home. I felt exhausted, and even though the day seemed long as hell, I didn't want it to end.

Shepley carried America up the stairs on his back, but I stayed behind, tugging on Abby's arm. I watched our friends until they went into the apartment, and then fidgeted with Abby's hands in mine. "I owe you an apology for today, so I'm sorry."

"You've already apologized. It's fine."

"No, I apologized for Parker. I don't want you thinking I'm some psycho that goes around attacking people over the tiniest thing," I said, "but I owe you an apology because I didn't defend you for the right reason."

"And that would be . . . ," she prompted.

"I lunged at him because he said he wanted to be next in line, not because he was teasing you."

"Insinuating there is a line is plenty reason for you to defend me, Trav."

"That's my point. I was pissed because I took that as him wanting to sleep with you."

Abby thought for a moment, and then grabbed the sides of my shirt. She pressed her forehead against my T-shirt, into my chest. "You know what? I don't care," she said, looking up at me with a smile. "I don't care what people are saying, or that you lost your temper, or why you messed up Chris's face. The last thing I want is a bad reputation, but I'm tired of explaining our friendship to everyone. To hell with 'em."

The corners of my mouth turned up. "Our *friendship*? Sometimes I wonder if you listen to me at all."

"What do you mean?"

The bubble she surrounded herself with was impenetrable, and I wondered what would happen if I ever did make it through. "Let's go in. I'm tired."

She nodded, and we walked together up the stairs, and into the apartment. America and Shepley were already murmuring happily in their bedroom, and Abby disappeared into the bathroom. The pipes shrieked, and then the water in the shower beat against the tile.

Toto kept me company while I waited. She didn't waste time; her nightly routine was complete within the hour.

She lay on the bed, her wet hair resting on my arm. She breathed out a long, relaxing breath. "Just two weeks left. What are you going to do for drama when I move back to Morgan?"

"I don't know," I said. I didn't want to think about it.

"Hey." She touched my arm. "I was kidding."

I willed my body to relax against the mattress, reminding myself that for the moment, she was still next to me. It didn't work. Nothing worked. I needed her in my arms. Enough time had been wasted. "Do you trust me, Pidge?" I asked, a little nervous.

"Yeah, why?"

"C'mere," I said, pulling her against me. I waited for her to protest, but she only froze for a few moments before letting her body melt into mine. Her cheek relaxed against my chest.

Instantly, my eyes felt heavy. Tomorrow I would try to think of a way to postpone her departure, but in that moment, sleeping with her in my arms was the only thing I wanted to do.

CHAPTER FIFTEEN

Tomorrow

TWO WEEKS. THAT WAS ALL I HAD LEFT TO EITHER ENJOY our remaining time together, or somehow show Abby that I could be who she needed.

I put on the charm; pulled out all the stops; spared no expense. We went bowling, on dinner dates, lunch dates, and to the movies. We also spent as much time at the apartment as possible: renting movies, ordering in, anything to be alone with her. We didn't have a single fight.

Adam called a couple of times. Even though I made a good show, he was unhappy with how short the fights lasted. Money was money, but I didn't want to waste any time away from Pidge.

She was happier than I'd ever seen her, and for the first time, I felt like a normal, whole human being instead of some broken, angry man.

At night we would lie down and snuggle like an old married couple. The closer it came to her last night, the more of a struggle it was to stay upbeat and pretend I wasn't desperate to keep our lives the way they were.

The night before her last night, Abby opted for dinner at the Pizza Shack. Crumbs on the red floor, the smell of grease and spices in the air, minus the obnoxious soccer team, it was perfect.

Perfect, but sad. It was the first place we'd had dinner together. Abby laughed a lot, but she never opened up. Never mentioned our time together. Still in that bubble. Still oblivious. That my efforts were being ignored was at times infuriating, but being patient and keeping her happy were the only ways I had any chance of succeeding.

She fell asleep fairly quickly that night. As she slept just a few inches away, I watched her, trying to burn her image into my memory. The way her lashes fell against her skin; the way her wet hair felt against my arm; the fruity, clean smell that wafted from her lotioned body; the barely audible noise her nose made when she exhaled. She was so peaceful, and had become so comfortable sleeping in my bed.

The walls surrounding us were covered with pictures of Abby's time in the apartment. It was dark, but each one was committed to my memory. Now that it finally felt like home, she was leaving.

The morning of Abby's last day, I felt like I would be swallowed whole by grief, knowing we would pack her up the next morning for Morgan Hall. Pidge would be around, maybe visit occasionally, probably with America, but she would be with Parker. I was on the brink of losing her.

The recliner creaked a bit as I rocked back and forth, waiting for her to wake. The apartment was quiet. Too quiet. The silence weighed down on me.

Shepley's door whined as it open and closed, and my cousin's bare feet slapped against the floor. His hair was sticking up in places, his eyes squinty. He made his way to the love seat and watched me a while from under the hood of his sweatshirt.

It might have been cold. I didn't notice.

"Trav? You're going to see her again."

"I know."

"By the look on your face, I don't think you do."

"It won't be the same, Shep. We're going to live different lives. Grow apart. She'll be with Parker."

"You don't know that. Parker will show his ass. She'll wise up."

"Then someone else like Parker."

Shepley sighed and pulled one leg onto the couch, holding it up by the ankle. "What can I do?"

"I haven't felt like this since Mom died. I don't know what to do," I choked out. "I'm going to lose her."

Shepley's brows pulled together. "So you're done fighting, huh?"

"I've tried everything. I can't get through to her. Maybe she doesn't feel the same way about me that I do about her."

"Or maybe she's just trying not to. Listen. America and I will make ourselves scarce. You still have tonight. Do something special. Buy a bottle of wine. Make her some pasta. You make damn good pasta."

One side of my mouth turned up. "Pasta isn't going to change her mind."

Shepley smiled. "You never know. Your cooking is why I decided to ignore the fact that you're fucking nuts and move in with you."

I nodded. "I'll give it a try. I'll try anything."

"Just make it memorable, Trav," Shepley said, shrugging. "She might come around."

Shepley and America volunteered to pick up a few things

from the grocery store so I could cook dinner for Abby. Shepley even agreed to stop by a department store to pick up some new silverware so we didn't have to use the mix and match shit we had in our drawers.

My last night with Abby was set.

AS I SET OUT THE NAPKINS THAT NIGHT, ABBY CAME AROUND the corner in a pair of holey jeans and a loose, flowing white shirt.

"I have been salivating. Whatever you're making smells so good."

I poured the Alfredo and pasta into her deep plate, and slid the blackened Cajun chicken on top, and then sprinkled over it some diced tomatoes and green onions.

"This is what I've been cooking," I said, setting the plate in front of Abby's chair. She sat down, and her eyes widened, and then she watched me fill my own plate.

I tossed a slice of garlic bread onto her plate, and she smiled. "You've thought of everything."

"Yes, I did," I said, popping the cork on the wine. The dark red liquid splashed a bit as it flowed into her glass, and she giggled.

"You didn't have to do all of this, you know."

My lips pressed together. "Yes. I did."

Abby took a bite, and then another, barely pausing to swallow. A small hum emanated from her lips. "This is really good, Trav. You've been holding out on me."

"If I told you before, you would have expected it every night." The contrived smile I'd somehow managed quickly faded.

"I'm going to miss you, too, Trav," she said, still chewing.

"You're still gonna come over, right?"

"You know I will. And you'll be at Morgan's, helping me study, just like you did before."

"But it won't be the same." I sighed. "You'll be dating Parker, we're going to get busy . . . go in different directions."

"It's not going to change that much."

I laughed once. "Who would have thought from the first time we met that we'd be sitting here? You couldn't have told me three months ago that I'd be this miserable over saying goodbye to a girl."

Abby's face fell. "I don't want you to be miserable."

"Then don't go."

Abby swallowed, and her eyebrows moved in infinitesimally. "I can't move in here, Travis. That's crazy."

"Says who? I just had the best two weeks of my life."

"Me, too."

"Then why do I feel like I'm never gonna see you again?"

She watched me for a moment, but didn't reply. Instead Abby stood up and walked around the breakfast bar, sitting on my lap. Everything in me wanted to look her in the eyes, but I was afraid if I did, I'd try to kiss her, and our night would be ruined.

She hugged me, her soft cheek pressing against mine. "You're going to realize what a pain in the ass I was, and then you'll forget all about missing me," she whispered in my ear.

I rubbed my hand in circles between her shoulder blades, trying to choke back the sadness. "Promise?"

Abby looked into my eyes, touching each side of my face with her hands. She caressed my jaw with her thumb. Thoughts of begging her to stay crossed my mind, but she wouldn't hear me. Not from the other side of her bubble.

Abby closed her eyes and leaned down. I knew she meant to kiss the corner of my mouth, but I turned so that our lips met. It was my last chance. I had to kiss her goodbye.

She froze for a moment, but then her body relaxed, and she let her lips linger on mine.

Abby finally pulled away, playing it off with a smile. "I have a big day tomorrow. I'm going to clean up the kitchen, and then I'm going to head to bed."

"I'll help you."

We did the dishes together in silence, with Toto asleep at our feet. I dried the last dish and set it in the rack, and then reached down for her hand to lead her down the hall. Each step was agony.

Abby pushed down her jeans, and then lifted her shirt over her head. Grabbing one of my T-shirts from the closet, she let the worn gray cotton slide over her head. I stripped down to my boxers like I'd done dozens of times with her in the room, but this time solemnness hung over the room.

We climbed into bed, and I switched off the lamp. I immediately wrapped my arms around her and sighed, and she nestled her face into my neck.

The trees outside my window cast a shadow across the walls. I tried to concentrate on their shapes and the way the light wind changed the shape of their silhouette against the different angles of the wall. Anything to keep my mind off the numbers on the clock, or how close we were to the morning.

Morning. My life was going to change for the worse in just a few hours. Jesus Christ. I couldn't bear it. I squeezed my eyes shut, trying to block that train of thought.

"Trav? Are you okay?"

It took me a while to form the words. "I've never been less okay in my life."

She pressed her forehead against my neck again, and I squeezed her tighter.

"This is silly," she said. "We're going to see each other every day."

"You know that's not true."

Her head tilted just a tiny bit upward. I wasn't sure if she was staring at me, or getting ready to say something. I waited in the darkness, in the silence, feeling like the world was going to crash around me at any second.

Without warning, Abby puckered her lips and touched them to my neck. Her mouth opened as she tasted my skin, and the warm wetness of her mouth lingered in that spot.

I looked down at her, completely taken off guard. A familiar spark burned behind the window of her eyes. Unsure of how it happened, I'd finally gotten through to her. Abby finally realized my feelings for her, and the light had suddenly come on.

I leaned down, pressing my lips against hers, soft and slow. The longer our mouths were melded together, the more overwhelmed I became by the reality of what was happening.

Abby pulled me closer to her. Each movement she made was further affirmation of her answer. She felt the same. She cared about me. She wanted me. I wanted to run around the block screaming in celebration, and at the same time, didn't want to move my mouth from hers.

Her mouth opened, and I moved my tongue inside, tasting and searching softly.

"I want you," she said.

Her words sunk in, and I understood what she meant. One part of me wanted to rip off every piece of fabric between us, the other set off full lights and sirens. We were finally on the same page. No need to rush it now.

I pulled back a bit, but Abby only became more determined. I retreated all the way upright on my knees, but Abby stayed with me.

I gripped her shoulders to hold her at bay. "Wait a sec," I whispered, breathing hard. "You don't have to do this, Pidge. This isn't what tonight is about."

Even though I wanted to do the right thing, Abby's unexpected intensity coupled with the fact that I hadn't been laid in a length of time that was sure to be my all-time record, my dick was proudly standing against my boxers.

Abby leaned in again, and this time I let her come close enough to touch her lips to mine. She looked up at me, serious and resolute. "Don't make me beg," she whispered against my mouth.

No matter how noble I'd intended to be, those words coming from her mouth destroyed me. I grabbed the back of her head and sealed my lips against hers.

Abby's fingers ran down the length of my back and settled on the elastic of my boxers, before seeming to contemplate her next move. Six weeks of pent-up sexual tension overwhelmed me, and we crashed into the mattress. My fingers tangled in her hair as I positioned myself between her open knees. Just as our mouths met again, she slid her hand down the front of my boxers. When her soft fingers touched my bare skin, a low groan erupted. It was the best fucking feeling I could imagine.

The old gray T-shirt Abby wore was the first thing to go.

Thankfully the full moon lit the room just enough that I could appreciate her bare breasts for just a few seconds before I impatiently moved on to the rest of her. My hand gripped her panties, and then slipped them down her legs. I tasted her mouth as I followed the inside line of her leg, and traveled the length of her thigh. My fingers slipped between Abby's soft, wet skin, and she let out a long, faltering breath. Before I went further, a conversation we'd had not too long before replayed in my mind. Abby was a virgin. If this was what she really wanted, I had to be gentle. The last thing I wanted to do was hurt her.

Her knees arched and twitched with each movement of my hand. I licked and sucked different spots on her neck while I waited for her to make a decision. Her hips moved from side to side, and rocked back and forth, reminding me of the way she danced against me at the Red. Her bottom lip pulled in, and she bit it, digging her fingers into my back at the same time.

I positioned myself above her. My boxers were still on, but I could feel her bare skin against me. She was so fucking warm, holding back was the hardest thing I'd ever made myself do. Not even an inch more and I could have pushed through my boxers and been inside her.

"Pigeon," I said, panting, "it doesn't have to be tonight. I'll wait until you're ready."

Abby reached for the top drawer of the nightstand, pulling it open. Plastic crackled in her hand, and then she ripped the square package open with her teeth. That was a green light if I'd ever seen one.

My hand left her back, and I pulled my boxers down, kicking them violently. Any patience I'd had was gone. The only thing I could think about was being inside of her. I slipped the latex on, and then lowered my hips between her thighs, touching the most sensitive parts of my skin to hers.

"Look at me, Pigeon," I breathed.

Her big, round, gray eyes peered up at me. It was so surreal. This was what I had dreamed about since the first time she rolled her eyes at me, and it was finally happening. I tilted my head, and then leaned down to kiss her tenderly. I moved forward and tensed, pushing myself inside as gently as I could. When I pulled back, I looked into Abby's eyes. Her knees held my hips like a vise grip, and she bit her bottom lip harder than before, but her fingers were pressing into my back, pulling me closer. When I rocked into her again, she clenched her eyes shut.

I kissed her, softly, patiently. "Look at me," I whispered.

She hummed, and groaned, and cried out. With each noise she made, it became more difficult to control my movements. Abby's body finally relaxed, allowing me to move against her in a more rhythmic motion. The faster I moved, the less in control I felt. I touched every part of her skin, and licked and kissed her neck, cheek, and lips.

She pulled me into her over and over, and each time I pressed deeper inside.

"I've wanted you for so long, Abby. You're all I want," I breathed against her mouth.

I grabbed her thigh with one hand and propped myself up with my elbow. Our stomachs slid easily against each other as beads of sweat began to form on our skin. I thought about turning her over, or pulling her on top of me, but decided I'd rather sacrifice creativity for being able to look into her eyes, and staying as close to her as I could.

Just when I thought I could make it last all night, Abby sighed.

"Travis."

The sound of her breathing my name unguarded me and put me over the edge. I had to go faster, press farther until every muscle in my body tensed. I groaned and jerked a few times before finally collapsing.

I breathed in through my nose against her neck. She smelled like sweat, and her lotion . . . and me. It was fucking fantastic.

"That was some first kiss," she said with a tired, contented expression.

I scanned her face and smiled. "Your last first kiss."

Abby blinked, and then I fell onto the mattress beside her, reaching across her bare middle. Suddenly the morning was something to look forward to. It would be our first day together, and instead of packing in poorly concealed misery, we could sleep in, spend a ridiculous amount of the morning in bed, and then just enjoy the day as a couple. That sounded pretty damn close to heaven to me.

Three months ago, no one could have convinced me that I would feel that way. Now, there was nothing else I wanted more.

A big, relaxing breath moved my chest up and down slowly as I fell asleep next to the second woman I'd ever loved.

CHAPTER SIXTEEN

Space and Time

At first, I didn't panic. At first, a sleepy haze provided just enough confusion to foster a sense of calm. At first, when I reached for Abby across the sheets and didn't feel her there, I felt just a small bit of disappointment, followed by curiosity.

She was probably in the bathroom, or maybe eating cereal on the couch. She'd just given her virginity to me, someone with whom she'd spend a lot of time and effort pretending not to have more than platonic feelings. That was a lot to take in.

"Pidge?" I called. I lifted only my head, hoping she would crawl back in bed with me. But after several moments, I gave in, and sat up.

Having no idea what was in store, I slipped on the boxers I'd kicked off the night before, and slipped a T-shirt over my head.

My feet dragged down the hall to the bathroom door, and I knocked. The door opened a bit. I heard no movement but I called for her, anyway. "Pigeon?"

Opening the door wider revealed what was expected. Empty and dark. I then went into the living room, fully expecting to see her in the kitchen or on the couch, but she was nowhere.

"Pigeon?" I called, waiting for an answer.

Panic started to swell inside of me, but I refused to freak out until I knew what the hell was going on. I stomped into Shepley's room and opened the door without knocking.

America lay next to Shepley, tangled in his arms the way I imagined Abby would have been in mine at that point.

"Have you guys seen Abby? I can't find her."

Shepley raised himself up onto his elbow, rubbing his eye with his knuckle. "Huh?"

"Abby," I said, impatiently flipping on the light switch. Shepley and America both recoiled. "Have you seen her?"

Different scenarios ran through my mind, all causing different degrees of alarm. Maybe she had let out Toto, and someone had taken her, or hurt her, or maybe she'd fallen down the stairs. But Toto's claws were clicking against the floor down the hall, so that couldn't be it. Maybe she went to get something out of America's car.

I rushed to the front door and looked around. Then I jogged down the stairs, my eyes searching every inch between the front door of the apartment and America's car.

Nothing. She'd vanished.

Shepley appeared in the doorway, squinting and hugging himself from the cold.

"Yeah. She woke us up early. She wanted to go home."

I took the stairs back up two at a time, grabbing Shepley's bare shoulders, pushing him back all the way to the opposite side of the room, and grinding him into the wall. He gripped my T-shirt, a half-frowning, half-stunned expression on his face.

"What the—" he began.

"You took her home? To Morgan? In the middle of the fucking night? Why?"

"Because she asked me to!"

I shoved him against the wall again, blinding rage beginning to take over my system.

America came out of the bedroom, her hair ratted and her mascara smeared below her eyes. She was in her robe, tightening the belt around her waist. "What the hell is going on?" she asked, pausing midstep at the sight of me.

Shepley jerked out his arm and held out his hand. "Mare, stay back."

"Was she angry? Was she upset? Why did she leave?" I asked through my teeth.

America took another step. "She just hates goodbyes, Travis! I wasn't surprised at all that she wanted to leave before you woke up!"

I held Shepley against the wall and looked to America. "Was she . . . was she crying?"

I imagined Abby disgusted that she'd allowed some asshole like me, someone she didn't give a shit about, taking her virginity, and then I thought maybe I'd somehow, accidentally hurt her.

America's face twisted from fear, to confusion, to anger. "Why," she said. Her tone was more an accusation than a question. "Why would she be crying or upset, Travis?"

"Mare," Shepley warned.

America took another step. "What did you do?"

I released Shepley, but he took a fistful of my shirt as I faced his girlfriend.

"Was she crying?" I demanded.

America shook her head. "She was fine! She just wanted to go home! What did you do?" she yelled.

"Did something happen?" Shepley asked.

Without thinking, I flipped around and swung, nearly missing Shepley's face.

America screamed, covering her mouth with her hands. "Travis, stop!" she said through her hands.

Shepley wrapped his arms around mine at the elbows, his face just a couple of inches from mine. "Call her!" he yelled. "Fucking calm down, and call Abby!"

Quick, light footsteps ran down the hall and back. America returned, her hand outstretched, holding my phone. "Call her."

I snatched it from her hand and dialed Abby's number. It rang until the voice mail picked up. I hung up and dialed again. And again. And again. She wasn't answering. She hated me.

I dropped the phone to the ground, my chest heaving. When tears burned my eyes, I picked up the first thing my hands touched, and launched it across the room. Whatever it was splintered into large pieces.

Turning, I saw the stools situated directly across from each other, reminding me of our dinner. I picked one up by the legs and smashed it against the refrigerator until it broke. The refrigerator door popped open, and I kicked it. The force caused it to spring open again, so I kicked it again, and again, until Shepley finally rushed over to keep it closed.

I stomped to my room. The messy sheets on the bed mocked me. My arms flung in every direction as I ripped them off the mattress—fitted sheet, top sheet, and blanket—and then returned to the kitchen to throw them in the trash, and then I did the same with the pillows. Still insane with anger, I stood in my room, willing myself to calm down, but there was nothing to calm down for. I'd lost everything.

Pacing, I stopped in front of the nightstand. The thought of Abby reaching into the drawer came to mind. The hinges squeaked when I opened it, revealing the fishbowl full of condoms. I had barely delved into them since I'd met Abby. Now that she'd made her choice, I couldn't imagine being with anyone else.

The glass was cold in my hand as I picked it up and launched it across the room. It made contact with the wall beside the door and shattered, spraying small foil packages in every direction.

My reflection in the mirror above my dresser looked back at me. My chin was down, and I stared into my eyes. My chest heaved, I was shaking, and by anyone's standards looked insane, but control was so far out of my reach at that point. I reared back and slammed my fist into the mirror. Shards stabbed into my knuckles, leaving behind a bloody circle.

"Travis, stop!" Shepley said from the hall. "Stop it, God dammit!"

I rushed him, pushed him back, and then slammed my door shut. I pressed my hands flat against the wood, and then took a step back, kicking it until my foot made a dent at the bottom. I yanked on the sides until it came off the hinges, and then I tossed it across the room.

Shepley's arms grabbed me again. "I said stop!" he screamed. "You're scaring America!" The vein in his forehead popped out, the one that appeared only when he was enraged.

I shoved him, and he shoved me back. I took another swing, but he ducked.

"I'll go see her!" America pleaded. "I'll find out if she's okay, and I'll have her call you!"

I let my hands fall to my sides. Despite the cold air filling the apartment from the open front door, sweat was dripping from my temples. My chest heaved as if I'd run a marathon.

America ran to Shepley's room. Within five minutes, she was dressed, knotting her hair into a bun. Shepley helped her slip on her coat and then kissed her goodbye, offering a nod of assurance. She grabbed her keys and let the door slam behind her.

"Sit. The fuck. Down," Shepley said, pointing to the recliner.

I closed my eyes, then did what he commanded. My hands shook as I brought them to my face.

"You're lucky. I was two seconds away from calling Jim. And every brother you've got."

I shook my head. "Don't call Dad," I said. "Don't call him." Salty tears burned my eyes.

"Talk."

"I bagged her. I mean, I didn't *bag* her, we . . ."

Shepley nodded. "Last night was tough for both of you. Who's idea was it?"

"Hers." I blinked. "I tried to pull away. Offered to wait, but she all but begged me."

Shepley looked as confused as I felt.

I threw up my hands and let them fall to my lap. "Maybe I hurt her, I don't know."

"How did she act after? Did she say anything?"

I thought for a moment. "She said it was some first kiss."

"Huh?"

"She let it slip a few weeks ago that a first kiss makes her nervous, and I made fun of her."

Shepley's brows pushed together. "That doesn't sound like she was upset."

"I said it was her last first kiss." I laughed once and used the bottom of my T-shirt to pinch the moisture from my nose. "I thought everything was good, Shep. That she had finally let me in. Why would she ask me to . . . and then just leave?"

Shepley shook his head slowly, as confused as I was. "I don't know, cousin. America will find out. We'll know something soon."

I stared at the floor, thinking about what could possibly happen next. "What am I gonna do?" I asked, looking up at him.

Shepley gripped my forearm. "You're going to clean up your mess to keep you busy until they call."

I walked into my room. The door was lying on my bare mattress, pieces of mirror and shattered glass on the floor. It looked like a bomb had gone off.

Shepley appeared in the doorway with a broom, a dustpan, and a screwdriver. "I'll get the glass. You get the door."

I nodded, pulling the large wooden plank from the bed. Just after making the last turn on the screwdriver, my cell phone rang. I scrambled off the floor to snap it up from the night table.

It was America.

"Mare?" I choked out.

"It's me." Abby's voice was small and nervous.

I wanted to beg her back, to beg for her forgiveness, but I wasn't sure what I'd done wrong. Then, I got angry.

"What the fuck happened to you last night? I wake up this morning, and you're gone and you . . . you just leave and don't say goodbye? *Why?*"

"I'm sorry. I—"

"You're *sorry*? I've been going crazy! You don't answer your phone, you sneak out and—wh-*why*? I thought we finally had everything figured out!"

"I just needed some time to think."

"About what?" I paused, afraid of how she might answer the question I was about to ask. "Did I . . . did I hurt you?"

"No! It's nothing like that! I'm really, really sorry. I'm sure America told you. I don't do goodbyes."

"I need to see you," I said, desperate.

Abby sighed. "I have a lot to do today, Trav. I have to unpack and I have piles of laundry."

"You regret it."

"It's not . . . that's not what it is. We're friends. That's not going to change."

"*Friends?* Then what the fuck was last night?"

I could hear her breath catch. "I know what you want. I just can't do that right now."

"So you just need some time? You could have told me that. You didn't have to run out on me."

"It just seemed like the easiest way."

"Easier for who?"

"I couldn't sleep. I kept thinking about what it would be like in the morning, loading Mare's car . . . and I couldn't do it, Trav."

"It's bad enough that you aren't going to be here anymore. You can't just drop out of my life."

"I'll see you tomorrow," she said, trying hard to sound casual. "I don't want anything to be weird, okay? I just need to sort some stuff out. That's all."

"Okay," I said. "I can do that."

The line went silent, and Shepley watched me, wary. "Travis . . . you just got the door hung. No more messes, okay?"

My entire face crumpled, and I nodded my head. I tried to be angry, that was much easier to control than the overwhelming, physical pain in my chest, but all I felt was wave after wave of sadness. I was too tired to fight it.

"What did she say?"

"She needs time."

"Okay. So, that's not the end. You can work with that, right?"

I took a deep breath. "Yeah. I can work with that."

The dustpan jingled with the shards of glass as Shepley walked with it down the hall. Left alone in the bedroom, surrounded by pictures of me and Abby, made me want to break something again, so I went into the living room to wait for America.

Thankfully, it didn't take her long to return. I imagined that she was probably worried about Shepley.

The door opened, and I stood. "Is she with you?"

"No. She's not."

"Did she say anything else?"

America swallowed, hesitating to answer. "She said she'll keep her promise, and that by this time tomorrow, you won't miss her."

My eyes drifted to the floor. "She's not coming back," I said falling to the couch.

America stepped forward. "What does that mean, Travis?"

I cupped the top of my head with both hands. "What happened last night wasn't her way of saying she wanted to be together. She was saying goodbye."

"You don't know that."

"I know her."

"Abby cares about you."

"She doesn't love me."

America took a breath, and any reservations she'd had about my temper vanished as a sympathetic expression softened her face. "You don't know that, either. Listen, just give her some space. Abby isn't like the girls you're used to, Trav. She gets freaked out easy. The last time someone mentioned getting serious she moved an entire state away. This isn't as bad as it seems."

I looked up at America, feeling the tiniest bit hopeful. "You don't think so?"

"Travis, she left because her feelings for you scare her. If you knew everything, it would be easier to explain, but I can't tell you."

"Why not?"

"Because I promised Abby, and she's my best friend."

"Doesn't she trust me?"

"She doesn't trust herself. You, however, need to trust *me*." America grabbed my hands and pulled me to stand. "Go take a long, hot shower, and then we're going out to eat. Shepley told me it's poker night at your dad's."

I shook my head. "I can't do poker night. They'll ask about Pigeon. Maybe we could go see Pidge?"

America blanched. "She won't be home."

"You guys going out?"

"She is."

"With who?" It only took me a few seconds to figure it out. "Parker."

America nodded.

"That's why she thinks I won't miss her," I said, my voice breaking. I couldn't believe she was going to do that to me. It was just cruel.

America didn't hesitate to intercept another rage. "We'll go to a movie, then, a comedy, of course, and then we'll see if the go-kart place is still open, and you can run me off the track again."

America was smart. She knew the go-kart track was one of the few places I hadn't been with Abby. "I didn't run you off the track. You just can't drive worth a shit."

"We'll see," America said, pushing me toward the bathroom. "Cry if you must. Scream. Get it all out of your system, and then we'll have fun. It won't last forever, but it will keep you busy for tonight."

I turned around in the bathroom doorway. "Thanks, Mare."

"Yeah, yeah . . . ," she said, returning to Shepley.

I turned on the water, letting the steam warm the room before stepping in. The reflection in the mirror startled me. Dark circles under my tired eyes, my once confident posture sagging; I looked like hell.

Once in the shower, I let the water run over my face, keeping my eyes closed. The delicate outlines of Abby's features were burned behind my eyelids. It wasn't the first time; I saw her every time my eyes closed. Now that she was gone, it was like being stuck in a nightmare.

I choked back something welling up in my chest. Every few minutes, the pain renewed itself. I missed her. God, I missed her, and everything we'd gone through played over and over inside my head.

My palms flat against the wall of the tile, I clenched my eyes shut. "Please come back," I said quietly. She couldn't hear me, but it didn't stop me from wishing she would come and save me from the terrible pain I felt without her there.

After wallowing in my despair under the water, I took a few

deep breaths, and got myself together. The fact that Abby left shouldn't have been such a surprise, even after what happened the night before. What America said made sense. Abby was just as new at this and as scared as I was. We both had a piss-poor way of dealing with our emotions, and I knew the second I realized I'd fallen for her that she was going to rip me apart.

The hot water washed away the anger and the fear, and a new optimism came over me. I wasn't some loser that had no clue how to get a girl. Somewhere in my feelings for Abby, I'd forgotten that fact. It was time to believe in myself again, and remember that Abby wasn't just a girl that could break my heart; she was also my best friend. I knew how to make her smile, and her favorite things. I still had a dog in this fight.

OUR MOODS WERE LIGHT WHEN WE RETURNED FROM THE go-kart track. America was still giggling about beating Shepley four times in a row, and Shepley was pretending to sulk.

Shepley fumbled with the key in the dark.

I held my cell phone in my hands, fighting the urge to call Abby for the thirteenth time.

"Why don't you just call her already?" America asked.

"She's still on the date, probably. I better not . . . interrupt," I said, trying to push the thought of what might be happening from my mind.

"You shouldn't?" America asked, genuinely surprised. "Didn't you say you wanted to ask her to go bowling tomorrow? It's rude to ask a girl on a date the day of, you know."

Shepley finally found the keyhole and opened the door, letting us inside.

I sat on the couch, staring at Abby's name on my call list.

"Fuck it," I said, touching her name.

The phone rang once, and then again. My heart pounded against my rib cage, more than it ever did before a fight.

Abby answered.

"How's the date goin', Pidge?"

"What do you need, Travis?" she whispered. At least she wasn't breathing hard.

"I wanna go bowling tomorrow. I need my partner."

"*Bowling?* You couldn't have called me later?" She meant her words to sound sharp, but the tone in her voice was the opposite. I could tell she was glad I'd called.

My confidence soared to a new level. She didn't want to be there with Parker.

"How am I supposed to know when you're gonna get done? Oh. That didn't come out right . . . ," I joked.

"I'll call you tomorrow and we can talk about it then, okay?"

"No, it's not okay. You said you wanna be friends, but we can't hang out?" She paused, and I imagined her rolling those gorgeous gray eyes. I was jealous that Parker could see them firsthand. "Don't roll your eyes at me. Are you coming or not?"

"How did you know I rolled my eyes? Are you stalking me?"

"You always roll your eyes. Yes? No? You're wasting precious date time."

"Yes!" she said in a loud whisper, a smile in her voice. "I'll go."

"I'll pick you up at seven."

The phone made a muffled thud when I tossed it to the end of the couch, and then my eyes traveled to America.

"You got a date?"

"I do," I said, leaning back against the cushion.

America tossed her legs off of Shepley, teasing him about their last race while he surfed through the channels. It didn't take her long to get bored. "I'm going back to the dorm."

Shepley frowned, never happy about her departure. "Text me."

"I will," America said, smiling. "See ya, Trav."

I was envious that she was leaving, that she had something to do. I'd already finished days earlier the only two papers I had due.

The clock above the television caught my eye. Minutes rolled by slowly, and the more I told myself to stop paying attention, the more my eyes drifted to the digital numbers in the box. After an eternity, only half an hour had passed. My hands fidgeted. I felt more bored and restless until even seconds were torture. Pushing thoughts of Abby and Parker from my head became a constant struggle. Finally I stood.

"Leaving?" Shepley asked with a trace of a smile.

"I can't just sit here. You know how Parker's been frothing at the mouth for her. It's driving me crazy."

"You think they . . . ? Nah. Abby wouldn't. America said she was . . . never mind. My mouth is going to get me in trouble."

"A virgin?"

"You know?"

I shrugged. "Abby told me. You think because we . . . that she'd . . . ?"

"No."

I rubbed the back of my neck. "You're right. I think you're right. I mean, I hope. She's capable of doing some crazy shit to push me away."

"Would it? Push you away, I mean?"

I looked up into Shepley's eyes. "I love her, Shep. I know what I'd do to Parker if he took advantage of her, though."

Shepley shook his head. "It's her choice, Trav. If that's what she decided, you're going to have to let it go."

I took my bike keys and clenched my fingers around them, feeling the sharp edges of the metal as it dug into my palm.

Before climbing on the Harley, I called Abby.

"You home, yet?"

"Yeah, he dropped me off about five minutes ago."

"I'll be there in five more."

I hung up before she could protest. The frigid air that rushed against my face as I drove helped to numb the anger that thoughts of Parker sparked, but a sick feeling still descended on my gut the closer I came to campus.

The bike engine seemed loud as the noise bounced off the brick of Morgan Hall. Compared to the dark windows and the abandoned parking lot, me and my Harley made the night seem abnormally quiet, and the wait exceptionally long. Finally Abby appeared in the doorway. Every muscle in my body tensed as I waited for her to smile or freak out.

She did neither. "Aren't you cold?" she asked, pulling her jacket tighter.

"You look nice," I said, noting she wasn't in a dress. She obviously wasn't trying to look all sexy for him, and that was a relief. "Did you have a good time?"

"Uh . . . yeah, thanks. What are you doing here?"

I gunned the engine. "I was going to take a ride to clear my head. I want you to come with me."

"It's cold, Trav."

"You want me to go get Shep's car?"

"We're going bowling tomorrow. Can't you wait until then?"

"I went from being with you every second of the day to seeing you for ten minutes if I'm lucky."

She smiled and shook her head. "It's only been two days, Trav."

"I miss you. Get your ass on the seat and let's go."

She contemplated my offer, and then zipped up her jacket and climbed on the seat behind me.

I pulled her arms around me without apology, tight enough that it was difficult to expand my chest enough to fully inhale, but for the first time all night, I felt like I could breathe.

CHAPTER SEVENTEEN

Lowball

THE HARLEY TOOK US NOWHERE IN PARTICULAR. WATCHing out for traffic and the sporadic police cruiser that crossed our path was enough to keep my thoughts occupied at first, but after a while we were the only ones on the road. Knowing the night would eventually end, I decided the moment I dropped her off at Morgan would be when I put in my last-ditch effort. Regardless of our platonic bowling dates, if she continued to see Parker, eventually those would stop, too. Everything would stop.

Pressuring Abby was never a good idea, but unless I laid all my cards on the table, I stood a very good chance of losing the only pigeon I'd ever met. What I would say and how I would say it played over and over in my mind. It would have to be direct, something Abby couldn't ignore, or pretend she didn't hear or understand.

The needle had been flirting with the empty end of the gas gauge for several miles, so I pulled into the first open gas station we came across.

"You want anything?" I asked.

Abby shook her head, climbing off the bike. She raked her fingers through the tangles of her long, shiny hair, and smiled sheepishly.

"Quit it. You're fucking beautiful."

"Just point me to the nearest 1980s rock video."

I laughed, and then yawned, placing the nozzle into the Harley's gas tank opening.

Abby pulled out her cell phone to check the time. "Oh my God, Trav. It's three in the morning."

"You wanna go back?" I asked, my stomach sinking.

"We better."

"We're still going bowling tonight?"

"I told you I would."

"And you're still going to Sig Tau with me in a couple weeks, right?"

"Are you insinuating that I don't follow through? I find that a little insulting."

I pulled the nozzle from the gas tank and hooked it on its base. "I just never know what you're going to do anymore."

I sat on the bike and then helped Abby to climb on behind me. She wrapped her arms around me, this time on her own, and I sighed, lost in thought before starting the engine. I gripped the handlebars, took a breath, and just when I got the balls to tell her, decided a gas station was not the appropriate backdrop to bare my soul.

"You're important to me, you know," Abby said, tensing her arms.

"I don't understand you, Pigeon. I thought I knew women, but you're so fucking confusing I don't know which way is up."

"I don't understand you, either. You're supposed to be this

school's ladies' man. I'm not getting the full freshmen experience they promised in the brochure."

I couldn't help but feel offended. Even if it was true. "Well, that's a first. I've never had a girl sleep with me to get me to leave her alone."

"That's not what it was, Travis."

I started the engine and pulled out into the street without saying another word. The drive to Morgan was excruciating. In my head, I talked myself in and out of confronting Abby so many times. Even though my fingers were numb from the cold, I drove slowly, dreading the moment when Abby knew everything, and then rejecting me for the final time.

When we pulled in front of the entrance to Morgan Hall, my nerves felt like they had been cut, lit on fire, and left in a raw, mangled mess. Abby stepped off the bike, and her sad expression made subdued panic blaze inside me. She might tell me to go to hell before I had a chance to say anything.

I walked Abby to the door, and she pulled out her keys, keeping her head down. Unable to wait another second, I took her chin gently in my hand, and lifted it, waiting patiently as her eyes rose to meet mine.

"Did he kiss you?" I asked, touching my thumb to her soft lips.

She pulled away. "You really know how to screw up a perfect night, don't you?"

"You thought it was perfect, huh? Does that mean you had a good time?"

"I always do when I'm with you."

My eyes fell, and I felt my features compress into a frown. "Did he kiss you?"

"Yes." She sighed, irritated.

My eyes closed tight, knowing my next question could result in disaster. "Is that all?"

"That is *none* of your business!" she said, yanking open the door.

I pushed it closed and stood in her way. "I need to know."

"No you don't! Move, Travis!" she jabbed her elbow into my side, trying to get by.

"Pigeon . . ."

"You think because I'm no longer a virgin, I'll screw anyone that'll have me? *Thanks!*" she said, shoving my shoulder.

"I didn't say that, damn it! Is it too much to ask for a little peace of mind?"

"*Why* would it give you peace of mind to know if I'm sleeping with Parker?"

"How can you not know? It's obvious to everyone else but you!"

"I guess I'm just an idiot, then. You're on a roll tonight, Trav," she said, reaching for the door handle.

I cupped her shoulders. She was doing it again, the oblivious routine I'd become so accustomed to. The time to show my cards was now. "The way I feel about you . . . it's crazy."

"You got the crazy part right," she snapped, pulling away from me.

"I practiced this in my head the whole time we were on the bike, so just hear me out."

"Travis—"

"I know we're fucked up, all right? I'm impulsive and hot tempered, and you get under my skin like no one else. You act like you hate me one minute, and then you need me the next. I never get anything right, and I don't deserve you . . . but I fucking *love* you, Abby. I love you more than I've loved anyone or anything, ever. When you're around, I don't need booze or money or the fighting or the one-night stands . . . all I need is you. You're all I think about. You're all I dream about. You're all I want."

She didn't speak for several seconds. Her eyebrows raised, and her eyes looked dazed as she processed everything I'd said. She blinked a few times.

I cupped each side of her face and looked into her eyes. "Did you sleep with him?"

Abby's eyes glossed over, and then she shook her head no. Without another thought, my lips slammed into hers, and I slipped my tongue inside her mouth. She didn't push me away; instead her tongue challenged mine, and she gripped my T-shirt in her fists, pulling me close. An involuntary hum emanated from my throat, and I wrapped my arms around her.

When I knew I had my answer, I pulled back, breathless. "Call Parker. Tell him you don't wanna see him anymore. Tell him you're with me."

She closed her eyes. "I *can't* be with you, Travis."

"Why the hell not?" I asked, letting go.

Abby shook her head. She had proven herself unpredictable a million times before, but the way she kissed me had meant more than friendship, and had too much behind it to just be sympathy. That left me with only one conclusion.

"Unbelievable. The one girl I want, and she doesn't want me."

She hesitated before she spoke. "When America and I moved out here, it was with the understanding that my life was going to turn out a certain way. Or, that it *wouldn't* turn out a certain way. The fighting, the gambling, the drinking . . . it's what I left behind. When I'm around you it's all right there for me in an irresistible, tattooed package. I didn't move hundreds of miles away to live it all over again."

"I know you deserve better than me. You think I don't know that? But if there was any woman made for me . . . it's you. I'll do whatever I have to do, Pidge. Do you hear me? I'll do anything."

She turned away from me, but I wouldn't give up. She was finally talking, and if she walked away this time, we might not get another chance.

I held the door shut with my hand. "I'll stop fighting the second I graduate. I won't drink a single drop again. I'll give you the happy ever after, Pigeon. If you just believe in me, I can do it."

"I don't *want* you to change."

"Then tell me what to do. Tell me and I'll do it," I pleaded.

"Can I borrow your phone?" she asked.

I frowned, unsure what she would do. "Sure." I pulled my phone from my pocket, handing it to her.

She fingered the buttons for a moment, and then dialed, closing her eyes as she waited.

"I'm sorry for calling you so early," she stammered, "but this couldn't wait. I . . . can't go to dinner with you on Wednesday."

She had called Parker. My hands trembled with apprehension, wondering if she was going to ask him to pick her up—to save her—or something else.

She continued, "I can't see you at all, actually. I'm . . . pretty sure I'm in love with Travis."

My whole world stopped. I tried to replay her words over. Had I heard them correctly? Did she really just say what I thought she had, or was it just wishful thinking?

Abby handed the phone back to me, and then reluctantly peered up into my eyes.

"He hung up," she said with a frown.

"You love me?"

"It's the tattoos," she said, flippant and shrugging, as if she hadn't just said the one thing I'd ever wanted to hear.

Pigeon loved me.

A wide smile stretched across my face. "Come home with me," I said, enveloping her in my arms.

Abby's eyebrows shot up. "You said all that to get me in bed? I must have made quite an impression."

"The only thing I'm thinking about right now is holding you in my arms all night."

"Let's go."

I didn't hesitate. Once Abby was securely on the back of my bike, I raced home, taking every shortcut, rushing every yellow light, and weaving in and out of the little traffic there was at that time of the morning.

When we reached the apartment, turning off the engine and lifting Abby into my arms seemed simultaneous.

She giggled against my lips as I fumbled with the bolt lock on the front door. When I set her down and closed the door behind us, I let out a long, relieved sigh.

"It hasn't seemed like home since you left," I said, kissing her again.

Toto scampered down the hall and wagged his shaggy tail, pawing at Abby's legs. He'd missed her almost as much as I had.

Shepley's bed squeaked, and then his feet stomped across the floor. His door flew open as he squinted from the light. "Fuck no,

Trav, you're not pulling this shit! You're in love with Ab . . ."—his eyes focused and he recognized his mistake—"by. Hey, Abby."

"Hey, Shep," Abby said with an amused smile, setting Toto on the floor.

Before Shepley could ask questions, I pulled Abby down the hall. We crashed into each other. I hadn't planned on anything but having her next to me in the bed, but she yanked my shirt up and over my head with intention. I helped her with her jacket, and then she stripped off her sweater and tank top. There was no questioning the look in her eyes, and I wasn't about to argue.

Soon we were both completely naked, and the small voice inside of me wanting to savor the moment and take things slow was easily overpowered by Abby's desperate kisses and the soft hums she made whenever I touched her pretty much anywhere.

I lowered her to the mattress, and her hand shot out toward the nightstand. Instantly, I remembered my unceremonious breaking of the fishbowl of condoms to pledge my intended celibacy.

"Shit," I said, panting. "I got rid of them."

"*What? All* of them?"

"I thought you didn't . . . if I wasn't with you, I wasn't going to need them."

"You're kidding me!" she said, letting her head fall against the headboard in frustration.

I leaned down, breathing hard, resting my forehead against her chest. "Consider yourself the opposite of a foregone conclusion."

The next moments were a blur. Abby did some weird counting, concluding that she couldn't get pregnant that particular week, and before I knew it, I was inside of her, feeling every part of her against every part of me. I had never been with a girl without that thin sheath of latex, but apparently a fraction of a millimeter made a lot of difference. Every movement created equally overpowering conflicting feelings: delaying the inevitable, or giving in because it felt so fucking good.

When Abby's hips rose against mine, and her uncontrolled groans and whimpers escalated to a loud, satisfied cry, I couldn't hold back anymore.

"Abby," I whispered, desperate. "I need a . . . I need to . . ."

"Don't stop," she begged. Her fingernails dug into my back.

I rocked into her again one last time. I must have been loud, because Abby's hand flew up to my mouth. I closed my eyes, letting everything go, feeling my eyebrows press together while my body convulsed and stiffened. Breathing hard, I looked into Abby's eyes. Wearing only a tired, satisfied smile, she peered up at me, waiting for something. I kissed her over and over, and then cupped each side of her face with my hands, kissing her again, this time more tenderly.

Abby's breathing slowed, and she sighed. I leaned my body to the side, relaxing next to her, and then pulled her against me. She rested her cheek against my chest, her hair cascading down my arm. I kissed her forehead once more, locking my fingers together at the small of her back.

"Don't leave this time, okay? I wanna wake up just like this in the morning."

Abby kissed my chest, but didn't look up. "I'm not going anywhere."

THAT MORNING, LYING WITH THE WOMAN I LOVED, A SIlent promise was formed in my head. I was going to be a better man for her, someone she deserved. No more flying off the handle. No more temper tantrums, or violent outbursts.

Every time I pressed my lips against her skin, waiting for her to wake up, I repeated that promise in my mind.

Dealing with life outside the apartment while trying to stay true to that promise proved to be a struggle. For the first time, I not only gave a shit about someone, but I was also desperate to keep them. Feelings of overprotection and jealousy chipped away at the oath I'd made just a few hours before.

By lunchtime, Chris Jenks had pissed me off and I regressed. Abby was thankfully patient and forgiving, even when I threatened Parker not twenty minutes later.

Abby had proved more than once that she could accept me for who I was, but I didn't want to be the violent asshole everyone was used to. Mixing my rages with these new feelings of jealousy was more difficult to control than I could have imagined.

I resorted to avoiding situations that could throw me into a rage, and remaining oblivious to the knowledge that not only was Abby insanely hot, every dick on campus was curious how she had tamed the one man they thought would never settle down. It seemed they were all waiting for me to fuck up so they could try her out, which only made me more agitated and cantankerous.

To keep my mind occupied, I focused on making it clear to the coeds that I was off the market, which had pissed off half the school's female population.

Walking into the Red with Abby on Halloween, I noticed that the sharp, late fall air didn't hinder the number of women wearing an array of slutty costumes. I hugged my girlfriend to my side, grateful that she wasn't one to dress up as Prostitute Barbie, or a football-player-slash-transvestite-whore, which meant that the number of threats I would have to make for staring at her tits or worrying about her bending over would be kept to a minimum.

Shepley and I played pool while the girls looked on. We were winning again, after having already pocketed $360 from the last two games.

From the corner of my eye, I saw Finch approach America and Abby. They giggled for a while, and then Finch pulled them onto the dance floor. Abby's beauty stood out, even amid the bare skin, glitter, and glaring cleavage of the naughty Snow Whites and sleazy referees around her.

Before the song was over, America and Abby left Finch on the dance floor and headed toward the bar. I stretched up onto my toes to find the tops of their heads in the sea of people.

"You're up," Shepley said.

"The girls are gone."

"They probably went to pick up drinks. Get to stickin', lover boy."

With hesitation, I bent down, focused on the ball, but then missed.

"Travis! That was an easy shot! You're killin' me!" Shepley complained.

I still couldn't see the girls. Knowing about the two sexual assault incidents the year before, it made me nervous to let Abby and America walk around alone. Drugging an unsuspecting girl's drink was not unheard of, even in our small college town.

I set my pool stick on the table and made my way across the wooden dance floor.

Shepley's hand fell on my shoulder. "Where are you going?"

"To find the girls. You remember what happened last year to that Heather chick."

"Oh. Yeah."

When I finally found Abby and America, I saw two guys buying them drinks. Both short, one was thicker around the middle, with a week's worth of scruff on his sweaty face. Jealousy should have been the last thing I would feel when looking at him, but the fact that he was clearly hitting on my girlfriend made this less about his looks and more about my ego—even if he didn't know she was with me, he should have assumed by looking at her that she wouldn't be alone. My jealousy mixed with annoyance. I'd told Abby a dozen times not to do something so potentially dangerous as accept a drink from a stranger; anger quickly took over.

The one guy yelling to Abby over the music leaned in. "You wanna dance?"

Abby shook her head. "No, thanks. I'm here with my—"

"Boyfriend," I said, cutting her off. I glared down at the men. It was almost laughable trying to intimidate two men wearing togas, but I still unleashed my full-on *I Will Kill You* expression. I nodded across the room. "Run along, now."

The men cowered, and then looked to America and Abby before retreating behind the curtain of the crowd.

Shepley kissed America. "I can't take you anywhere!" She giggled, and Abby smiled at me.

I was too angry to smile back.

"What?" she asked, taken aback.

"Why did you let him buy your drink?"

America let go of Shepley. "We didn't, Travis. I told them not to."

I took the bottle from Abby's hand. "Then what's this?"

"Are you serious?" she asked.

"Yes, I'm fucking serious," I said, tossing the beer in the trash can by the bar. "I've told you a hundred times . . . you can't take drinks from random guys. What if he put something in it?"

America held up her glass. "The drinks were never out of our sight, Trav. You're overreacting."

"I'm not talking to you," I said, glaring at Abby.

Her eyes flashed, mirroring my anger. "Don't talk to her like that."

"Travis," Shepley warned, "let it go."

"I don't like you letting other guys buy you drinks," I said.

Abby raised an eyebrow. "Are you trying to pick a fight?"

"Would it bother you to walk up to the bar and see me sharing a drink with some chick?"

"Okay. You're oblivious to all women, now. I get it. I should be making the same effort."

"It would be nice," I said, my teeth clenched.

"You're going to have to tone down the jealous-boyfriend thing, Travis. I didn't do anything wrong."

"I walk up here, and some guy is buying you a drink!"

"Don't yell at her!" America said.

Shepley put his hand on Travis's shoulder. "We've all had a lot to drink. Let's just get out of here."

Abby's anger turned up a notch. "I have to tell Finch we're leaving," she grumbled, shouldering past me to the dance floor.

I took her by the wrist. "I'll go with you."

She twisted from my grip. "I am fully capable of walking a few feet by myself, Travis. What is *wrong* with you?"

Abby pushed her way out to Finch, who was flinging his

arms around and jumping around in the middle of the wooden floor. Sweat was pouring down his forehead and from his temples. At first he smiled, but when she yelled her goodbyes, he rolled his eyes.

Abby had mouthed my name. She had blamed it on me, which only made me more mad. Of course I would get angry if she did something that could get her hurt. She didn't seem to mind so much when I was bashing Chris Jenks's head in, but when I got pissed about her taking drinks from strangers, she had the audacity to get mad.

Just as my anger boiled to rage, some asshole in a pirate costume grabbed Abby and pressed himself against her. The room blurred, and before I knew it, my fist was in his face. The pirate fell to the floor, but when Abby went with him, I snapped back to reality.

Her palms flat on the dance floor, she looked stunned. I was frozen in shock, watching her, in slow motion, turn her hand over to see that it was covered in bright red blood gushing from the pirate's nose.

I scrambled to pick her up. "Oh shit! Are you all right, Pidge?"

When Abby got to her feet, she yanked her arm from my grip. "Are you *insane*?"

America grabbed Abby's wrist and pulled her through the crowd, only letting go when we were outside. I had to walk double-time to keep up.

In the parking lot, Shepley unlocked the Charger and Abby slid into her seat.

I tried pleading with her. She was beyond pissed. "I'm sorry, Pigeon, I didn't know he had a hold of you."

"Your fist was two inches from my face!" she said, catching the oil-stained towel Shepley had thrown at her. She wiped the blood from her hand, wringing the cloth around each finger, clearly revolted.

I winced. "I wouldn't have swung if I thought I could have hit you. You know that right?"

"Shut up, Travis. Just shut up," she said, staring at the back of Shepley's head.

"Pidge . . ."

Shepley hit his steering wheel with the heel of his hand. "Shut up, Travis! You said you're sorry, now shut the fuck up!"

I couldn't say anything back. Shepley was right: I had FUBARed the entire night, and suddenly Abby kicking me to the curb became a frightening possibility.

When we reached the apartment, America kissed her boyfriend good night. "I'll see you tomorrow, baby."

Shepley nodded in resignation and kissed her. "Love you."

I knew they were leaving because of me. Otherwise, the girls would be staying the night at the apartment like they did every weekend.

Abby walked past me to America's Honda without saying a word.

I jogged to her side, trying an awkward smile in an attempt to defuse the situation. "C'mon. Don't leave mad."

"Oh, I'm not leaving mad. I'm furious."

"She needs some time to cool off, Travis," America warned, unlocking her door.

When the passenger side lock popped, I panicked, holding my hand against the door. "Don't leave, Pigeon. I was out of line. I'm *sorry*."

Abby held up her hand, showing the remnants of dried blood on her palm. "Call me when you grow up."

I leaned against the door with my hip. "You can't leave."

Abby raised an eyebrow, and Shepley jogged around the car beside us. "Travis, you're drunk. You're about to make a huge mistake. Just let her go home, cool off . . . you can both talk tomorrow when you're sober."

"She can't leave," I said, desperately staring into Abby's eyes.

"It's not going to work, Travis," she said, tugging on the door. "Move!"

"What do you mean it's not gonna work?" I asked, grabbing her arm. The fear of Abby saying the words, ending it right there made me react without thinking.

"I mean the sad face. I'm not falling for it," she said, pulling away.

A short-lived relief came over me. She wasn't going to end it. At least, not yet.

"Abby," Shepley said. "This is the moment I was talking about. Maybe you should—"

"Stay out of it, Shep," America snapped, starting the car.

"I'm gonna fuck up. I'm gonna fuck up a lot, Pidge, but you have to forgive me."

"I'm going to have a huge bruise on my ass in the morning! You hit that guy because you were pissed at *me*! What should that tell me? Because red flags are going up *all* over the place right now!"

"I've never hit a girl in my life," I said, surprised she would ever think I could ever lay a hand on her—or any other woman for that matter.

"And I'm not about to be the first one!" she said, tugging on the door. "Move, damn it!"

I nodded, taking a step back. The last thing I wanted was for her to leave, but it was better than her getting so pissed off that she ended up telling me to fuck off.

America put the car in reverse, and I watched Abby through the window.

"You're going to call me tomorrow, right?" I asked, touching the windshield.

"Just go, Mare," she said, looking straight ahead.

When the brake lights were no longer visible, I retreated into the apartment.

"Travis," Shepley warned. "No messes, bro. I mean it."

I nodded, trudging to my room in defeat. It seemed that just when I was getting a handle on things, my fucking temper would rear its ugly head. I had to get it under control, or I was going to lose the best thing that ever happened to me.

To pass the time, I cooked some pork chops and mashed potatoes, but just rolled it all around on my plate, unable to eat. Laundry helped to knock out an hour, and then I decided to give Toto a bath. We played for a while, but then even he gave up and curled up on the bed. Staring at the ceiling, obsessing about how stupid I'd been, wasn't appealing, so I decided to pull all the dishes out of the cabinet and wash them by hand.

Longest night of my life.

The clouds began to turn colors, signaling the sun. I grabbed the bike keys and went for a drive, ending up in front of Morgan Hall.

Harmony Handler was just leaving for a jog. She watched me for a moment, keeping her hand on the door.

"Hey, Travis," she said with her typical small smile. It quickly faded. "Wow. Are you sick or something? Do you need me to take you somewhere?" I must have looked like hell. Harmony had always been a sweetheart. Her brother was a Sig Tau, so I didn't know her all that well. Little sisters were off-limits.

"Hey, Harmony," I said, trying a smile. "I wanted to surprise Abby with breakfast. Think you could let me in?"

"Uh," she trailed off, looking back through the glass door. "Nancy might freak. Are you sure you're okay?"

Nancy was Morgan Hall's dorm mom. I'd heard of her, but never seen her, and doubted she would even notice. The word around campus was that she drank more than the residents and was seldom seen outside of her room.

"Just a long night. C'mon." I smiled. "You know she won't care."

"Okay, but it wasn't me."

I held my hand to my heart. "I promise."

I made my way upstairs, knocking softly on Abby's door.

The knob turned quickly, but the door opened slowly, gradually revealing Abby and America across the room. Kara's hand slipped from the doorknob back under the covers of her bed.

"Can I come in?"

Abby sat up quickly. "Are you okay?"

I walked in and fell to my knees before her. "I'm so sorry, Abby. I'm sorry," I said, wrapping my arms around her middle and burying my head in her lap.

Abby cradled my head in her arms.

"I'm uh . . . ," America stuttered, "I'm gonna go."

Abby's roommate Kara stomped around the room, getting her shower supplies. "I'm always very clean when you're around, Abby," she said, slamming the door behind her.

I looked up at Abby. "I know I get crazy when it comes to you, but God knows I'm tryin', Pidge. I don't wanna screw this up."

"Then don't," she said simply.

"This is hard for me, ya know. I feel like any second you're going to figure out what a piece of shit I am and leave me. When you were dancing last night, I saw a dozen different guys watching you. You go to the bar, and I see you thank that guy for your drink. Then that douche bag on the dance floor grabs you."

"You don't see me throwing punches every time a girl talks to you. I can't stay locked up in the apartment all the time. You're going to have to get a handle on your temper."

"I will," I said, nodding. "I've never wanted a girlfriend before, Pigeon. I'm not used to feeling this way about someone . . . about *anyone*. If you'll be patient with me, I swear I'll get it figured out."

"Let's get something straight; you're not a piece of shit, you're amazing. It doesn't matter who buys me drinks or who asks me to dance or who flirts with me. I'm going home with you. You've asked me to trust you, and you don't seem to trust me."

I frowned. "That's not true."

"If you think I'm going to leave you for the next guy that comes along, then you don't have much faith in me."

I tightened my grip. "I'm not good enough for you, Pidge. That doesn't mean I don't trust you, I'm just bracing for the inevitable."

"Don't say that. When we're alone, you're perfect. We're perfect. But then you let everyone else ruin it. I don't expect a 180, but you have to pick your battles. You can't come out swinging every time someone looks at me."

I nodded, knowing she was right. "I'll do anything you want. Just . . . tell me you love me." I was fully aware of how ridiculous I sounded, but it just didn't matter anymore.

"You know I do."

"I need to hear you say it."

"I love you," she said. She touched her lips to mine, and then pulled a few inches away. "Now quit being such a baby."

Once she kissed me, my heart slowed, and every muscle in my body relaxed. How much I needed her terrified me. I couldn't imagine love was like this for everyone, or men would be walking around like lunatics the second they were old enough to notice girls.

Maybe it was just me. Maybe it was just me and her. Maybe together we were this volatile entity that would either implode or meld together. Either way, it seemed the moment I met her, my life had been turned upside down. And I didn't want it any other way.

CHAPTER EIGHTEEN

Lucky Thirteen

HALF EXCITED, HALF NERVOUS AS HELL, I WALKED INTO my father's home, my fingers intertwined with Abby's. Smoke from my father's cigar and my brothers' cigarettes drifted from the game room, mixing with the faint, musky smell of carpet older than I was.

Even though Abby was initially pissed that she didn't have much notice before meeting my family, she looked more at ease than I felt. Bringing home a girlfriend was not a habit of the Maddox men, and any prediction of their reaction was unreliable at best.

Trenton came into view first. "Holy Christ! It's the asshat!"

Any hope of my brothers even pretending not to be anything but feral was a waste of time. I loved them anyway, and knowing Abby, she would, too.

"Hey, hey . . . watch the language around the young lady," Dad said, nodding to Abby.

"Pidge, this is my dad, Jim Maddox. Dad, this is Pigeon."

"Pigeon?" Jim asked, an amused expression on his face.

"Abby," she said, shaking his hand.

I pointed to my brothers, all of them nodding when I said their name. "Trenton, Taylor, Tyler, and Thomas."

Abby seemed a bit overwhelmed. I couldn't blame her; I'd never really talked about my family, and five boys would be mind-boggling to anybody. In fact, five Maddoxes were downright frightening to most.

Growing up, the neighborhood kids learned early not to mess with one of us, and only once did someone make the mistake of taking on all of us. We were broken, but came together as a solid fortress if necessary. That was clear even to those we didn't mean to intimidate.

"Does Abby have a last name?" Dad asked.

"Abernathy," she said, nodding politely.

"It's nice to meet you, Abby," Thomas said with a smile. Abby wouldn't have noticed, but Thomas's expression was a front for what he was really doing: analyzing her every word and movement. Thomas was always on the lookout for someone that could potentially rock our already rickety boat. Waves weren't welcome, and Thomas had always made it his job to calm potential storms.

Dad can't take it, he used to say. None of us could argue with that logic. When one or a few of us found ourselves in trouble, we would go to Thomas, and he would take care of it before Dad could find out. Years of fostering a bunch of rowdy, violent boys made a man out of Thomas far earlier than anyone should be expected to be. We all respected him for it, including my father, but years of being our protector left him a little overbearing at times. But Abby stood, smiling and oblivious to the fact that she was now a target, under scrutiny by the family guardian.

"Really nice," Trenton said, his eyes roving over places that would have gotten anyone else killed.

Dad slapped the back of Trenton's head and he yelped.

"What'd I say?" he said, rubbing the back of his head.

"Have a seat, Abby. Watch us take Trav's money," Tyler said.

I pulled out a chair for Abby, and she sat. I glared at Trenton, and he responded with only a wink. Smart-ass.

"You knew Stu Unger?" Abby asked, pointing to a dusty photo.

I couldn't believe my ears.

Dad's eyes brightened. "You know who Stu Unger is?"

Abby nodded. "My dad's a fan, too."

Dad stood up, pointing to the dusty picture beside it. "And that's Doyle Brunson, there."

Abby smiled. "My dad saw him play, once. He's unbelievable."

"Trav's granddaddy was a professional. We take poker very seriously around here." Dad smiled.

Not only had Abby never mentioned the fact that she knew anything about poker, it was also the first time I'd ever heard her speak of her dad.

As we watched Trenton shuffle and deal, I tried to forget what had just happened. With her long legs, slight but perfectly proportioned curves, and big eyes, Abby was stunningly gorgeous, but knowing Stu Unger by name already made her a huge hit with my family. I sat up a little taller in my seat. No way would any of my brothers bring home anyone that could top *that*.

Trenton raised an eyebrow. "You wanna play, Abby?"

She shook her head. "I don't think I should."

"You don't know how?" Dad asked.

I leaned over to kiss her forehead. "Play . . . I'll teach you."

"You should just kiss your money goodbye, now, Abby." Thomas laughed.

Abby pressed her lips together and dug into her purse, pulling out two fifties. She held them out to Dad, waiting patiently while he traded them for chips. Trenton smiled, eager to take advantage of her confidence.

"I have faith in Travis's teaching skills," Abby said.

Taylor clapped. "Hells yeah! I'm going to get rich tonight!"

"Let's start small this time," Dad said, throwing in a five-dollar chip.

Trenton dealt, and I fanned out Abby's hand. "Have you ever played?"

"It's been a while." She nodded.

"Go Fish doesn't count, Pollyanna," Trenton said, looking at his cards.

"Shut your hole, Trent," I growled, throwing him a quick threatening look before returning to Abby's cards. "You're shooting for higher cards, consecutive numbers, and if you're really lucky, in the same suit."

We lost the first few rounds, but then Abby refused to let me help her. After that, she started to pick it up pretty quickly. Three hands later, she had kicked all of their asses without blinking.

"Bullshit!" Trenton whined. "Beginner's luck sucks!"

"You've got a fast learner, Trav," Dad said, moving his mouth around his cigar.

I took a sip of my beer, feeling like the king of the world. "You're makin' me proud, Pigeon!"

"Thanks."

"Those that cannot do, teach," Thomas said, smirking.

"Very funny, asshole," I murmured.

"Get the girl a beer," Dad said, an amused smile lifting his already puffy cheeks.

I gladly hopped up, pulled a bottle from the fridge, and used the already cracked edge of the countertop to pop off the cap. Abby smiled when I placed the beer in front of her and didn't hesitate to take one of her signature man-size swigs.

She wiped her lips with the back of her hand, and then waited on my dad to put in his chips.

Four hands later, Abby had tipped back the last of her third beer and watched Taylor closely. "The action's on you, Taylor. You gonna be a baby or you going to put in like a man?"

It was getting very difficult for me to keep from being excited in other places. Watching Abby own my brothers—and a poker veteran like my father—hand after hand was turning me on. I'd never seen a women so sexy in my life, and this one happened to be my girlfriend.

"Fuck it," Taylor said, throwing the last of his chips in.

"Whatdya got, Pigeon?" I asked with a grin. I felt like a kid at Christmas.

"Taylor?" Abby prompted, her face completely blank.

A wide grin spread across his face. "Flush!" He smiled, spreading his cards faceup on the table.

We all looked to Abby. Her eyes scanned the men around the table, and then she slammed her cards down. "Read 'em and weep, boys! Aces and eights!"

"A full house? What the fuck?" Trenton cried.

"Sorry. I've always wanted to say that," Abby said, giggling as she pulled in her chips.

Thomas's eyes narrowed. "This isn't just beginner's luck. She plays."

I watched Thomas for a moment. He wasn't taking his eyes from Abby.

I looked to her, then. "Have you played before, Pidge?"

She pressed her lips together and shrugged, letting a sweet smile turn up the corners of her mouth. My head fell back, and I burst into laughter. I started to tell her how proud I was, but the words were held hostage by the uncontrollable cackling shaking my entire body. I hit the table with my fist a few times, trying to get a hold of myself.

"Your girlfriend just fucking hustled us!" Taylor said, pointing in my direction.

"NO FUCKING WAY!" Trenton wailed, standing up.

"Good plan, Travis. Bring a card shark to poker night," Dad said, winking at Abby.

"I didn't know!" I said, shaking my head.

"Bullshit," Thomas said, his eyes still dissecting my girlfriend.

"I didn't!" I said.

"I hate to say it, bro. But I think I just fell in love with your girl," Tyler said.

Suddenly my laughter was gone, and I frowned. "Hey, now."

"That's it. I was going easy on you, Abby, but I'm winning my money back, now," Trenton warned.

I sat out the last few rounds, watching the boys try to win back their money. Hand after hand, Abby steamrolled them. She didn't even pretend to go easy on them.

Once my brothers were broke, Dad called it a night, and Abby returned a hundred dollars to each of them, except Dad, who wouldn't take it.

I took Abby's hand, and we walked to the door. Watching my girlfriend de-sack my brothers was entertaining, but I was still disappointed that she returned some of their money.

She squeezed my hand. "What's wrong?"

"You just gave away four hundred bucks, Pidge!"

"If this was poker night at Sig Tau, I would have kept it. I can't rob your brothers the first time I meet them."

"They would have kept your money!"

"And I wouldn't have lost a second of sleep over it, either," Taylor said.

From the corner of my eye, I caught Thomas staring at Abby from the recliner in the corner of the living room. He'd been even more quiet than usual.

"Why do you keep starin' at my girl, Tommy?"

"What did you say your last name was?" Thomas asked.

Abby shifted nervously but didn't answer.

I put my arm around her waist, and turned to my brother, not sure what he was getting at. He thought he knew something, and was getting ready to make his move.

"It's Abernathy. What of it?"

"I can see why you didn't put it together before tonight, Trav, but now you don't have an excuse," Thomas said, smug.

"What the fuck are you talking about?" I asked.

"Are you related to Mick Abernathy by any chance?" Thomas asked.

All heads turned to wait for Abby's response.

She raked her hair back with her fingers, clearly nervous. "How do you know Mick?"

My neck craned even more in her direction. "He's only one of the best poker players that ever lived. Do you know him?"

"He's my father," she said. It looked almost painful for her to answer.

The entire room exploded.

"NO FUCKING WAY!"

"I KNEW IT!"

"WE JUST PLAYED MICK ABERNATHY'S DAUGHTER!"

"MICK ABERNATHY? HOLY SHIT!"

The words rang in my ears, but it still took me several seconds to process. Three of my brothers were jumping up and down and screaming, but to me the entire room was frozen, and the world silent.

My girlfriend, who also happened to be my best friend, was the daughter of a poker legend—someone my brothers, father, and even my grandfather idolized.

Abby's voice brought me back to the present. "I told you guys I shouldn't play."

"If you would have mentioned you were Mick Abernathy's daughter, I think we would have taken you more seriously," Thomas said.

Abby peeked over at me from under her lashes, waiting for a reaction.

"You're Lucky Thirteen?" I asked, dumbfounded.

Trenton stood and pointed. "Lucky Thirteen is in our house! No way! I don't fucking believe it!"

"That was the nickname the papers gave me. And the story wasn't exactly accurate," Abby said, fidgeting.

Even amid the booming commotion from my brothers, the only thing I could think about was how fucking hot it was that the girl I'm in love with was practically a celebrity. Even better, she was famous for something outrageously badass.

"I need to get Abby home, guys," I said.

Dad peered at Abby over his glasses. "Why wasn't it accurate?"

"I didn't take my dad's luck. I mean, how ridiculous." She chuckled, twisting her hair nervously around her finger.

Thomas shook his head. "No, Mick gave that interview. He said at midnight on your thirteenth birthday his luck ran dry."

"And yours picked up," I added.

"You were raised by mobsters!" Trent said, smiling with excitement.

"Uh . . . no." She laughed once. "They didn't raise me. They were just . . . around a lot."

"That was a damn shame, Mick running your name through the mud like that in all the papers. You were just a kid," Dad said, shaking his head.

"If anything it was beginner's luck," Abby said.

I could tell by the look on her face she was bordering on feeling mortification from all of the attention.

"You were taught by Mick Abernathy," Dad said, shaking his head in awe. "You were playing pros, and winning, at thirteen years old for Christ's sakes." He looked at me and smiled. "Don't bet against her, son. She doesn't lose."

My mind instantly returned to the fight when Abby bet against me, knowing she would lose, and have to live with me for a month if she did. All that time I thought she didn't care about me, and just then I realized it couldn't have been true.

"Uh . . . we gotta go, Dad. Bye, guys."

I raced through the streets, weaving in and out of traffic.

The faster the needle inched up on the speedometer, the tighter Abby's thighs clamped, making me even more eager to reach the apartment.

Abby didn't say a word when I parked the Harley and led her upstairs, and still wasn't speaking when I helped her with her jacket.

She let her hair down, and I stood, watching her in awe. It was almost like she was a different person, and I couldn't wait to get my hands on her.

"I know you're mad," she said, her eyes to the floor. "I'm sorry I didn't tell you, but it's not something I talk about."

Her words stunned me. "Mad at you? I am so turned on I can't see straight. You just robbed my asshole brothers of their money without batting an eyelash, you have achieved legend status with my father, and I know for a fact that you purposely lost that bet we made before my fight."

"I wouldn't say that . . ."

"Did you think you were going to win?"

"Well . . . no, not exactly," she said, pulling off her heels.

I could barely contain the smile that inched across my face. "So you *wanted* to be here with me. I think I just fell in love with you all over again."

Abby kicked her heels into the closet. "How are you not mad right now?"

I sighed. Maybe I should've been mad. But I just . . . wasn't. "That's pretty big, Pidge. You should have told me. But I understand why you didn't. You came here to get away from all of that. It's like the sky opened up. Everything makes sense, now."

"Well, that's a relief."

"Lucky Thirteen," I said, grabbing the hem of her shirt and pulling it over her head.

"Don't call me that, Travis. It's not a good thing."

"You're fucking famous, Pigeon!" I unbuttoned her jeans and pulled them down around her ankles, helping her to step out of them.

"My father *hated* me after that. He still blames me for all his problems."

I yanked off my shirt and hugged her to me, impatient to feel her skin against mine. "I still can't believe the daughter of Mick Abernathy is standing in front of me, and I've been with you this whole time and had no idea."

She pushed me away. "I'm not *Mick Abernathy's daughter*, Travis! That's what I left behind. I'm Abby. *Just* Abby!" she said, walking over to the closet. She yanked a T-shirt off its hanger and pulled it over her head.

"I'm sorry. I'm a little starstruck."

"It's just me!" She held the palm of her hand to her chest, an edge of desperation in her voice.

"Yeah, but . . ."

"But *nothing*. The way you're looking at me right now? This is exactly why I didn't tell you." She closed her eyes. "I won't live like that anymore, Trav. Not even with you."

"Whoa! Calm down, Pigeon. Let's not get carried away." I took her in my arms, suddenly worried where the conversation was going. "I don't care what you were or what you're not anymore. I just want you."

"I guess we have that in common, then."

I pulled her gently to the bed, and then snuggled next to her, taking in the faint smell of cigar mixed with her shampoo. "It's just you and me against the world, Pidge."

She curled up beside me, seeming satisfied with my words. When she relaxed against my chest, she sighed.

"What's wrong?" I asked.

"I don't want anyone to know, Trav. I didn't want *you* to know."

"I love you, Abby. I won't mention it again, okay? Your secret's safe with me," I said, pressing my lips gently against her temple.

She nuzzled her cheek against my skin, and I pulled her tight. The night's events seemed like a dream. The first time I bring a girl home, and not only is she the daughter of a famous poker player, but she could also easily bankrupt us all in a single hand. For being the family fuckup, I felt like I had finally gained a little respect from my older brothers. And it was all because of Abby.

I lie in bed awake, unable to stop my mind long enough to doze off. Abby's breathing had evened out half an hour before.

My cell lit up and buzzed just once, signaling a text message. I opened it up, and immediately frowned. The sender's name scrolled across: Jason Brazil.

Dude. Parker's talkin smack.

Very carefully, I pulled my arm out from under Abby's head to use both hands to type a message back.

Says who?

Says me hes sittin right here.

Oh yeah? Whats he sayin?

Its about Pigeon. U sure u wanna know?

Dont b a dick.

He sd shes still calling him.

Negative.

Sd earlier hes waiting 4 u to screw up, and shes just waitin for a good time to kick u 2 the curb.

Did he now?

Sd just now that she told him the other day she was really unhappy but u were kinda crazy and she was worried about when to do it.

If she wasnt laying next to me id come over there n beat his fkn ass

Not worth it. We all know hes full of shit.

Still pisses me off

I heard that. Don't worry about the douche canoe. U got ur girl next 2 u.

Had Abby not been sleeping beside me, I would have jumped on my bike and went straight to the Sig Tau house and shoved my fist through Parker's five-thousand-dollar grill. Maybe taken a bat to his Porsche.

Half an hour passed before the rage shakes finally began to subside. Abby hadn't moved. That same subtle noise that she made with her nose when she slept helped to slow my heart rate, and before long I was able to take her back into my arms and relax.

Abby wasn't calling Parker. If she was unhappy, she would have told me. I took a deep breath and watched the shadow of the tree outside dance against the wall.

"HE DIDN'T," SHEPLEY SAID, STOPPING MIDSTEP.

The girls left us at the apartment alone so they could shop for a dress for the date party, so I talked Shepley into driving us to the local furniture store.

"He sure as shit did." I turned my phone for Shepley to see. "Brazil texted me last night and ratted his ass out."

Shepley sighed and shook his head. "He had to know that would get back to you. I mean . . . how could it not? Those guys are bigger gossips than the girls."

I stopped, seeing a couch that caught my eye. "I bet that's why he did it. Hoping it would get back to me."

Shepley nodded. "Let's face it. The old you would have gone into a jealous rage and scared her right into Parker's arms."

"Bastard," I said as a salesman approached.

"Good morning, gentleman. Can I help you find something in particular?"

Shepley threw himself onto the couch, and then bounced a few times before nodding his head. "I approve."

"Yeah. I'll take this one," I said.

"You'll take it?" he said, a little surprised.

"Yeah," I said, a little surprised myself at his reaction. "Do you deliver?"

"Yes, sir, we do. Would you like to know the price?"

"It says right here, doesn't it?"

"Yes."

"So, I'll take it. Where do I pay?"

"Right this way, sir."

The salesman tried unsuccessfully to talk me into some more items that matched the couch, but I had a few more things to buy that day.

Shepley gave them our address, and the salesman thanked me for being the easiest sale of the year.

"Where are we going now?" he asked, trying to keep pace with me to the Charger.

"Calvin's."

"You getting new ink?"

"Yep."

Shepley watched me, wary. "What are you doing, Trav?"

"What I always said I would do if I met the right girl."

Shepley stepped in front of the passenger door. "I'm not sure this is a good idea. Don't you think you should discuss it with Abby first . . . you know, so she doesn't freak out?"

I frowned. "She might say no."

"It's better she says no than you do it and she runs out of the apartment because you scared her off. Things have been going good between you two. Why don't you just let it ride for a while?"

I cupped my hands on Shepley's shoulders. "That doesn't sound like me at all," I said, and then moved him aside.

Shepley jogged around the front of the Charger, and then slid into the driver's seat. "I'm still taking the official position that this is a bad idea."

"Noted."

"Then where?"

"Steiner's."

"The jewelry store?"

"Yep."

"Why, Travis?" Shepley said, his voice more stern than before.

"You'll see."

He shook his head. "Are you *trying* to run her off?"

"It's going to happen, Shep. I just want to have it. For when the time is right."

"No time anytime soon is right. I am so in love with America that it drives me crazy sometimes, but we're not old enough for that shit, yet, Travis. And . . . what if she says no?"

My teeth clenched at the thought. "I won't ask her until I know she's ready."

Shepley's mouth pulled to the side. "Just when I think you can't get any more insane, you do something else to remind me that you are far beyond bat shit crazy."

"Wait until you see the rock I'm getting."

Shepley craned his neck slowly in my direction. "You've already been over there shopping, haven't you?"

I smiled.

CHAPTER NINETEEN

Daddy's Home

FRIDAY. THE DAY OF THE DATE PARTY, THREE DAYS after Abby smiled about the new couch and then minutes later turned to whiskey over my tats.

The girls were gone doing what girls do on the day of date parties, and I was sitting in front of the apartment, on the steps, waiting for Toto to take a dump.

For reasons I couldn't pinpoint, my nerves were shot. I'd already taken a couple swigs of whiskey to try to settle my ass down, but it was no use.

I stared at my wrist, hoping whatever ominous feeling I had was just a false alarm. As I started to tell Toto to hurry up because it was fucking cold outside, he hunched over and did his business.

"It's about time, little man!" I said, scooping him up and walking inside.

"Just called the florist. Well, florists. The first one didn't have enough," Shepley said.

I smiled. "The girls are going to shit. Did you make sure they would deliver before they get home?"

"Yeah."

"What if they come home early?"

"They'll be here in plenty of time."

I nodded.

"Hey," Shepley said with a half smile. "You nervous about tonight?"

"No," I said, frowning.

"You are, too, you pussy! You're nervous about date night!"

"Don't be a dick," I said, retreating to my room.

My black shirt was already pressed and waiting on its hanger. It wasn't anything special—one of two button-down shirts that I owned.

The date party would be my first, yes, and I was going with my girlfriend for the first time, but the knot in my stomach was from something else. Something I couldn't quite put my finger on. As if something terrible was lurking in the immediate future.

On edge, I went back into the kitchen and poured another shot of whiskey. The doorbell rang, and I looked up from the counter to see Shepley jogging across the living room from his room, a towel around his waist.

"I could've gotten it."

"Yeah, but then you would have had to stop crying in your Jim Beam," he grumbled, pulling on the door. A small man carrying two mammoth bouquets bigger than he was stood in the doorway.

"Uh, yeah . . . this way, buddy," Shepley said, opening the door wider.

Ten minutes later, the apartment was beginning to look the way I'd imagined. The thought of getting Abby flowers before the date party had come to mind, but one bouquet wasn't enough.

Just as one delivery guy left, another arrived, and then another. Once every surface in the apartment proudly displayed at least two or three ostentatious bouquets of red, pink, yellow, and white roses, Shepley and I were satisfied.

I took a quick shower, shaved, and was slipping on a pair of jeans as the Honda's engine whirred loudly in the parking lot. A few moments after it shut off, America pushed through the front door, and then Abby. Their reaction to the flowers was immediate, and Shepley and I were grinning like idiots as they squealed in delight.

Shepley looked around the room, standing proud. "We went to buy you two flowers, but neither of us thought just one bouquet would do it."

Abby wrapped her arms around my neck. "You guys are . . . you're amazing. Thank you."

I smacked her ass, letting my palm linger on the gentle curve just above her upper thigh. "Thirty minutes until the party, Pidge."

The girls dressed in Shepley's room while we waited. It took me all of five minutes to button up my shirt, find a belt, and slip on socks and shoes. The girls, however, took for fucking ever.

Shepley, impatient, knocked on the door. The party had started fifteen minutes earlier.

"Time to go, ladies," Shepley said.

America walked out in a dress that looked like a second skin, and Shepley whistled, sparking an instant smile on her face.

"Where is she?" I asked.

"Abby's having some trouble with her shoe. She'll be out in just a sec," America explained.

"The suspense is killin' me, Pigeon!" I called.

The door squeaked, and out walked Abby, fidgeting with her short, white dress. Her hair was swept to one side, and even though her tits were carefully hidden, they were accentuated by the tight-fitting fabric.

America elbowed me, and I blinked. "Holy shit."

"Are you ready to be freaked out?" America asked.

"I'm not freaked out—she looks amazing."

Abby smiled with mischief in her eyes, and then slowly turned around to show the steep dip of the fabric in the back.

"Okay, now I'm freakin' out," I said, walking over to her and turning her away from Shepley's eyes.

"You don't like it?" she asked.

"You need a jacket." I jogged to the rack and hastily draped Abby's coat over her shoulders.

"She can't wear that all night, Trav." America chuckled.

"You look beautiful, Abby," Shepley said, trying to apologize for my behavior.

"You do," I said, desperate to be heard and understood without causing a fight. "You look incredible . . . but you can't wear that. Your skirt is . . . wow, your legs are . . . your skirt is too short and it's only half a dress! It doesn't even have a back on it!"

"That's the way it's made, Travis." Abby smiled. At least she wasn't pissed.

"Do you two live to torture each other?" Shepley frowned.

"Do you have a longer dress?" I asked.

Abby looked down. "It's actually pretty modest in the front. It's just the back that shows off a lot of skin."

"Pigeon," I said, wincing, "I don't want you to be mad, but I can't take you to my frat house looking like that. I'll get in a fight the first five minutes."

She leaned up and kissed my lips. "I have faith in you."

"This night is gonna suck," I groaned.

"This night is going to be fantastic," America said, offended.

"Just think of how easy it will be to get it off later," Abby said. She pushed up on the balls of her feet to kiss my neck.

I stared up at the ceiling, trying not to let her lips, sticky from her lip gloss, weaken my case. "That's the problem. Every other guy there will be thinking the same thing."

"But you're the only one that gets to find out," she lilted. When I didn't respond, she leaned back to look me in the eyes. "Do you really want me to change?"

I scanned her face, and every other part of her, and then exhaled. "No matter what you wear, you're gorgeous. I should just get used to it, now, right?" Abby shrugged, and I shook my head. "All right, we're already late. Let's go."

I KEPT MY ARMS AROUND ABBY AS WE WALKED ACROSS the lawn to the Sigma Tau house. Abby was shivering, so I walked quickly and awkwardly with her in tow, trying to get her out of the cold as fast as her high heels would allow. The second we pushed through the thick, double doors, I immediately popped a cigarette in my mouth to add to the typical frat party haze. The bass from the speakers downstairs buzzed like a heartbeat under our feet.

After Shepley and I took care of the girls' coats, I led Abby to the kitchen, with Shepley and America just behind. We stood there, beers in hand, listening to Jay Gruber and Brad Pierce discuss my last fight. Lexie pawed at Brad's shirt, clearly bored with the man talk.

"Dude, you got your girl's name on your wrist? What in the hell possessed you to do that?" Brad said.

I turned over my hand to reveal Abby's nickname. "I'm crazy about her," I said, looking down at Abby.

"You barely know her," Lexie scoffed.

"I know her."

In my peripheral vision, I saw Shepley pull America toward the stairs, so I took Abby's hand and followed. Unfortunately, Brad and Lexie did the same. In a line, we descended the stairs to the basement, the music growing louder with each step.

The second my feet hit the last stair, the DJ played a slow song. Without hesitation, I pulled Abby onto the concrete dance floor, lined with furniture that had been pushed to the side for the party.

Abby's head fit perfectly in the crook of my neck. "I'm glad I never went to one of these things before," I said in her ear. "It's right that I've only brought you."

Abby pressed her cheek against my chest, and her fingers pressed into my shoulders.

"Everyone's staring at you in this dress," I said. "I guess it's kinda cool . . . being with the girl everyone wants."

Abby leaned back to make a show of rolling her eyes. "They don't want me. They're curious why *you* want me. And anyway, I feel sorry for anyone that thinks they have a chance. I am hopelessly and completely in love with you."

How could she even wonder? "You know why I want you? I didn't know I was lost until you found me. I didn't know what alone was until the first night I spent without you in my bed. You're the one thing I've got right. You're what I've been waiting for, Pigeon."

Abby reached up to take my face between her hands, and I wrapped my arms around her, lifting her off the floor. Our lips pressed together gently, and as she worked her lips against mine, I made sure to silently communicate how much I loved her in that kiss, because I could never get it right with just words.

After a few songs and one hostile, yet entertaining moment between Lexie and America, I decided it was a good time to head upstairs. "C'mon, Pidge. I need a smoke."

Abby followed me up the stairs. I made sure to grab her coat before continuing to the balcony. The second we stepped outside, I paused, as did Abby, and Parker, and the makeup-spackled girl he was fingering.

The first move was made by Parker, who pulled his hand from underneath the girl's skirt.

"Abby," he said, surprised and breathless.

"Hey, Parker," Abby replied, choking back a laugh.

"How, uh . . . how have you been?"

She smiled politely. "I've been great, you?"

"Uh"—he looked at his date—"Abby this is Amber. Amber . . . Abby."

"*Abby* Abby?" she asked.

Parker gave one quick, uncomfortable nod. Amber shook Abby's hand with a disgusted look on her face, and then eyed me as if she had just encountered the enemy. "Nice to meet you . . . I guess."

"Amber," Parker warned.

I laughed once, and then opened the doors for them to walk through. Parker grabbed Amber's hand and retreated into the house.

"That was . . . awkward," Abby said, shaking her head and folding arms around her. She looked over the edge at the few couples braving the winter wind.

"At least he's moved on from trying his damndest to get you back," I said, smiling.

"I don't think he was trying to get me back so much as trying to keep me away from you."

"He took *one* girl home for me *once*. Now he acts like he's made a habit of swooping in and saving every freshman I bagged."

Abby shot me a wry look from the corner of her eye. "Did I ever tell you how much I *loathe* that word?"

"Sorry," I said, pulling her into my side. I lit a cigarette and took a deep breath, turning over my hand. The delicate but thick black lines of ink weaved together to form *Pigeon*. "How weird is it that this tat isn't just my new favorite, but it makes me feel at ease to know it's there?"

"Pretty weird," Abby said. I shot her a look, and she laughed. "I'm kidding. I can't say I understand it, but it's sweet . . . in a Travis Maddox sort of way."

"If it feels this good to have this on my arm, I can't imagine how it's going to feel to get a ring on your finger."

"Travis . . ."

"In four, or maybe five years," I said, inwardly cringing that I went that far.

Abby took a breath. "We need to slow down. Way, way down."

"Don't start this, Pidge."

"If we keep going at this pace, I'm going to be barefoot and pregnant before I graduate. I'm not ready to move in with you, I'm not ready for a ring, and I'm certainly not ready to settle down."

I gently cupped her shoulders. "This isn't the 'I wanna see other people' speech, is it? Because I'm not sharing you. No fucking way."

"I don't want anyone else," she said, exasperated.

I relaxed and released her shoulders, turning to grip the railing. "What are you saying, then?" I asked, terrified of her answer.

"I'm saying we need to slow down. That's *all* I'm saying."

I nodded, unhappy.

Abby reached for my arm. "Don't be mad."

"It seems like we take one step forward and two steps back, Pidge. Every time I think we're on the same page, you put up a wall. I don't get it . . . most girls are hounding their boyfriends to get serious, to talk about their feelings, to take the next step . . ."

"I thought we established that I'm not *most girls*?"

I dropped my head, frustrated. "I'm tired of guessing. Where do you see this going, Abby?"

She pressed her lips against my shirt. "When I think about my future, I see you."

I hugged her to my side, every muscle in my body immediately relaxing with her words. We both watched the night clouds move across the starless, black sky. The laughter and humming of the voices below sparked a smile across Abby's face. I watched the same partygoers she did, huddling together and rushing into the house from the street.

For the first time that day, the ominous feeling hovering over me began to fade away.

"Abby! There you are! I've been looking all over for you!" America said, bursting through the door. She held up her cell phone. "I just got off the phone with my dad. Mick called them last night."

Abby's nose wrinkled. "Mick? Why would he call them?"

America raised her eyebrows. "Your mother kept hanging up on him."

"What did he want?"

America pressed her lips together. "To know where you were."

"They didn't tell him, did they?"

America's face fell. "He's your father, Abby. Dad felt he had a right to know."

"He's going to come here," Abby said, her voice swelling with panic. "He's going to come here, Mare!"

"I know! I'm sorry!" America said, trying to comfort her friend. Abby pulled away from her and covered her face with her hands.

I wasn't sure what the hell was going on, but I touched Abby's shoulders. "He won't hurt you, Pigeon," I said. "I won't let him."

"He'll find a way," America said, watching Abby with heavy eyes. "He always does."

"I have to get out of here." Abby pulled her coat tight, and then pulled at the handles of the French doors. She was too upset to slow down long enough to first push down the handles before pulling the doors. As tears fell down her cheeks, I covered her hands with mine. After helping her open the doors, Abby looked at me. I wasn't sure if her cheeks were flush with embarrassment or from the cold, but all I wanted was to make it go away.

I took Abby under my arm, and together we went through

the house, down the stairs and through the crowd to the front door. Abby moved quickly, desperate to get to the safety of the apartment. I had only heard about Mick Abernathy's accolades as a poker player from my father. Watching Abby run like a frightened little girl made me hate any time my family wasted being in awe of him.

Midstep, America's hand shot out and grabbed Abby's coat. "Abby!" she whispered, pointing to a small group of people.

They were crowded around an older, slovenly man, unshaven and dirty to the point where he looked like he smelled. He was pointing to the house, holding a small picture. The couples were nodding, discussing the photo among themselves.

Abby stormed over to the man and pulled the photo from his hands. "*What* in the *hell* are you doing here?"

I looked down at the picture in her hand. She couldn't have been more than fifteen, scrawny, with mousy hair and sunken eyes. She must have been miserable. No wonder she wanted to get away.

The three couples around him backed away. I glanced back at their stunned faces, and then waited for the man to answer. It was Mick fucking Abernathy. I recognized him by the unmistakable sharp eyes nestled in that dirty face.

Shepley and America stood on each side of Abby. I cupped her shoulders from behind.

Mick looked at Abby's dress and clicked his tongue in disapproval. "Well, well, Cookie. You can take the girl out of Vegas—"

"Shut up. Shut up, Mick. Just turn around," she pointed behind him, "and go back to wherever you came from. I don't want you here."

"I can't, Cookie. I need your help."

"What else is new?" America sneered.

Mick narrowed his eyes at America, and then returned his attention to his daughter. "You look awful pretty. You've grown up. I wouldn't've recognized you on the street."

Abby sighed. "What do you want?"

He held up his hands and shrugged. "I seemed to have gotten myself in a pickle, kiddo. Old Dad needs some money."

Abby's entire body tensed. "How much?"

"I was doing good, I really was. I just had to borrow a bit to get ahead and . . . you know."

"I know," she snapped. "How much do you need?"

"Twenty-five."

"Well, shit, Mick, twenty-five hundred? If you'll get the hell outta here . . . I'll give that to you now," I said, pulling out my wallet.

"He means twenty-five thousand," Abby said, her voice cold.

Mick's eyes rolled over me, from my face to my shoes. "Who's this clown?"

My eyebrows shot up from my wallet, and instinctively, I leaned in toward my prey. The only thing stopping me was feeling Abby's small frame between us, and knowing that this skeevy little man was her father. "I can see, now, why a smart guy like yourself has been reduced to asking your teenage daughter for an allowance."

Before Mick could speak, Abby pulled out her cell phone. "Who do you owe this time, Mick?"

Mick scratched his greasy, graying hair. "Well, it's a funny story, Cookie—"

"*Who?*" Abby shouted.

"Benny."

Abby leaned into me. "Benny? You owe *Benny*? What in the

hell were you . . ." She paused. "I don't have that kind of money, Mick."

He smiled. "Something tells me you do."

"Well, I don't! You've really done it this time, haven't you? I knew you wouldn't stop until you got yourself killed!"

He shifted; the smug grin on his face had vanished. "How much ya got?"

"Eleven thousand. I was saving for a car."

America's eyes darted in Abby's direction. "Where did you get eleven thousand dollars, Abby?"

"Travis's fights."

I tugged on her shoulders until she looked at me. "You made *eleven thousand* off my fights? When were you betting?"

"Adam and I had an understanding," she said casually.

Mick's eyes were suddenly animated. "You can double that in a weekend, Cookie. You could get me the twenty-five by Sunday, and Benny won't send his thugs for me."

"It'll clean me out, Mick. I have to pay for school," Abby said, a tinge of sadness in her voice.

"Oh, you can make it back in no time," he said, waving his hand dismissively.

"When is your deadline?" Abby asked.

"Monday mornin'. Midnight," he said, unapologetically.

"You don't have to give him a fucking dime, Pigeon," I said.

Mick grabbed Abby's wrist. "It's the least you could do! I wouldn't be in this mess if it weren't for you!"

America slapped his hand away and then shoved him. "Don't you dare start that shit again, Mick! She didn't make you borrow money from Benny!"

Mick glared at Abby. The light of hatred in his eyes made any connection with her as his daughter disappear. "If it weren't for her, I woulda had my own money. You took everything from me, Abby. I have nothin'!"

Abby choked back a cry. "I'll get your money to Benny by Sunday. But when I do, I want you to leave me the *hell* alone. I won't do this again, Mick. From now on, you're on your own, do you hear me? Stay. Away."

He pressed his lips together and then nodded. "Have it your way, Cookie."

Abby turned around and headed for the car.

America sighed. "Pack your bags, boys. We're going to Vegas." She walked toward the Charger, and Shepley and I stood, frozen.

"Wait. What?" He looked to me. "Like Las Vegas, Vegas? As in Nevada?"

"Looks that way," I said, shoving my hands in my pockets.

"We're just going to book a flight to Vegas," Shepley said, still trying to process the situation.

"Yep."

Shepley walked over to open America's door to let her and Abby in on the passenger side, and then slammed it shut, blank faced. "I've never been to Vegas."

An impish grin pulled one side of my mouth to the side. "Looks like it's time to pop that cherry."

CHAPTER TWENTY

You Win Some, You Lose Some

ABBY BARELY SPOKE WHILE WE PACKED, AND EVEN LESS on the way to the airport. She stared off into space most of the time unless one of us asked her a question. I wasn't sure if she was drowning in despair, or just focused on the looming challenge ahead.

Checking in to the hotel, America did all the talking, flashing her fake ID, as if she had done it a thousand times before.

It occurred to me, then, that she probably *had* done it before. Vegas was where they had procured such flawless IDs, and why America never seemed to worry about what Abby could handle. They'd seen it all before, in the bowels of the city of sin.

Shepley was an unmistakable tourist, his head leaned back, gawking at the ostentatious ceiling. We pulled our luggage into the elevator, and I pulled Abby to my side.

"You okay?" I asked, touching my lips to her temple.

"I don't want to be here," she choked out.

The doors opened, revealing the intricate pattern of the rug that lined the hallway. America and Shepley went one way, Abby and I the other. Our room was at the end of the hall.

Abby shoved the card key into the slot, and then pushed open the door. The room was large, dwarfing the king-size bed in the middle of the room.

I left the suitcase against the wall, pressing all the switches until the thicker curtain separated to reveal the busy, blinking lights and traffic of the Las Vegas Strip. Another button pulled away a second set of sheer curtains.

Abby didn't pay attention to the window. She didn't even bother to look up. The glitter and gold had lost its luster for her years before.

I set our carry-on bags on the floor and looked around the room. "This is nice, right?" Abby glared at me. "What?"

She opened her suitcase in one motion, and shook her head. "This isn't a vacation, Travis. You shouldn't be here."

In two steps, I was behind her, crossing my arms around her middle. She was different here, but I wasn't. I could still be someone she could count on, someone who could protect her from the ghosts of her past.

"I go where you go," I said against her ear.

She leaned her head back against my chest and sighed. "I have to get on the floor. You can stay here or check out the Strip. I'll see you later, okay?"

"I'm going with you."

She turned to face me. "I don't want you there, Trav."

I didn't expect that from her, especially not the cold tone of her voice.

Abby touched my arm. "If I'm going to win fourteen thousand dollars in one weekend, I have to concentrate. I don't like who I'm going to be while I'm at those tables, and I don't want you to see it, okay?"

I brushed her hair from her eyes, and then kissed her cheek. "Okay, Pidge." I couldn't pretend to understand what she meant, but I would respect it.

America knocked on the door and then traipsed in wearing the same nude number she wore to the date party. Her heels were sky high, and she had put on two extra layers of makeup. She looked ten years older.

I waved to America, and then grabbed the extra card key off the table. America was already building Abby up for her night, reminding me of a trainer offering a pep talk to his fighter before a big boxing match.

Shepley was standing in the hall, staring at three trays of half-eaten food on the floor left there by guests across the hall.

"What do you want to do first?" I asked.

"I'm definitely not marrying you."

"You're fucking hilarious. Let's go downstairs."

The elevator door opened, and the hotel came alive. It was like the hallways were the veins, and the people were its lifeblood. Groups of women dressed like porn stars, families, foreigners, the occasional bachelor party, and hotel employees followed each other in organized chaos.

It took a while to get past the stores that lined the exits and reach the boulevard, but we broke out onto the street and walked until we saw a crowd gathered in front of one of the casinos. The fountains were on, performing to some patriotic song. Shepley was mesmerized, seemingly unable to move while he watched the water dance and spray.

We must have caught the last the two minutes, because the lights soon dimmed, the water fizzled, and the crowd immediately dispersed.

"What was that about?" I asked.

Shepley still stared at the now calm pond. "I don't know, but it was cool."

The streets were lined with Elvis, Michael Jackson, showgirls, and cartoon characters, all readily available to take a picture for a price. At one point, I kept hearing a flapping noise, and then I pinpointed where it was coming from. Men were standing on the sidewalk, snapping a stack of cards in their hands. They handed one to Shepley. It was a picture of a ridiculously big-breasted woman in a seductive pose. They were selling hookers and strip clubs. Shepley tossed the card to the ground. The sidewalk was covered in them.

A girl walked past, eyeing me with a drunken smile. She carried her heels in her hand. As she ambled by, I noticed her blackened feet. The ground was filthy, the foundation for the glitz and glamour above.

"We're saved," Shepley said, walking over to a street vendor selling Red Bull and whatever liquor you could imagine. Shepley ordered two with vodka, and smiled when he took his first sip. "I may never wanna leave."

I checked the time on my cell phone. "It's been an hour. Let's head back."

"Do you remember where we were? Because I don't."

"Yeah. This way."

We retraced our steps. I was glad when we finally ended up

at our hotel, because in truth I wasn't exactly sure how to get back, either. The Strip wasn't hard to navigate, but there were a lot of distractions along the way, and Shepley was definitely in vacation mode.

I searched the poker tables for Abby, knowing that's where she would be. I caught a glimpse of her caramel hair; she sat upright and confident at a table full of old men, and America; the girls were a stark contrast from the rest of those camped out in the poker area.

Shepley waved me over to a blackjack table, and we played a while to pass the time.

Half an hour later, Shepley nudged my arm. Abby was standing, talking to a guy with olive skin and dark hair, in a suit and tie. He had her by the arm, and I immediately stood.

Shepley grabbed my shirt. "Hold up, Travis. He works here. Just give it a minute. You might get us all kicked out if you don't keep your head."

I watched them. He was smiling, but Abby was all business. He acknowledged America, then.

"They know him," I said, trying to read their lips to figure out the distant conversation. The only thing I could make out was *have dinner with me* from the douche in the suit, and Abby saying *I'm here with someone.*

Shepley couldn't hold me back this time, but I stopped a few feet away when I saw the suit kiss Abby's cheek.

"It was good to see you again. See you tomorrow . . . five o'clock all right? I'm on the floor at eight," he said.

My stomach sank, and my face felt like it was on fire. America tugged on Abby's arm, noting my presence.

"Who was that?" I asked.

Abby nodded in the suit's direction. "That is Jesse Viveros. I've known him a long time."

"How long?"

She glanced back at her empty chair at the poker table. "Travis, I don't have time for this."

"I guess he chucked the youth minister idea," America said, sending a flirtatious grin in Jesse's direction.

"That's your ex-boyfriend?" I asked, instantly angry. "I thought you said he was from Kansas?"

Abby shot America an impatient glare, and then took my chin in her hand. "He knows I'm not old enough to be in here, Trav. He gave me until midnight. I will explain everything later, but for now I have to get back to the game, all right?"

My teeth clenched, and I closed my eyes. My girlfriend had just agreed to go out with her ex-boyfriend. Everything inside me wanted to throw a typical Maddox tantrum, but Abby needed me to man up for the moment. Acting against my instincts, I decided to let it go, and leaned down to kiss her. "All right. I'll see you at midnight. Good luck."

I turned, pushing my way through the crowd, hearing Abby's voice surge at least two octaves. "Gentlemen?"

It reminded me of those girls who would talk like children when they tried to get my attention, hoping to come across as innocent.

"I don't understand why she had to make any deals with that Jesse guy," I growled.

"So she could stay, I guess?" Shepley asked, staring up at the ceiling again.

"There are other casinos. We can just go to another one."

"She knows people here, Travis. She probably came here because she knew if she got caught, they wouldn't rat her out to the cops. She has a fake ID, but I bet it wouldn't take long for security to recognize her. These casinos pay high dollar for people to point out the hustlers, right?"

"I guess," I said, frowning.

We met Abby and America at the table, watching as America gathered Abby's winnings.

Abby looked at her watch. "I need more time."

"Wanna try the blackjack tables?"

"I can't lose money, Trav."

I smiled. "You can't lose, Pidge."

America shook her head. "Blackjack's not her game."

"I won a little," I said, digging in my pockets. "I'm up six hundred. You can have it."

Shepley handed Abby his chips. "I only made three. It's yours."

Abby sighed. "Thanks, guys, but I'm still short five grand." She looked at her watch again and then looked up to see Jesse approaching.

"How did you do?" he asked, smiling.

"I'm five K short, Jess. I need more time."

"I've done all I can, Abby."

"Thanks for letting me stay."

Jesse offered an uncomfortable smile. He was obviously just as scared of these people as Abby. "Maybe I can get my dad to talk to Benny for you?"

"It's Mick's mess. I'm going to ask him for an extension."

Jesse shook his head. "You know that's not going to happen, Cookie, no matter how much you come up with. If it's less than what he owes, Benny's going to send someone. You stay as far away from him as you can."

"I have to try," Abby said, her voice broken.

Jesse took a step forward, leaning in to keep his voice low. "Get on a plane, Abby. You hear me?"

"I hear you," she snapped.

Jesse sighed, and his eyes grew heavy with sympathy. He wrapped his arms around Abby and then kissed her hair. "I'm sorry. If my job wasn't at stake, you know I'd try to figure something out."

The hairs on the back of my neck stood on end, something that only happened when I felt threatened and was about to unleash my full wrath on someone.

Just before I tackled him, Abby pulled away.

"I know," she said. "You did what you could."

Jesse lifted her chin with his finger. "I'll see you tomorrow at five." He bent down to kiss the corner of her mouth, and then walked away.

It was then that I noticed my body was leaning forward, and Shepley was once again gripping my shirt, his knuckles white.

Abby's eyes were stuck to the floor.

"What's at five?" I seethed.

"She agreed to dinner if Jesse would let her stay. She didn't have a choice, Trav," America said.

Abby peered up at me with her big, apologetic eyes.

"You had a choice," I said.

"Have you ever dealt with the Mob, Travis? I'm sorry if your feelings are hurt, but a free meal with an old friend isn't a high price to pay to keep Mick alive."

I clamped my jaw closed, refusing to let it open for words to spill out that I would regret later.

"C'mon, you guys, we have to find Benny," America said, pulling Abby by the arm.

Shepley walked beside me as we followed the girls down the Strip to Benny's building. It was one block away from the bright lights, but it was somewhere the gold had never touched—and wasn't meant to. Abby paused, and then walked up a few steps to a large, green door. She knocked, and I held her other hand to keep it from trembling.

The doorman appeared in the open doorway. He was enormous—black, intimidating, and as wide as he was tall—with the stereotypical Vegas sleazeball standing next to him. Gold chains, suspicious eyes, and a gut from eating too much of his mother's cooking.

"Benny," Abby breathed.

"My, my . . . you're not Lucky Thirteen anymore, now, are ya? Mick didn't tell me what a looker you've grown into. I've been waiting for you, Cookie. I hear you have a payment for me."

Abby nodded, and Benny gestured to the rest of us. "They're with me," she said, her voice surprisingly strong.

"I'm afraid your companions will have to wait outside," the doorman said in an abnormally deep bass tone.

I took Abby by the arm, turning my shoulder in a protective stance. "She's not going in there alone. I'm coming with her."

Benny eyed me for a moment, and then smiled to his doorman. "Fair enough. Mick will be glad to know you have such a good friend with you."

We followed him inside. I kept a firm grip on Abby's arm, making sure to stand between her and the biggest threat—the doorman. We walked behind Benny, followed him into an elevator, and then traveled up four floors.

When the doors opened, a large mahogany desk came into view. Benny hobbled to his plush chair and sat down, gesturing for us to take the two empty seats facing his desk. I sat, but adrenaline was streaming through my veins, making me twitch and fidget. I could hear and see everything in the room, including the two thugs standing in the shadows behind Benny's desk.

Abby reached over to grab my hand, and I gave her a reassuring squeeze.

"Mick owes me twenty-five thousand. I trust you have the full amount," Benny said, scribbling something on a notepad.

"Actually," Abby paused, clearing her throat, "I'm five K short, Benny. But I have all day tomorrow to get that. And five thousand is no problem, right? You know I'm good for it."

"Abigail," Benny said, frowning, "You disappoint me. You know my rules better than that."

"P-please, Benny. I'm asking you to take the nineteen-nine, and I'll have the rest for you tomorrow."

Benny's beady eyes darted from Abby to me, and then back again. The thugs stepped out of their dark corners, and the hairs on the back of my neck were standing on end again.

"You know I don't take anything but the full amount. The fact that you're trying to hand me less tells me something. You know what it tells me? That you're not sure if you can get the full amount."

The thugs took another step forward. I took stock of their pockets and any shape under their clothing that screamed weapon. They both had some sort of knife, but I didn't see any guns. That didn't mean they didn't have one stuffed in a boot, but I doubted either one was as fast as me. If I needed to, I could get it away from them and get us the hell out of there.

"I can get your money, Benny," Abby giggled nervously. "I won eighty-nine hundred in six hours."

"So are you saying you'll bring me eighty-nine hundred in six more hours?" Benny smiled his devilish grin.

"The deadline isn't until midnight tomorrow," I said, glancing behind us and watching the approaching shadow men.

"W-what are you doing, Benny?" Abby asked, her posture rigid.

"Mick called me tonight. He said you're taking care of his debt."

"I'm doing him a favor. I don't owe you any money," she said sternly.

Benny leaned both of his fat, stubby elbows onto his desk. "I'm considering teaching Mick a lesson, and I'm curious just how lucky you are, kiddo."

Instinctively, I shot out of my chair, pulling Abby with me. I jerked her behind me, backing up toward the door.

"Josiah is outside the door, young man. Where exactly do you think you're going to escape to?"

"Travis," Abby warned.

There would be no more talking. If I let either of these goons past me, they would hurt Abby. I moved her behind me.

"I hope you know, Benny, that when I take out your men, I mean no disrespect. But I'm in love with this girl, and I can't let you hurt her."

Benny burst into a loud cackle. "I gotta hand it to you, son.

You've got the biggest balls of anyone that's come through those doors. I'll prepare you for what you're about to get. The rather large fella to your right is David, and if he can't take you out with his fists, he's going to use that knife in his holster. The man to your left is Dane, and he's my best fighter. He's got a fight tomorrow, as a matter of fact, and he's never lost. Mind you don't hurt your hands, Dane. I've got a lot of money riding on you."

Dane smiled at me with wild, amused eyes. "Yes, sir."

"Benny, stop! I can get you the money!" Abby cried.

"Oh no . . . this is going to get interesting very fast." Benny chuckled, settling back into his seat.

David rushed me. He was clumsy and slow, and before he even had a chance to reach for his knife, I incapacitated him, shoving his nose straight down into my knee. I then threw two punches into his rat face. Knowing this wasn't a basement fight, and that I was fighting to get me and Abby out alive, I put everything I had into each swing. It felt good, as if every bit of pent-up rage inside me was finally allowed an outlet. Two more punches and an elbow later, David was lying on the floor in a bloody heap.

Benny's head fell back, laughing hysterically and pounding his desk with the delight of a child watching Saturday morning cartoons. "Well, go on, Dane. He didn't scare you, did he?"

Dane approached me more carefully, with the focus and precision of a professional fighter. His fist flew at my face, but I stepped to the side, ramming my shoulder into him at full force. We stumbled back together, and fell onto Benny's desk.

Dane grabbed me with both arms, hurling me to the ground. He was faster than I had anticipated, but not fast enough. We scuffled on the floor for a moment while I bought time to get a good grip, but then Dane gained ground, positioning himself to get in a few punches on me while I was trapped beneath him on the floor.

I grabbed Dane's nuts and twisted. It shocked him and he cried out, pausing just long enough for me to get the upper hand. I kneeled over him, holding him by his long hair, loading punch after punch into the side of his head. Dane's face rammed into the front of Benny's desk with each blow, and then he scrambled to his feet, disoriented and bleeding.

I watched him for a moment, and then attacked again, letting my rage flow through me with every strike. Dane dodged once and landed his knuckles to my jaw.

He may have been a fighter, but Thomas hit a lot harder than he did. This was going to be cake.

I smiled and held up my index finger. "That's your one."

Benny's unrestrained laughter filled the room while I finished his goon off. My elbow landed in the center of Dane's face, knocking him out before he hit the ground.

"Amazing young man! Simply amazing!" Benny said, clapping with delight.

Immediately I grabbed for Abby, pulling her behind me when Josiah filled the doorway with his massive frame.

"Should I take care of this, sir?" Josiah asked. His voice was deep but innocent, as if he was just doing the only job he was good at, and didn't truly desire to hurt either of us.

"No! No, no . . . ," Benny said, still giddy with the impromptu performance. "What is your name?"

"Travis Maddox," I said between breaths. I wiped Dane's and David's blood off of my hands and onto my jeans.

"Travis Maddox, I believe you can help your little girlfriend out."

"How's that?" I puffed.

"Dane was supposed to fight tomorrow night. I had a lot of cash riding on him, and it doesn't look like Dane will be fit to win a fight anytime soon. I suggest you take his place, make my bankroll for me, and I'll forgive the remaining fifty-one hundred of Mick's debt."

I turned to Abby. "Pigeon?"

"Are you all right?" she asked, wiping the blood from my face. She bit her lip, her face crumpling around her mouth. Her eyes filled with tears.

"It's not my blood, baby. Don't cry."

Benny stood. "I'm a busy man, son. Pass or play?"

"I'll do it," I said. "Give me the when and where and I'll be there."

"You'll be fighting Brock McMann. He's no wallflower. He was barred from the UFC last year."

I knew the name. "Just tell me where I need to be."

Benny gave me the information, then a shark's grin spread across his face. "I like you, Travis. I think we'll be good friends."

"I doubt it," I said. I opened the door for Abby and sustained a protective stance beside her until we cleared the front door.

"Jesus Christ!" America cried upon seeing the splattered blood covering my clothing. "Are you guys okay?" She grabbed Abby's shoulders and scanned her face.

"I'm okay. Just another day at the office. For both of us," Abby said, wiping her eyes.

With her hand in mine, we rushed to the hotel, with Shepley and America close behind.

The only people that seemed to notice my blood-spattered clothes was the kid in the elevator.

Once we were all back in my and Abby's room, I stripped down and went into the bathroom to wash the sleaze off me.

"What in the hell happened in there?" Shepley finally asked.

I could hear their voices murmuring as I stood under the water, recalling the last hour. As scary as it was for Abby to be in such real danger, it felt fucking amazing to unleash on Benny's two goons David and Dane. It was like the best drug in existence.

I wondered if they had come to yet, or if Benny just had them dragged outside and left in the alley.

A strange calm came over me. Pummeling Benny's men was an outlet for every bit of anger and frustration that had accumulated over the years, and now I almost felt normal.

"I'm gonna kill him! I'm going to kill that sorry son of a bitch!" America shouted.

I shut off the shower and wrapped a towel around my waist.

"One of the guys I knocked out had a fight tomorrow night," I said to Shepley. "I'm taking his place and in return Benny will forgive the last five K Mick owes."

America stood up. "This is ridiculous! Why are we helping Mick, Abby? He threw you to the wolves! I'm going to *kill* him!"

"Not if I kill him first," I seethed.

"Get in line," Abby said.

Shepley shifted nervously. "So you're fighting tomorrow?"

I nodded once. "At a place called Zero's. Six o'clock. It's Brock McMann, Shep."

Shepley shook his head. "No way. No fucking way, Trav. The guy's a maniac!"

"Yeah," I said, "but he's not fighting for his girl, is he?" I took Abby in my arms, kissing the top of her hair. She was still trembling. "You okay, Pigeon?"

"This is wrong. This is wrong on so many levels. I don't know which one to talk you out of first."

"Did you not see me tonight? I'm going to be fine. I've seen Brock fight before. He's tough, but not unbeatable."

"I don't want you to do this, Trav."

"Well, I don't want you to go to dinner with your ex-boyfriend tomorrow night. I guess we both have to do something unpleasant to save your good-for-nothing father."

CHAPTER TWENTY-ONE

Slow Death

Shepley sat beside me on a bench in a small but well-lit room. It was the first time I wouldn't walk out into a basement for a staged fight. The audience would consist of the shadow people of Vegas: locals, mobsters, drug dealers, and their arm candy. The crowd outside was a dark army, exponentially louder, and far more thirsty for blood. I would be surrounded by a cage instead of people.

"I still don't think you should do this," America said from the other side of the room.

"Not now, baby," Shepley said. He was helping me wrap tape around my hands.

"Are you nervous?" she asked, uncharacteristically quiet.

"No. I'd be better if Pidge was here, though. Have you heard from her?"

"I'll text her. She'll be here."

"Did she love him?" I asked, wondering what their dinner conversation consisted of. He was obviously no preacher man now, and I wasn't sure what he expected in return for his favor.

"No," America said. "She never said so, anyway. They grew up together, Travis. He was the only person she could count on for a long time."

I wasn't sure if that made me feel better or worse. "Did she text you back yet?"

"Hey," Shepley said, smacking my cheek. "Hey! You have Brock McMann waiting for you. Your head needs to be in this one hundred percent. Quit being a pussy and focus!"

I nodded, trying to remember the few times I'd seen Brock fight. He'd been banned from the UFC for sucker punches and a rumor that he'd accosted the UFC president. It had been a while, but he was a notoriously dirty fighter and pulled blatantly illegal shit just out of sight of the ref. The key would be to not get in that position. If he locked his legs around me, it could go downhill pretty fast.

"You're gonna play this safe, Trav. Let him attack first. Kind of the same way you fought the night you were trying to win your bet with Abby. You're not fighting some varsity wrestling reject. This isn't the Circle, and you're not trying to create a show for the crowd."

"The hell if I'm not."

"You've gotta win, Travis. You're fighting for Abby, don't forget that."

I nodded. Shepley was right. If I lost, Benny wouldn't get his money, and Abby would still be in danger.

A tall, large man in a suit and greasy hair walked in. "You're up. Your trainer can join you on the outside of the cage, but the girls . . . where's the other girl?"

A lined formed between my eyebrows. "She's coming."

". . . they have reserved seats on the end of the second row on your corner."

Shepley turned back to America. "I'll walk you there." He looked to the suit. "Nobody touches her. I will fucking kill the first person that does."

The suit offered a ghost of a smile. "Benny already said no distractions. We'll have eyes on her at all times."

Shepley nodded, and then held out his hand for America. She took it, and they quietly followed me through the door.

The announcers amplified voice echoed through huge speakers placed at each corner of the vast room. It looked like a small concert hall, easily seating a thousand people, and they were all on their feet, either cheering or eyeing me suspiciously as I walked out.

The gate to the cage opened, and I stepped inside.

Shepley watched the suit seat America, and once he was satisfied that she was okay, turned to me. "Remember: play it smart. Let him attack first, and the goal is to win for Abby."

I nodded.

Seconds later, music blared from the speakers, and both the motion and volume from the stands exploded into a frenzy. Brock McMann emerged from a hallway as a spotlight in the rafters illuminated the severe expression on his face. He had an entourage that kept the spectators at bay while he bounced up and down to stay loose. I figured he'd probably been training for this fight for weeks if not months.

That was okay. I'd been beat up by my brothers my whole life. I'd had plenty of training.

I turned to check in with America. She shrugged, and I

frowned. The biggest fight of my life was minutes away, and Abby wasn't there. Just when I turned to watch Brock enter the cage, I heard Shepley's voice.

"Travis! Travis! She's here!"

I turned, desperately searching for Abby, to see her running down the steps at full speed. She stopped just short of the cage, slamming her hands into the chain-link to stop herself.

"I'm here! I'm here," she breathed.

We kissed through the space between the fence, and she held my face in her hands with the few fingers she could fit through. "I love you." She shook her head. "You don't have to do this, you know."

I smiled. "Yeah, I do."

"Let's do this, Romeo. I don't have all night," Brock called from the other side.

I didn't turn around, but Abby glanced over my shoulder. When she caught sight of Brock, her cheeks flushed with anger, and her expression turned cold. Less than a second later, her eyes returned to mine, warming again. She smiled an impish grin.

"Teach that asshole some manners."

I winked at her and smiled. "Anything for you, baby."

Brock met me in the center of the ring, toe to toe.

"Be smart!" Shepley yelled.

I leaned over to whisper in Brock's ear. "I just want you to know I'm a big fan, even though you're kind of a prick and a cheat. So don't take it personally when you get KTFO'd tonight."

Brock's square jaws worked violently under the skin, and his eyes lit up—not with anger, but with stunned confusion.

"Be *smart,* Travis!" Shepley yelled again, seeing the look in my eyes.

The bell sounded, and I immediately attacked. Using every bit of force, I let the same fury free that I'd unleashed on Benny's goons.

Brock stumbled backward, trying to position himself to guard or kick me, but I gave him no time, using both of my fists to run him into the ground.

It was an extraordinary release not to hold back. Relishing the pure adrenaline ripping through me, I forgot myself, and Brock dodged my blow, coming back with a right hook. His throws had a lot more bite than the amateurs I went up against at school—and it was fucking awesome. Fighting Brock brought back memories of some of the more serious disagreements I'd had with my brothers, when words escalated to an ass whipping.

I felt right at home trading punches with Brock; in that moment, my rage had a purpose and a place.

Each time Brock's fists landed a blow, it only served to amp up my adrenaline, and I could feel my already powerful punches picking up more steam.

He tried to wrestled me to the ground, but I planted my feet in a squatlike position, stabilizing myself against his desperate movements to throw me off balance. While he thrashed around, my clenched hand made contact with his head, ears, and temple numerous times.

The once white tape around my knuckles was now crimson, but I felt no pain, only the sheer pleasure of unleashing every negative emotion that had weighed me down for so long. I remembered how relaxing it felt to beat the hell out of Benny's men. Win or lose, I looked forward to what kind of person I would be after this fight.

The referee, Shepley, and Brock's trainer surrounded me, pulling me off of my opponent.

"Bell, Travis! Stop!" Shepley said.

Shepley dragged me to one corner, and Brock was pulled to the other. I turned to look at Abby. She was wringing her hands together, but her wide smile told me she was okay. I winked at her, and she blew me a kiss. The gesture reenergized me, and I returned to the middle of the cage with renewed determination.

Once the bell rang, I attacked again, this time taking more care to dodge just as many times as I threw a punch. Once or twice, Brock wrapped his arms around me, breathing hard, and tried to bite me or knee me in the balls. I'd just push him off and hit him harder.

In the third round, Brock stumbled, swung or kicked and missed. He was running out of steam fast. Feeling winded myself, I was taking more breaks between swings. The adrenaline that had once surged through my body felt tapped out, and my head was beginning to pound.

Brock landed a punch, and then another. I blocked a third, and then, ready for it to end, went in for the kill. With my remaining strength, I dodged Brock's knee and then swung around, planting my elbow straight into his nose. His head flew back, looking straight upward, he took a few steps, and then fell to the ground.

The noise from the crowd was deafening, but I could only hear one voice.

"Oh my God! Yes! Yay, baby!" Abby screamed.

The referee checked Brock, and then walked over to me, lifting my hand. Shepley, America, and Abby were all let into the cage, and they swarmed me. I picked up Abby and planted my lips on hers.

"You did it," she said, cupping my face in her hands.

The celebration was cut short when Benny and a fresh batch of bodyguards entered the cage. I set Abby on her feet, and took a defensive stance in front of her.

Benny was all smiles. "Well done, Maddox. You saved the day. If you have a minute, I'd like to talk to you."

I looked back at Abby, who grabbed my hand. "It's okay. I'll meet you at that door," I said, nodding to the closest door, "in ten minutes."

"Ten?" she asked with worry in her eyes.

"Ten," I said, kissing her forehead. I looked to Shepley. "Keep an eye on the girls."

"I think maybe I should go with you."

I leaned into Shepley's ear. "If they want to kill us, Shepley, there's not much we can do about it. I think Benny has something else in mind." I leaned back and slapped his arm. "I'll see you in ten."

"Not eleven. Not fifteen. Ten," Shepley said, pulling a reluctant Abby away.

I followed Benny to the same room I had waited in before the fight. To my surprise, he made his men wait outside.

He held out his hands, gesturing to the room. "I thought this would be better. So you could see that I'm not always this . . . bad man that maybe I'm made out to be."

His body language and tone were relaxed, but I kept my ears and eyes open for any surprises.

Benny smiled. "I have a proposition for you, son."

"I'm not your son."

"True," he conceded. "But after I offer you a hundred and fifty grand a fight, I think you might want to be."

"What fights?" I asked. I figured he would try to say that Abby still owed him. I had no clue he'd try to offer me a job.

"You are obviously a very vicious, very talented young man. You belong in that cage. I can make that happen . . . and I can also make you a very rich man."

"I'm listening."

Benny grinned wider. "I'll schedule one fight a month."

"I'm still in college."

He shrugged. "We'll schedule around it. I'll fly you out, and Abby if you wish, first class, on weekends, if that's what you want. Making money like this, though, you might want to put a hold on the college education."

"Six figures a fight?" I did the math, trying not to let my surprise show. "To fight and what else?"

"That's it, kid. Just fight. Make me money."

"Just fight . . . and I can quit when I want."

He smiled. "Well, sure, but I don't see that happening anytime soon. You love it. I saw you. You were drunk with it, in that cage."

I stood there for a moment, mulling over his offer. "I'll think about it. Let me talk to Abby."

"Fair enough."

I SET OUR SUITCASES ON THE BED AND COLLAPSED BESIDE them. I'd mentioned Benny's offer to Abby, but she wasn't receptive at all. Then the plane ride home was a little tense, so I decided to leave it alone until we got home.

Abby was drying off Toto after giving him a bath. He'd been staying with Brazil, and she was revolted with the way he smelled.

"Oh! You smell so much better!" She giggled as he shook, spraying water all over her and the floor. He stood up on his hind legs, covering her face with tiny puppy kisses. "I missed you, too, little man."

"Pigeon?" I asked, nervously knotting my fingers together.

"Yeah?" she said, rubbing Toto with the yellow towel in her hands.

"I wanna do this. I want to fight in Vegas."

"No," she said, smiling at Toto's happy face.

"You're not listening. I'm gonna do it. You'll see in a few months that it was the right decision."

She looked up at me. "You're going to work for Benny."

I nodded nervously and then smiled. "I just wanna take care of you, Pidge."

Tears glossed her eyes. "I don't want anything bought with that money, Travis. I don't want anything to do with Benny or Vegas or anything that goes along with it."

"You didn't have a problem with the thought of buying a car with the money from my fights here."

"That's different, and you know it."

I frowned. "It's gonna be okay, Pidge. You'll see."

She watched me for a moment, and then her cheeks flushed. "Why did you even ask me, Travis? You were going to work for Benny no matter what I said."

"I want your support on this, but it's too much money to turn down. I would be crazy to say no."

She paused for a long time, her shoulders fell, and then nodded. "Okay, then. You've made your decision."

My mouth stretched into a wide smile. "You'll see, Pigeon. It's going to be great." I pushed off the bed, walked over to Abby and kissed her fingers. "I'm starved. You hungry?"

She shook her head.

I kissed her hairline before making my way to the kitchen. My lips hummed a chipper tune from a random song while I grabbed two slices of bread and some salami and cheese. *Man, she's missing out,* I thought, squeezing spicy mustard onto the bread slices.

It took about three bites for me to finish, and then I washed it down with a beer, wondering what else there was to eat. I didn't realize how spread thin my body felt until we'd gotten home. Aside from the fight, nerves probably also had something to do with it. Now that Abby knew my plans and it was settled, the nerves went away just enough for me to have an appetite again.

Abby padded down the hall and then rounded the corner, suitcase in hand. She didn't look at me when she crossed the living room to the door.

"Pigeon?" I called.

I walked to the still-open door, seeing Abby approaching America's Honda.

When she didn't answer, I jogged down the stairs and across the grass to where Shepley, America, and Abby stood.

"What are you doing?" I asked, gesturing to the suitcase.

Abby smiled awkwardly. It was immediately obvious something wasn't right.

"Pidge?"

"I'm taking my stuff to Morgan. They have all those washers and dryers and I have a ridiculous amount of laundry to do."

I frowned. "You were going to leave without telling me?"

"She was coming back in, Trav. You're so freakin' paranoid," America said.

"Oh," I said, still unsure. "You staying here tonight?"

"I don't know. I guess it depends on when my laundry gets done."

Although I knew she was probably still uneasy with my decision about Benny, I let it go, smiled, and pulled her against me. "In three weeks, I'll pay someone to do your laundry. Or you can just throw away your dirty clothes and buy new ones."

"You're fighting for Benny again?" America asked, shocked.

"He made me an offer I couldn't refuse."

"Travis," Shepley began.

"Don't you guys start on me, too. If I'm not changing my mind for Pidge, I'm not changing my mind for you."

America traded glances with Abby. "Well, we better get you back, Abby. That pile of clothes is gonna take you forever."

I leaned down to kiss Abby's lips. She pulled me close and kissed me hard, making me feel a little better about her unease. "See you later," I said, holding the door open while she sat in the passenger seat. "Love you."

Shepley lifted Abby's suitcase into the hatchback of the Honda, and America slid into her seat, reaching over to pull across her seat belt.

I shut Abby's door, and then folded my arms across my chest.

Shepley stood beside me. "You're not really going to fight for Benny, are you?"

"It's a lot of money, Shepley. Six figures a fight."

"*Six* figures?"

"Could you say no?"

"I would if I thought America would dump my ass over it."

I laughed once. "Abby's not going to *dump* me over this."

America backed out of the parking lot, and I noticed tears spilling down Abby's cheeks.

I jogged to her window, tapping on the glass. "What's wrong, Pidge?"

"Go, Mare," she mouthed, wiping her eyes.

I jogged alongside the car, slamming my palm against the glass. Abby wouldn't look at me, and absolute terror sunk into my bones. "Pigeon? America! Stop the fucking car! Abby, don't do this!"

America turned onto the main road and pressed on the gas.

I sprinted after them, but when the Honda was nearly out of sight, I turned and ran for my Harley. I dug my hand in my pocket for my keys as I ran, and leaped onto the seat.

"Travis, don't," Shepley warned.

"She's fucking leaving me, Shep!" I yelled, barely starting the bike before revving the throttle into a 180, and flying down the street.

America had just shut her door when I made it into Morgan Hall's parking lot. I nearly laid my bike over coming to a halt and failing to root the kickstand on the first try. I ran over to the Honda and jerked open the passenger door. America's teeth were clenched, ready for whatever I might throw at her.

I looked to Morgan's brick and mortar, knowing Abby was somewhere inside. "You gotta let me in, Mare," I begged.

"I'm sorry," she said. She put the car in reverse and backed out of the parking space.

Just as I raced up the steps, taking two at a time, a girl I hadn't seen before was walking out. I grabbed the door, but she blocked my way.

"You can't come in without an escort."

I pulled out my bike keys and jingled them in her face. "My girlfriend, Abby Abernathy, left her car keys at my apartment. I'm just bringing them by."

The girl nodded, unsure, and then moved out of my way.

Leaping up several steps at a time in the stairwell, I finally reached Abby's floor and her dorm room door. I took a few deep breaths. "Pidge?" I said, trying to be quiet. "You gotta let me in, baby. We've got to talk about this."

She didn't answer.

"Pigeon, please. You're right. I didn't listen to you. We can sit down and discuss this some more, okay? I just . . . please answer the door. You're scarin' me to death."

"Go away, Travis," Kara said from the other side.

I pounded on the door with the side of my fist. "Pidge? Open the fucking door, dammit! I'm not leaving until you talk to me! Pigeon!"

"What?" Kara growled, opening the door. She pushed her glasses up, and sniffed. For such a tiny girl, she had a very severe expression.

I sighed, relieved that at least I would be able to see Abby. Looking over Kara's shoulder, Abby wasn't in my direct line of sight.

"Kara," I said, trying to stay calm. "Tell Abby I need to see her. Please."

"She's not here."

"She's here," I said, quickly losing my patience.

Kara's weight shifted. "I haven't seen her tonight. I haven't seen her in several days, actually."

"I know she's here!" I yelled. "Pigeon?"

"She's not . . . Hey!" Kara said, shrieking when I shouldered past her.

The door cracked against the wall. I pulled the knob and looked behind it, and then in the closets, even under the bed. "Pigeon! Where is she?"

"I haven't seen her!" Kara shouted.

I walked into the hall, looking in both directions, and Kara slammed the door shut behind me, followed by the click of the bolt lock.

The wall felt cold against my back, and I suddenly realized I didn't have a coat on. Slowly sliding down the concrete block wall to my ass, I covered my face with my hands. She might have hated me at the moment, but she had to come home sometime.

After twenty minutes, I pulled out my phone and shot her a text.

Pidge, please. i know ur pissed, but we can still talk about this

And then another.

Please come home.

And another.

Please? i love you.

She didn't respond. I waited another half hour, and then sent her more.

im @ Morgan would u @ least call me to let me know if ur coming home 2nite?

Pigeon I'm so fuckin sorry. Please come home. I need 2 c u.

U know im not the 1 being unreasonable here. U could @ least answer me.

i don't fucking deserve this ok so im an asshat 4 thinking i could solve all our problems with money but @least i don't run away every time we have 1

im sorry i didn't mean that

what do u want me 2 do? i will do whatever u want me 2 ok? just please talk 2 me.

this is bullshit

im in love with u. i don't understand how u can just walk away

Just before sunrise, when I was sure I'd officially made a total ass of myself and Abby was probably certain that I was insane, I picked myself up off the floor. The fact that security had never showed to escort me out was amazing in itself, but if I was still sitting in the hallway when the girls started leaving for class, that luck would more than likely run out.

After trudging down the stairs in defeat, I sat on my bike, and even though a T-shirt was the only thing between my skin and the frigid winter air, I ignored it. Hoping to see Abby in history class, I went straight home to thaw my skin under a hot shower.

Shepley stood at the doorway of my bedroom while I got dressed.

"What do you want, Shep?"

"Did you talk to her?"

"No."

"At all? Text? Anything?"

"I said no," I snapped.

"Trav." Shepley sighed. "She's probably not going to be in class today. I don't want me and America in the middle of this, but that's what she said."

"Maybe she will," I said, buckling my belt. I put on Abby's favorite cologne, and then slipped on my coat before grabbing my backpack.

"Hold up, I'll drive you."

"No, I'll take the bike."

"Why?"

"In case she agrees to come back to the apartment with me so we can talk."

"Travis, I think it's time you consider the fact that she might not—"

"Shut the fuck up, Shep," I said, glancing over to him. "Just this one time, don't be reasonable. Don't try to save me. Just be my friend, okay?"

Shepley nodded once. "You got it."

America came out of Shepley's room, still in her pj's. "Travis, it's time to let her go. She was done the second you made it clear you were working for Benny."

When I didn't reply, she continued, "Travis . . ."

"Don't. No offense, Mare, but I can't even look at you right now."

Without waiting for a response, I slammed the door behind me. Theatrics were worth it just to vent a little of the anxiety I felt about seeing Abby. Better than getting on my hands and knees in a panic to beg her back in the middle of class. Not that I wouldn't go that far if that was what it would take to change her mind.

Walking slowly to class and even taking the stairs didn't keep me from being a half hour early. I hoped Abby would show up, and we'd have time to talk before, but when the previous class let out, she still wasn't there.

I sat down, next to her empty seat, and picked at my leather bracelet while the other students filtered into the classrooms and took their seats. It was just another day for them. Watching their world continue while mine was coming to an end was disturbing.

Except for a few stragglers sneaking in behind Mr. Chaney, everyone was accounted for—everyone but Abby. Mr. Chaney flipped open his book, greeted the classroom, and then started his lecture. His words blurred together as my heart knocked against my chest, swelling more with each breath. My teeth clenched and my eyes watered as thoughts of Abby being somewhere else, relieved to be away from me, amplified my anger.

I stood and stared at Abby's empty desk.

"Er . . . Mr. Maddox? Are you feeling well?" Mr. Chaney asked.

I kicked over her desk and then mine, barely registering the gasps and shrieks of the students watching.

"GOD DAMMIT!" I screamed, kicking my desk again.

"Mr. Maddox," Mr. Chaney said in a strangely calm voice. "I think it's best you get some fresh air."

I stood over the toppled desks, breathing hard.

"Leave my classroom, Travis. Now," Chaney said, this time his voice more firm.

I jerked my backpack from the floor and shoved open the door, hearing the wood crash against the wall behind it.

"Travis!"

The only detail that registered about the voice was that it was female. I flipped around, for half a second hopeful that it was Abby.

Megan sauntered down the hall, stopping next to me. "I thought you had class?" She smiled. "Doing anyone exciting this weekend?"

"What do you need?"

She raised an eyebrow, her eyes bright with recognition. "I know you. You're pissed. Things didn't work out with the nun?"

I didn't answer.

"I could have told you that." She shrugged, and then took a step closer, whispering in my ear so close her full lips brushed against my ear. "We're the same, Travis: not good for anybody."

My eyes darted to hers, traveled down to her lips, and then back. She leaned in with her trademark small, sexy smile.

"Fuck off, Megan."

Her smile vanished, and I walked away.

CHAPTER TWENTY-TWO

Not Good for Anybody

THE NEXT WEEK SEEMED ENDLESS. AMERICA AND I DEcided it would be best if she stayed at Morgan for a while. Shepley reluctantly agreed. Abby missed all three days of history and found somewhere else other than the cafeteria to eat. I tried to catch up with her after a few of her classes, but she either never went to them or had left early. She wouldn't answer her phone.

Shepley assured me that she was okay, and nothing had happened to her. As agonizing as it was to know I was two degrees from Abby, it would have been worse to be cut off from her completely and have no idea if she was dead or alive. Even though it seemed she wanted nothing to do with me, I couldn't stop hoping that at some point soon she would forgive me or start missing me as much as I missed her and show up at the apartment. Thinking about never seeing her again was too painful, so I decided to keep waiting.

On Friday, Shepley knocked on my door.

"Come in," I said from the bed, staring up at the ceiling.

"You going out tonight, buddy?"

"No."

"Maybe you should call Trent. Go get a couple of drinks and get your mind off things for a while."

"No."

Shepley sighed. "Listen, America's coming over, but . . . and I hate to do this to you . . . but you can't bug her about Abby. I barely talked her into coming. She just wants to stay in my room. Okay?"

"Yeah."

"Call Trent. And you need to eat something and take a shower. You look like shit."

With that, Shepley shut the door. It still didn't shut right from the time I had kicked it down. Every time someone closed it, the time I destroyed the apartment over Abby leaving came to mind, and the fact that she came back to me not long after, leading to our first time.

I closed my eyes, but like every other night that week, couldn't sleep. How people like Shepley went through this torment over and over with different girls was insane. Meeting someone after Abby, even if that girl were to somehow measure up, I couldn't imagine putting my heart out there again. Not just so I could feel like this all over again. Like a slow death. Turns out I'd had it right all along.

Twenty minutes later, I could hear America's voice in the living room. The sounds of them talking quietly as they hid from me in Shepley's room echoed throughout the apartment.

Even America's voice was too much to take. Knowing she had probably just spoken to Abby was excruciating.

I forced myself to stand up and make my way to the bathroom to take care of showering and other basic hygiene rituals

I'd neglected over the last week. America's voice was drowned out by the water, but the second I turned the lever off, I could hear her again.

I got dressed, and grabbed my bike keys, set to take a long ride. I'd probably end up at Dad's to break the news.

Just as I passed Shepley's bedroom door, America's phone rang. It was the ringtone she'd assigned to Abby. My stomach sank.

"I can come pick you up and take you somewhere for dinner," she said.

Abby was hungry. She might go to the cafeteria.

I jogged out to the Harley and raced out of the parking lot, speeding and running red lights and stop signs all the way to campus.

When I got to the cafeteria, Abby wasn't there. I waited a few more minutes, but she never showed. My shoulders sagged, and I trudged in darkness toward the parking lot. It was a quiet night. Cold. Opposite of the night I walked Abby to Morgan after I won our bet, reminding me of how empty it felt not having her beside me.

A small figure some yards away appeared, walking toward the cafeteria alone. It was Abby.

Her hair was pulled up into a bun, and when she got closer, I noticed she wasn't wearing any makeup. Her arms crossed against her chest, she didn't have a coat on, only a thick, gray cardigan to ward off the cold.

"Pigeon?" I said, walking into the light from the shadows.

Abby jerked to a stop, and then relaxed a bit when she recognized me.

"Jesus, Travis! You scared the hell out of me!"

"If you would answer your phone when I call I wouldn't have to sneak around in the dark."

"You look like hell," she said.

"I've been through there once or twice this week."

She pulled her arms tighter around her, and I had to stop myself from hugging her to keep her warm.

Abby sighed. "I'm actually on my way to grab something to eat. I'll call you later, okay?"

"No. We have to talk."

"Trav—"

"I turned Benny down. I called him Wednesday and told him no."

I was hoping she would smile, or at least show some sign that she approved.

Her face remained blank. "I don't know what you want me to say, Travis."

"Say you forgive me. Say you'll take me back."

"I can't."

My face crumpled.

Abby tried to walk around. Instinctively, I stepped in front of her. If she walked away this time, I would lose her. "I haven't slept, or ate . . . I can't concentrate. I *know* you love me. Everything will be the way it used to be if you'd just take me back."

She closed her eyes. "We are dysfunctional, Travis. I think you're just obsessed with the thought of owning me more than anything else."

"That's not true. I love you more than my life, Pigeon."

"That's exactly what I mean. That's crazy talk."

"It's not crazy. It's the truth."

"Okay . . . so what exactly is the order for you? Is it money, me, your life . . . or is there something that comes before money?"

"I realize what I've done, okay? I see where you'd think that, but if I'd known that you were gonna leave me, I would have never . . . I just wanted to take care of you."

"You've said that."

"Please don't do this. I can't stand feeling like this . . . it's . . . it's killin' me," I said, on the verge of panic. The wall Abby kept around her when we were just friends was back up, stronger than before. She wasn't listening. I couldn't get through to her.

"I'm done, Travis."

I winced. "Don't say that."

"It's *over*. Go home."

My eyebrows pulled in. "*You're* my home."

Abby paused, and for a moment I felt like I'd actually gotten through to her, but her eyes lost focus, and the wall was up again. "You made your choice, Trav. I've made mine."

"I'm going to stay the hell out of Vegas, and away from Benny . . . I'm going to finish school. But I need you. I *need* you. You're my best friend."

For the first time since I was a little kid, hot tears burned in my eyes and dripped down one of my cheeks. Unable to restrain myself, I reached out for Abby, wrapped her small frame in my arms, and planted my lips on hers. Her mouth was cold and stiff, so I cradled her face in my hands, kissing her harder, desperate to get a reaction.

"Kiss me," I begged.

Abby's kept her mouth taut, but her body was lifeless. If I

let her go, she would have fallen. "Kiss me!" I pleaded. "Please, Pigeon! I told him no!"

Abby shoved me away. "Leave me *alone,* Travis!"

She shouldered passed me, but I grabbed her wrist. She kept her arm straight, outstretched behind her, but she didn't turn around.

"I am *begging* you." I fell to my knees, her hand still in mine. My breath puffed out in white steam as I spoke, reminding me of the cold. "I'm begging you, Abby. Don't do this."

Abby glanced back, and then her eyes drifted down her arm to mine, seeing the tattoo on my wrist. The tattoo that bared her name.

She looked away, toward the cafeteria. "Let me go, Travis."

The air knocked out of me, and with all hope obliterated, I relaxed my hand, and let her slip out of my fingers.

Abby didn't look back as she walked away from me, and my palms fell flat on the sidewalk. She wasn't coming back. She didn't want me anymore, and there was nothing I could do or say to change it.

Several minutes passed before I could gain the strength to stand. My feet didn't want to move, but somehow I forced them to cooperate long enough to get me to the Harley. I sat on the seat, and let my tears fall. Loss was something I'd only experienced once before in my life, but this felt more real. Losing Abby wasn't a story I remembered from early childhood—it was in my face, debilitating me like a sickness, robbing me of my senses and physically, excruciatingly painful.

My mother's words echoed in my ear. Abby was the girl I had to fight for, and I went down fighting. None of it was ever going to be enough.

A red Dodge Intrepid pulled up next to my bike. I didn't have to look up to see who it was.

Trenton killed the engine, resting an arm out of the open window. "Hey."

"Hey," I said, wiping my eyes with my jacket sleeve.

"Rough night?"

"Yeah," I nodded, staring at the Harley's fuel tank.

"I just got off work. I need a fuckin' drink. Ride with me to the Dutch."

I took a long, faltering breath. Trenton, like Dad and the rest of my brothers, always knew how to handle me. We both knew I shouldn't drive in my condition.

"Yeah."

"Yeah?" Trenton said with a small, surprised smile.

I swung my leg backward over the seat, and then walked around to the passenger side of Trenton's car. The heat from the vents made my skin burn, and for the first time that night I felt how biting cold the air was, and recognized that I didn't have nearly enough clothes on for the temperature.

"Shepley called you?"

"Yep." He backed out from the parking space and slowly weaved through the lot, finding the street at a turtle's pace. He looked over at me. "I guess a guy named French called his girl? Said you and Abby were fighting outside the cafeteria."

"We weren't fighting. I was just . . . trying to get her back."

Trenton nodded once, pulling into the street. "That's what I figured."

We didn't speak again until we took our stools at the bar of the Dutch. The crowd was rough, but Bill, the owner and bartender, knew Dad well from when we were kids, and most of the regulars watched us grow up.

"Good to see you boys. It's been a while," Bill said, wiping down the counter before setting a beer and a shot on the bar in front of each of us.

"Hey, Bill," Trenton said, immediately tossing back his shot.

"You feeling okay, Travis?" Bill asked.

Trenton answered for me. "He'll feel better after a few rounds."

I was grateful. In that moment, if I spoke, I might have broken down.

Trenton continued buying me whiskey until my teeth were numb and I was on the verge of passing out. I must have done so sometime between the bar and the apartment, because I woke up the next morning on the couch in my clothes, unsure of how in the hell I got there.

Shepley closed the door, and I heard the familiar sound of America's Honda rev up and pull away.

I sat up and closed one eye. "Did you guys have a good night."

"Yeah. Did you?"

"I guess so. Did you hear me come in?"

"Yeah, Trent carried your ass upstairs and threw you on the couch. You were laughing, so I'd say it was a successful night."

"Trent can be a dick, but he's a good brother."

"That he is. You hungry?"

"Fuck no," I groaned.

"Alrighty, then. I'm gonna make me some cereal."

I sat on the couch, going over the night before in my mind. The last hours were hazy, but when I backed up to the moment I saw Abby on campus, I winced.

"I told Mare we had plans today. I thought we'd go to the lumber place to replace your creaky ass door."

"You don't have to babysit me, Shep."

"I'm not. We're leaving in half an hour. Wash the stank off you, first," he said, sitting in the recliner with his bowl of Mini Wheats. "And then we're going to come home and study. Finals."

"Fuck," I said with a sigh.

"I'll order pizza for lunch, and we can just eat leftovers for dinner."

"Thanksgiving is coming up, remember? I'll be eating pizza three meals a day for two days straight. No, thank you."

"Okay, Chinese, then."

"You're micromanaging," I said.

"I know. Trust me, it helps."

I nodded slowly, hoping he was right.

THE DAYS PASSED SLOWLY, BUT STAYING UP LATE TO study with Shepley, and sometimes America, helped to shorten the sleepless nights. Trenton promised not to tell Dad or the rest of the Maddox boys about Abby until after Thanksgiving, but I still dreaded it, knowing I'd already told them all she would come. They would ask about her, and then see right through me when I lied.

After my last class on Friday, I called Shepley. "Hey, I know this is supposed to be off-limits, but I need you to find out where Abby is going for break."

"Well, that's easy. She'll be with us. She spends the holidays at America's."

"Really?"

"Yeah, why?"

"Nothing," I said, abruptly hanging up the phone.

I walked around campus in the light rain, waiting for Abby's class to let out. Outside the Hoover building, I saw a few people from Abby's calculus class congregated outside. The back of Parker's head came into view, and then Abby.

She was huddled inside her winter coat, seeming uncomfortable as Parker babbled on.

I pulled down my red ball cap and jogged in their direction. Abby's eyes drifted to mine; recognition made her eyebrows raise infinitesimally.

The same mantra played on repeat in my head. *No matter what smart-ass comment Parker makes, play it cool. Don't fuck this up. Don't. Fuck. This. Up.*

To my surprise, Parker left without saying a word to me.

I shoved my hands into the front pockets of my hoodie. "Shepley said you're going with him and Mare to Wichita tomorrow."

"Yeah?"

"You're spending the whole break at America's?"

She shrugged, trying too hard to be unaffected by my presence. "I'm really close with her parents."

"What about your mom?"

"She's a drunk, Travis. She won't know it's Thanksgiving."

My stomach lurched, knowing the answer to my next question was going to be my last chance. Thunder rolled above us and I looked up, squinting as the large drops fell against my face.

"I need to ask you for a favor," I said, ducking from the hard rain. "C'mere." I pulled Abby under the closest awning so she wouldn't get soaked from the sudden downpour.

"What kind of favor?" she asked, clearly suspicious. It was hard to hear her over the rain.

"My uh . . ." I shifted my weight, my nerves attempting to get the best of me. My mind screamed *abort!*, but I was determined to at least try. "Dad and the guys are still expecting you on Thursday."

"Travis!" Abby whined.

I looked to my feet. "You said you would come."

"I know, but . . . it's a little inappropriate now, don't you think?"

"You said you would come," I said again, trying to keep my voice calm.

"We were still together when I agreed to go home with you. You *knew* I wasn't going to come."

"I *didn't* know, and it's too late, anyway. Thomas is flying in, and Tyler took off work. Everyone's looking forward to seeing you."

Abby cringed, twirling a piece of her wet hair around her finger. "They were going to come anyway, weren't they?"

"Not everyone. We haven't had all of us there for Thanksgiving in years. They all made an effort to be there, since I promised them a real meal. We haven't had a woman in the kitchen since Mom died and . . ."

"That's not sexist or anything,"

"That's not what I meant, Pidge, c'mon. We all want you there. That's all I'm sayin'."

"You haven't told them about us, have you?"

"Dad would ask why, and I'm not ready to talk to him about it. I'd never hear the end of how stupid I am. Please come, Pidge."

"I have to put the turkey in at six in the morning. We'd have to leave here by five . . ."

"Or we could stay there."

Her eyebrows shot up. "No way! It's bad enough that I'm going to have to lie to your family and pretend we're still together."

Her reaction, although anticipated, still stung my ego a little. "You act like I'm asking you to light yourself on fire."

"You should have told them!"

"I will. After Thanksgiving . . . I'll tell them."

She sighed and then looked away. Waiting for her answer was like pulling out my fingernails one by one.

"If you promise me that this isn't some stunt to try and get back together, I'll do it."

I nodded, trying not to be too eager. "I promise."

Her lips formed a hard line, but there was the tiniest hint of a smile in her eyes. "I'll see you at five."

I leaned down to kiss her cheek. I'd just meant to give her a quick peck, but my lips had missed her skin, and it was hard to pull away. "Thanks, Pigeon."

After Shepley and America headed out for Wichita in the Honda, I cleaned the apartment, folded the last load of laundry, smoked half a pack of cigarettes, packed an overnight bag, and then cussed the clock for being so slow. When four thirty finally rolled around, I jogged down the steps to Shepley's Charger, trying not to speed all the way to Morgan.

When I arrived at Abby's door, her confused expression took me by surprise.

"Travis," she breathed.

"Are you ready?"

Abby raised an eyebrow. "Ready for what?"

"You said pick you up at five."

She folded her arms across my chest. "I meant five in the *morning*!"

"Oh. I guess I should call Dad and let him know we won't be staying after all."

"Travis!" she wailed.

"I brought Shep's car so we didn't have to deal with our bags on the bike. There's a spare bedroom you can crash in. We can watch a movie or—"

"I'm *not* staying at your dad's!"

My face fell. "Okay. I'll uh . . . I'll see you in the morning."

I took a step back, and Abby shut the door. She would still come, but my family would definitely know something was up if she didn't show up tonight like I'd said she would. I walked down the hall slowly as I punched in Dad's number. He was going to ask why, and I didn't want to outright lie to him.

"Travis, wait."

I flipped around to see Abby standing in the hallway.

"Give me a minute to pack a few things."

I smiled, nearly overwhelmed with relief. We walked together back to her room, and I waited in the doorway while she shoved a few things in a bag. The scene reminded me of the night I'd won the bet, and I realized that I wouldn't have traded a single second we spent together.

"I still love you, Pidge."

She didn't look up. "Don't. I'm not doing this for you."

I sucked in a breath, physical pain shooting in all directions in my chest. "I know."

CHAPTER TWENTY-THREE

Acceptance Speech

THE EASY CONVERSATIONS WE USED TO HAVE WERE lost on me. Nothing that came to mind seemed appropriate, and I was worried about pissing her off before we got to Dad's.

The plan was for her to play the part, start to miss me, and then maybe I would get another chance to beg her back. It was a long shot, but the only thing I had going for me.

I pulled into the wet gravel drive, and carried our bags to the front porch.

Dad answered the door with a smile.

"Good to see ya, son." His smiled broadened when he looked at the damp but beautiful girl standing beside me. "Abby Abernathy. We're looking forward to dinner tomorrow. It's been a long time since . . . Well. It's been a long time."

Inside the house, Dad rested his hand on his protruding belly and grinned. "I set you two up in the guest bedroom, Trav. I didn't figure you would wanna fight with the twin bed in your room."

Abby looked to me. "Abby's uh . . . she's going to uh . . . going to take the guest room. I'm going to crash in mine."

Trenton walked up, his face screwed into disgust. "*Why?* She's been staying at your apartment, hasn't she?"

"Not lately," I said, trying not to lunge at him. He knew exactly why.

Dad and Trenton traded glances.

"Thomas's room has been storage for years now, so I was going to let him take your room. I guess he can sleep on the couch," Dad said, looking at its ratty, discolored cushions.

"Don't worry about it, Jim. We were just trying to be respectful," Abby said, touching my arm.

Dad's laughter bellowed throughout the house, and he patted her hand. "You've met my sons, Abby. You should know it's damn near impossible to offend me."

I nodded toward the stairs, and Abby followed. I gently pushed open the door with my foot and sat our bags on the floor, looking at the bed and then turning to Abby. Her gray eyes were big as they scanned the room, stopping on a picture of my parents that hung from the wall.

"I'm sorry, Pidge. I'll sleep on the floor."

"Damn straight you will," she said, pulling her hair up into a ponytail. "I can't believe I let you talk me into this."

I sat on the bed, realizing just how unhappy she was about the situation. I guess part of me hoped she'd be as relieved as I was to be together. "This is going to be a fucking mess. I don't know what I was thinking."

"I know exactly what you were thinking. I'm not stupid, Travis."

I looked up and offered a tired smile. "But you still came."

"I have to get everything ready for tomorrow," she said, opening the door.

I stood. "I'll help you."

As Abby prepared the potatoes, pies, and turkey, I was busy fetching and handing her things, and completed the small cooking tasks she assigned to me. The first hour was awkward, but when the twins arrived, everyone seemed to congregate in the kitchen, helping Abby to relax. Dad told Abby stories about us boys, and we laughed about tales of previous disastrous Thanksgivings when we attempted to do something other than order pizza.

"Diane was a hell of a cook," Dad mused. "Trav doesn't remember, but there was no sense trying after she passed."

"No pressure, Abby," Trenton said. He chuckled, and then grabbed a beer from the fridge. "Let's get out the cards. I want to try to make back some of my money that Abby took."

Dad waved his finger. "No poker this weekend, Trent. I brought down the dominoes; go set those up. No betting, dammit. I mean it."

Trenton shook his head. "All right, old man, all right." My brothers meandered from the kitchen, and Trenton followed, stopping to look back. "C'mon, Trav."

"I'm helping Pidge."

"There's not much more to do, baby," Abby said. "Go ahead."

I knew she had only said it for show, but it didn't change the way it made me feel. I reached for her hip. "You sure?"

She nodded and I leaned over to kiss her cheek, squeezing her hip with my fingers before following Trenton into the game room.

We sat down in the card room, settling in for a friendly game of dominoes.

Trenton broke out the box, cursing the cardboard for slicing the underside of his fingernail before dealing out the bones.

Taylor snorted. "You're such a fucking baby, Trent, just deal."

"You can't count anyway, douche. What are you so eager about?"

I laughed at Trenton's comeback, drawing his attention to me.

"You and Abby are getting along well," he said. "How did this all work out?"

I knew what he meant, and I shot him a glare for broaching the subject in front of the twins. "With much persuasion."

Dad arrived and sat down. "She's a good girl, Travis. I'm happy for you, son."

"She is," I said trying not to let the sadness show on my face.

Abby was busy cleaning in the kitchen, and it seemed I spent every second fighting the urge to join her. It may have been a family holiday, but I wanted to spend every spare moment with her that I could.

A half hour later, grinding noises alerted me to the fact that the dishwasher had been started. Abby walked by to wave quickly before making her way to the stairs. I jumped up and took her hand.

"It's early, Pidge. You're not going to bed, are ya?"

"It's been a long day. I'm tired."

"We were getting ready to watch a movie. Why don't you come back down and hang out?"

She looked up the stairs and then down to me. "Okay."

I led her by the hand to the couch, and we sat together as the opening credits rolled.

"Shut off that light, Taylor," Dad ordered.

I reached behind Abby, resting my arm on the back of the couch. I fought wrapping both my arms around her. I was wary about her reaction, and I didn't want to take advantage of the situation when she was doing me a favor.

Halfway through the movie, the front door flew open, and Thomas rounded the corner, bags in hand.

"Happy Thanksgiving!" he said, setting his luggage on the floor.

Dad stood up and hugged him, and everyone but me stood to greet him.

"You're not going to say hi to Thomas?" Abby whispered.

I watched my dad and brothers hug and laugh. "I got one night with you. I'm not going to waste a second of it."

"Hi there, Abby. It's good to see you again." Thomas smiled.

I touched Abby's knee. She looked down, and then back to me. Noticing her expression, I took my hand off her leg and interlocked my fingers in my lap.

"Uh-oh. Trouble in paradise?" Thomas asked.

"Shut up, Tommy," I grumbled.

The mood in the room shifted, and all eyes fell on Abby, waiting for an explanation. She smiled nervously, and then took my hand into both of hers.

"We're just tired," she said, smiling. "We've been working all evening on the food." Her cheek pressed into my shoulder.

I looked down at our hands and then squeezed, wishing there was some way I could say then how much I appreciated what she'd done.

"Speaking of tired, I'm exhausted." Abby breathed. "I'm gonna head to bed, baby." She looked to everyone else. "Good night, guys."

"Night, sis," Dad said.

My brothers all said good night, and watched Abby make her way up the stairs.

"I'm gonna turn in, too," I said.

"I bet you are," Trenton teased.

"Lucky bastard," Tyler grumbled.

"Hey. We're not going to talk about your sister like that," Dad warned.

Ignoring my brothers, I jogged up the stairs, catching the bedroom door just before it closed. Realizing she might want to get dressed, and wouldn't be comfortable doing it in front of me anymore, I froze. "Did you want me to wait in the hall while you dressed for bed?"

"I'm going to hop in the shower. I'll just get dressed in the bathroom."

I rubbed the back of my neck. "All right. I'll make a pallet, then."

Her big eyes were solid steel as she nodded, her wall obviously impenetrable. She picked out a few things from her bag before making her way to the bathroom.

Digging in the closet for sheets and a blanket, I spread out the linens on the floor beside the bed, thankful we'd at least have some time alone to talk. Abby emerged from the bathroom, and I dropped a pillow on the floor at the head of the pallet, and then took my turn in the shower.

I wasted no time, quickly scrubbing the soap all over my body, letting the water rinse away the suds as soon as they lathered. Within ten minutes, I was already dried off and dressed, walking back into the bedroom.

Abby lay in bed when I returned, the sheets as high on her

chest as she could get them. The pallet wasn't nearly as inviting as a bed with Abby snuggled up inside. I realized my last night with her was going to be spent awake, listening to her breathe just inches away, unable to touch her.

I turned off the light, and situated myself on the floor. "This is our last night together, isn't it?"

"I don't wanna fight, Trav. Just go to sleep."

I turned over to face her, propping up my head with my hand. Abby turned over, too, and our eyes met.

"I love you."

She watched me for a moment. "You promised."

"I promised this wasn't a stunt to get back together. It wasn't." I reached up a hand to touch hers. "But if it meant being with you again, I can't say I wouldn't consider it."

"I care about you. I don't want you to hurt, but I should have followed my gut in the first place. It would've never worked."

"You did love me, though, right?"

She pressed her lips together. "I still do."

Every emotion washed over me in waves, so strong that I couldn't tell one from the other. "Can I ask you for a favor?"

"I'm sort of in the middle of the last thing you asked me to do," she said with a smirk.

"If this is really it . . . if you're really done with me . . . will you let me hold you tonight?"

"I don't think it's a good idea, Trav."

My hand gripped tight over hers. "Please? I can't sleep knowing you're just a foot away, and I'm never gonna get the chance again."

Abby stared at me for a few seconds, and then frowned. "I'm not having sex with you."

"That's not what I'm asking."

Abby's eyes darted around the floor for a bit as she contemplated her answer. Finally shutting her eyes tight, she scooted from the edge of the bed, and turned down the covers.

I crawled into the bed beside her, hastily pulling her tight into my arms. It felt so incredible that coupled with the tension in the room, I struggled not to break down.

"I'm going to miss this," I said.

I kissed her hair and pulled her closer, burying my face into her neck. She rested her hand on my back, and I sucked in another breath, trying to breathe her in, to let that moment of time burn into my brain.

"I . . . I don't think I can do this, Travis," she said, trying to wriggle free.

I didn't mean to restrain her, but if holding on meant avoiding that deep burning pain I'd felt for days on end, it just made sense to hang on.

"I can't do this," she said again.

I knew what she meant. Being together like that was heartbreaking, but I didn't want it to end.

"Then don't," I said against her skin. "Give me another chance."

After one last attempt to break free, Abby covered her face with both hands and cried in my arms. I looked up at her, tears burning my eyes.

I pulled one hand gently away and kissed her palm. Abby took a staggered breath as I looked at her lips, and then back to her eyes. "I'll never love anyone the way I love you, Pigeon."

She sniffed and touched my face, offering an apologetic expression. "I can't."

"I know," I said, my voice breaking. "I never once convinced myself that I was good enough for you."

Abby's face crumpled and she shook her head. "It's not just you, Trav. We're not good for each other."

I shook my head, wanting to disagree, but she was half right. She deserved better, what she'd wanted all along. Who the fuck was I to take that from her?

With that recognition, I took a deep breath, and then rested my head against her chest.

I AWOKE, HEARING COMMOTION DOWNSTAIRS.

"Ow!" Abby yelped from the kitchen.

I jogged down the stairs, pulling a T-shirt over my head.

"You okay, Pidge?" The cold floor sent shock waves through my body, starting with my feet. "Shit! The floor's fucking freezing!" I jumped on one foot, and then the other, causing Abby to stifle a giggle.

It was still early, probably five or six, and everyone else was asleep. Abby bent over to push the turkey into the oven, and my morning tendency to protrude through my shorts had even more of a reason to do so.

"You can go back to bed. I just had to put the turkey in," she said.

"Are you coming?"

"Yeah."

"Lead the way," I said, sweeping my hand toward the stairs.

I yanked my shirt off as we both shoved our legs under the

covers, pulling the blanket up to our necks. I tightened my arms around her as we shivered, waiting for our body heat to warm the small space between our skin and the covers.

I looked out the windows, seeing large snowflakes fall from the gray sky. I kissed Abby's hair, and she seemed to melt against me. In that embrace, it felt like nothing had changed.

"Look, Pidge. It's snowing."

She turned to face the window. "It kind of feels like Christmas," she said, lightly pressing her cheek against my skin. A sigh from my throat prompted her to look at me. "What?"

"You won't be here for Christmas."

"I'm here, now."

I pulled my mouth into a half smile, and then leaned down to kiss her lips. Abby pulled back and shook her head.

"Trav . . ."

I held on tight and lowered my chin. "I've got less than twenty-four hours with you, Pidge. I'm gonna kiss you. I'm gonna kiss you a lot today. *All* day. Every chance I get. If you want me to stop, just say the word, but until you do, I'm going to make every second of my last day with you count."

"Travis—" Abby began, but after a few seconds of thought, her line of sight lowered from my eyes to my lips.

Not wanting to hesitate, I immediately bent down to kiss her. She kissed me back, and although I'd just meant for it to be short and sweet, my lips parted, making her body react. Her tongue slipped into my mouth, and every part of me that was warm-blooded male screamed for me to go full steam ahead. I pulled her against me, and Abby let her leg fall to one side, welcoming my hips to fit tightly between her thighs.

Within moments, she was naked beneath me, and it took just two quick motions for me to remove my clothes. Pressing my mouth against hers, hard, I gripped the iron vines of the headboard with both hands, and in one quick movement, pushed myself inside her. My body instantly felt hot, and I couldn't stop moving or rocking against her, unable to control myself. I moaned into Abby's mouth when she arched her back to move her hips against mine. At one point she flattened her feet on the bed so she could raise up to let me slip inside of her fully.

With one hand on the iron, and the other on the nape of Abby's neck, I rocked into her over and over, everything that had happened between us, all the pain I'd felt, forgotten. The light from the window poured in as beads of sweat began to form on our skin, making it a little easier to slide back and forth.

I was just about to finish when Abby's legs began to quiver, and her nails dug into my back. I held my breath and thrust into her one last time, groaning with the intense spasms throughout my body.

Abby relaxed against the mattress, her hairline damp, and her limbs limp.

I breathed as if I'd just finished a marathon, sweat dripping from the hair above my ear and down the side of my face.

Abby's eyes lit up when she heard voices murmuring downstairs. I turned on my side, scanning her face with pure adoration.

"You said you were just going to kiss me." She looked at me the way she used to, making it easy to pretend.

"Why don't we just stay in bed all day?"

"I came here to cook, remember?"

"No, you came here to help *me* cook, and I don't report for duty for another eight hours."

She touched my face, her expression preparing me for what she might say. "Travis, I think we—"

"Don't say it, okay? I don't want to think about it until I have to." I stood up and pulled on my boxers, walking over to Abby's bag. I tossed her clothes to the bed, and then yanked my T-shirt over my head. "I want to remember this as a good day."

It seemed not long after we awoke, it was lunchtime. The day raced by, far too fucking fast. I dreaded every minute, cursing the clock as it approached the evening.

Admittedly, I was all over Abby. It didn't even matter that she was putting on a show, I refused to even consider the truth while she was next to me.

When we sat down for dinner, Dad insisted that I carve the turkey, and Abby smiled with pride as I stood up to do the honors.

The Maddox clan annihilated Abby's hard work, and showered her with compliments.

"Did I make enough?" She laughed.

Dad smiled, pulling his fork through his lips to get it clean for dessert. "You made plenty, Abby. We just wanted to tide ourselves over until next year . . . unless you'd like to do this all over again at Christmas. You're a Maddox, now. I expect you at every holiday, and not to cook."

With Dad's words, the truth seeped in, and my smile faded.

"Thanks, Jim."

"Don't tell her that, Dad," Trenton said. "She's gotta cook. I haven't had a meal like this since I was five!" He shoveled half a slice of pecan pie into his mouth, humming with satisfaction.

While my brothers cleared the table and washed the dishes, I sat with Abby on the couch, trying not to hold her too tight.

Dad had already turned in, his belly full, making him too tired to attempt to stay awake.

I pulled Abby's legs onto my lap, and slipped off her shoes, massaging the soles of her feet with my thumbs. She loved that, and I knew it. I might have been trying to subtly remind her about how good we were together, even though I knew deep down that it was time for her to move on.

Abby did love me, but she also cared about me too much to send me packing when she should. Even though I'd told her before that I couldn't walk away from her, I finally realized that I loved her too much to fuck up her life by staying, or to lose her completely by forcing us both to hang on until we hated each other.

"This was the best Thanksgiving we've had since Mom died," I said.

"I'm glad I was here to see it."

I took a deep breath. "I'm different," I said, conflicted about what I would say next. "I don't know what happened to me in Vegas. That wasn't me. I was thinking about everything we could buy with that money, and that was *all* I was thinking about. I didn't see how much it hurt you for me to want to take you back there, but deep down, I think I knew. I deserved for you to leave me. I deserved all the sleep I lost and the pain I've felt. I needed all that to realize how much I need you, and what I'm willing to do to keep you in my life.

"You said you're done with me, and I accept that. I'm a different person since I met you. I've changed . . . for the better. But no matter how hard I try, I can't seem to do right by you. We were friends first, and I can't lose you, Pigeon. I will always love you, but if I can't make you happy, it doesn't make much sense for me to try to get you back. I can't imagine being with anyone else, but I'll be happy as long as we're friends."

"You want to be friends?"

"I want you to be happy. Whatever that takes."

She smiled, breaking the part of my heart that wanted to take back everything I'd just said. Part of me hoped she would tell me to shut the fuck up because we belonged together.

"Fifty bucks says you'll be thanking me for this when you meet your future wife."

"That's an easy bet," I said. I couldn't imagine a life without her, and she was already thinking about our separate futures. "The only woman I'd ever wanna marry just broke my heart."

Abby wiped her eyes and then stood up. "I think it's time you took me home."

"C'mon, Pigeon. I'm sorry, that wasn't funny."

"It's not that, Trav. I'm just tired, and I'm ready to go home."

I sucked in a breath and nodded, standing up. Abby hugged my brothers goodbye, and asked Trenton to say goodbye to Dad. I stood at the door with our bags, watching them all agree to come home for Christmas.

When I slowed to a stop at Morgan Hall, I felt the tiniest bit of closure, but it didn't stop my heart from shattering.

I leaned over to kiss her cheek, and then held the door open, watching as she walked inside. "Thanks for today. You don't know how happy you made my family."

Abby stopped at the bottom of the stairs and turned. "You're going to tell them tomorrow, aren't you?"

I glanced at the Charger, trying to hold back the tears. "I'm pretty sure they already know. You're not the only one with a poker face, Pidge."

I left her on the steps alone, refusing to look back. From now on, the love of my life was only an acquaintance. I wasn't sure what expression I had on my face, but I didn't want her to see it.

The Charger whined as I drove far beyond the speed limit back to my father's. I stumbled into the living room, and Thomas handed me a bottle of whiskey. They all had some in a glass.

"You told them?" I asked Trenton, my voice broken.

Trenton nodded.

I collapsed to my knees, and my brothers surrounded me, placing their hands on my head and shoulders for support.

CHAPTER TWENTY-FOUR

Forget

"TRENT'S CALLING AGAIN! ANSWER YOUR DAMN PHONE!" Shepley yelled from the living room.

I kept my cell on top of the television. The farthest point from my bedroom in the apartment.

The first torturous days without Abby, I locked it in the glove box of the Charger. Shepley brought it back in, arguing that it should be in the apartment in case my dad called. Unable to deny that logic, I agreed, but only if it stayed on the TV.

The urge to pick it up and call Abby was maddening otherwise.

"Travis! Your phone!"

I stared up at the white ceiling, thankful that my other brothers had gotten the hint, and felt annoyed that Trenton hadn't. He'd kept me busy or drunk at night, but was under the impression he had to also call me during every break while he was at work. I felt I was on some sort of Maddox suicide watch.

Two and a half weeks into winter break, the urge to call Abby had turned into need. Any access at all to my phone seemed like a bad idea.

Shepley pushed open the door and threw the small, black rectangle into the air. It landed on my chest.

"Jesus, Shep. I told you . . ."

"I know what you said. You have eighteen missed calls."

"All Trent?"

"One is from Panty Wearers Anonymous."

I picked up the phone from my stomach, straightened my arm, and then opened my hand, letting the hard plastic fall to the floor. "I need a drink."

"You need a shower. You smell like shit. You also need to brush your damn teeth, shave, and put deodorant on."

I sat up. "You talk a lot of shit, Shep, but I seem to remember doing your laundry and making you soup for three entire months after Anya."

He sneered. "At least I brushed my teeth."

"I need you to schedule another fight," I said, falling back onto the mattress.

"You just had one two nights ago, and another a week before that. Numbers were down because of break. Adam won't schedule another until classes resume."

"Then bring in the locals."

"Too risky."

"Call Adam, Shepley."

Shepley walked over to my bed, picked up my cell phone, clicked a few buttons, and then threw the phone back onto my stomach. "Call him yourself."

I held up the phone to my ear.

"Asshat! What've you been doing? Why haven't you answered your phone? I wanna go out tonight!" Trenton said.

I narrowed my eyes at the back of my cousin's head, but he left my room without looking back.

"I don't feel like it, Trent. Call Cami."

"She's a bartender. It's New Year's Eve. We can go see her though! Unless you have other plans . . ."

"No. I don't have other plans."

"You just wanna lay there and die?"

"Pretty much." I sighed.

"Travis, I love you little brother, but you are being a huge pussy. She was the love of your life. I get it. It sucks. I know. But like it or not, life's gotta go on."

"Thank you, Mr. Rogers."

"You aren't old enough to know who that even is."

"Thomas made us watch reruns, remember?"

"No. Listen. I get off at nine. I'm gonna pick you up at ten. If you aren't dressed and ready, and I mean *showered and shaved* ready, I'm going to call a bunch of people and tell them you're having a party at your house with six free kegs and hookers."

"Damn it, Trenton, don't."

"You know I will. Last warning. Ten o'clock, or by eleven you'll have guests. Ugly ones."

I groaned. "I fucking hate you."

"No you don't. See you in ninety minutes."

The phone grated in my ear before it hung up. Knowing Trenton, he was probably calling from his boss's office, kicked back with his feet on the desk.

I sat up, looking around the room. The walls were empty, devoid of the pictures of Abby that had once crowded the white paint. The sombrero hung above my bed again, proudly displayed after the shame of being replaced by the framed black-and-white photo of Abby and me.

Trenton was really going to make me do this. I imagined myself sitting at the bar, the world celebrating around me, ignoring the fact that I was miserable and—according to Shepley and Trenton—being a pussy.

Last year I danced with Megan and ended up taking home Kassie Beck, who would've been a good one to keep on the list had she not thrown up in the hall closet.

I wondered what plans Abby had for the night but tried not to allow my mind to wander too far into the realm of who she might be meeting. Shepley hadn't mentioned America having plans. Unsure if that was being kept from me on purpose, pushing the issue just seemed too masochistic, even for me.

The night table drawer squeaked when I pulled it open. My fingers padded across the bottom and paused at the corners of a small box. Carefully I pulled it out, holding it in my hands against my chest. My chest rose and fell with a sigh, and then I opened the box, wincing at the sight of the sparkling diamond ring inside. There was only one finger that belonged inside that white gold circle, and with each passing day, that dream seemed less and less possible.

I knew when I bought the ring that it would be years before I gave it to Abby, but it made sense to keep it just in case the perfect moment happened to arise. Knowing it was there gave me something to look forward to, even now. Inside that box was the little bit of hope I had left.

After putting away the diamond, and giving myself a long mental pep talk, I finally trudged down the hall to the bathroom, intentionally keeping my eyes from my reflection in the mirror. The shower and shave didn't improve my mood, and neither (I would later point out to Shepley) did brushing my teeth. I put on a buttoned-up black shirt and blue jeans, and then slipped on my black boots.

Shepley knocked on my door and walked in, dressed and ready to go as well.

"You're going?" I asked, buckling my belt. I'm not sure why I was surprised. Without America there, he wouldn't have plans with anyone other than us.

"Is that okay?"

"Yeah. Yeah, I just . . . I guess you and Trent worked this out before."

"Well, yeah," he said, skeptical and maybe a little amused that I had just figured it out.

The Intrepid's horn honked outside, and Shepley pointed to the hallway with his thumb. "Let's roll."

I nodded once and followed him out. Trenton's car smelled like cologne and cigarettes. I popped a Marlboro in my mouth and lifted up my ass so I could get into my pocket for a lighter.

"So, the Red's packed, but Cami told the door guy to let us in. They've got a live band, I guess, and pretty much everyone is home. Should be a good one."

"Hanging out with our drunken, loser high school classmates in a dead college town. Score," I grumbled.

Trenton smiled. "I got a friend coming. You'll see."

My eyebrows pulled in. "Tell me you didn't."

A few people were huddled outside the door, waiting for people to leave so they could enter. We slipped past them, ignoring their complaints while we paid and walked straight in.

A table sat by the entrance, once full of New Year's Eve party hats, glasses, Glow Sticks, and kazoos. The freebies had been mostly picked through, but it didn't stop Trenton from finding a ridiculous pair of glasses that were shaped into the numbers of the new year. Glitter was all over the floor, and the band was playing "Hungry Like the Wolf."

I glowered at Trenton, who pretended not to notice. Shepley and I followed my older brother to the bar, where Cami was decapping bottles and shaking drinks at full speed, pausing only momentarily to type in numbers into the register or write down an addition to someone's tab. Her tip jars were overflowing, and she had to shove down the greenbacks into the glass every time someone added a bill.

When she saw Trenton, her eyes lit up. "You made it!" Cami grabbed three bottles of beer, popped the tops, and sat them on the bar in front of him.

"I said I would." He smiled, leaning over the counter to peck her lips.

That was the end of their conversation, as she quickly turned to slide another beer bottle down the bar and strained to hear another order.

"She's good," Shepley said, watching her.

Trenton smiled. "She damn sure is."

"Are you . . . ?" I began.

"No," Trent said, shaking his head. "Not yet. I'm working on it. She's got some asshole college boy in Cali. He just needs to piss her off one last time and she's going to figure out what a pecker head he is."

"Good luck with that," Shepley said, taking a swig of his beer.

Trenton and I intimidated a small group enough for them to

leave their table, so we nonchalantly commandeered it to start our night of drinking and people watching.

Cami took care of Trenton from afar, sending over a waitress regularly with full shot glasses of tequila and beer bottles. I was glad it was my fourth shot of Cuervo when the second 1980s ballad of the night began.

"This band sucks ass, Trent," I yelled over the noise.

"You just don't appreciate the legacy of hair bands!" he yelled back. "Hey. Looky there," he said, pointing to the dance floor.

A redhead sauntered across the crowded space, a glossed smile brightening her pale face.

Trenton stood up to hug her, and her smile grew wider. "Hey, T! How've you been?"

"Good! Good! Working. You?"

"Great! I'm living in Dallas, now. Working at a PR firm." Her eyes scanned our table, to Shepley and then to me. "Oh my God! Is this your baby brother? I used to babysit you!"

My eyebrows pulled together. She had double Ds and curves like a 1940s pinup model. I was sure if I had spent any time with her in my formative years, I would have remembered.

Trent smiled. "Travis, you remember Carissa, don't you? She graduated with Tyler and Taylor."

Carissa held out her hand, and I shook it once. I put the filter end of a cigarette between my front teeth, and flicked the lighter. "I don't think I do," I said, sticking the nearly empty pack in my front shirt pocket.

"You weren't very old." She smiled.

Trenton gestured to Carissa. "She just went through a bad divorce with Seth Jacobs. You remember Seth?"

I shook my head, already tired of the game Trenton was playing.

Carissa took the full shot glass that was in front of me and slurped it dry, and then she sidestepped until she was next to me. "I heard you've gone through a rough time lately, too. Maybe we could keep each other company tonight?"

By the look in her eyes, I could see she was drunk . . . and lonely. "Not looking for a babysitter," I said, taking a drag.

"Well, maybe just a friend? It's been a long night. I came here alone because all of my girlfriends are married now, ya know?" She giggled nervously.

"Not really."

Carissa looked down, and I felt a small bit of guilt. I was being a dick, and she hadn't done anything to deserve that from me.

"Hey, I'm sorry," I said. "I don't really wanna be here."

Carissa shrugged. "Me, either. But I didn't want to be alone."

The band stopped playing, and the lead singer began counting down from ten. Carissa looked around, and then back to me, her eyes glossing over. Her line of sight fell to my lips, and then in unison the crowd screamed, "HAPPY NEW YEAR!"

The band played a rough version of "Auld Lang Syne," and then Carissa's lips smashed into mine. My mouth moved against hers for a moment, but her lips were so foreign, so different from what I was used to, it only made Abby's memory more vivid, and the realization that she was gone more painful.

I pulled away and wiped my mouth with my sleeve.

"I'm so sorry," Carissa said, watching me leave the table.

I pushed through the crowd to the men's bathroom and locked myself in the only stall. I pulled out my phone and held it in my hands, my vision blurry and the rotten twang of tequila on my tongue.

Abby's probably drunk, too, I thought. *She wouldn't care if I called. It's New Year's Eve. She might even be waiting for my call.*

I scrolled over the names in my address book, stopping on Pigeon. I turned over my wrist, seeing the same inked into my skin. If Abby wanted to talk to me, she would have called. My chance had come and gone, and I told her at Dad's I would let her move on. Drunk or not, calling her was selfish.

Someone knocked on the stall door. "Trav?" Shepley asked. "You okay?"

I unlocked the door and stepped outside, my phone still in my hand.

"Did you call her?"

I shook my head, and then looked to the tile wall across the room. I reared back, and then launched my phone, watching it shatter into a million pieces and scatter on the floor. Some poor bastard standing at the urinal jumped, his shoulders flying up to his ears.

"No," I said. "And I'm not going to."

Shepley followed me back to the table without a word. Carissa was gone, and three new shots were waiting for us.

"I thought she might get your mind off things, Trav, I'm sorry. It always makes me feel better to bag a really hot chick when I've been where you're at," Trenton said.

"Then you haven't been where I'm at," I said, slamming the tequila to the back of my throat. I stood up quickly, grabbing the edge of the table for stability. "Time for me to go home and pass out, boys."

"You sure?" Trenton asked, looking mildly disappointed.

After Trenton got Cami's attention long enough to say goodbye, we made our way to the Intrepid. Before he started the car, he looked over at me.

"You think she'll ever take you back?"

"No."

"Then maybe it's time you accept that. Unless you don't want her in your life at all."

"I'm trying."

"I mean when classes start. Pretend it's like it was before you saw her naked."

"Shut up, Trent."

Trenton turned over the engine and put the car in reverse. "I was just thinking," he said, turning the wheel, and then shoving the shifter into drive, "that you were happy when you guys were friends, too. Maybe you could go back to that. Maybe you thinking you can't is why you're so miserable."

"Maybe," I said, staring out the window.

THE FIRST DAY OF SPRING SEMESTER FINALLY ARRIVED. I hadn't slept all night, tossing and turning, both dreading and eagerly anticipating seeing Abby again. Regardless of my sleepless night, I was determined to be all smiles, never letting on how much I'd suffered, to Abby or anyone else.

At lunch, my heart nearly exploded out of my chest when I saw her. She looked different, but the same. The difference was that she seemed like a stranger. I couldn't just walk up to her and kiss her or touch her like before. Abby's big eyes blinked once when she saw me, and I smiled and winked back, sitting at the end of our usual table. The football players were busy bitching about their loss to State, so I tried to relieve their angst by telling them some of my more colorful experiences over break, like watching Trenton salivate over Cami, and the time that his Intrepid broke down and we were almost arrested for public intoxication while walking home.

From the corner of my eye, I saw Finch hug Abby to his side, and for a moment I wondered if she wished I would go away, or if she might be upset.

Either way, I hated not knowing.

Throwing the last bite of something deep-fried and disgusting into my mouth, I tossed my tray and walked up behind Abby, resting my hands on her shoulders.

"How's your classes, Shep?" I asked, willing my voice not to sound anything but casual.

Shepley's face pinched. "First day sucks. Hours of syllabi and class rules. I don't even know why I show up the first week. How about you?"

"Eh . . . it's all part of the game. How 'bout you, Pidge?" I tried not to let the tension in my shoulders affect my hands.

"The same." Her voice was small, distant.

"Did you have a good break?" I asked, playfully swaying her from side to side.

"Pretty good."

Yeah. This was awkward as fuck.

"Sweet. I've got another class. Later." I walked out of the cafeteria quickly, reaching for the Marlboro box in my pocket before I even shouldered through the metal doors.

The next two classes were torture. The only place that felt like a safe haven was my bedroom, away from campus, away from everything that reminded me that I was alone, and away from the rest of the world, which was continuing on, not giving a shit that I was in so much pain it was palpable. Shepley kept telling me it wouldn't be so bad after a while, but it didn't seem to be letting up.

I met my cousin in the parking lot in front of Morgan Hall, trying hard not to stare at the entrance. Shepley seemed on edge and didn't talk much on the ride to the apartment.

When he pulled into his parking spot, he sighed. I debated whether or not to ask him if he and America were having problems, but I didn't think I could handle his shit *and* mine.

I grabbed my backpack from the backseat and pushed the door open, stopping only long enough to unlock the door.

"Hey," Shepley said, shutting the door behind him. "You all right?"

"Yeah," I said from the hallway, not turning around.

"That was kind of awkward in the cafeteria."

"I guess," I said, taking another step.

"So, uh . . . I should probably tell you something I overheard. I mean . . . hell, Trav, I don't know if I should tell you or not. I don't know if it'll make it worse or better."

I turned around. "Overheard from who?"

"Mare and Abby were talking. It was . . . mentioned that Abby's been miserable all break."

I stood in silence, trying to keep my breathing even.

"Did you hear what I said?" Shepley asked, his brows pulling together.

"What does that mean?" I asked, throwing my hands up. "She's been miserable without me? Because we're not friends anymore? What?"

Shepley nodded. "Definitely a bad idea."

"Tell me!" I yelled, feeling myself shake. "I can't . . . I can't keep feeling like this!" I threw my keys down the hall, hearing a loud crack when they made contact with the wall. "She barely acknowledged me today, and you're telling me she wants me back? As a friend? The way it was before Vegas? Or is she just miserable in general?"

"I don't know."

I let my bag fall to the floor and kicked it in Shepley's general direction. "Wh-why are you doing this to me, man? Do you think I'm not suffering enough, because I promise you, it's too much."

"I'm sorry, Trav. I just thought I'd wanna know . . . if it were me."

"You're not me! Just fucking . . . leave it alone, Shep. Leave it the hell alone." I slammed my door and sat on my bed, my head resting on my hands.

Shepley cracked open the door. "I'm not trying to make it worse, if that's what you think. But I knew if you found out later, you would have kicked my ass for not telling you. That's all I'm sayin'."

I nodded once. "Okay."

"You think . . . you think if maybe you focused on all the bullshit you had to endure with her, that'd make it easier?"

I sighed. "I've tried. I keep coming back to the same thought."

"What's that?"

"Now that it's over, I wish I could have all the bad stuff back . . . just so I could have the good."

Shepley's eyes bounced around the room, trying to think of something else comforting to say, but he was clearly all out of advice. His cell phone beeped.

"It's Trent," Shepley said, reading the display screen. His eyes lit up. "You want to grab some drinks with him at the Red? He gets off at five today. His car broke down and he wants you to take him to see Cami. You should go, man. Take my car."

"All right. Let him know I'm comin'." I sniffed, and wiped my nose before standing up.

Sometime between me leaving the apartment and pulling into the gravel lot of the tattoo parlor Trenton worked at, Shepley had alerted Trenton to my shitty day. Trenton gave it away when he insisted on going straight to the Red Door as soon as he slid into the passenger seat of the Charger, instead of wanting to go home to change first.

When we arrived, we were alone except for Cami, the owner, and some guy stocking Cami's bar, but it was the middle of the week—prime college bar time and coin beer night. It didn't take long for the room to fill with people.

I was already lit by the time Lexi and some of her friends had made a drive-by, but it wasn't until Megan stopped by that I even bothered to look up.

"Looking pretty sloppy, Maddox."

"Nah," I said, trying to get my numb lips to form around my words.

"Let's dance," she whined, tugging on my arm.

"I don't think I can," I said, swaying.

"I don't think you should," Trenton said, amused.

Megan bought me a beer and took the stool next to mine. Within ten minutes, she was pawing at my shirt, and not so subtly touching my arms, and then my hands. Just before closing, she had given up her stool to stand next to me—or more like straddle my thigh.

"So I didn't see the bike outside. Did Trenton drive you?"

"Nope. I brought Shepley's car."

"I love that car," she cooed. "You should let me drive you home."

"You wanna drive the Charger?" I asked, slurring.

I glanced over to Trenton, who was stifling a laugh. "Probably not a bad idea, little brother. Be safe . . . in every way."

Megan pulled me off the stool, and then out of the bar into the parking lot. She wore a sequined tube top with a jean skirt and boots, but she didn't seem to mind the cold—if it was cold. I couldn't tell.

She giggled as I threw my arm around her shoulders to help steady myself as I walked. When we reached the passenger side of Shepley's car, she stopped giggling.

"Some things never change, huh, Travis?"

"Guess not," I said, staring at her lips.

Megan wrapped her arms around my neck and pulled me in, not even hesitating to stick her tongue into my mouth. It was wet and soft, and vaguely familiar.

After a few minutes of playing grab ass and trading spit, she hiked her leg up, wrapping it around me. I grabbed her thigh, and rammed my pelvis into hers. Her ass slammed against the car door, and she moaned into my mouth.

Megan always liked it rough.

Her tongue made a trail down my neck, and it was then that I noticed the cold, feeling the warmth left behind by her mouth cool quickly from the winter air.

Megan's hand reached between us, and she grabbed my dick, smiling that I was right where she wanted me to be. "Mmmmm, Travis," she hummed, biting my lip.

"Pigeon." The word came out muffled as I crashed my mouth against hers. At that stage of the night, it was easy enough to pretend.

Megan giggled. "What?" In true Megan fashion, she didn't demand an explanation when I didn't respond. "Let's go to your apartment," she said, grabbing the keys from my hand. "My roommate is sick."

"Yeah?" I asked, pulling on the door handle. "You really wanna drive the Charger?"

"Better me than you," she said, kissing me one last time before leaving me for the driver's side.

While Megan drove, she laughed and talked about her break all while opening my jeans and reaching inside. It was a good thing I was drunk, because I hadn't been laid since Thanksgiving. Otherwise, by the time we reached the apartment, Megan would have had to catch a cab and call it a night.

Halfway home, the empty fishbowl flashed in my mind. "Wait a sec. Wait a sec," I said, pointing down the street. "Stop at the Swift Mart. We gotta pick up some . . ."

Megan reached into her purse and pulled out a small box of condoms. "Gotcha covered."

I leaned back and smiled. She really was my kind of girl.

Megan pulled up into Shepley's parking spot, having been to the apartment enough times to know. She jogged around in tiny steps, trying to hurry along in her stilettos.

I leaned on her to walk up the stairs, and she laughed against my mouth when I finally figured out the door was already unlocked and shoved through it.

Midkiss, I froze. Abby was standing in the front room, holding Toto.

"Pigeon," I said, stunned.

"Found it!" America said, jogging out of Shepley's room.

"What are you doing here?" I asked.

Abby's expression morphed from surprise to anger. "It's good to see you're feeling like your old self, Trav."

"We were just leaving," America snarled. She grabbed Abby's hand as they slid past me and Megan.

It took me a moment to react, but I made my way down the steps, for the first time noticing America's Honda. A string of expletives ran through my mind.

Without thinking, I grabbed a fistful of Abby's coat. "Where are you going?"

"Home," she snapped, straightening her coat in a huff.

"What are you doing here?"

The packed snow crunched under America's feet as she walked up behind Abby, and suddenly Shepley was beside me, his wary eyes fixed on his girlfriend.

Abby lifted her chin. "I'm sorry. If I knew you were going to be here, I wouldn't have come."

I shoved my hands in my coat pockets. "You can come here anytime you want, Pidge. I never wanted you to stay away."

"I don't want to *interrupt*." She looked to the top of the stairs, where Megan of course stood to watch the show. "Enjoy your evening," she said, turning away.

I grabbed her arm. "Wait. You're *mad*?"

She yanked her coat from my grip. "You know"—she laughed once—"I don't even know why I'm surprised."

She might have laughed, but she had hatred in her eyes. No matter what I did—moving on without her, or lying in my bed agonizing over her—she would have hated me. "I can't win with you. I can't *win* with you! You say you're done . . . I'm fucking miserable over here! I had to break my phone into a million pieces to keep from calling you every minute of the damn day—I've had to play it off like everything is just fine at school so you can be happy . . . and you're fucking *mad* at me? You *broke* my *fuckin'* heart!" I screamed.

"Travis, you're drunk. Let Abby go home," Shepley said.

I grabbed Abby's shoulders and pulled her closer, looking into her eyes. "Do you want me or not? You can't keep doing this to me, Pidge!"

"I didn't come here to see you."

"I don't want her," I said, staring at her lips. "I'm just so fucking unhappy, Pigeon." I leaned in to kiss her, but she grabbed my chin and held me away.

"You've got her lipstick on your mouth, Travis," she said, disgusted.

I took a step back and lifted my shirt, wiping my mouth. Red streaks left behind made it impossible to deny. "I just wanted to forget. Just for one fuckin' night."

One tear spilled over onto Abby's cheek, but she quickly wiped it away. "Then don't let me stop you."

She turned to walk away, but I grabbed her arm again.

A blond blur was suddenly in my face, lashing out and striking at me with small but vicious fists.

"Leave her alone, you bastard!"

Shepley grabbed America, but she pushed him away, turning to slap my face. The sound of her hand against my cheek was quick and loud, and I flinched with the noise. Everyone froze for a moment, shocked at America's sudden rage.

Shepley grabbed his girlfriend again, holding her wrists, and pulling her to the Honda while she thrashed about.

She fought him violently, her blond hair whipping around as she attempted to get away.

"How *could* you? She deserved better from you, Travis!"

"America, STOP!" Shepley yelled, louder than I'd ever heard him.

Her arms fell to her side as she glared at Shepley in disgust. "You're *defending* him?"

Although he was scared as hell, he stood his ground. "Abby broke up with *him*. He's just trying to move on."

America's eyes narrowed, and she pulled her arm from his grip. "Well then, why don't you go find a random WHORE"—she looked at Megan—"from the Red and bring her home to fuck, and then let me know if it helps you get over me."

"Mare." Shepley grabbed for her, but she evaded him, slamming the door as she sat behind the wheel. Abby opened the passenger door and sat next to her.

"Baby, don't leave," Shepley begged, leaning down into the window.

America started the car. "There is a right side and a wrong side here, Shep. And *you* are on the *wrong* side."

"I'm on your side," he said, his eyes desperate.

"Not anymore, you're not," she said, backing out.

"America? America!" Shepley yelled.

When the Honda was out of sight, Shepley turned around, breathing hard.

"Shepley, I'm—"

Before I could get a word out, Shepley reared back and launched his fist into my jaw.

I took the blow, touched my face, and then nodded. I deserved that.

"Travis?" Megan called from the stairs.

"I'll take her home," Shepley said.

I watched the taillights of the Honda get smaller as it took Abby farther away, feeling a lump form in my throat. "Thanks."

CHAPTER TWENTY-FIVE

Possession

SHE'S GOING TO BE THERE.

Showing up would be a mistake.

It would be awkward.

She's going to be there.

What if someone asks her to dance?

What if she meets her future husband and I'm there to witness it?

She doesn't want to see me.

I might get drunk and do something to piss her off.

She might get drunk and do something to piss me off.

I shouldn't go.

I had to go. She was going to be there.

I mentally listed the pros and cons for going to the Valentine's party but kept coming back to the same conclusion: I needed to see Abby, and that's where she would be.

Shepley was getting ready in his room, barely speaking to me since he and America had finally gotten back together. In part because they stayed holed up in his room making up for lost time, and he still blamed me for the five weeks they'd spent apart.

America never missed a moment to let me know she hated my guts, especially after the most recent time I'd broken Abby's heart. I had talked Abby into leaving her date with Parker to come with me to a fight. Of course I wanted her there, but I made the mistake of admitting it was also that I had primarily asked her so I could win a pissing contest. I wanted Parker to know he had no hold on her. Abby felt I'd taken advantage of her feelings for me, and she was right.

All of those things were enough to feel guilty about, but the fact that Abby had been attacked in a place where I'd taken her made it nearly impossible to look anyone in the eye. Adding to all of that our close call with the law totaled up to me being a gigantic fuckup.

Regardless of my constant apologies, America spent her days in the apartment shooting dirty looks in my direction, and snapping unwarranted shitty remarks. Even after all that, I was glad Shepley and America had reconciled. If she wouldn't have taken him back, Shepley might have never forgiven me.

"I'm going," Shepley said. He walked into my room, where I sat in my boxers, still conflicted about what to do. "Picking up Mare at the dorm."

I nodded once. "Abby's still going?"

"Yeah. With Finch."

I managed a half smile. "Should that make me feel better?"

Shepley shrugged. "It would me." He looked around my walls and nodded. "You put the pictures back up."

I looked around, nodding once. "I don't know. It didn't feel right to just have them sitting in a bottom drawer."

"I guess I'll see you later."

"Hey, Shep?"

"Yeah," he said, not turning around.

"I really am sorry, cousin."

Shepley sighed. "I know."

The second he left, I walked into the kitchen to pour the last of the whiskey. The liquid amber sat still in the glass, waiting to offer comfort.

I shot it back and closed my eyes, considering a trip to the liquor store. But there wasn't enough whiskey in the universe to help me make my decision.

"Fuck it," I said, grabbing my bike keys.

After a stop at Ugly Fixer Liquor's, I drove the Harley over the curb and parked in the front yard of the fraternity house, opening the half-pint I'd just bought.

Finding courage at the bottom of the bottle, I walked into Sig Tau. The entire house was covered in pink and red; cheap decorations were hung from the ceiling, and glitter covered the floor. The bass from the speakers downstairs hummed throughout the house, muffling the laughter and constant drone of conversation.

Standing room only, I had to turn and maneuver my way through the crowd of couples, keeping an eye out for Shepley, America, Finch, or Abby. Mostly Abby. She wasn't standing in the kitchen, or in any of the other rooms. She wasn't on the balcony, either, so I made my way downstairs. My breath caught when I saw her.

The beat of the music slowed, and her angel's smile was noticeable even across the dim basement. Her arms wrapped around Finch's neck, and he awkwardly moved with her to the music.

My feet propelled me forward, and before I knew what I was doing, or stopped to think about the consequences, I found myself standing inches away from them.

"Mind if I cut in, Finch?"

Abby froze, her eyes flashing with recognition.

Finch's eyes bounced between me and Abby. "Sure."

"Finch," she hissed as he walked away.

I pulled her against me and took a step.

Abby kept dancing but kept as much space between us as possible. "I thought you weren't coming."

"I wasn't, but I knew you were here. I had to come."

With each passing minute, I expected her to walk away, and every minute she stayed in my arms felt like a miracle. "You look beautiful, Pidge."

"Don't."

"Don't what? Tell you you're beautiful?"

"Just . . . don't."

"I didn't mean it."

"Thanks," she snapped.

"No . . . you look beautiful. I meant that. I was talking about what I said in my room. I'm not going to lie. I enjoyed pulling you from your date with Parker . . ."

"It wasn't a date, Travis. We were just eating. He won't speak to me now, thanks to you."

"I heard. I'm sorry."

"No you're not."

"Y-you're right," I said, stuttering when I noticed she was getting angry. "But I . . . that wasn't the only reason I took you to the fight. I wanted you there with me, Pidge. You're my good luck charm."

"I'm not your anything." She glared up at me.

My eyebrows pulled in and I stopped midstep. "You're my *everything*."

Abby's lips formed a hard line, but her eyes softened.

"You don't really hate me . . . do you?" I asked.

Abby turned away, putting more distance between us. "Sometimes I wish that I did. It would make everything a whole hell of a lot easier."

A cautious, small smile spread across my lips. "So what pisses you off more? What I did to make you wanna hate me? Or knowing that you can't?"

In a flash, Abby's anger returned. She shoved past me, running up the stairs to the kitchen. I stood alone in the middle of the floor, both dumbfounded and disgusted that I'd somehow managed to reignite her hatred for me all over again. Trying to speak to her at all seemed futile, now. Every interaction just added to the growing snowball of clusterfucks that was our relationship.

I walked up the stairs and made a beeline for the keg, cursing my greediness and the empty bottle of whiskey lying somewhere in Sig Tau's front lawn.

After an hour of beer and monotonous, drunken conversation with frat brothers and their dates, I glanced over at Abby, hoping to catch her eye. She was already looking at me, but looked away. America seemed to be in the middle of an attempt to cheer her up, and then Finch touched her arm. He was obviously ready to leave.

She drank the remainder of her beer in a quick swig, and then took Finch's hand. She walked two steps, and then froze when the same song that we had danced to at her birthday party floated up the stairs. She reached out and grabbed Finch's bottle, taking another swig.

I wasn't sure if it was the whiskey talking, but something

about the look in her eyes told me the memories the song triggered were just as painful for her as they were for me.

She still cared about me. She had to.

One of my frat brothers leaned against the counter beside Abby and smiled. "Wanna dance?"

It was Brad, and although I knew he had probably just noticed the forlorn look on her face and was trying to cheer her up, the hairs on the back of my neck stood on end. Just as she shook her head to say no, I was next to her, and my stupid fucking mouth was moving before my brain could tell it to stop.

"Dance with me."

America, Shepley, and Finch were all staring at Abby, waiting for her answer as anxiously as I was.

"Leave me alone, Travis," she said, crossing her arms.

"This is our song, Pidge."

"We don't have a song."

"Pigeon . . ."

"No."

She looked to Brad and forced a smile. "I would love to dance, Brad."

Brad's freckles stretched across his cheeks as he smiled, gesturing with his hand for Abby to lead the way to the stairs.

I staggered backward, feeling like I'd just been punched in the gut. A combination of anger, jealousy, and sadness boiled in my blood.

"A toast!" I yelled, climbing onto a chair. On my way to the top, I stole someone's beer and held it out in front of me. "To douche bags!" I said, gesturing to Brad. "And to girls that break your heart." I bowed to Abby. My throat tightened. "And to the absolute fucking horror of losing your best friend because you were stupid enough to fall in love with her."

I tilted back the beer, finishing what was left, and then tossed it to the floor. The room was silent except for the music playing in the basement, and everyone stared at me in mass confusion.

Abby's quick movement drew my attention when she grabbed Brad's hand, leading him downstairs to the dance floor.

I jumped off the chair and started for the basement, but Shepley put the side of his fist against my chest, leaning into me. "You need to stop," he said in a hushed voice. "This is only going to end badly."

"If it ends, what does it matter?" I shoved past Shepley and down the stairs to where Abby was dancing with Brad. The snowball was too big to stop, so I decided just to roll with it. There was no shame in going balls out. We couldn't go back to being friends, so making one of us hate the other seemed like a good idea.

I pushed my way through the couples on the dance floor, stopping beside Abby and Brad. "I'm cutting in."

"No, you're not. Jesus!" Abby said, ducking her head with embarrassment.

My eyes bore into Brad's. "If you don't back away from my girl, I'll rip out your fucking throat. Right here on the dance floor."

Brad seemed conflicted, his eyes nervously darting from me to his dance partner. "Sorry, Abby," he said, slowly pulling his arms away. He retreated to the stairs.

"How I feel about you right now, Travis . . . it very closely resembles hate."

"Dance with me," I pleaded, shifting to keep my balance.

The song ended and Abby sighed. "Go drink another bottle of whiskey, Trav." She turned to dance with the only single guy on the dance floor.

The tempo was faster, and with every beat, Abby moved closer and closer to her new dance partner. David, my least favorite Sig Tau brother, danced behind her, grabbing her hips. They smiled as they two-timed her, putting their hands all over her body. David grabbed her hips and dug his pelvis into her ass. Everyone stared. Instead of feeling jealous, guilt washed over me. This is what I had reduced her to.

In two steps, I bent down and wrapped my arm around Abby's legs, throwing her over my shoulder, shoving David to the ground for being such an opportunistic dick.

"Put me down!" Abby said, pounding her fists into my back.

"I'm not going to let you embarrass yourself over me," I growled, taking the stairs two at a time.

Every pair of eyes we passed watched Abby kick and scream as I carried her across the room. "You don't think," she said while she struggled, "this is embarrassing? Travis!"

"Shepley! Is Donnie outside?" I yelled, ducking from her flailing limbs.

"Uh . . . yeah?" he said.

"Put her down!" America said, taking a step toward us.

"America," Abby said, squirming, "don't just stand there! *Help* me!"

America's mouth turned up and she laughed once. "You two look ridiculous."

"Thanks a lot, *friend*!" she said, incredulous. Once we were outside, Abby only fought harder. "Put me down, dammit!"

I walked over to Donnie's waiting car, opened the back door, and tossed Abby inside. "Donnie, you're the DD tonight?"

Donnie turned around, nervously watching the chaos from the driver's seat. "Yeah."

"I need you to take us to my apartment," I said as I got in beside her.

"Travis . . . I don't think . . ."

"Do it, Donnie, or I'll shove my fist through the back of your head, I swear to God."

Donnie immediately put the car into gear and pulled away from the curb. Abby lunged for the door handle. "I'm not going to your apartment!"

I grabbed one of her wrists, and then the other. She leaned down, sinking her teeth into my forearm. It hurt like hell, but I just closed my eyes. When I was sure she'd broken the skin and it felt like fire was shooting up my arm, I growled to offset the pain.

"Do your worst, Pidge. I'm tired of your shit."

She released me and then thrashed around again, trying to hit me, more for being insulted than trying to get away. "*My* shit? Let me out of this fucking car!"

I pulled her wrists close to my face. "I love you, dammit! You're not going anywhere until you sober up and we figure this out!"

"You're the only one that hasn't figured it out, Travis!"

I released her wrists, and she crossed her arms, pouting the rest of the way to the apartment.

When the car slowed to a stop, Abby leaned forward. "Can you take me home, Donnie?"

I opened the door, and then pulled Abby out by the arm,

swinging her over my shoulder again. "Night, Donnie," I said, carrying her up the stairs.

"I'm calling your dad!" Abby cried.

I couldn't help but laugh. "And he'd probably pat me on the shoulder and tell me that it's about damn time!"

Abby's body writhed while I pulled the keys from my pocket. "Knock it off, Pidge, or we're going to fall down the stairs!"

Finally the door opened, and I stomped straight into Shepley's room.

"Put. Me. *Down*!" Abby screamed.

"Fine," I said, dropping her onto Shepley's bed. "Sleep it off. We'll talk in the morning."

I imagined how pissed she must have been, but even though my back was throbbing from being lambasted by Abby's fists for the last twenty minutes, it was a relief to have her in the apartment again.

"You can't tell me what to do anymore, Travis! I don't belong to you!"

Her words ignited a deep anger inside me. I stomped to the bed, planted my hands on the mattress on each side of her thighs, and leaned into her face.

"Well, I belong to you!" I screamed. I put so much force behind my words, I could feel all the blood rush to my face. Abby met my glare, refusing to even flinch. I looked at her lips, panting. "I belong to you," I whispered, my anger fading as desire took over.

Abby reached out, but instead of slapping my face, she grabbed each of my cheeks and slammed her mouth into mine. Without hesitation, I lifted her into my arms and carried her into my bedroom, letting us both fall into my mattress.

Abby grabbed at my clothes, desperate to remove them. I unzipped her dress with one smooth movement, and then watched as she pulled it quickly over her head, tossing it to the floor. Our eyes met, and then I kissed her, moaning into her mouth when she kissed me back.

Before I'd even had the chance to think, we were both naked. Abby grabbed my ass, anxious to pull me inside of her, but I resisted, the adrenaline burning through the whiskey and beer. My senses returned, and thoughts of permanent consequences began flashing though my mind. I had been an ass, I had pissed her off, but I never wanted Abby to wonder if I'd taken advantage of this moment.

"We're both drunk," I said, breathing hard.

"Please."

Her thighs squeezed my hips, and I could feel the muscles under her soft skin quiver in anticipation.

"This isn't right." I fought against the alcohol haze that told me that the next few hours with her was worth whatever was on the other side of that moment.

I pressed my forehead against hers. As much as I wanted her, the painful thought of making Abby take the walk of shame in the morning was stronger than what my hormones were telling me to do. If she really wanted to go through with this, I needed solid proof.

"I want you," she whispered against my mouth.

"I need you to say it."

"I'll say whatever you want."

"Then say that you belong to me. Say that you'll take me back. I won't do this unless we're together."

"We've never really been apart, have we?"

I shook my head, sweeping my lips across hers. Not good enough. "I need to hear you say it. I need to know you're mine."

"I've been yours since the second we met," she said, begging.

I stared into her eyes for a few seconds, and then felt my mouth turn up into a half smile, hoping her words were true and not just spoken in the moment. I leaned down and kissed her tenderly, and then she slowly pulled me into her. My entire body felt like it was melting inside of her.

"Say it again." Part of me couldn't believe it was all really happening.

"I'm yours." She breathed. "I don't ever want to be apart from you again."

"Promise me," I said, groaning with another thrust.

"I love you. I'll love you forever." She looked straight into my eyes when she spoke, and it finally clicked that her words weren't just an empty promise.

I sealed my mouth over hers, the rhythm of our movements picking up momentum. Nothing else needed to be said, and for the first time in months, my world wasn't upside down. Abby's back arched, and her legs wrapped around my back, hooked at the ankles. I tasted every part of her skin I could reach as if I'd been starving for it. A part of me was. An hour passed, and then another. Even when I was exhausted, I kept going, afraid if we stopped I would wake up, and it would all be just a dream.

I SQUINTED AGAINST THE LIGHT POURING INTO THE room. I couldn't sleep all night, knowing when the sun came up, it would all be over. Abby stirred, and my teeth clenched. The few hours we spent together wasn't enough. I wasn't ready.

Abby nuzzled her cheek against my chest. I kissed her hair, and then her forehead, and then her cheeks, neck, shoulders, and then I brought her hand to my mouth and tenderly kissed her wrist, palm, and fingers. I wanted to squeeze her but restrained myself. My eyes filled with hot tears for the third time since I'd brought her to my apartment. When she woke, she was going to be mortified, angry, and then leave me forever.

I'd never been so afraid to see the different shades of gray in her irises.

Her eyes still closed, Abby smiled, and I brought my mouth back to hers, terrified for the realization to hit.

"Good morning," she said against my mouth.

I moved halfway above her and then continued to touch my lips to various spots on her skin. My arms dug beneath her, between her back and the mattress, and I buried my face in her neck, taking in her scent before she bolted out the door.

"You're quiet this morning," she said, running her hands over the bare skin of my back. She slid her palms over my ass, and then hooked her leg over my hip.

I shook my head. "I just want to be like this."

"Did I miss something?"

"I didn't mean to wake you up. Why don't you just go back to sleep?"

Abby leaned back against the pillow, pulling up my chin to face her.

"What in the hell is wrong with you?" she asked, her body suddenly tense.

"Just go back to sleep, Pigeon. Please?"

"Did something happen? Is it America?" With the last question, she sat up.

I sat up with her, wiping my eyes.

"No . . . America's fine. They got home around four this morning. They're still in bed. It's early, let's just go back to sleep."

Her eyes bounced around to different points of my room as she remembered the night before. Knowing any moment she would recall the fact that I'd dragged her out of the party and made a spectacle, I put both hands on each side of her face and kissed her one last time.

"Have you slept?" she asked, wrapping her arms around my middle.

"I . . . couldn't. I didn't wanna . . ."

She kissed my forehead. "Whatever it is, we'll get through it, okay? Why don't you get some sleep? We'll figure it out when you wake up."

That was not what I expected. My head popped up and I scanned her face. "What do you mean? That *we'll* get through it?"

Her eyebrows pulled in. "I don't know what's going on, but I'm here."

"You're here? As in you're staying? With me?"

Her expression scattered in different directions. "Yes. I thought we discussed this last night?"

"We did." I probably looked like a total tool, but I nodded emphatically.

Abby's eyes narrowed. "You thought I was going to wake up pissed at you, didn't you? You thought I was going to leave?"

"That *is* what you're famous for."

"Is that what you're so upset about? You stayed up all night worrying about what would happen when I woke up?"

I shifted. "I didn't mean for last night to happen like that. I was a little drunk, and I followed you around the party like some fucking stalker, and then I dragged you out of there, against your will . . . and then we . . ." I shook my head, disgusted with myself.

"Had the best sex of my life?" Abby said, smiling and squeezing my hand.

I laughed once, astounded at how well the conversation was going. "So we're okay?"

Abby held my face and kissed me tenderly. "Yes, dummy. I promised, didn't I? I told you everything you wanted to hear, we're back together, and you're still not happy?"

My breath faltered, and I choked back tears. It still didn't seem real.

"Travis, stop. I love you," she said, using her thin fingers to smooth lines around my eyes. "This absurd standoff could have been over at Thanksgiving, but . . ."

"Wait . . . what?" I interrupted, leaning back.

"I was fully prepared to give in on Thanksgiving, but you said you were done trying to make me happy, and I was too proud to tell you that I wanted you back."

"Are you fucking kidding me? I was just trying to make it easier on you! Do you know how *miserable* I've been?"

Abby frowned. "You looked just fine after break."

"That was for you! I was afraid I'd lose you if I didn't pretend to be okay with being friends. I could have been with you this whole time? What the *fuck*, Pigeon?"

"I . . . I'm sorry."

"You're *sorry*? I damn near drank myself to death, I could

barely get out of bed, I shattered my phone into a million pieces on New Year's Eve to keep from calling you . . . and you're *sorry*?"

Abby bit her bottom lip and nodded, ashamed. "I'm so . . . *so* sorry."

"You're forgiven," I said without hesitation. "Don't ever do it again."

"I won't. I promise."

I shook my head, grinning like an idiot. "I fucking love you."

CHAPTER TWENTY-SIX

Panic

LIFE HAD RETURNED TO NORMAL—MAYBE MORE FOR Abby than for me. On the surface we were happy, but I could feel a wall of caution building around me. Not a second with Abby was taken for granted. If I looked over at her and wanted to touch her, I did. If she wasn't at the apartment and I missed her, I went to Morgan. If we were at the apartment, she was in my arms.

Returning to school as a couple for the first time since the fall had the expected effect. As we walked around together, holding hands, laughing, and occasionally kissing—okay, more than occasionally—the gossip spiked to an all-time high. As always at this school, whispers and tabloid-worthy stories continued until another scandal rocked the campus.

On top of the unrest I already felt about my and Abby's relationship, Shepley was growing increasingly irritable about the last fight of the year. I wasn't far behind. We both depended on the winnings from that fight to fund our living expenses for the summer, not to mention part of the fall. Since I'd decided the last fight of the year was also my last fight for good, we would need it.

Spring break inched closer, but still no word from Adam. Shepley had finally heard through multiple lines of communication that Adam was lying low after the arrests following the most recent fight.

On the Friday before break, the campus mood felt lighter, even with the fresh batch of snow that had been dumped onto the state overnight. On our way to the cafeteria for lunch, Abby and I had barely escaped a public snowball fight; America, not so much.

We all chatted and laughed, waiting in line for trays of God-knows-what, and then sat at our regular seats. Shepley comforted America while I amused Brazil with the story of how Abby hustled my brothers on poker night. My phone buzzed, but it didn't register until Abby pointed it out.

"Trav?" she said.

I turned, tuning everything out the second she said my name.

"You might want to get that."

I looked down at the cell phone and sighed. "Or not." Part of me needed that last fight, but part of me knew it would be time spent away from Abby. After she was attacked at the last one, there was no way I could concentrate if she came to this one without protection—and I couldn't concentrate fully if she wasn't there, either. The last fight of the year was always the biggest, and I couldn't afford to have my head somewhere else.

"It could be important," Abby said.

I held the phone to my ear. "What's up, Adam?"

"Mad Dog! You're gonna love this. It's done. I got John fucking Savage! He's planning to go pro next year! Chance of a goddamn lifetime, my friend! Five figures. You'll be set for a while."

"This is my last fight, Adam."

The other end of the line was quiet. I could imagine his jaw working under the skin. More than once he'd accused Abby of threatening his cash flow, and I was sure he would blame her for my decision.

"Are you bringing her?"

"I'm not sure yet."

"You should probably leave her at home, Travis. If this really is your last fight, I need you all in."

"I won't go without her, and Shep's leaving town."

"No fucking around this time. I mean it."

"I know. I heard you."

Adam sighed. "If you really won't consider leaving her at home, maybe you could call Trent. That would probably set your mind at ease, and then you could concentrate."

"Hmmm . . . that's not a bad idea, actually," I said.

"Think about it. Let me know," Adam said, hanging up the phone.

Abby stared at me expectantly.

"It's enough to pay rent for the next eight months. Adam got John Savage. He's trying to go pro."

"I haven't seen him fight, have you?" Shepley asked, leaning forward.

"Just once in Springfield. He's good."

"Not good enough," Abby said. I leaned in and kissed her forehead. "I can stay home, Trav."

"No," I said, shaking my head.

"I don't want you to get hit like you did last time because you're worried about me."

"No, Pidge."

"I'll wait up for you." She smiled, but it was obviously forced, making me even more determined.

"I'm going to ask Trent to come. He's the only one I'd trust so I can concentrate on the fight."

"Thanks a lot, asshole," Shepley grumbled.

"Hey, you had your chance," I said, only half teasing.

Shepley's mouth pulled to the side. He could pout all day long, but he dropped the ball at Hellerton, letting Abby get away from him like that. If he'd been paying attention, it would have never happened, and we all knew it.

America and Abby swore that it was a fluke accident, but I didn't hesitate to tell him otherwise. He was watching the fight instead of Abby, and if Ethan had finished what he started, I would be in jail for murder. Shepley apologized to Abby for weeks, but then I took him aside and told him to knock it off. None of us liked reliving it every time his guilt got the best of him.

"Shepley, it wasn't your fault. You pulled him off of me, remember?" Abby said, reaching around America to pat his arm. She turned to me. "When is the fight?"

"Next week sometime. I want you there. I need you there." If I'd been any less of an asshole, I would have insisted she stay home, but it had already been established on numerous occasions that I wasn't. My need to be around Abby Abernathy overruled any rational thought. It had always been that way, and I imagined it always would.

Abby smiled, resting her chin on my shoulder. "Then I'll be there."

I dropped Abby off at her final class, kissing her goodbye before meeting Shepley and America at Morgan. The campus was quickly emptying, and I finally resorted to smoking my cigarettes around the corner so I wouldn't have to dodge a coed carrying luggage or laundry every three minutes.

I pulled my cell phone from my pocket and dialed Trenton's number, listening to each ring with increasing impatience. Finally, his voice mail picked up. "Trent, it's me. I need a huge favor. It's time sensitive, so call me back ASAP. Later."

I hung up, seeing Shepley and America pushing through the glass doors of the dorm, each holding two of her bags.

"Looks like you're all set."

Shepley smiled; America didn't.

"They're really not that bad," I said, nudging her with my elbow. Her scowl didn't disappear.

"She'll feel better once we get there," Shepley said, more to encourage his girlfriend than to convince me.

I helped them pack the trunk of the Charger, and then we waited for Abby to finish her midterm and find us in the parking lot.

I pulled my beanie over my ears and lit a cigarette, waiting. Trenton still hadn't called back, and I was getting nervous that he wouldn't be able to come. The twins were halfway to Colorado with some of their fellow Sig Tau alums, and I didn't trust anyone else to keep Abby safe.

I took several drags, working out the different scenarios in my head if Trenton didn't call back, and how fucking selfish I was being, requiring her presence in a place where I knew she could be in danger. Complete concentration was needed to win this fight, and that depended on two things: Abby's presence, and Abby's safety. If Trenton had to work or didn't call me back, I'd have to call off the fight. That was the only option.

I took a final drag off the last cigarette in the pack. I'd been so wrapped up in worry, I hadn't realized how much I'd been smoking. I looked down at my watch. Abby should have gotten out of class by now.

Just then, she called my name.

"Hey, Pigeon."

"Everything okay?"

"It is now," I said, pulling her against me.

"Okay. What's up?"

"Just have a lot on my mind." I sighed. When she made it known that my answer wasn't good enough, I continued, "This week, the fight, you being there . . ."

"I told you I would stay home."

"I need you there, Pidge," I said, flicking my cigarette to the ground. I watched it disappear into a deep footprint in the snow, and then took Abby's hand.

"Have you talked to Trent?" she asked.

"I'm waiting for him to call me back."

America rolled down the window and poked her head out of Shepley's Charger. "Hurry up! It's freaking freezing!"

I smiled and opened the door for Abby. While I stared out the window Shepley and America repeated the same conversation they'd had since she learned she would be meeting his parents. Just as we pulled into the parking lot of the apartment, my phone rang.

"What the fuck, Trent?" I asked, seeing his name on the display. "I called you hours ago. It's not like you're productive at work or anything."

"It hasn't been *hours*, and I'm sorry. I've been at Cami's."

"Whatever. Listen, I need a favor. I've got a fight next week. I need you to go. I don't know when it is, but when I call you, I need you there within an hour. Can you do that for me?"

"I don't know. What's in it for me?" he teased.

"Can you do it or not, douche bag? Because I need you to keep an eye on Pigeon. Some asshole put his hands on her last time and—"

"What the fuck, Chuck? Are you serious?"

"Yeah."

"Who did it?" Trenton asked, his tone immediately grave.

"I took care of it. So if I call . . . ?"

"Yeah. I mean, of course, little brother, I'll be there."

"Thanks, Trent." I clicked my phone shut and leaned my head against the back of the seat.

"Relieved?" Shepley asked, watching my anxiety unwind inside the rearview mirror.

"Yeah. I wasn't sure how I was going to do it without him there."

"I told you—" Abby began, but I stopped her.

"Pidge, how many times do I have to say it?"

She shook her head at my impatient tone. "I don't understand it, though. You didn't need me there before."

I turned to her, my finger touching her cheek. She clearly had no idea how deep my feelings ran. "I didn't know you before. When you're not there, I can't concentrate. I'm wondering where you are, what you're doing . . . if you're there and I can see you, I can focus. I know it's crazy, but that's how it is."

"And crazy is exactly the way I like it," she said, leaning up to kiss my lips.

"Obviously," America muttered under breath.

Before the sun set too far into the horizon, America and Shepley took the Charger south.

Abby shook the Honda keys and smiled. "At least we don't have to freeze on the Harley."

I smiled.

Abby shrugged. "Maybe we should, I don't know, consider getting our own car?"

"After the fight, we'll go shopping for one. How about that?"

She jumped up, wrapped her arms and legs around me, and covered my cheeks, mouth, and neck with kisses.

I walked up the stairs to the apartment, making a beeline to the bedroom.

Abby and I spent the next four days snuggled up either in the bed, or on the couch with Toto, watching old movies. It made waiting on Adam's call tolerable.

Finally on Tuesday night, between *Boy Meets World* reruns, Adam's number lit up my cell phone's display. My eyes met Abby's.

"Yeah?"

"Mad Dog. You're up in an hour. Keaton Hall. Bring your game face, sweet pea, he's Hulk Hogan on steroids."

"See you then." I stood up, bringing Abby with me. "Change into something warm, baby. Keaton is an old building, and they've probably shut off the heaters for break."

Abby did a little happy dance before jogging down the hall to the bedroom. The corners of my mouth turned up. What other woman would be that excited to see her boyfriend trade punches? No wonder I fell in love with her.

I slipped on a hoodie and my boots, and waited for Abby by the front door.

"Coming!" she called, strutting around the corner. She gripped each side of the door jamb and shifted her hip to the side.

"What do you think?" she asked, pouting her lips attempting to imitate a model . . . or a duck. I wasn't sure which.

My eyes traveled down from her long, heather gray cardigan, white T, and tight blue jeans tucked inside tall black boots. She meant it as a joke, thinking she looked frumpy, but my breath caught at the sight of her.

Her body relaxed, and she let her hands fall to her thighs. "That bad?"

"No," I said, trying to find the words. "Not bad at all."

With one hand I opened the door, and held out the other. With a bounce in her walk, Abby crossed the living room and intertwined her fingers in mine.

The Honda was slow to start, but we made it to Keaton in plenty of time. I called Trenton on the way, hoping to God he would come through for me like he'd promised.

Abby stood with me, waiting for Trenton beside the tall, seasoned north wall of Keaton. The east and west walls were protected with steel scaffolding. The university was preparing to give their oldest building a face-lift.

I lit a cigarette and took a drag, blowing smoke out of my nose.

Abby squeezed my hand. "He'll be here."

People were already filtering in from every direction, parking blocks away in different lots. The closer it came to fight time, the more people could be seen scaling the south fire escape.

I frowned. The building choice hadn't been thought through. The last fight of the year always brought the more serious punters out, and they always came early so they could place their bets and secure a good view. The size of the pot also brought out the less experienced spectators, who showed up late and ended up flattened against the walls. This year's was exceptionally large. Keaton was on the outskirts of campus, which was preferred, but its basement was one of the smallest.

"This is one of the worst ideas Adam has had yet," I grumbled.

"It's too late to change it now," Abby said, her eyes traveling up the concrete blocks.

I popped open my cell and shot a sixth text to Trenton, and then snapped the phone shut.

"You seem nervous tonight," Abby whispered.

"I'll feel better when Trent gets his punk ass here."

"I'm here, you whiny little girl," Trenton said in a hushed voice.

I sighed with relief.

"How ya been, sis?" Trenton asked Abby, hugging her with one arm, and then playfully shoving me with the other.

"I'm good, Trent," she said, amused.

I led Abby by the hand to the back of the building, glancing back to Trenton as we walked. "If the cops show and we get separated, meet me at Morgan Hall, okay?"

Trenton nodded just as I stopped next to an open window low to the ground.

"You're fuckin' with me," Trenton said, staring down at the window. "Abby's barely gonna fit through there."

"You'll fit," I assured him, crawling down into the blackness inside.

Now accustomed to breaking and entering, Abby didn't hesitate to crawl on the frozen ground and inch backward through the window, falling into my arms.

We waited for a few moments, and then Trenton grunted as he pushed off the ledge and landed on the floor, nearly losing his balance as his feet hit the concrete.

"You're lucky I love Abby. I wouldn't do this shit for just anyone," he grumbled, brushing off his shirt.

I jumped up, shutting the window with one quick pull. "This way," I said, leading Abby and my brother through the dark.

We weaved farther into the building until a small flicker of light could be seen ahead. A low hum of voices came from the same point, as our three pairs of feet grated against the loose concrete on the floor.

Trenton sighed after the third turn. "We're never gonna find our way out of here."

"Just follow me out. It'll be fine," I said.

It was easy to discern how close we were by the growing volume of the crowd waiting in the main room. Adam's voice came over the bullhorn, yelling names and numbers.

I stopped in the next room, glancing around at the desks and chairs covered in white sheets. A sick feeling came over me. The venue was a mistake. Almost as big as bringing Abby somewhere so dangerous. If a fight broke out, Abby would be protected by Trenton, but the usual safe haven away from the crowd was full of furniture and equipment.

"So how you're gonna play this?" Trenton asked.

"Divide and conquer."

"Divide what?"

"His head from the rest of his body."

Trenton nodded quickly. "Good plan."

"Pigeon, I want you to stand by this doorway, okay?" Abby looked into the main room, her eyes wide as she took in the chaos. "Pigeon, did you hear me?" I asked, touching her arm.

"What?" she asked, blinking.

"I want you to stand by this doorway, okay? Keep hold of Trent's arm at all times."

"I won't move," she said. "I promise."

I smiled at her sweet, overwhelmed expression. "Now *you* look nervous."

She glanced to the doorway, and then back at me. "I don't have a good feeling about this, Trav. Not about the fight, but . . . something. This place gives me the creeps."

I couldn't disagree. "We won't be here long."

Adam's voice came over the horn, starting his opening announcement.

I touched each side of Abby's face, and looked into her eyes. "I love you." A ghost of a smile touched her lips, and I pulled her into me, holding her tight against my chest.

". . . so don't use your hos to scam the system, boys!" Adam's voice said, amplified by the bullhorn.

I hooked Abby's arm around Trenton's. "Don't take your eyes off her. Even for a second. This place'll get crazy once the fight starts."

". . . so let's welcome tonight's contender—JOHN SAVAGE!"

"I'll guard her with my life, little brother," Trenton said, lightly tugging Abby's arm for emphasis. "Now go kick this guy's ass and let's get out of here."

"Shake in your boots, boys, and drop your panties, ladies! I give you: TRAVIS 'MAD DOG' MADDOX!"

At Adam's introduction, I stepped into the main room.

Arms flailed, and the voices of many boomed in unison. The sea of people parted before me, and I slowly made my way out to the Circle.

The room was lit only with lanterns hanging from the ceiling. Still trying to keep a low profile from nearly getting busted before, Adam didn't want bright lights tipping anyone off.

Even in the dim light, I could see the severity of John Savage's expression. He towered over me, his eyes wild and eager. He bounced from one foot to the other a few times, and then stood still, glowering down at me with murder in mind.

Savage was no amateur, but there were only three ways to win: knockout, submission, and decision. The reason the advantage had always been in my favor was because I had four brothers, who all fought different ways.

If John Savage fought like Trenton, he would rely on offense, speed, and surprise attacks—which I had trained for my entire life.

If he fought like the twins—with combinations of punches and kicks, or switching up his tactics to land blows—I had trained for that all my life.

Thomas was the most lethal. If Savage fought smart, and he probably did, judging by the way he was sizing me up, he would fight with the perfect balance of strength, speed, and strategy. I'd only traded blows with my eldest brother a handful of times in my life, but by the time I was sixteen, he couldn't defeat me without help from my other brothers.

No matter how hard John Savage had trained, or what advantage he thought he had, I had fought him before. I had fought everyone that could fight worth a damn before . . . and I had won.

Adam blew the bullhorn, and Savage took a short step back before powering a blow in my direction.

I dodged. He would definitely fight like Thomas.

Savage got too close, so I pulled up my boot and launched him back into the crowd. They pushed him back into the circle, and he approached me with renewed purpose.

He landed two punches in a row, and then I grabbed him, shoving his face down into my knee. John stumbled backward, got his wits about him, and then charged again.

I swung and missed, and then he tried to wrap his arms around my middle. Already sweaty, it was easy to slip from his grasp. When I turned, his elbow met with my jaw, and the world stopped for less than a second before I shook it off and answered him with a left and right hook, landing one right after the other.

Savage's bottom lip split and splattered. Drawing first blood heightened the volume in the room to a deafening decibel.

My elbow reared back, and my fist followed all the way through, making a short pit stop at Savage's nose. I didn't hold back, purposefully stunning him so I would have time to look back and check on Abby. She stood where I'd asked her to, her arm still hooked around Trenton's.

Satisfied she was okay, I focused on the fight again, dodging quickly when Savage threw a wobbly punch, and then threw his arms around me, yanking us both to the ground.

John landed under me, and without even trying, my elbow rammed into his face. He put my body in a vise grip with his legs, locking them together at the ankles.

"I'm going to end you, you fucking punk!" John growled.

I smiled, and then pushed off the ground, lifting both of us.

Savage struggled to take me off balance, but it was time to get Abby home.

Trenton's voice erupted over the rest of the crowd. "Slam his ass, Travis!"

I fell forward and slightly to the side, slamming John's back and head against the concrete in a devastating blow. My opponent now dazed, I reared back my elbow and shoved my fists into his face and the sides of his head over and over until a pair of arms hooked under my mine and pulled me away.

Adam threw a red square on Savage's chest, and the room exploded as Adam grabbed my wrist and raised my hand in the air.

I looked to Abby, who was bobbing up and down, heads above the rest of the crowd, held up by my brother.

Trenton was yelling something, a huge smile on his face.

Just as the crowd began to disperse, I caught a horrified look on Abby's face, and seconds later, a collective cry from the crowd sparked panic. A hanging lantern in the corner of the main room had fallen, catching a white sheet on fire. The blaze spread quickly to the sheet beside it, starting a chain reaction.

The screaming crowd rushed to the mouth of the stairs as smoke quickly filled the room. Frightened faces, both male and female, were highlighted by flames.

"Abby!" I screamed, realizing just how far away she was, and just how many people were between us. If I couldn't get to her, she and Trenton would have to find their way back to the window through the maze of dark hallways. Terror dug into my core, spurring me to wildly push through whoever got in my way.

The room darkened, and a loud popping noise sounded from the other side of the room. The other lanterns were igniting and adding to the blaze in small explosions. I caught a glimpse of

Trenton, who was grabbing at Abby's arm, pulling her behind him as he tried to force his way through the crowd.

Abby shook her head, pulling back.

Trenton looked around, forming a plan of escape while they stood in the center of the confusion. If they tried to go out the fire escape, they would be the last ones out. The fire was growing fast. They wouldn't make it through the crowd to get to the exit in time.

Any attempt I made to get to Abby was thwarted as the crowd surged and pushed me farther away. The excited cheering that filled the room before was replaced by horrified shrieks of fear and desperation as everyone fought to reach the exits.

Trenton pulled Abby to the doorway, but she struggled against him to look back. "Travis!" she yelled, reaching out for me.

I took a breath to yell back, but smoke filled my lungs. I coughed, waving the smoke away.

"This way, Trav!" Trenton yelled.

"Just get her out of here, Trent! Get Pigeon out!"

Abby's eyes widened, and she shook her head. "Travis!"

"Just go!" I said. "I'll catch up to you outside!"

Abby paused for a moment before her lips formed a hard line. Relief came over me. Abby Abernathy had a strong survival instinct, and it had just kicked in. She grabbed Trenton's sleeve and pulled him back into the darkness, away from the fire.

I turned, looking for my own way out. Dozens of spectators were clawing their way to the narrow access to the stairs, screaming and fighting one another to get to the exit.

The room was nearly black with smoke, and I felt my lungs struggling for air. I kneeled to the ground, trying to remember the different doors that lined the main room. I turned back to the stairway. That was the way I wanted to go, away from the fire, but I refused to panic. There was a second exit that led to the fire escape, one only a few people would think to go through. I crouched and ran toward where I remembered it being, but I stopped.

Thoughts of Abby and Trenton getting lost flashed in my mind, pulling me away from the exit.

I heard my name, and squinted toward the sound.

"Travis! Travis! This way!" Adam stood in the doorway, waving me toward him.

I shook my head. "I'm going to get Pigeon!"

The path to the smaller room where Trenton and Abby escaped through was almost clear, so I sprinted across the room, hitting someone head-on. It was a girl, a freshman by the looks of her, her face covered with black streaks. She was terrified and scrambled to her feet.

"H-help me! I can't . . . I don't know the way out!" she said, coughing.

"Adam!" I yelled. I pushed her toward the direction of the exit. "Help her out of here!"

The girl raced for Adam, and he grabbed her hand before they disappeared through the exit before the smoke totally obscured it from view.

I pushed off the floor and ran toward Abby. Others were running around in the dark mazes too, crying and panting as they tried to find a way out.

"Abby!" I yelled into the darkness. I was terrified they had taken a wrong turn.

A small group of girls stood in the end of a hallway, crying. "Have you seen a guy and a girl go through here? Trenton's about this tall, looks like me?" I said, holding a hand to my forehead.

They shook their heads.

My stomach sank. Abby and Trenton had gone the wrong way.

I pointed past the frightened group. "Follow that hall until you get to the end. There is a stairwell with a door at the top. Take it, and then turn left. There's a window you can get out of."

One of the girls nodded, wiped her eyes, and then barked at her friends to follow.

Instead of backtracking down the halls from where we came, I turned left, running through the blackness, hoping that I would get lucky and run into them somehow.

I could hear screaming from the main room as I pushed on, determined to make sure Abby and Trenton had found their way out. I wouldn't leave until I knew for sure.

After running through several hallways, I felt panic weighing down my chest. The smell of smoke had caught up to me, and I knew that with the construction, the aged building, the furniture, and the sheets that covered them feeding the fire, the entire basement level would be swallowed by the flames in minutes.

"Abby!" I yelled again. "Trent!"

Nothing.

CHAPTER TWENTY-SEVEN

Fire and Ice

THE SMOKE HAD BECOME INESCAPABLE. NO MATTER what room I found myself in, every breath was shallow and hot, burning my lungs.

I leaned down and grabbed my knees, panting. My sense of direction was weakened, both by the darkness, and the real possibility of not being able to find my girlfriend or brother before it was too late. I wasn't even sure if I could find my *own* way out.

Between bouts of coughing, I heard a knocking sound coming from the adjacent room.

"Help me! Somebody help me!"

It was Abby. Renewed resolve came over me, and I scrambled toward her voice, feeling through the blackness. My hands touched a wall, and then I stopped when I felt a door. It was locked. "Pidge?" I yelled, yanking on the door.

Abby's voice became more shrill, spurring me to take a step back and kick at the door until it flew open.

Abby stood on a desk just under a window, banging her hands against the glass so desperately, she didn't even realize I'd broken into the room.

"Pigeon?" I said, coughing.

"Travis!" she cried, scrambling down from the desk and into my arms.

I cupped her cheeks. "Where's Trent?"

"He followed them!" she bawled, tears streaming down her face. "I tried to get him to come with me, but he wouldn't come!"

I looked down the hall. The fire was barreling toward us, feeding on the covered furniture that lined the walls.

Abby gasped at the sight, and then coughed. My eyebrows pulled in, wondering where in the hell he was. If he was at the end of that hallway, he couldn't have made it. A sob welled up in my throat, but the look of terror in Abby's eyes forced it away.

"I'm gonna get us outta here, Pidge." I pressed my lips against hers in one quick, firm movement, and then climbed on top of her makeshift ladder.

I pushed at the window, the muscles of my arms quivering as I used all of my remaining strength against the glass.

"Get back, Abby! I'm gonna break the glass!"

Abby took one step away, her entire body shaking. My elbow bent as I reared back my fist, and I let out a grunt as I rammed it into the window. Glass shattered, and I reached out my hand.

"Come on!" I yelled.

The heat from the fire took over the room. Motivated by pure fear, I lifted Abby from the floor with one arm, and pushed her outside.

She waited on her knees as I climbed out, and then helped me to my feet. Sirens blared from the other side of the building, and red and blue lights from fire engines and police cruisers danced across the brick on the adjacent buildings.

I pulled Abby with me, sprinting to where a crowd of people

stood in front of the building. We scanned the soot-covered faces for Trenton while I yelled his name. Each time I called out, my voice became more broken. He wasn't there. I checked my phone, hoping he'd called. Seeing that he hadn't, I slammed it shut.

Nearing hopelessness, I covered my mouth, unsure of what to do next. My brother had gotten lost in the burning building. He wasn't outside, leading to only one conclusion.

"TRENT!" I screamed, stretching my neck as I searched the crowd.

Those that had escaped were hugging and whimpering behind the emergency vehicles, watching in horror as the pumper trucks shot water through the windows. Firefighters ran inside, pulling hoses behind them.

"He didn't get out," I whispered. "He didn't get out, Pidge." Tears streamed down my cheeks, and I fell to my knees.

Abby followed me to the ground, holding me in her arms.

"Trent's smart, Trav. He got out. He had to have found a different way."

I fell forward into Abby's lap, gripping her shirt with both fists.

An hour passed. The cries and wailing from the survivors and spectators outside the building had softened to an eerie quiet. Firefighters brought out just two survivors, and then continuously came out empty-handed. Each time someone emerged from the building, I held my breath, part of me hoping it was Trenton, the other fearing that it was.

Half an hour later, the bodies they returned with were lifeless. Instead of performing CPR, they simply laid them next to the other victims and covered their bodies. The ground was lined with casualties, far outnumbering those of us that had escaped.

"Travis?"

Adam stood beside us. I got up, pulling Abby along with me.

"I'm glad to see you guys made it out," Adam said, looking stunned and bewildered. "Where's Trent?"

I didn't answer.

Our eyes returned to the charred remains of Keaton Hall, the thick black smoke still billowing from the windows. Abby buried her face into my chest and gripped my shirt in her small fists.

It was a nightmarish scene, and all I could do was stare.

"I have to uh . . . I have to call my dad," I said, furrowing my brow.

"Maybe you should wait, Travis. We don't know anything, yet," Abby said.

My lungs burned, just like my eyes. The numbers blurred together as tears overflowed and poured down my cheeks. "This ain't fucking right. He shoulda never been there."

"It was an accident, Travis. You couldn't have known something like this was going to happen," Abby said, touching my cheek.

My face compressed, and I clenched my eyes shut. I was going to have to call my father and tell him that Trenton was still inside a burning building, and that it was my fault. I didn't know if my family could handle another loss. Trenton had lived with my dad while trying to get back on his feet, and they were a little closer than the rest of us.

My breath caught as I punched in the numbers, imagining my father's reaction. The phone felt cold in my hand, and so I pulled Abby against me. Even if she didn't know it yet, she had to be freezing.

The numbers turned into a name, and my eyes widened. I was getting another call.

"Trent?"

"Are you okay?" Trent yelled in my ear, his voice thick with panic.

A surprised laugh escaped my lips as I looked at Abby. "It's Trent!"

Abby gasped and squeezed my arm.

"Where are you?" I asked, desperate to find him.

"I'm at Morgan Hall, you dumb fuck! Where you told me to meet you! Why aren't you here?"

"What do you mean you're at Morgan? I'll be there in a second, don't you fucking move!"

I took off in a sprint, dragging Abby behind me. When we reached Morgan, we were both coughing and gasping for breath. Trenton ran down the steps, crashing into both of us.

"Jesus H. Christ, brother! I thought you were toast!" Trenton said, squeezing us tight.

"You asshole!" I screamed, shoving him away. "I thought you were fucking dead! I've been waiting for the firefighters to carry your charred body from Keaton!"

I frowned at Trenton for a moment, and then pulled him back into a hug. My arm shot out, fumbling around until I felt Abby's sweater, and then pulled her back into a hug as well. After several moments, I let Trenton go.

Trenton looked at Abby with an apologetic frown. "I'm sorry, Abby. I panicked."

She shook her head. "I'm just glad you're okay."

"*Me?* I would have been better off dead if Travis had seen me come out of that building without you. I tried to find you after you ran off, but then I got lost and had to find another way. I walked along the outside wall looking for that window, but I ran into some cops and they made me leave. I've been flippin' the fuck out over here!" he said, running his hand over his head.

I wiped Abby's cheeks with my thumbs, and then pulled up my shirt, using it to wipe the soot from my face. "Let's get out of here. The cops are going to be crawling all over the place soon."

After hugging my brother again, he headed to his car, and we walked to America's Honda. I watched Abby buckle her seat belt, and then frowned when she coughed.

"Maybe I should take you to the hospital. Get you checked out."

"I'm fine," she said, interlacing her fingers in mine. She looked down, seeing a deep cut across my knuckles. "Is that from the fight or the window?"

"The window," I answered, frowning at her bloodied nails.

Her eyes turned soft. "You saved my life, you know."

My eyebrows pushed together. "I wasn't leaving without you."

"I knew you'd come."

I kept Abby's hand in mine until we arrived at the apartment. Abby took a long shower, and with shaky hands, I poured us both a glass of bourbon.

She padded down the hallway, and then collapsed onto the bed in a daze.

"Here," I said, handing her a full glass of amber liquid. "It'll help you relax."

"I'm not tired."

I held out the glass again. She might have grown up around mobsters in Vegas, but we'd just seen death—a lot of it—and barely escaped it ourselves. "Just try to get some rest, Pidge."

"I'm almost afraid to close my eyes," she said, taking the glass and gulping the liquid down.

I took the empty glass and sat it on the nightstand, then sat beside her on the bed. We sat in silence, reflecting on the last few hours. It didn't seem real.

"A lot of people died tonight," I said.

"I know."

"We won't find out until tomorrow just how many."

"Trent and I passed a group of kids on the way out. I wonder if they made it. They looked so scared . . ."

Abby's hands began to tremble, so I comforted her the only way I knew how. I held her.

She relaxed against my chest and sighed. Her breathing evened out, and she nuzzled her cheek deeper into my skin. For the first time since we'd gotten back together, I felt completely at ease with her, as if we'd returned to the way things were before Vegas.

"Travis?"

I lowered my chin and whispered into her hair. "What, baby?"

Our phones rang in unison, and she simultaneously answered hers while she handed me mine.

"Hello?"

"Travis? You all right, man?"

"Yeah, buddy. We're okay."

"I'm okay, Mare. We're all okay," Abby said, reassuring America on the other line.

"Mom and Dad are freaking out. We're watching it on the news right now. I didn't tell them you would be there. What?" Shepley pulled his face away from the phone to answer his parents. "No, Mom. Yeah, I'm talking to him! He's fine! They're at the apartment! So," he continued, "what the hell happened?"

"Fucking lanterns. Adam didn't want any bright lights drawing attention and getting us busted. One caught the whole fucking place on fire . . . it's bad, Shep. A lot of people died."

Shepley breathed deep. "Anyone we know?"

"I don't know, yet."

"I'm glad you're okay, brother. I'm . . . Jesus, I'm glad you're okay."

Abby described the horrific moments when she was stumbling through the dark, trying to find her way out.

I winced when she recounted how she dug her fingers into the window when she tried to get it open.

"Mare, don't leave early. We're fine," Abby said. "We're fine," she said again, this time with emphasis. "You can hug me on Friday. I love you, too. Have a good time."

I pressed my cell phone tight against my ear. "Better hug your girl, Shep. She sounds upset."

Shepley sighed. "I just . . ." He sighed again.

"I know, man."

"I love you. You're as much a brother as I could ever have."

"Me, too. See you soon."

After Abby and I hung up our phones, we sat in silence, still processing what had happened. I leaned back against the pillow, and then pulled Abby against my chest.

"America all right?"

"She's upset. She'll be okay."

"I'm glad they weren't there."

I could feel Abby's jaw working against my skin, and I inwardly cursed myself for giving her more gruesome thoughts.

"Me, too," she said with a shiver.

"I'm sorry. You've been through a lot tonight. I don't need to add anything else to your plate."

"You were there, too, Trav."

I thought about what it was like, searching for Abby in the dark, not knowing if I would find her, and then finally kicking through that door and seeing her face.

"I don't get scared very often," I said. "I was scared the first morning I woke up and you weren't here. I was scared when you left me after Vegas. I was scared when I thought I was going to have to tell my dad that Trent had died in that building. But when I saw you across the flames in that basement . . . I was terrified. I made it to the door, was a few feet from the exit, and I couldn't leave."

"What do you mean? Are you *crazy*?" she asked, her head jerking up to look into my eyes.

"I've never been so clear about anything in my life. I turned around, made my way to that room you were in, and there you were. Nothing else mattered. I didn't even know if we would make it out or not, I just wanted to be where you were, whatever that meant. The only thing I'm afraid of is a life without you, Pigeon."

Abby leaned forward, softly kissing my lips. When our mouths parted, she smiled. "Then you have nothing to be afraid of. We're forever."

I sighed. "I'd do it all over again, you know. I wouldn't trade one second if it meant we were right here, in this moment."

She took in a deep breath, and I gently kissed her forehead.

"This is it," I whispered.

"What?"

"The moment. When I watch you sleeping . . . that peace on

your face? This is it. I haven't had it since before my mom died, but I can feel it again." I took another deep breath and pulled her closer. "I knew the second I met you that there was something about you I needed. Turns out it wasn't something about you at all. It was just you."

Abby offered a tired smile as she buried her face into my chest. "It's *us,* Trav. Nothing makes sense unless we're together. Have you noticed that?"

"*Noticed*? I've been telling you that all year!" I teased. "It's official. Bimbos, fights, leaving, Parker, Vegas . . . even fires . . . our relationship can withstand anything."

She lifted her head, her eyes fixed on mine. I could see a plan forming behind her irises. For the first time, I didn't worry what her next step would be, because I knew in my core whatever path she chose, it would be a path we walked together.

"Vegas?" she asked.

I frowned, forming a line between my brows. "Yeah?"

"Have you thought about going back?"

My eyebrows shot up in disbelief. "I don't think that's a good idea for me."

"What if we just went for a night?"

I glanced around the dark room, confused. "A night?"

"Marry me," she blurted out. I heard the words, but it took a second for them to register.

My mouth widened into a ridiculous grin. She was full of shit, but if that was what helped get her mind off what we'd just gone through, I was happy to play along.

"When?"

She shrugged. "We can book a flight tomorrow. It's spring break. I don't have anything going on tomorrow, do you?"

"I'm callin' your bluff," I said, reaching for my phone. Abby lifted her chin, making a show of her stubborn side. "American Airlines," I said, watching her reaction closely. She didn't flinch.

"American Airlines, how can I help you?"

"I need two tickets to Vegas, please. Tomorrow."

The woman looked up a flight time, and then asked how long we were going to stay.

"Hmmmm . . ." I waited for Abby to give in, but she didn't. "Two days, round-trip. Whatever you have."

She rested her chin on my chest with a big smile, waiting for me to finish the call.

The woman asked for my payment information, so I asked Abby for my wallet. That was the point I thought she would laugh and tell me to hang up the phone, but she happily pulled out the card from my wallet and handed it to me.

I gave my credit card numbers to the agent, glancing up at Abby after each set. She just listened, amused. I said the expiration date, and it crossed my mind that I was about to pay for two plane tickets we probably wouldn't use. Abby did have a hell of a poker face, after all. "Er, yes ma'am. We'll just pick them up at the desk. Thank you."

I handed Abby the phone, and she placed it on the night stand.

"You just asked me to marry you," I said, still waiting for her to admit she wasn't serious.

"I know."

"That was the real deal, you know. I just booked two tickets to Vegas for noon tomorrow. So that means we're getting married tomorrow night."

"Thank you."

My eyes narrowed. "You're going to be Mrs. Maddox when you start classes on Monday."

"Oh," she said, looking around.

I raised an eyebrow. "Second thoughts?"

"I'm going to have some serious paperwork to change next week."

I nodded slowly, cautiously hopeful. "You're going to marry me tomorrow?"

She grinned. "Uh-huh."

"You're serious?"

"Yep."

"I fucking *love* you!" I grabbed each side of her face, slamming my lips against hers. "I love you so much, Pigeon," I said, kissing her over and over. Her lips had trouble keeping up.

"Just remember that in fifty years when I'm still kicking your ass in poker." She giggled.

"If it means sixty or seventy years with you, baby . . . you have my full permission to do your worst."

She raised one eyebrow. "You're gonna regret that."

"I bet I won't."

Her sweet grin turned into the expression of the confident Abby Abernathy I saw hustling pros at the poker table in Vegas. "Are you confident enough to bet that shiny bike outside?"

"I'll put in everything I have. I don't regret a single second with you, Pidge, and I never will."

She held out her hand and I took it without hesitation, shaking it once, and then bringing it to my mouth, pressing my lips tenderly against her knuckles.

"Abby Maddox . . . ," I said, unable to stop smiling.

She hugged me, tensing her shoulders as she squeezed. "Travis and Abby Maddox. Has a nice ring to it."

"Ring?" I said, frowning.

"We'll worry about rings later. I sort of sprung this on you."

"Uh . . ." I trailed off, remembering the box in the drawer. I wondered if giving it to her was even a good idea. A few weeks ago, maybe even a few days ago, Abby might have freaked out, but we were past that now. I hoped.

"What?"

"Don't freak out," I said. "I kind of . . . already took care of that part."

"What part?"

I stared up at the ceiling and sighed, realizing my mistake too late. "You're going to freak out."

"Travis . . ."

I reached for the drawer of the nightstand, and felt around for a moment.

Abby frowned, and then blew her damp hair from her eyes. "What? You bought condoms?"

I laughed once. "No, Pidge," I said, reaching farther into the drawer. My hand finally touched the familiar corners, and I watched Abby's expression as I pulled the small box from its hiding place.

Abby looked down as I placed the small velvet square on my chest, reaching behind me to rest my head on my arm.

"What's that?" she asked.

"What does it look like?"

"Okay. Let me rephrase the question: When did you get that?"

I inhaled. "A while ago."

"Trav—"

"I just happened to see it one day, and I knew there was only one place it could belong . . . on your perfect little finger."

"One day when?"

"Does it matter?"

"Can I see it?" she smiled, her gray irises shining.

Her unexpected reaction caused another wide smile to stretch across my face. "Open it."

Abby lightly touched the box with one finger, and then grasped the golden seal with both hands, slowly pulling the lid open. Her eyes widened, and then she slammed the lid shut.

"Travis!" she wailed.

"I knew you'd freak out!" I said, sitting up and cupping my hands over hers.

"Are you *insane*?"

"I know. I know what you're thinking, but I had to. It was The One. And I was right! I haven't seen one since that was as perfect as this one!" I inwardly cringed, hoping she didn't pick up on the fact that I'd just admitted how often I actually looked at rings.

Her eyes popped open, and then she slowly peeled her hands from the case. Trying again, she pulled open the lid, and then plucked the ring from the slit that held it in place.

"It's . . . my God, it's amazing," she whispered as I took her left hand in mine.

"Can I put it on your finger?" I asked, peering up at her. When she nodded, I pressed my lips together, and then slid the silver band over her knuckle, holding it in place for just a second or two before letting go. "*Now* it's amazing."

We both stared at her hand for a moment. It was finally where it belonged.

"You could have put a down payment on a car for this," she said quietly, as if she had to whisper in the ring's presence.

I touched her ring finger to my lips, kissing the skin just ahead of her knuckle. "I've imagined what this would look like on your hand a million times. Now that it's there . . ."

"What?" She smiled, hoping for me to finish.

"I thought I was going to have to sweat five years before I'd feel like this."

"I wanted it as much as you did. I've just got a hell of a poker face," she said, pressing her lips against mine.

As much as I wanted to undress her until the only thing she had on was my ring, I nestled back against the pillow, and let her rest her body against mine. If there was a way to focus on something other than the horror of that night, we'd managed it.

CHAPTER TWENTY-EIGHT

Mr. and Mrs.

ABBY STOOD ON THE CURB, HER HAND HOLDING THE only two fingers I had free. The rest were gripping bags or trying to flag down America.

We had driven the Honda to the airport two days prior, so Shepley had to drop his girlfriend off at her car. America insisted on being the one to pick us up, and everyone knew why. When she pulled up to the curb, she looked straight ahead. She didn't even get out to help with the bags.

Abby hobbled to the passenger seat and got in, babying the side she'd just inked with my last name.

I tossed the bags in the hatchback, and then pulled on the handle of the backseat. "Uh . . . ," I said, pulling on it again. "Open the door, Mare."

"I don't think I will," she said, whipping her head around to glare at me.

She pulled forward a bit, and Abby tensed. "Mare, stop."

America slammed on the brakes, and raised an eyebrow. "You nearly get my best friend killed at one of your stupid fights, then you bring her to Vegas and marry her when I'm out of town, so not only can I not be the maid of honor, but I can't even *witness* it?"

I pulled on the handle again. "C'mon, Mare. I wish I could say I'm sorry, but I'm married to the love of my life."

"The love of your life is a Harley!" America seethed. She pulled forward again.

"Not anymore!" I begged.

"America Mason . . . ," Abby began. She tried to sound intimidating, but America shot a glare in her direction so severe, it left Abby cowering against the door.

The cars behind us honked, but America was too enraged to pay attention.

"Okay!" I said, holding up one hand. "Okay. What if we uh . . . what if we have another wedding this summer? The dress, the invites, the flowers, everything. You can help her plan it. You can stand next to her, throw her a bachelorette party, whatever you want."

"It's not the same!" America growled, but then the tension in her face relaxed a bit. "But it's a start." She reached behind her and pulled up the lock.

I yanked on the handle and slid into the seat, careful not to speak again until we reached the apartment.

Shepley was wiping down his Charger when we pulled into the apartment parking lot. "Hey!" He smiled and hugged me first, and then Abby. "Congratulations, you two."

"Thanks," Abby said, still feeling uneasy from America's temper tantrum.

"I guess it's a good thing America and I were already discussing getting our own place."

"Oh, you were," Abby said, cocking her head at her friend.

"Looks like we weren't the only ones making decisions on our own."

"We were going to talk about it with you," America said defensively.

"No hurry," I said. "But I would like some help today getting the rest of Abby's stuff moved over."

"Yeah, sure. Brazil just got home. I'll tell him we need his truck."

Abby's eyes darted between the three of us. "Are we going to tell him?"

America couldn't contain her smug smile. "It'll be hard to deny with that big-ass rock on your finger."

I frowned. "You don't want anyone to know?"

"Well, no, it's not that. But, we eloped, baby. People are going to freak out."

"You're Mrs. Travis Maddox, now. Fuck 'em," I said without hesitation.

Abby smiled at me, and then looked down at her ring. "That I am. Guess I better represent the family appropriately."

"Oh, shit," I said. "We gotta tell Dad."

Abby's face turned white. "We do?"

America laughed. "You sure are expecting a lot from her already. Baby steps, Trav, Jesus."

I sneered at her, still irritated that she wouldn't let me in the car at the airport.

Abby waited for an answer.

I shrugged. "We don't have to do it today, but pretty soon, okay? I don't want him hearing it from anyone else."

She nodded. "I understand. Let's just take the weekend and

enjoy our first few days as newlyweds without inviting everyone into our marriage just yet."

I smiled, pulling our luggage from the hatchback of the Honda. "Deal. Except one thing."

"What's that?"

"Can we spend the first few days looking for a car? I'm pretty sure I promised you a car."

"Really?" She smiled.

"Pick a color, baby."

Abby jumped on me again, wrapping her legs and arms around me and covering my face with kisses.

"Oh, stop it, you two," America said.

Abby dropped to her feet, and America pulled on her wrist. "Let's go in. I wanna see your tat!"

The girls rushed up the stairs, leaving me and Shepley to the luggage. I helped him with America's numerous, heavy bags, grabbing mine and Abby's as well.

We heaved the luggage up the stairs and were grateful that the door had been left open.

Abby was lying on the couch, her jeans unbuttoned and folded over, looking down as America inspected the delicate, black curves along Abby's skin.

America looked up at Shepley, who was red-faced and sweating. "I'm so glad we're not crazy, baby."

"Me, too," Shepley said. "I hope you wanted these in here, because I'm not taking them back out to the car."

"I did, thank you." She smiled sweetly, returning to Abby's ink.

Shepley puffed as he disappeared into his bedroom, bringing out a bottle of wine in each hand.

"What's that?" Abby said.

"Your reception," Shepley said with a wide grin.

ABBY PULLED SLOWLY INTO AN EMPTY PARKING SPACE, carefully checking each side. She had chosen a brand-new, silver Toyota Camry the day before, and the few times I could get her behind the wheel, she drove it as if she were secretly borrowing someone's Lamborghini.

After two stops, she finally put the gearshift in Park, and turned off the engine.

"We'll have to get a parking sticker," she said, checking the space on her side again.

"Yes, Pidge. I'll take care of it," I said for the fourth time.

I wondered to myself if I should have waited another week or so before adding the stress of a new car. We both knew by the end of the day that the school's rumor mill would be spreading the news of our marriage, along with a fictional scandal or two. Abby purposefully wore skinny jeans and a tight-fitting sweater to ward off the inevitable questions about a pregnancy. We might have gotten married on the fly, but kids were a whole new level, and we were both content to wait.

A few drops fell from the gray, spring sky as we started our trek to our classes across campus. I pulled my red ball cap low on my forehead, and Abby opened her umbrella. We both stared at Keaton Hall as we passed, noting the yellow tape and blackened brick above each window. Abby grabbed at my coat, and I held her, trying not to think about what had happened.

Shepley heard that Adam had been arrested. I hadn't said anything to Abby, afraid that I was next, and that it would cause her needless worry.

Part of me thought that the news about the fire would keep unwanted attention from Abby's ring finger, but I knew that the news of our marriage would be a welcome distraction from the grim reality of losing classmates in such a horrific way.

Like I expected, when we arrived at the cafeteria, my frat brothers and the football team were congratulating us on our wedding and our impending son.

"I'm not pregnant," Abby said, shaking her head.

"But . . . you guys are married, right?" Lexi said, dubious.

"Yes," Abby said simply.

Lexi raised an eyebrow. "I'll guess we'll find out the truth soon enough."

I jerked my head to the side. "Beat it, Lex."

She ignored me. "I guess you both heard about the fire?"

"A little bit," Abby said, clearly uncomfortable.

"I heard students were having a party down there. That they've been sneaking into basements all year."

"Is that so?" I asked. From the corner of my eye I could see Abby looking up at me, but I tried not to look too relieved. If that was true, maybe I'd be off the hook.

The rest of the day was spent either being stared at or congratulated. For the first time, I wasn't stopped between classes by different girls wanting to know my plans for the weekend. They just watched as I walked by, hesitant to approach someone else's husband. It was actually kinda nice.

My day was going pretty well, and I wondered if Abby could

say the same. Even my psych professor offered me a small smile and nod when she overhead my answer to questions about whether the rumor was true.

After our last class, I met Abby at the Camry, and tossed our bags into the backseat. "Was it as bad as you thought?"

"Yes." She breathed.

"I guess today wouldn't be a good day to break it to my dad, then, huh?"

"No, but we'd better. You're right, I don't want him hearing the news somewhere else."

Her answer surprised me, but I didn't question it. Abby tried to get me to drive, but I refused, insisting she get comfortable behind the wheel.

The drive to Dad's from campus didn't take long—but longer than if I'd driven. Abby obeyed all traffic laws, mostly because she was nervous about getting pulled over and accidentally handing the cop the fake ID.

Our little town seemed different as it passed by, or maybe it was me that wasn't the same. I wasn't sure if it was being a married man that made me feel a little more relaxed—laid-back, even—or if I had finally settled into my own skin. I was now in a situation where I didn't have to prove myself, because the one person that fully accepted me, my best friend, was now a permanent fixture in my life.

It seemed like I had completed a task, overcome an obstacle. I thought about my mother, and the words she said to me almost a lifetime ago. That's when it clicked: she had asked me not to settle, to fight for the person I loved, and for the first time, I did what she expected of me. I had finally lived up to who she wanted me to be.

I took a deep, cleansing breath, and reached over to rest my hand on Abby's knee.

"What is it?" she asked.

"What is what?"

"The look on your face."

Her eyes shifted between me and the road, extremely curious. I imagined it was a new expression, but I couldn't begin to explain what it might look like.

"I'm just happy, baby."

Abby half hummed, half laughed. "Me, too."

Admittedly I was a little nervous about telling my dad about our eventful getaway to Vegas, but not because he would be mad. I couldn't quite put my finger on it, but the butterflies in my stomach swirled faster and harder with every block closer that we came to Dad's house.

Abby pulled into the gravel driveway, soggy from the rain, and stopped beside the house.

"What do you think he'll say?" she asked.

"I don't know. He'll be happy, I know that."

"You think so?" Abby asked, reaching for my hand.

I squeezed her fingers between mine. "I know so."

Before we could make it to the front door, Dad stepped out onto the porch.

"Well, hello there, kids" he said, smiling. His eyes scrunched as his cheeks pushed up the puffy bags under his eyes. "I wasn't sure who was out here. Did you get a new car, Abby? It's nice."

"Hey, Jim." Abby smiled. "Travis did."

"It's ours," I said, pulling off my ball cap. "We thought we'd stop by."

"I'm glad you did . . . glad you did. We're getting some rain, I guess."

"I guess," I said, my nerves stifling any ability I had for small talk. What I thought were nerves was really just excitement to share the news with my father.

Dad knew something was amiss. "You had a good spring break?"

"It was . . . interesting," Abby said, leaning into my side.

"Oh?"

"We took a trip, Dad. We skipped on over to Vegas for a couple of days. We decided to uh . . . we decided to get married."

Dad paused for a few seconds, and then his eyes quickly searched for Abby's left hand. When he found the validation he was looking for, he looked to Abby, and then to me.

"Dad?" I said, surprised by the blank expression on his face.

My father's eyes glossed a bit, and then the corners of his mouth slowly turned up. He outstretched his arms, and enveloped me and Abby at the same time.

Smiling, Abby peeked over at me. I winked back at her.

"I wonder what Mom would say if she were here," I said.

Dad pulled back, his eyes wet with happy tears. "She'd say you did good, son." He looked at Abby. "She'd say thank you for giving her boy back something that left him when she did."

"I don't know about that," Abby said, wiping her eyes. She was clearly overwhelmed by Dad's sentiment.

He hugged us again, laughing and squeezing at the same time. "You wanna bet?"

EPILOGUE

The walls dripped with rainwater from the streets above. The droplets plopped down into deepening puddles, as if they were crying for him, the bastard lying in the middle of the basement in a pool of his own blood.

I breathed hard, looking down at him, but not for long. Both of my Glocks were pointed in opposite directions, holding Benny's men in place until the rest of my team arrived.

The earpiece buried deep in my ear buzzed. "ETA ten seconds, Maddox. Good work." The head of my team, Henry Givens, spoke quietly, knowing as well as I did that with Benny dead, it was all over.

A dozen men with automatic rifles and dressed in black from head to toe rushed in, and I lowered my weapons. "They're just bag men. Get 'em the hell out of here."

After holstering my pistols, I pulled the remaining tape from my wrists and trudged up the basement stairs. Thomas waited for me at the top, his khaki coat and hair drenched from the storm.

"You did what you had to do," he said, following me to the

car. "You all right?" he said, reaching for the cut on my eyebrow.

I'd been sitting in that wooden chair for two hours, getting my ass kicked while Benny questioned me. They'd figured me out that morning—all part of the plan, of course—but the end of his interrogation was supposed to result in his arrest, not his death.

My jaws worked violently under the skin. I had come a long way from losing my temper and beating the hell out of anyone that sparked my rage. But in just a few seconds, all of my training had been rendered worthless, and it just took Benny speaking her name for that to happen.

"I've gotta get home, Tommy. I've been away for weeks, and it's our anniversary . . . or what's left of it."

I yanked open the car door, but Thomas grabbed my wrist. "You need to be debriefed, first. You've spent years on this case."

"Wasted. I've wasted years."

Thomas sighed. "You don't wanna bring this home with you, do you?"

I sighed. "No, but I have to go. I promised her."

"I'll call her. I'll explain."

"You'll lie."

"It's what we do."

The truth was always ugly. Thomas was right. He practically raised me, but I didn't truly know him until I was recruited by the FBI. When Thomas left for college, I thought he was studying advertising, and later he told us he was an advertising executive in California. He was so far away, it was easy for him to keep his cover.

Looking back, it made sense, now, why Thomas had decided

to come home for once without needing a special occasion—the night he met Abby. Back then, when he'd first started investigating Benny and his numerous illegal activities, it was just blind luck that his little brother met and fell in love with the daughter of one of Benny's borrowers. Even better that we ended up entangled in his business.

The second I graduated with a degree in criminal justice, it just made sense for the FBI to contact me. The honor was lost on me. It never occurred to me or Abby that they had thousands of applications a year, and didn't make a habit of recruiting. But I was a built-in undercover operative, already having connections to Benny.

Years of training and time away from home had culminated to Benny lying on the floor, his dead eyes staring up at the ceiling of the underground. The entire magazine of my Glock was buried deep in his torso.

I lit a cigarette. "Call Sarah at the office. Tell her to book me the next flight. I want to be home before midnight."

"He threatened your family, Travis. We all know what Benny is capable of. No one blames you."

"He knew he was caught, Tommy. He knew he had nowhere to go. He baited me. He baited me, and I fell for it."

"Maybe. But detailing the torture and death of the wife of his most lethal acquaintance wasn't exactly good business. He had to know he couldn't intimidate you."

"Yeah," I said through clenched teeth, remembering the vivid picture Benny painted of kidnapping Abby and stripping the flesh away from her bones piece by piece. "I bet he wishes he wasn't such a good storyteller, now."

"And there is always Mick. He's next on the list."

"I told you, Tommy. I can consult on that one. Not a good idea for me to participate."

Thomas only smiled, willing to wait another time for that discussion.

I slid into the backseat of the car that was waiting to take me to the airport. Once the door closed behind me, and the driver pulled away from the curb, I dialed Abby's number.

"Hi, baby," Abby lilted.

Immediately, I took a deep, cleansing breath. Her voice was all the debriefing I needed.

"Happy anniversary, Pigeon. I'm on my way home."

"You are?" she asked, her voice rising an octave. "Best present, ever."

"How's everything?"

"We're over at Dad's. James just won another hand of poker. I'm starting to worry."

"He's your son, Pidge. Does it surprise you that he's good at cards?"

"He beat *me*, Trav. He's good."

I paused. "He beat you?"

"Yes."

"I thought you had a rule about that."

"I know." She sighed. "I know. I don't play anymore, but he had a bad day, and it was a good way to get him to talk about it."

"How's that?"

"There's a kid at school. Made a comment about me today."

"Not the first time a boy made a pass at the hot math teacher."

"No, but I guess it was particularly crude. Jay told him to shut up. There was a scuffle."

"Did Jay beat his ass?"

"Travis!"

I laughed. "Just asking!"

"I saw it from my classroom. Jessica got there before I did. She might have . . . humiliated her brother. A little. Not on purpose."

I closed my eyes. Jessica, with her big honey-brown eyes, long dark hair, and ninety pounds of mean, was my mini-me. She had an equally bad temper and never wasted time with words. Her first fight was in kindergarten, defending her twin brother, James, against a poor, unsuspecting girl who was teasing him. We tried to explain to her that the little girl probably just had a crush, but Jessie wouldn't have any of it. No matter how many times James begged her to let him fight his own battles, she was fiercely protective, even if he was eight minutes older.

I puffed. "Let me talk to her."

"Jess! Dad's on the phone!"

A sweet, small voice came over the line. It was amazing to me that she could be as savage as I ever was, and still sound—and look—like an angel.

"Hi, Daddy."

"Baby . . . did you find some trouble today?"

"It wasn't my fault, Daddy."

"It never is."

"Jay was bleeding. He was pinned down."

My blood boiled, but steering my kids in the right direction came first. "What did Papa say?"

"He said, 'It's about time someone humbled Steven Matese.'"

I was glad she couldn't see me smile at her spot-on Jim Maddox impression.

"I don't blame you for wanting to defend your brother, Jess, but you have to let him fight some battles on his own."

"I will. Just not when he's on the ground."

I choked back another swell of laughter. "Let me talk to Mom. I'll be home in a few hours. Love you bunches, baby."

"Love you, too, Daddy!"

The phone scratched a bit as it made the transition from Jessica to Abby, and then my wife's smooth voice was back on the line.

"You didn't help at all, did you?" she asked, already knowing the answer.

"Probably not. She had a good argument."

"She always does."

"True. Listen, we're pulling up to the airport. I'll see you soon. Love you."

When the driver parked next to the curb in the terminal, I rushed to pull out my bag from the trunk. Sarah, Thomas's assistant, just sent through an email with my itinerary, and my flight was leaving in half an hour. I rushed through check-in and security, and made it to the gate just as they were calling the first group.

The flight home seemed to last an eternity, as they always did. Even though I used a quarter of it to freshen up and change clothes in the bathroom—which was always a challenge—the time left over still dragged by.

Knowing my family was waiting for me was brutal, but the fact that it was my and Abby's eleventh anniversary made it even worse. I just wanted to hold my wife. It was all I had ever wanted to do. I was just as in love with her in our eleventh year as I was in the first.

Every anniversary was a victory, a middle finger to everyone who thought we wouldn't last. Abby tamed me, marriage settled me down, and when I became a father, my entire outlook changed.

I stared down at my wrist and pulled back my cuff. Abby's nickname was still there, and it still made me feel better knowing it was there.

The plane landed, and I had to keep myself from sprinting through the terminal. Once I got to my car, my patience had expired. For the first time in years, I ran stoplights and weaved in and out of traffic. It was actually kind of fun, reminding me of my college days.

I pulled into the drive and turned off the headlights. The front porch light flipped on as I approached.

Abby opened the door, her caramel hair just barely grazing her shoulders, and her big gray eyes, although a little tired, showed how relieved she was to see me. I pulled her into my arms, trying not to squeeze her too tightly.

"Oh my God," I sighed, burying my face in her hair. "I missed you so much."

Abby pulled away, touching the cut on my brow. "Did you take a fall?"

"It was a rough day at work. I might have run into the car door when I was leaving for the airport."

Abby pulled me against her again, digging her fingers into my back. "I'm so glad you're home. The kids are in bed, but they refuse to go to sleep until you tuck them in."

I pulled back and nodded, and then bent at the waist, cupping Abby's round stomach. "How about you?" I asked my third child. I kissed Abby's protruding belly button, and then stood up again.

Abby rubbed her middle in a circular motion. "He's still cooking."

"Good." I pulled a small box from my carry-on and held it in front of me. "Eleven years today, we were in Vegas. It's still the best day of my life."

Abby took the box, and then tugged on my hand until we were in the entryway. It smelled like a combination of cleaner, candles, and kids. It smelled like home.

"I got you something, too."

"Oh, yeah?"

"Yeah." She smiled. She left me for a moment, disappearing into the office, and then came out with a manila envelope. "Open it."

"You got me mail? Best wife, ever," I teased.

Abby simply smiled.

I opened the lip, and pulled out the small stack of papers inside. Dates, times, transactions, even emails. To and from Benny, to Abby's father, Mick. He'd been working for Benny for years. He'd borrowed more money from him, and then had to work off his debt so he wouldn't get killed when Abby refused to pay it off.

There was only one problem: Abby knew I worked with Thomas . . . but as far as I knew, she thought I worked in advertising.

"What's this?" I asked, feigning confusion.

Abby still had a flawless poker face. "It's the connection you need to tie Mick to Benny. This one right here," she said, pulling the second paper from the pile, "is the nail in the coffin."

"Okay . . . but what am I supposed to do with it?"

Abby's expression morphed into a dubious grin. "Whatever you do with these things, honey. I just thought if I did a little digging, you could stay home a little longer this time."

My mind raced, trying to figure a way out of this. I had somehow blown my cover. "How long have you known?"

"Does it matter?"

"Are you mad?"

Abby shrugged. "I was a little hurt at first. You have quite a few white lies under your belt."

I hugged her to me, the papers and envelope still in my hand. "I'm so sorry, Pidge. I'm so, so sorry." I pulled away. "You haven't told anyone, have you?"

She shook her head.

"Not even America or Shepley? Not even Dad or the kids?"

She shook her head again. "I'm smart enough to figure it out, Travis. You think I'm not smart enough to keep it to myself? Your safety is at stake."

I cupped her cheeks in my hand. "What does this mean?"

She smiled. "It means you can stop saying you have yet another convention to go to. Some of your cover stories are downright insulting."

I kissed her again, tenderly touching my lips to hers. "Now what?"

"Kiss the kids, and then you and I can celebrate eleven years of in-your-face-we-made-it. How about that?"

My mouth stretched into a wide grin, and then looked down at the papers. "Are you going to be okay with this? Helping take down your dad?"

Abby frowned. "He's said it a million times. I was the end of him. At least I can make him proud about being right. And the kids are safer this way."

I laid the papers on the end of the entryway table. "We'll talk about this later."

I walked down the hall, pulling Abby by the hand behind me. Jessica's room was the closest, so I ducked in and kissed her cheek, careful not to wake her, and then I crossed the hall to James's room. He was still awake, lying there quietly.

"Hey, buddy," I whispered.

"Hey, Dad."

"I hear you had a rough day. You all right?" He nodded. "You sure?"

"Steven Matese is a douche bag."

I nodded. "You're right, but you could probably find a more appropriate way to describe him."

James pulled his mouth to the side.

"So. You beat Mom at poker today, huh?"

James smiled. "Twice."

"She didn't tell me that part," I said, turning to Abby. Her dark, curvy silhouette graced the lit doorway. "You can give me the play-by-play tomorrow."

"Yes, sir."

"I love ya."

"Love you, too, Dad."

I kissed my son's nose and then followed his mom down the hall to our room. The walls were full of family and school portraits, and framed artwork.

Abby stood in the middle of the room, her belly full with our third child, dizzyingly beautiful, and happy to see me, even after she learned what I'd been keeping from her for the better part of our marriage.

I had never been in love before Abby, and no one had even piqued my interest since. My life was the woman standing before me, and the family we'd made together.

Abby opened the box, and looked up at me, tears in her eyes. "You always know just what to get. It's perfect," she said, her graceful fingers touching the three birthstones of our children. She slipped it on her right ring finger, holding out her hand to admire her new bauble.

"Not as good as you getting me a promotion. They're going to know what you did, you know, and it's going to get complicated."

"It always seems to with us," she said, unaffected.

I took a deep breath, and shut the bedroom door behind me. Even though we'd put each other through hell, we'd found heaven. Maybe that was more than a couple of sinners deserved, but I wasn't going to complain.

ACKNOWLEDGMENTS

I HAVE TO START BY THANKING MY INCREDIBLE HUSband, Jeff. Without fail he has offered his support and encouragement, and has kept the children happy and busy so mommy can work. I wouldn't be able to do this without him, and I truly mean that. He takes care of me so completely, I literally just have to sit in my office and write. My husband possesses seemingly endless patience and understanding that I wish I had just a fraction of. He loves me on my worst days, and refuses to let me believe there is anything I can't do. Thank you for loving me so perfectly that I can funnel that into my writing to let others experience a little bit of what you've given me. I'm so lucky to have you.

My two sweet girls, who let mommy work for hours into the night without complaining so that I could meet my first real deadline on time, and to the most handsome man in the world, my son, for waiting until I typed "The End" to make his appearance into the world.

Beth Petrie, my most treasured friend, who is the closest thing to a sister I could have. Three years ago she said I could finish a novel during X-ray school with two kids and a job. She said I would accomplish everything I wanted to, and she's still saying it. I've said this a million times, but I'll say it again: if it weren't for Beth, I wouldn't have written a single word of *Beautiful Disaster,* or *Providence,* or any of my other novels. It did not occur to me to write a novel until she said, "Do it. Go sit down at your computer right now and start typing." She is the sole reason I have traveled down this magical path that has freed me in so many ways. She has saved me in even more ways than that. Thank you. Thank you, thank you, thank you.

Rebecca Watson, my film and literary agent, for her hard work and dedication, for taking me on when I was still an up-and-coming author, and to E L James for introducing us.

Abbi Glines, my sweet friend and fellow writer, who took a look at *Walking Disaster* in its infancy and assured me that yes, I was doing the male POV right.

Colleen Hoover, Tammara Webber, and Elizabeth Reinhardt, for making my editor's job a bit easier. You teach me something almost every day, whether it's writing, my career, or life lessons.

The women of FP, my writers group, and on some days my rock and salvation. I cannot say enough how much your friendship means to me. You have been with me through every up-and-down, disappointment, and celebration this year. Your advice is invaluable, and your encouragement has gotten me through so many rough days.

Nicole Williams, my friend and fellow writer. Thank you for being so gracious and kind. The way you handle every aspect of your career is an inspiration to me, and I can't wait to see what life has in store for you.

Tina Bridges, RN and former hospice angel. When I needed answers to some very tough questions, she didn't hesitate to let me dig as deep and dark as I needed to get to the unpleasant truth about death and dying. You are an amazing person for helping so many children get through unimaginable loss. I applaud you for your courage and compassion.

Foreign literary agents and staff of the Intercontinental Literary Agency. Everything you've accomplished has been so far beyond the spectrum of what I could have done for myself. Thank you so much for bringing my book to more than twenty countries in as many languages!

Maryse Black, book blogger, genius, supermodel, and friend. You have brought Travis to so many wonderful people who love him almost as much as you do. No wonder he loves you so much. I've watched your blog grow from something fun to a force of nature, and I'm so glad we began our journeys around the same time. It's amazing to see where we've been, where we are, and where we'll go!

I'd also like to thank my editor Amy Tannenbaum for not only loving and believing in this unconventional love story as much as I do, but for being such a joy to work with, and making the entire transition to traditional publishing so positive.

My publicist Ariele Fredman, who has walked me through an unknown (to me) jungle of press and interviews, and for taking such great care of me.

Judith Curr, my publisher, for her constant words of encouragement and validation that I was a part of the Atria family not only through her words, but through her actions.

Julia Scribner and the rest of the Atria staff for working so hard on production, marketing, sales, and everything else that goes into getting this novel from my computer to the readers' hands. I'm not sure what I expected from traditional publishing, but I'm so glad my path led me to Atria Books!